Foolish Expectations

An April May Snow

Southern Paranormal Fiction Thriller

By

M. Scott Swanson

April May Snow Titles

Foolish Aspirations
Foolish Beliefs
Foolish Cravings
Foolish Desires
Foolish Expectations
Foolish Fantasies

The Gifts Awaken

Seven Title Prequel Series

Throw the Bouquet

Throw the Cap

Throw the Dice

Throw the Elbow

Throw the Fastball

Throw the Gauntlet

Throw the Hissy

Never miss an April May Snow release.

Join the reader's club!

www.mscottswanson.com

Author's Note- This is a work of fiction. Character names, businesses, locations, crime incidents, and hauntings are purely imagination. Where the public names of locations are used, please know it is from a place of love and respect from this author. Any resemblance to actual people living or dead, or to private events or establishments is entirely coincidental.

Lonely shadows following me

Lonely ghosts come a-calling

Lonely voices talking to me

Now I'm gone, now I'm gone, now I'm gone

Barns Courtney-

"Fire"

Chapter 1

There is an intermittent draft in the old playroom cutting through my sweatshirt on its way to chill my bones. Scanning the severely angled ceiling and cracked plaster sidewalls, I attempt to locate the opening to the night air for what must be the hundredth time this evening.

Thankful Liza was thoughtful enough to have brought me a chair to sit on during tonight's investigation too, I readjust my sore butt in my lawn chair. I can only imagine how cranky I would feel now if my numb tush had spent the last four hours on the wood floor—flooring so dusty it appears to have enough of the gray dirt to plant flower seeds.

Of course, for seeds to grow, the lighting would need to be changed to grow lights. That would be a significant improvement from the hazy yellow glow the circa 1930 incandescent fixtures cast in the cavernous space.

The seeds still wouldn't grow. You need water for them to germinate.

Still, given the pervasive scent of black mold, which in conjunction with the copious amounts of silt-like gray dust threaten a doozy of a sinus infection in my near future, I feel the suspect roof may provide enough leakage to support life in the attic. That would be the only life up here. Besides Liza and me. I haven't seen so much as a bug move.

Somebody kill me. I'm so bored.

"Lord, these assignments are tedious when there's no action," I complain.

My partner, Liza Ingle, doesn't bother to look up from her drawing. "Chill. These quiet assignments are comp pay for the crazy dangerous investigations we've had this year."

Liza has the right of it. Paranormal investigations do run hot and cold.

When there aren't any disturbances, like tonight, your employer is burning research money on a bad lead.

Our employer is my older brother, Dusty. Dusty is a self-made millionaire paranormal author. He can afford to pay Liza and me to sit in an ancient attic where nothing is happening tonight.

Tonight does balance out the level of danger to the pay in comparison to the other assignments. The assignments where there is a supernatural imprint or where some twisted degenerate decides to make a pact with the devil. Those assignments are incredibly challenging and have no shortage of occupational dangers. Those assignments often culminate with some great life-or-death confrontation.

Yes. I agree with Liza's point that tonight's assignment means an easy money project for the two of us. But dang it, the time sure does pass a whole lot quicker when something is going on.

My boredom has officially poisoned my attitude, and I feel myself becoming catty. I don't even like myself when I become this grouchy.

"I'm so bored," I whine.

Liza continues to shade in her colored pencil drawing of the playroom. Until a few weeks ago, I didn't even know that Liza's hobby of choice is drawing.

"You don't have any excursion details that you can write up for Dusty's book?" She pushes one of her long black bangs away from her dark mascaraed eyes. The red colored pencil she holds stands in sharp contrast to her porcelain white skin.

"No. Dusty seems to have gotten his writing mojo back since the last book. So now he's Mr. Control Freak again."

"Hmm … I would've thought Dusty would at least let you continue to edit."

"He did. I reviewed three stories this week." I twirl my finger through the air. "There wasn't anything wrong with any of them. Fantastic, gripping writing and not a single mistake."

"Good for Dusty. I'm sure he's relieved he's back on track."

"Yay for Dusty," I grouse.

"Honestly, April. Life doesn't have to be edge-of-your seat excitement all the time. Be thankful for the quiet times, too. They help to keep you sane."

As if. There'll be plenty of quiet time when I'm dead. Which might not be too long from now since I'm on the verge of dying from boredom.

Liza didn't even favor me a glance during her comments. Her full attention remains on her drawing.

I lean closer to Liza to better my view of the pad she holds in her lap. Her tattooed hand makes quick, horizontal strokes that appear to be no more than errant squiggles to me.

She changes colors and applies a few more lines, drawn lightning fast. I grin as I am able to make out the outline of the rocking horse, seconds before she begins to color it in with a gray pencil—because everything up here is covered with gray dust. Lots of it.

I continue to watch her in companionable silence. Liza can have that effect on me when I'm open to it. Being with her can often calm my heart rate and, more importantly, all the incessant thoughts that ricochet around in my mind.

After she completes a life-like drawing of the old crib in the corner, I'm surprised when she begins to make long, diagonal strokes across the drawing with a yellow pencil. Looking up from her sketch, I realize she captures the same weird pale-yellow glow the old lighting fixtures cast on the scene in the attic.

It is magical. Her drawing mimics a photo with a yellow enhancement filter.

I wish I had a talent like Liza's. She is really quite impressive.

"Do you girls have something up there?" Luis's voice cracks across the two-way radio.

Thankful for the additional distraction, I grab the radio. Before I answer him, I make another cursory scan of the room. Nothing. "We're all clear up here, Luis."

There is a pause before he answers. "Okay—just keep your eyes open. Because I've been seeing some sudden EMF spikes. They're short-lived and dissipate quickly. I'll check the power supply to the equipment. I'm sure we're just getting some harmonics through the line."

"My vote is definitely with Luis having equipment issues," Liza mumbles. "I haven't felt anything since we've been up here."

She raises her head and looks around the room. "Except for that stupid draft that keeps blowing in."

Yeah, I would like to figure out where that stupid draft is coming from, too. "Sure thing, Luis. We'll let you know if anything changes up here."

Luis, the team's lead tech, is tall, lean, and blessed with a perpetual tan. He would be a typecast for one of those Latin lover parts. Surprisingly, even though he is charming and handsome, I have rarely known him to date.

I get it, though. What woman wants to compete with his level of physical perfection? Geez. It would be exhausting and probably give rise to eating disorders or an addiction to plastic surgery.

Good looks aside, he is an excellent technician. Even the best at their trades have an occasional off day. So, maybe Liza is correct and the safe bet is the EMF spikes are caused by some damaged shielding on one of the electronic cables.

We all have our roles on Dusty's research team. Luis is our electronic recorder, audio and video, and EMF metering specialist. The Early brothers, Jason and Travis, and Chet Lambert are the brawn for carrying and setting up the heavy paranormal recording equipment required for our research. They also help Luis monitor the signals.

Miles is our researcher and historian extraordinaire. It is his responsibility to identify storylines and complete a full brief before a research excursion.

My brother Dusty is the brainchild of the operation and the bestselling author. He's a good boss, although sometimes he may get a tad too much tunnel vision when we are chasing a story.

Tonight, the rest of the team members are distributed throughout the late-nineteenth-century home in the Englewood subdivision of Birmingham, Alabama. Liza and I were assigned the playroom—AKA, the attic.

The positioning makes sense. Both Liza and I have clairvoyant skill sets. The reported activity in the deteriorating mansion has been chiefly in the playroom. If there are spirits in the playroom, they most likely will reach out to one of us as they so often yearn to be heard.

"You know, it's almost unnaturally quiet," I remark.
Liza's pencil stops in mid-stroke. "Perfectly quiet."

I've come to learn that on a scale of one to ten, ten being the strongest, Liza's clairvoyance is about a four.

Mine is a solid eleven.

I often pick up on the electrical impressions people leave behind, even if they are decades old. I also am constantly bombarded by passionate discussions and arguments that never really clear out of the air—lending extra weight to Granny's favorite saying about not being able to take back words spoken in anger.

Tonight, I feel and hear nothing. It is as if we exist in a vacuum.

Well, other than the occasional biting-cold draft in the attic. I certainly *feel* that.

While she has paused, I study Liza's drawing in greater detail.

"It looks like you got a little bit of mirror image going on here." I point to the top of the toybox she drew. "You swapped those two."

Liza pins her blue pencil to the tablet with her thumb as she stares at the toy box. She checks her drawing, then raises her head again, this time squinting at the toybox twenty-five feet in front of us. "I didn't."

I tap the ugly clown doll she has expertly drawn, true to every creepy detail, including the long-toed pointy shoes. "See, you drew him on the left side of the play chest and the ball on the right-hand side." I look up just to double-check myself. "See, they're actually both on the right-hand side." The ball is sitting next to the clown.

Liza shoots me a sideways glance. "I didn't do that. When I started drawing the clown, it *was* on the left-hand side."

A cold chill runs up my spine, causing all the hairs on my neck to stand up. "Are you sure?"

"Of course, I'm sure."

I feared that. Liza's not much of a kidder, but I hoped maybe just this once she had gotten a wild hair and decided to play a joke.

Reaching down the collar of my sweatshirt, I pull out the ornate Gothic cross Liza gifted me early on in our friendship. I rub it vigorously as I keep a watchful eye on the play chest.

"I don't think that's gonna help you any," Liza whispers. "Something tells me this one is all in your skill set grouping."

Thanks! "Why do you say that?"

Liza tucks a blue pencil behind her ear. "Because I don't feel anything, silly. Remember?"

"I don't feel anything, either," I argue.

Another blast of arctic wind forces me to cross my arms as I curl forward to retain my body warmth. The wind this time is so forceful and loud I would expect there to be a manhole-sized void in the wall behind me when I jerk around in my chair to inspect the old plaster for openings.

"That wind is icy cold," Liza says.

Before I can agree, the radio crackles again.

"Hey, girls. I'm getting all kinds of weird readings from your location." Luis's voice sounds an octave higher than usual.

I raise the radio to answer Luis, and Liza motions for me to hand her the radio. Reluctantly, I give it to her. She immediately clicks in. "Luis, you need to check the shielding on your wires. You've either got a problem there, or a capacitor is screwing up. The only thing we have is some sort of a hole in the roof letting in a draft that we can't locate."

Liza hands me the radio with a satisfied smile. "Boys and their toys. It never ever occurs to them that they might have broken their equipment when they were lugging it in here."

"What about the clown doll changing positions," I ask.

"So, I misdrew it. I didn't think I did, but you don't feel anything, and I don't feel anything—it's not well-lit in here, and it is a little after two in the morning…"

Her explanation sounds weak to me, but maybe she is right. Things were a little hazy for me, too, earlier. Now I'm wide awake.

Liza pulls the blue pencil out from behind her ear and begins shading in another area on the tablet sheet. After a few strokes, the marks start to form as a young child, possibly five years old, dressed in light-blue footed pajamas.

"Trying to liven it up with some kids in the playroom?" I quip.

Liza quits shading the figure, making a face at her drawing. She looks in my direction, her eyes wide with fright. "Why did I draw that, April? Tell me."

I look in the direction of where the little boy would be in relation to her sketch of the playroom. I don't see anything.

I'll count that as a positive.

It's not like two grown women should fear the ghost of a five-year-old wearing powder-blue footies. Especially considering some of the dangers Liza and I have thwarted together. Still, I'd be lying if I said my pulse isn't racing and I'm not finding it difficult to pull in a full breath now that I realize what Liza is drawing. No matter how often I'm exposed to the supernatural, it still tweaks my heart and respiratory rates into double-time each occurrence.

"Maybe you're just sensing residual currents. It's not that far-fetched to think that there might've been some little boy up here at some time who experienced exceptional joy—or some other emotion."

"Except I don't normally have visions. I'm not like *you*, April." She frowns severely. "This isn't even a vision. I do not see anything. The rare times I have had visions, it's always a dream while I'm asleep."

I take note of the color rising in her cheeks as she shows the first sign of panic. "Don't worry, we'll figure out some logical explanation." I'm not sure we will, but it sounds comforting and necessary to say considering her obvious distress.

Liza's jaw drops as her eyes open wide. "Oh, no! What if I'm asleep. I could be asleep right now and dreaming. How do I know I'm not dreaming?"

It's an excellent question. Considering I had almost fallen asleep a few minutes earlier. Maybe I did. What if we're both asleep?

"Pinch your arm," I say.

Liza's face tightens as if she's bitten into something sour. "You pinch *your* arm."

"You're the one worried you're dreaming."

"I don't think pinching my skin is going to prove anything," Liza says.

I reach over and pinch the back of Liza's arm. *Hard.*

She rolls to the side to get away from me. "Ow! That smarts."

I give a nonchalant shrug of my shoulders. "Now you know you're not dreaming."

"I ought to pinch you on the back of the arm."

"That's stupid. We already know I'm awake." Otherwise, I wouldn't have been able to pinch her on the back of the arm and hear her scream.

Liza favors me her best "you will pay later" glare. She turns her attention back to her drawing.

I notice she abandons any further detail work on the little boy blue.

Our silence is no longer of the companionable design. I'm quickly irritated and bored again.

I turn my attention back to scanning the room as if I am standing guard—waiting. Waiting for what, I haven't a clue.

Morning. Breakfast. A three-hour ride home, once Dusty judges this trip as a failure.

The frigid breeze assaults me again. The odd thing is, it's as if the wind is blowing directly at my ponytail and finding its way inside the back collar of my sweatshirt. I inspect the wall hoping this time to find a large, gaping hole that has previously gone undetected in the steeply slanted ceiling.

Nope. Still no visible entry point for the frigid air.

I adjust my position in the lawn chair as I turn to face forward again. Something isn't quite right. Something has changed.

"Liza?"

"What?" Her curt tone signaling she remains perturbed with me.

"Something's different. I can't tell what." My anxiety ratchets up a few notches.

Liza breaks away from her drawing and scans the room. Her underbite, more prominent than usual, is a standard "tell" that she is concentrating.

"Yeah. There's something—I'm—sort of confused here. I can't tell if I'm sensing something real or if I'm just starting to get a little freaked."

I have already accounted for my anxiety level working its way up the panic ladder. Something malicious is disturbing the energy around us. No, in front of us.

The disturbance is right in front of my nose. I just *feel* it.

"Hey girls, I'm getting a real heavy spike now." Miles's voice on the radio startles me.

Picking up the radio, I press the button. "Hey, keep silent for a moment, guys."

The room is expansive for an attic, roughly twenty feet by fifty feet. The majority was converted into a playroom with two doors on either end, leading to oversized storage closets jammed full of discarded remnants of the last century.

Despite the size of the room, it is possible to feel claustrophobic due to the ceilings being only seven feet tall at the center of the room and tapering down to four feet. It gives the room a squatty feeling. Still, it would have made the space perfect for young children in its day.

Miles's report on the property was that the family who owned it had left everything when they moved out of state. Odd, but true. The playroom remains full of the trappings of what I would expect to find in a privileged child's private amusement park. That is, if the child were born in the early 1930s and their room is frozen in time.

My eyes, checking the room once more, return to the toy chest on the far-right wall. My chest constricts. "Liza, toy chest."

In my peripheral vision, I watch her study the toy chest. She lurches backward, forced to catch her balance with her hands behind her as her chair tumbles. "What the heck, April?"

Fear builds in me. Direct confrontation can be much easier to manage than the subtle mind game scenery changes.

Once I become aware of the unexplained change of object locations, I can't take my eyes off them. There is no reasonable explanation on why the ball is now in the creepy clown doll's lap. Now, the only question is if I have the intestinal fortitude to hang out and see what happens next.

"You're still not getting anything?" I ask.

"No. I told you I don't think it's my skill set," Liza whispers.

Liza is referencing that although we are both clairvoyants, our skills are derived from dissimilar sources. Mine is best described as originating from animism, like the old druid religion. Because of this, it's easier for me to read residual energy prints and, for lack of a better term, hear the thoughts of spirits and ghosts.

All of Liza's skills are wrapped up in Catholicism Cannon. Her specialties are angels, demons, and mankind, who have signed a pact in trade with evil forces.

Truth be known, I'm glad that is her forte. Ghosts wig me out, but demons scare the living bejesus out of me.

We both gasp as the blue rubber ball rolls out of the clown's lap and bounces toward us. Before we gather our senses, the laughter of a young boy rings out through the playroom.

"What the frick!" Liza yells.

I see a faint wisp of smoke to my left. It floats toward the ball, rolling toward us, growing thicker and more prominent as it nears the sphere.

Smoke, Columbia blue in tint, materializes more details, similar to Liza's drawing. I can make out a highly transparent boy of approximately five years old. He intercepts the ball, lifting it above his head as he yells with glee.

Liza knocks over her chair and backpedals until she is bent over by the slant in the ceiling. "The ball is floating, April."

I'm suddenly amused by the young apparition. Although I've heard many reports of child spirits, I have not personally encountered many.

I clap my hands in praise. His upturned face lowers. Locking eyes with me, he turns slightly to the right. His arms lower in slow motion as he continues to stare at me as if confused. His face has the visual clarity of a blurry projection.

"Are you seeing something, April?"

"You don't see who has the ball?" I ask.

Liza crouches next to my chair, wrapping her hand around the armrest. "I just see the ball floating in the air."

"No, we have a little visitor. The little boy blue you drew earlier."

"What's he doing?" Her voice is full of anxiety.

"Right now, playing with a ball."

Liza exhales loudly. "I'm serious."

"Staring at me as if he just realized we are here."

Miles did an excellent job of researching 3613 Oaklawn

Drive. Because of his in-depth, pre-excursion briefing on the reported disturbances, I know precisely who has materialized in front of me.

The ghost, rubbing the sleep from his eyes, is still determining who I am, and more to the point, how he will react to me being in his space.

As we stare at one another, I hold my breath as Miles's information—I admit I wasn't giving it my totally undivided attention when he went over it—flows through my mind.

The homes in Oaklawn had once belonged to the upper management of Birmingham's first industrial age. They were not the homes of the entrepreneurs who owned the businesses. They weren't even close to the opulence of those residences. They were commanding in the monstrous size of the structures but lacked flair or any unique design that might be considered creative.

The once proud and exclusive neighborhood had fallen from grace and is now more apt to be, at best, housing for the homeless, and at the worst, a flophouse for heavy drug users.

Because of the high level of disrepair and vacancy, there are now more empty lots than homes left standing in the neighborhood. All of the houses, given their age and the duress of the current inhabitants, hold an abundance of emotional imprints, so many so that I was forced to increase the mental partitions in my mind to buffer the constant barrage against my mind.

Yet, since we arrived, 3613 has been uncharacteristically quiet. As if someone, or something, has wiped all the imprints off the home.

"Do you see him?" I whisper to Liza.

I see her shake her head in my periphery.

This home had a series of owners abandon it, the last leaving all their possessions. Eighty years later, while every other house has been pilfered or occupied, this one has been left alone. Even the dust, before tonight, appears not to have been disturbed for decades.

In the paranormal business, that's what we call a clue. Why else would an abandoned home remain untouched?

Jarvis Baron, CEO of one of the numerous water pipe foundry fitting producers in the area, completed the home in 1892. Jarvis, according to Miles, was extraordinarily successful at an early age and ordered the home in Oaklawn built for his wife, Babette. The couple lived in the house for only two years when they were blessed with a little boy. They named their son Moses.

In the late 1800s it was common for families of means to have many children. As I understand it, it was done to ensure they had at least some children survive into adulthood in case the parents needed help in their later years.

From the size of the home, Jarvis and Babette were ambitious in the family-producing department. The home could easily have housed a football team—offense and defense.

Five years after his birth, Moses remained an only child.

"You really can't see him?"

"I got nothing," Liza says.

Miles wasn't able to find much on Moses, other than his age. Babette's diary did report he was a precocious and affable boy. Not an unexpected mother's judgment of her young son.

There is much information about Moses's fifth birthday week, which coincided with the day after Thanksgiving. Moses disappeared into thin air and was never seen again.

It was a scandal that rocked the tight business community in Birmingham for the following year. The year after that, the Barons' divorce became the favorite salacious topic at cocktail parties. Tragically, in 1902 Babette hung herself in the barn on her maternal grandmother's farm.

Jarvis had sold 3613 Oaklawn in 1901 and followed his fortunes to Los Angeles by that time. Not much else is known about Jarvis.

The young boy's disappearance remained on the North Birmingham precinct captain's high priority list for the next six years until he took retirement. The new administration packed it away.

Mother dead and the father gone, why wouldn't they?

Miles found only two sketches of Moses Baron. He had enormous eyes and delicate features. There is no doubt it is Moses's ghost in front of me, studying me intently.

I want to call him by name, but I hesitate.

There's something peculiar about his body language. Something that unnerves me.

Still, it could be he who is unnerved. I am encroaching on his space, after all.

The little boy crosses his arms as he squints his eyes. It's not a hostile gesture. Still, I would have preferred a smile and a wave of his hand.

"Hi, Moses. Do you want to play ball?" I ask.

He favors me a smile, or maybe it's a smirk as he drops the ball, which bounces slowly toward me. Moses follows the progress of the ball until it rolls between my legs. He stops six inches from my chair and looks at me directly as he crooks his finger in a gesture beckoning me to lean forward.

Against my better judgment, I lean toward the three-foot-tall apparition.

Moses covers his mouth on both sides, forming a hand megaphone as he leans in close to my ear to share his secret. "The bad man's coming," he whispers.

I nearly pee myself.

Certain things in life are always red flags signaling I'm in imminent danger. I've never considered the possibility before, but if I had, I'm positive that having a small ghost whisper, "The bad man's coming," would be way up there on my danger list.

I pull back and wait for something awful to happen to Moses's face. I expect his head to grow and his jaw to dislocate so he can open his mouth wide like an anaconda to swallow me whole. Or maybe he will turn into some sort of insidious gas that will sear my lungs, leaving me writhing in pain on the floor. I'm amazed how many dreadful endings to my life I can dream up in a matter of ten fright-filled seconds.

All I know is I need to get the heck out of Dodge, and pronto. Besides, I've got a comfortable gig at a small law practice, and I don't have to be out here dealing with this creepy stuff.

"Liza, it's time we make ourselves scarce," I say.

She pops up from her chair without an argument. "Okay, what are you seeing?"

I lift the radio and hit the button to call Luis. "Luis, what do the meters show now?" I fold my lawn chair, tucking it under my arm.

If only it could record what I see. A young boy dressed in blue footies standing only inches from me.

The affable smile has faded. Moses's large eyes close until they are slits as he glares at me while shaking his head slowly from side to side.

"Don't leave. He wants to play, too," Moses growls.

The response from the radio clicks in, but it is just static. Considering the boys are only two floors below us, and we use shortwave radio for in-house communications, that makes no sense.

I lift the radio to try again.

"Come on, April. There's no point in trying to call them. Let's just go downstairs," Liza says as she backs toward the door.

Liza has a point. What the heck am I doing calling this in? We both turn to jog out of the attic.

As we near the door, it slams shut with such force I feel the reverberations in the floor planks. I freeze, considering what our next move should be to escape.

The distinct clicking noise of the old key lock engaging with no key in the keyhole chills my blood. That can't be a good sign. I'm guessing the door as a means of escape is out unless we can kick in a solid oak door.

"I don't like this. I don't like this one bit."

Liza, typically much more controlled during these excursions than me, appears to be going over "panic falls."

"No worries. The boys are downstairs. I'm sure the meters

are spiking like crazy now. Once we don't report in, they'll be up here and force the door open for us."

"I'm not so worried about getting out of here as I am about what I'm in here with." Liza points toward the toy chest.

Moses has lifted the clown doll and is walking the toy across the floor toward us. "That's the ghost. He's playing with the clown."

Liza shakes her head furiously. "No! Something's wrong. I've got to get out of here. I have to get out of here now!"

Despite having heard it lock, I go to the attic door to try my luck. I reach for the doorknob, and pain sears through my palm. I yank my hand back.

"Ow!" I curl my hand into my chest. "It's like the door's on fire."

I hear a slow clapping noise behind me. Rotating, I see Moses clapping his pudgy hands together in a slow, methodical cadence. I don't find him nearly as cute as he was a few minutes earlier. His smile has transformed into a snarl, *and* he is clearly mocking me.

"Liza, I need you to do a protection spell for us. Can you do that?"

"Something is coming, April. Can you feel it?"

No, I can't feel it. But I've been warned by the creepy little dude in the blue footies that the bad man is coming, and I don't plan to ignore his warning.

"I need you to do a protection spell for us. Liza, you have to give us time for the boys to get the door open."

She isn't listening. Her eyes are opened wide, and she is spinning in tight circles, looking around the playroom.

I grab her by the shoulders and shake her. "Liza, you have to do this for us!"

She calms down, drawing a long breath. She favors me a single nod of her head and starts a chant I have heard her use before.

The doorknob to one of the side storage closets clicks. Liza stops chanting, and I quit breathing.

As the door slowly inches open, it squeals as if it has been rusted shut for decades. Liza grabs me by the wrist.

I feel faint as the door continues to open. There is a rush of dark, oily feelings concealed behind it.

"Hurry, Liza. Finish the spell," I whisper breathlessly.

"I'm trying."

The door continues to open, stopping short at a forty-five-degree angle. It is open, but I can't see who is opening it from my vantage point. My blood pressure shoots up incredibly high, and I realize I still haven't drawn a breath.

There is a rustling of bells, like the jingle bells on the old-time sleighs.

I attempt to focus on the happy times that the sound has symbolized in the past for me: Christmas, presents, and family. Still, there is a twenty-pound spiked ball of fear in my gut telling me these jingle bells will not be the harbinger of anything I want.

A muffled shuffling noise comes from behind the ajar closet door. A pointy slipper with a tennis ball-sized bell on the toe appears. The shoe, an ill omen if I ever met one, is gold, orange, and impossibly large.

This is not going well.

Liza and I checked the closet when we set up last night. It is a small closet, just big enough for six winter coats.

I would have noticed size twenty-four elf shoes with bells.

"New playmates, Moses? I think they'll make excellent dolls. What a good boy you are." The deep voice with a giddy undertone causes the hair on my body to stand at attention.

I'm not sure what the voice behind the door is alluding to. Still, I have no intentions of waiting to find out.

Without thought, I make a run for the playroom's exit door, lowering my shoulder for impact. I strike the door squarely with my left shoulder.

The unyielding door reverses my momentum, bouncing me backward onto my butt.

That trick obviously only works in the movies. All I have to show for my brute force attempt is a sore derrière and what feels like a dislocated shoulder.

"Come now. It's an honor to dance for the King."

I know it is probably a poor decision—because I don't know how to control my "gifts"—but I try to burn the door down by throwing my energy toward it in hopes of burning the door open.

I would rather try an ill use of my "gifts" than go down without a fight.

"Let me take a closer look at you two," the creepy voice from behind the door continues.

My concentration is broken. I turn back toward the voice and freeze as I watch the horrific spectacle.

The size twenty-four clown shoes, ski boat size as my brothers would say, make an exaggerated step from behind the door lifting high into the air and waggling. The loud slapping noise the sole makes as it strikes the dusty wooden floor releases bitter acid from fear into my gut.

Long, stilted legs seemingly unpack from the closet as if the space had been incredibly too small for the clown. The oddly thin six-foot-long legs are adorned in baggy, blue-and-white spangled silk pants. The start of a slim torso stretches out as the legs continue to walk out from the closet as if in some absurd limbo game required to exit the closet.

The untucked tail of a red striped shirt precedes the tails of a magenta velvet waistcoat, both swaths of fabric dangling vertically to the floor below. Placed askew on the left lapel of the magenta coat, I recognize a black belladonna bloom.

I stand mesmerized with fear and disbelief as the spectacle continues to stretch closer to us.

The clown, much too large to be of any human, dead or otherwise, stops moving.

Blood pounds in my ears. I attempt to swallow and choke on the dryness of my mouth.

A loud cracking noise—the sound of breaking bones—has me suck in my breath. There is an abrupt jack-knifing motion from the clown as its torso rotates a full three hundred and sixty degrees at the waist. His painted face, one only a mad circus manager could possibly love, swings quickly out from the closet and stops a foot from Liza and me.

The gargantuan clown draws in an exaggerated breath. His preposterous red ball nose flexes inward. "My, you two smell absolutely delicious."

I'm simply struck stupid by the grotesque vision in front of me. By the way he was forced to bend at the waist to keep from hitting his head. I estimate the clown's height at ten feet.

I want to run and escape from this bizarre nightmare. But, with the door locked, there is no escape.

Liza and I will have to buy time and survive until the rest of the team can come to our aid.

Given his close proximity, I can't help but notice the trail of tattooed tears leading down from both eyes to his neck and under his collar. He chomps on the stubby remains of a cigar, the wrapping dark and shiny from saliva.

He takes the cigar from his mouth with one hand as he adjusts the circa 1910 leather football helmet on his head. A smirk forms on his blue lips, and I nearly pee myself.

Leaning forward, he blows a plume of sickly green smoke in my face. I gag and sputter. Not just from the cigar smoke. There is another dreadful scent blending with the tobacco. The smell is only present around large roadkill on the hottest of summer days.

The clown laughs. "You think you're awfully smart. But you don't know much. Maybe after I play with you for a while, you will understand."

Okay. The freeze part of the equation isn't working out, and the grotesquely oversized clown is way too big for me to consider fighting. I'm all in on the flight as my body comes back under my control.

"Liza!"

I turn to make sure she is still at my side. She has dropped to the floor and is making chalk marks on the floor.

"Give me a second," she yells.

I wish I could. I'm afraid we're out of time, and I'm not sure a warding spell would even work on this nightmare.

I attempt to calm myself. With a startling level of discipline, I draw more energy inward to my core.

The energy surges into me, and I feel like I may explode. With a violent push of my hands, I send the power coursing out. It rushes down my shoulders across my arms and out from my hands, all of it directed at the playroom's locked door. The door blocking our escape.

Two tiny sparks shoot out my index fingers. Well, that is underwhelming as well as embarrassing.

I look over my shoulder to see where my adversary is.

He's right behind me. Leastways, his face is...

"Whoa. I bet that would tickle, Sweetcakes." He runs a dark purple split tongue across his serrated yellow teeth.

"That's just a warmup. You might want to get your gangly butt back in that closet. I get better quick." I have no idea where the false bravado comes from. I seriously am at the "curl up and die" stage in my mind.

Mr. Creepy Clown's pitch-black eyes lock onto mine. His smirk informs me he isn't the slightest bit worried over my "gifts."

Lifting his right hand, he mimics a gun with his twelve-inch-long fingers. "I think I've got way more juice than you do." He rolls his hand over and points a bizarrely long pinky in the air. "In my pinky."

"Liza, we need that warding spell." Hey, I have my doubts, but the sparklers I'm creating aren't going to stop this maniac.

"It's done!" She points to the chalk pentagram drawn on the hardwood floor. "Step inside."

I eagerly step inside.

Mr. Creepy Clown laughs as if he just heard the best joke in the world. Again, I don't feel things are going well for Liza and me.

The clown, hunched over with his back scraping cobwebs

from the center of the ceiling, clomps his giant slippers over to Liza's pentagram. His red and gold slippers stop two inches outside of the circle. Mockingly, he forms an "O" shape with his lips as he raises his drawn-on, black-colored eyebrows as if he is fearful of the warding circle.

A loud scraping sound accompanied by the jingle of a bell fills the room as he drags the toe of his massive shoe across the line, breaking any warding power it might have held. Mr. Creepy Clown shrugs. "That's the strongest magic you have?"

Liza and I have seen some messed-up stuff in the past. Still, this clown has shot right up to the top of my scariest-thing-ever list. His legs, arms, and chest are implausibly gaunt. Still, his face would better belong to an overweight man in his late fifties—if he were inclined to paint his face white and put on a red nose.

Worse, while his height, cramped due to the seven-foot ceiling, has him hunched over, he appears to have to bend a little further with each passing moment to keep his leather helmet from scraping the plaster above us. Is he still growing?

"April, what are we going to do?" Liza asks.

"What are we going to do," he mocks.

His eyes are the most disquieting. Glossy pitch black, they are all wrong.

I can see my reflection in his right eye with Liza behind me as if I were looking into a black mirror. His left eye is endless. I'm forced to turn my gaze as I have the sudden feeling of looking over a cliff into a fiery pit ... and the sensation that someone is pushing me toward the flame.

Something ordinarily funny and lighthearted, requisitioned for evil, always puts an extra chill in my blood. There is no need for team jerseys to know Mr. Creepy Clown plays for the opposing team. He may even be one of their all-star players, one of them that plays for keeps.

"What you are going to do is join Rollo's collection of pretties," he says.

Uh ... no. No whacked-out clown talking in the third person

will be adding me to their collection today. I won't be a monster's play toy—and still be alive.

I return my attention to the most immediate issue, the solid oak door with the fouled-up locking mechanism trapping us in the room with repulsive Rollo. Gathering all the energy I dare hold centered in my core—then a little more—I point at the bedroom door and let all the power fly with no focus or constraints.

Flames flicker out from the tips of my fingers, sputtering weakly. As the tiny fire spouts stretch slowly toward the door, I bear down on my "gifts" with everything in me. I am aware this will be the only opportunity I have to bring my abilities to life.

The flames roll steadily from my finger and cover the wooden door in a cloud of angry, orange flames. Ferocious heat flashes across my face, and the smell of singed hair rises to my nostrils.

Now, I grin like a crazy woman as the heady emotional concoction of escaping death while harnessing such tremendous power fills me. At the apex of my exaltation, the fire from my fingertips ceases. It looks like the flame of a gas grill being turned off.

Small puffs of smoke lazily trail from my fingertips.

The door, charred black in the center, smokes lightly. It is not on fire

"Aww, look. Her itty-bitty doll finger won't make the fire for her anymore."

I turn in time to watch Rollo cross his arms. His preposterously long arms wrap around his chest no less than six times. Gorge rises from my gut. Odd, impossible details like that will bend my mind forever.

More scared than ever and without a plan, I step back from Rollo as he continues to *tsk-tsk*.

In my periphery, I see movement from Liza. She appears to have accepted the fact her warding pentagram failed. Ever resourceful, she has pulled her orthodox gothic cross from under her sweatshirt and is chanting a dispersal spell so fast it sounds like another language.

"A dispersing spell?" Rollo asks. "Isn't that for vampires? You do know I'm not a vampire, don't you?" He bares his teeth, exposing hundreds of serrated, ultra-pointed yellow teeth.

Liza recoils, and Rollo and Moses laugh uncontrollably.

Watching the macabre scene, a now twelve-foot-tall clown partnered with a five-year-old petulant boy ghost dressed in powder blue footies, I realize I'm going to die. Or worse, be added to some evil collection of undead playthings for these two evil creatures.

Liza steps closer to the enormous clown with her cross held out high. She continues to chant, "Lord deliver us safely from this abomination."

Rollo doesn't bother to unwrap his arms. He doesn't have to. He extends his long index finger in a snake-like motion touching the cross with his fingertip. "Oh, that tickles."

Moses laughs with glee. I wonder why I thought he was cute when we first met this evening.

Screw it. I decide to give the door another blast.

What? It's only insanity if you believe it will have a different result. I'm not deluding myself. Still, I don't want to die standing catatonic with my mouth hanging open.

Gathering every ounce of energy I can pull in from the room, including the abundance of excess evil—which is never a good idea—I force everything I have out of my hands.

The door disappears behind a blast of flames that reminds me of Sloss Furnaces. When the ball of flame blows back on me, I cut off the flow so I don't broil myself.

As my vision normalizes after the blast of blinding light, I grin. The door looks like a large rectangular chunk of glowing charcoal. The brass doorknob is misshapen, gleaming bright red.

Nana would have thrown a hissy fit if she knew I was throwing fire with no constraints. I'll be proud if she has the opportunity to scold me on the dangers later.

I kick at the door with the sole of my sneaker, fully expecting it to shatter into a hundred blackened shards.

It doesn't budge an inch. It's as if the door is made with asbestos-covered steel rather than wood.

"I've been cooped up in that closet for sooo long. I'm absolutely famished." Rollo unwraps his arms while rotating his waist to face Moses. "I'm ravenous, and they smell so good. Would you care, dear boy, if I eat one now? It will still leave one to add to our collection."

Moses let out a gleeful scream. The evil brat is obviously all in on the idea.

Eating is death. Yes, I had already deduced that being an undead plaything for this creepy duo would be an endless purgatory. Still, it sounded like it might take a little time and effort on Rollo's part to make our permanent bondage a reality. The time that would allow the boys to come to our aid.

Eating? That sounds more imminent. How long would it take a twelve-foot-tall clown to kill and eat one of us?

It's rhetorical.

And he certainly looks like he could use a few sandwiches.

It's stupid, even considering one of us is about to be a Rollo snack and the other turned into a toy for Moses for the rest of eternity. Still, let it never be said April May Snow went down without a fight.

"You'll never take me alive, creepy clown dude!" I scream.

Rollo and Moses screech with laughter, giving me the time I want. The time to pull all the pervasive evil energy of the room into my core.

The energy sickens me, yet the dark power feels especially powerful, tickling something in my mind.

"Perfect!" Rollo exclaims. "Then I'll eat the cute one with the cross, and the little boy haircut, then make you Moses's play..."

I let loose with a fire stream from my palms that would make a flamethrower envious.

Rollo backs away, screaming in agony. His long fingers cover his face as the back of his helmeted head smashes a hole into the ceiling.

My initial target, his face, now being through the roof, I concentrate the fire spouting from my palms at the black belladonna on his chest.

"No!" Moses screams. "Don't hurt him. He's my only friend."

I struggle to maintain my concentration and not look away to Moses. I must end this now.

Rollo yanks his head back inside the playroom. My attention breaks as I view the destruction from the flame I have created.

His bluish-blackened lips droop over his chin, while his red ball nose has been replaced by two nostril holes. Rollo's eyes are an abhorrent sight as the painted white flesh has burned away from them, leaving two black marbles the size of softballs in the scorched eye sockets. Despite his leather helmet burning fiercely, he makes no attempt to pull it off.

The stream of flames from my palms sputter then flame out. There will be no chance of me reigniting them as my concentration and energy are both exhausted.

I watch in horror as Rollo yells in full fury while his costume disintegrates in the yellow and blue flames.

The flames lick across the ceiling spanning the room. Finding oxygen in the hole created by Rollo's head, they increase every second.

I'm going to die. I'm going to frickin' burn to death in some stupid old attic in Birmingham, Alabama.

All those years of law school and now, because some bizarre clown wanted to eat me like a pimento cheese sandwich, I will be incinerated. Something about that just seems totally wrong.

"I'm going to tear your legs off and beat you to death with them!" Rollo threatens.

His threat rips me out of my feel-sorry-for-April mode. I search my mind for any other way out of this mess.

Nothing. I've got nothing.

I'm frozen as I watch the spectacle unfolding in front of me.

Rollo's clothing burns away, revealing that his body is not

flesh but some densely packed fabric. His long fingers, now super-heated, dribble onto the floor as if they are molded plastic.

"April, the protective bubble."

I tear my attention from Rollo. Liza's eyes, wide as saucers, implore me to call on one of my other "gifts."

I shake my head no. Protective bubbles might work against small-time wizards and other nuisances. Still, I have a sense Rollo's powers derive from something far too powerful to be turned back by the magical protective shield. I need something with a lot more punch. Plus, I would need a mega recharge on my energy source.

Rollo's right hand moves strangely fast, clutching Liza by the waist. His melting fingers smolder on her sweatshirt as they wrap all the way around her.

The demonic clown's jaw cracks and hinges open to the floor like an anaconda preparing to feed. He pulls Liza toward his gaping maw.

I must help Liza. Still, there is nothing I can do. I'm at a total loss on how to help her, and tears fill my eyes as I realize I'm going to lose my friend. This will be a moment that will haunt me forever.

Liza struggles for her life in Rollo's hand as he scoops her closer to her demise. But she is not struggling to free herself from his hand. She is pulling at the shoulder seam of her sweatshirt.

Her sleeve tears down from her shoulder. A brilliant light strobes once, filling the room with white light.

My eyes readjust. Nothing has changed.

Rollo pulls Liza closer to the edge of his mouth. Droplets of drool fall like rain from his yellow teeth.

He makes to bite Liza. A staff appears in her right hand, and she thrusts the wooden weapon into Rollo's upper palate. It sticks there, like an unseen toothpick in a club sandwich.

Rollo screams as he throws Liza across the room. Reaching frantically, he attempts to pull the staff out of his palate.

He is unable to grip the staff effectively. Rollo's thumbs are already melted to nubs.

Circling widely around the clown, I go to Liza. As I kneel to check her for injury, Moses rushes over to us and shakes his head while glowering at us. His forever-young face is the picture of hate.

I'm relieved when I find Liza's pulse. I haven't lost her.

"Go away," I tell Moses.

"I'm glad your friend is hurt. You hurt my friend," Moses says.

"Fine. Then we're even. Go away."

He doesn't, but it doesn't matter. I realize Liza and I have a more natural dilemma to deal with than an oversized clown and a ticked-off five-year-old ghost.

The entire playroom is engulfed in flames. With the door sealed, my earlier certainty that I would be burned alive is closer to realization. Still, it's a moderate upgrade from having Rollo eat us. I mean, if you have to play that silly "which way would you prefer to die" game.

I sit down next to Liza and put her head on my lap. I'm not surrendering to death. It's just the air is better down here, and I need to remain calm if I come up with an idea to save us. Screaming and acting a fool never helped anyone come up with a good plan of escape.

Moses continues to glower over us. I reciprocate his look and add a single-finger salute for good measure.

I know, not very classy, but I don't like him, and the gesture is effective as he turns around and walks through the flames back to the toy chest.

The center of the room had degenerated into a wall of flames and a lot of jerky movement. All of Rollo's clothes are now gone, except for the leather helmet that continues to burn. It makes him appear like he has red and yellow spiked hair. He sticks a flaming hand into his mouth periodically, attempting to pull Liza's staff from his mouth. Still, his fingers are now no more than exaggerated knuckles due to their melting, and he cannot get a grip on the staff.

Epiphany. Why didn't I remember this sooner?

Magic is magic, unless I misunderstood Nana's coaching. It takes the same thing for people to create magic, regardless if they are a first-year witch, fiftieth-year warlock, or one-hundred-plus-year creepy oversized demon doll. Concentration is the key.

Watching Rollo twitch, making weak attempts to put out the flames consuming him, I realize there is no way he can concentrate on the spells he cast earlier. Lord knows if my hair were on fire, which it may be soon, I wouldn't be able to focus on my magic.

Following the logical conclusion, assuming it was Rollo who made the radio malfunction earlier, whatever magic he cast to cause the squelch, he has allowed to lapse.

I slide Liza's head off my leg and bear crawl to my lawn chair where I left our two-way radio. "Luis. We need help."

"April? The video feed just cleared up. Is that fire we're seeing—"

"We need an ax, hatchet, or sledgehammer up here now!" I yell.

"What happened?"

I glance back over at Rollo, who is still running around like a giant torch setting every part of the playroom ablaze. "Can you not see the … Just get up here fast as you can. The door's stuck, and we can't get out."

"We're on our way. Hang in there."

Is that a fire? That gives me a sinking feeling. Which should be preposterous, being I'm in imminent danger of burning to death. Still, I'm disappointed to realize the cameras did not record anything in the playroom from the clown or the little boy in powder-blue footie pajamas.

This is a shame since I don't know I would ever be able to adequately describe Rollo. Assuming Liza and I survive this ordeal.

But the fact isn't lost on me that a few good pictures of this clown would spike Dusty's book sales.

Will this clown ever quit moving? His helmet, now burnt black, still has a low flame on it, but the rest of the clown's broomstick skeletal system only smolders. Rollo's face is worse for wear. His eyes have dried to raisins inside monstrous sockets, his nostril holes big enough to poke my head through.

Rollo reaches up with what is left of his super-heated plastic hand and jams his fist into his mouth. His wrist disappears into his mouth. The staff dangles out one of his nostril holes, and he pushes it out by swiping at it with his other fingerless hand.

"This stick and the fire have given me a great idea. I'm going to barbecue you alive and use this as a spit. I love the taste of barbecue," Rollo yells at me as he runs his dark-purple tongue over his lips. A large portion of his bottom lip falls off onto the hardwood floor.

Rollo and I stare down at the remnants of his lip. A thud against the playroom door draws our attention away from the morbid gummy snake Rollo dropped on the floor.

Rollo roars in frustration.

I dog crawl back to Liza with the radio.

The heat is becoming so oppressive that if I'm sweating, it evaporates off my skin before it gets the chance to trickle down my back. My hair rises on the heated drafts. I find it impossible to take anything but tiny, short breaths. Anything more, and I risk breaking into a hacking cough that will mimic bronchitis.

I've done everything I can do. Now I must have faith the boys can get to us in time.

If they don't, I plan to haunt them mercilessly for the rest of their short lives.

I hear a thump on the door again. Still no much-desired splintering of dumb solid oak door sound.

"Leave us alone!" Rollo screams at the door.

Moses runs across the room and adds his two cents towards the door, "Yeah. Go away!"

I thumb the radio, "That's not us, Luis. Keep swinging away

at the door."

"Who is that, April May?"

Aww, how sweet. It's my big brother who talked me into this idiotic research trip. He used my middle name, too. Which means he's *really* concerned.

I cough as the noxious black smoke fills my lungs. "I'll explain as soon as you get us out, Dusty."

"Hurry it up, guys!" Dusty's voice carries through the door.

"Conserve your breath. We'll be to you in no time," Dusty says through the radio.

I snort a laugh. All those times I've made fun of my brother's desire to play the hero. I'll gladly let Dusty and the boys save me now.

The room is filled with thick, swirling smoke. I have lost view of Rollo and Moses in the black fog.

Lying nearly prone on the floor, I feel it's best to get our butts to the door to wait—hope. Putting my arm around Liza, I slide toward the door. Pinch and pull, pinch and pull, I move us toward the exit.

It will be for naught if the boys can't break through the door in the next thirty seconds. I fear that since my lungs are burning from toxins and the flames are ever nearer, we will have already perished.

Reaching the door, I hear the unmistakable crack of the door splintering, and I cry out in joy. I sound more like a grievously injured animal.

On the next strike, a two-foot-wide gap opens in the center of the door. The boys gag and cough as they get a dose of Liza's and my current predicament, the gases of the fire rolling out the new source of oxygen to greet them.

"Down here. We're down here, guys." My skin feels like it is peeling off my face, and I'm not one hundred percent sure my hair hasn't been singed off.

Someone's hand pushes through the gap in the door. I start to warn them as their hand goes to the doorknob, but it is too late.

There is profuse cursing as the hand recoils back through the opening.

My hope fades. I don't know how they can get inside to help in time. The door is too solid.

I cough so hard a streamer of spittle runs from my mouth, and my eyes close shut from the burning sensation caused by the acrid smoke.

That's alright. I just want to lie down and take a nap. It's so hard to catch my breath, and I'm feeling exhausted.

Someone jerks me across the floor by the back collar of my sweatshirt. A second lurch, and I'm vaguely aware I'm being pulled out of the playroom and into the tiled bathroom across the hallway.

The old tile of the bathroom reeks of mildew and rat urine. I don't believe I have ever smelled anything so sweet in my life. I breathe in as much air as I dare, attempting to get my lungs back to normal operations.

Dusty hovers over me. Luis lays Liza down next to me.

"You gave us a heck of a scare, Tink. How are you?"

With my remaining strength, I pull myself upright and grab Dusty by the front of his shirt. "You have to seal that room or at least let this house burn down."

He squints his eyes. "Why?"

"Dusty, you just have to trust me on this."

"How is she?" Dusty says to Luis.

Luis stops checking Liza for burns. "Surprisingly well for being unconscious. Good pulse and breathing."

The sound of extinguishers comes from across the hall. I tug on Dusty's shirt. "Let it burn, Dusty!"

"What happened in there?" he asks.

I want to explain everything to him. But I'm exhausted, and my throat is burning. "Don't. We have to go."

He hesitates. Looking over his shoulder, he calls out, "Chet, give me a hand here."

Dusty returns his attention to me as he begins to scoop me up. I push against his chest.

"No, don't. I can walk," I complain.

"For once in your life, just be quiet." Dusty slides his arms behind my shoulders and kneecaps, lifting me as if I weigh nothing.

"You're going to have a lot of explaining to do on this one," he growls.

It would be easy for me to take offense to that comment from my brother. It isn't like Liza and I asked to be attacked by a creepy twelve-foot clown. To be fair about it, if Rollo and Moses were not being filmed by the video, the team didn't see the attic fire start.

Sometimes I wonder, especially when someone like Dusty sees supernatural on a sporadic basis, if some people's minds are wired to not see paranormal once things get too weird. I assume it was my hero brother who reached in and pulled Liza and me through the hole in the door.

How did he *not* see Rollo and Moses? For that matter, how did Liza see Rollo and never Moses? No matter how much coaching I receive from Nana Hirsch, I will never understand why my "gifts" are so sensitive compared to others.

We clear the third-floor stairs and turn to go down the second when we almost crash into the Early brothers taking the stairs two at a time. Each has a fire extinguisher in their hand.

"No!" I say, holding out my arm to block Travis's and Jason's progress to the playroom.

"Luis said to get the spares to help put out the fire, April," Jason explains as he brushes my arm aside.

"No. Let it burn. It's too powerful to leave alone," I plead.

Dusty's brow wrinkles as his face hardens. I believe I have finally gotten through to him. "Forget about it, guys. It's too far gone. See what we can strip out of the first floor as quickly as possible and meet on the front lawn."

Travis's eyes squint in disbelief. "At least let us try to put out the playroom, Dusty."

I feel Dusty's chest bow out as he stands up to his full height. "It's too dangerous. Get as much equipment out as you can downstairs and meet on the front lawn."

"Yeah, sure. Whatever you say, Dusty."

The Early brothers double-time it down the stairs.

Dusty leans back and yells up the stairs. "Luis, Chet, get Liza and get out of there. It's a goner, guys."

Dusty quickly steps down the stairs, runs out the front door, and sets me down on the lawn. As he returns, I see the Early brothers and Miles picking up equipment.

Luis sets Liza down on the lawn and runs back in to help the rest of the team salvage the equipment.

I sit next to Liza and grab hold of her wrist. I'm not checking for a pulse; I just need to touch someone. Still, when I feel the steady thump under my index finger, I relax. The last of the adrenaline ebbs from my body.

I watch our team scramble onto the porch then down to the lawn with equipment, only to return inside for another load.

Flames shoot from the top of the roof. Slowly they grow the hole where Rollo shoved his head through the ceiling. All I can think is, before too long, the third floor will fall onto the second.

Dusty hustles out with another camera. He lays it next to me.

"Dusty, let it go." I point in the direction of the rooftop.

He swivels to examine the roof. Dusty runs back to the door.

"Out! Everyone out now!" he yells.

I'm relieved. My brother is as brilliant as I often give him credit for.

Lying down next to Liza in the cool, damp weeds, I'm careful to keep my eyes on the doorway until everyone has escaped. My hearing fades as if someone put a noise-canceling headset on me. The only sound penetrating my senses is the faint sound of fire engine sirens far, far away.

The fire grows in brilliance. The intricate wood carving details of the house are more pronounced by the additional lighting.

A surge of paranormal energy pulls my attention to the

third-story window. At the lowest row of panes, there is a small face. The face of a five-year-old boy. Moses's face is light blue. He grins at me, then shoots me the bird. I suppose I deserve that.

Chapter 2

Waking up Sunday afternoon, every inch of my body feels either bruised or blistered. Puppy watches me speculatively as I groan and set my feet on the cold planks of my bedroom floor.

A cough racks my body, and I grimace at the charcoal, bloodied taste that fills my mouth. *Note to self, coughing hurts. Avoid it at all costs.*

The doctors at UAB's emergency room cleared me to go home the night of the fire. They chose to admit Liza for observation due to her concussion. Once again, I escape serious injury while another team member spends the night in the hospital.

I'm not sure if I'm that tough or just lucky. I'll guess it's luck since right now I feel puny—not tough.

Dusty and Luis stayed behind with Liza, and I rode home with Miles, Chet, and the Early brothers. It was dawn when we arrived home.

Running my tongue over my furry teeth, brushing them seems like an excellent idea. My sinuses are full of the odor of burnt plastic. I can't get the taste out of my mouth.

I trudge toward my tiny bathroom, stopping when I hear a knock on my apartment door. "Yes?"

"Are you hungry? Mama sent me over with a sandwich and some soup."

"I don't know. Maybe?" Puppy growls at the door. "Hush up. It's just Chase."

"I'm coming in," he announces.

I look down, basketball shorts and a sports bra. Good enough for Chase. "Okay." I continue my slow walk to the bathroom.

Chase opens the door. Puppy offers one quick bark. Jumping off the bed, he makes a beeline to Chase to inspect what he holds.

"Did you hear anything about when they were going to release Liza?" Chase asks.

I put toothpaste on my toothbrush. "No. I just got up. I'll give Dusty a call in a little while and see what I can find out."

Chase sets the plate on my makeshift dinette. He turns a chair and sits, straddling the back.

Without asking, he takes half of one of the two sandwiches and hands it to Puppy. Receiving his cut, my keeshond retreats to his doggie bed that he rarely uses for sleep.

"I swear, Fang will eat anything."

Fang is Chase's name for my dog. Everybody in the family has a different name for him. I gave up arguing about it a few months back once I realized it was an act of futility.

"He doesn't like green beans," I say.

Chase shrugs his shoulders. "I get that. I mean, they don't make me gag like Brussels sprouts or lima beans, but I'd just as soon not eat them."

I rinse my mouth and walk to my table. "What did Mama send?"

"Grilled cheese and tomato basil."

I didn't think I was hungry. But I'm easily convinced otherwise once I hear what comfort food my kind brother has just brought. I pull the plate and bowl to myself. "You want one of these halves?"

Chase shakes his head as if he has just returned from a thought. "No. Thanks. I've already eaten."

I finish most of the soup and all the sandwich halves as we

sit in companionable sibling silence. Having company is good. I hadn't thought about it, but I really don't want to be alone today—not after the recent close call.

"When Dusty called, he said it got a little out of control last night." Chase clasps his hands in front of the chair back.

That's an understatement. I accidentally let a laugh escape. "Is that what he said?"

My usually "devil may care" brother's sky-blue eyes lock in on me. I know he isn't going to let me skirt the topic. "Listen, I don't pretend to understand this stuff you two are always doing. I mean, if you two enjoy it and you both make a little money on the side from it, I say go for it. But you've been to the emergency room more often than I have since you've been home, April. That's an accomplishment."

"Aww, that's just because you've gotten so old and don't take as many stupid dares as you used to," I quip.

His lips thin to a narrow line. He bobs his chin once. "Okay. You can make light of the subject if you want. But I talked to Chet and the Earlys when you got home. They told me that you and Liza were trapped in a burning room. Chet said Dusty was barely able to get you two out, by their account."

"*Barely* being the operative word." I smile and raise my arms. "Here I am."

Chase gathers my empty plate and bowl. "Well, for Mama and Dad's sake, I would really appreciate it if, in the future, you could be more careful. I would hate for them to lose two of their kids."

"What do you mean, two?"

"If you get killed on one of Dusty's stupid research trips, I'd have to kill him. And even though everyone knows I'm their favorite child, I know it would still devastate our parents."

"You're a goofball." I laugh.

"I'm not kidding."

"Speaking of Mama and Daddy. Have you mentioned anything to them yet?"

Chase picks up the plates. "No. I'm not a rat. Just a concerned brother."

"Thank you. If you don't mind, please just keep it quiet for now."

"Sure." Chase taps his right eyebrow. "But they might ask you why you're missing your right eyebrow. I'm not judging, but it's not a very good look."

As soon as Chase closes the door, I race to my full-length mirror and inspect my face. Sure enough. The outer third of my right eyebrow is singed off.

Great. What do you do with that? Shave the outside third off the other and go with short eyebrows? Draw the outer third of the right eyebrow?

It's kind of funny. I'm sore all over, have blisters, and still, I wasn't totally ticked off until I just saw that I'm missing part of my eyebrow.

Now I'm salty about last night.

I throw myself onto my bed. My life is a complete joke. I am most assuredly trapped in some sort of bad nightmare—a six-month-long nightmare—but I have to be about ready to wake up at any time.

I will wake and be the high-dollar, prominent defense attorney with an exclusive client base I trained so hard to be. Not a glorified law clerk in a town with a population of five thousand working paranormal studies on the side for extra spending money. There is only one word that fits my life: pathetic.

I lie on my bed, staring at the ceiling. For some reason, feeling sorry for myself isn't nearly as enjoyable as it had once been.

Something has to give soon. I've been home for half a year! When I initially retreated home, my confidence shattered. I thought I might be home for a few weeks at the most. Never did I imagine half a year.

That's an important date, too, as the deferred undergraduate student loans I took out would be coming due soon. This is in addition to the loans I already pay from my Juris Doctorate degree.

Yet, I'm still here.

Why?

My confidence is back. It's well-earned from a few successful cases won at Snow and Associates and surviving a few near-death paranormal experiences that snap your life into perspective quickly.

The bird's wing has mended. Why is she still in the nest when she can fly?

Meh. Who knows?

I rub Puppy's mane. "How about we go check out what's going on over at the big house, Puppy."

He yaps, jumps off the bed, and rams through his doggie door before I can stand. "I meant together!" I yell at the flapping plastic door.

Sliding open the glass doors of my parents' kitchen, I notice the vampires and Frankenstein decorations have been replaced with pilgrims, Indians, and the occasional smiling turkey.

The smiling turkey is somewhat disturbing, but at least it signals Thanksgiving dinner is coming soon. Sorry, Tom Turkey.

That's why I'm still in Guntersville. I have just been working on the *revised* plan. The one where I spend the football and holiday season with my family one last time in Alabama and then get serious about finding a job in January.

Sort of a trip down memory lane. An April May Snow victory tour, if you will.

It is a solid plan. It has served me well this fall.

The problem is I'm beginning to believe I'm becoming entirely too comfortable with my routine. A routine that a twelve-foot-tall clown and a burned-off eyebrow remind me is not normal.

"Mama!" I call.

"In here, baby."

I pad into the family room. Mama is sitting on one of the brown leather sofas scribbling into a legal pad. "What are you doing?"

"Just mapping out the menu for next week. And then filling in the list of items for our Thanksgiving meal. Is there anything new you want to suggest?" Mama asks.

"Are we having broccoli cheese rice casserole?"

"Always."

The very thought of it makes me hungry even though I just ate. "As long as we have that and stuffing and gravy, I'm good."

Mama looks up, her dark hazel eyes flash with mischief. "Is there anything you want to try to make this year?"

"Like what?" What an odd question.

"A dish. Your signature holiday dish," she says.

It is a trick question. Everybody in my family is a cook, except me. In my defense, with everybody cooking, why in the world would I bother learning how to cook? Seriously, what would be the point? Besides, everybody else is a good cook already, so somebody has to bring up the rear, and it might as well be me.

"No. I think I'm good," I say.

Mama favors me her deadly frown of disappointment. Still, she doesn't verbalize her displeasure directly. "It would be a lot easier for you to learn a recipe to pass down to your children if you worked in the kitchen with us now, so we can help you."

"I'm not going to have any kids. Well, in all likelihood."

Mama shakes her head again. "I wish you would quit saying that."

"What, you know it's true. I'll probably be too busy with my career to stop and raise a family."

"The choice is yours, April. Still, you may come to regret that choice. I suppose time will tell. The offer still stands if you want to help out in the kitchen."

Let's see, slave over a hot stove and oven in the company of Mama, Nana, and Granny, or simply set the table for the family and eat. As generous as the cooking lesson offer is, I must decline. "Thank you, Mama. But I'm good."

"Are you wanting to invite any friends over for Thanksgiving dinner? Maybe a boyfriend?"

The whole boyfriend thing right now is a sore subject with me. It's not like I haven't been dating. I thought I had even possibly fallen in love with a Prince Charming or two a few times. Unfortunately, one by one, they all revealed themselves to be toads, or I pulled an "April" and pushed them away. At the rate I'm going, I'll be covered with warts.

"No, ma'am. I'll let you know if that changes."

"Well, don't hesitate if you think of somebody. By the way, Dusty told me to tell you that they were going to be releasing Liza later today." Her attention shifts from her list to my face again. "What happened last night?"

I give a quick shrug of my shoulders. "She bumped her head, and we were concerned she might've had a concussion. Better to err on the side of caution. Isn't that what Daddy always says?"

"That's it?"

"Yes, ma'am." I'll burn in Hades. I think lying to your mama is one of the mortal sins.

Mama eyes me. It isn't difficult to tell she doesn't believe my story. "Well, your Nana Hirsch called, too. She kept calling me all last night telling me she was worried about you."

That strikes me as odd. "What was she worried about?"

"Just some more of her mumbo-jumbo stuff."

"Why didn't she just call me?" I ask.

"Because I told her if you needed us, you would've called. Everybody needs their space to grow; you're no different," Mama says.

Oddly, they are both right. I appreciate how Mama mostly holds her opinions of me and what I should be doing to herself recently. It has given me room to operate and find myself.

Still, when things looked the bleakest last night, and the fire had surrounded Liza and me, I wish I could have called Nana. Maybe she could've helped me think of a way of stopping Rollo without burning down the old house.

"What are you planning the rest of the day?" Mama asks.

I was thinking lying around doing nothing was a swell idea.

"I've got a couple of cases I need to review tonight in preparation for Monday."

"Okay, your daddy is frying some chicken in the deep fryer tonight. I was going to make mashed potatoes and green beans."

If I had a date with Ryan Gosling tonight, I'd stand him up for fried chicken and mashed potatoes—or at least ask him to come over for dinner with my parents. "I'll try to break away from my work."

I step out to the back porch. I consider myself lucky that Mama was so distracted by her list-making. Her usual cross-examination skills would make the FBI envious.

Our oak tree's leaves have finally turned color. The elms and sycamores across the lake changed the week before. The dried leaves under my feet sound like potato chips crunching, and they release a warm cinnamon scent.

I love this time of year. There is something special about October fifteenth until Christmas that makes me smile. Even on the worst of days, I can't stay melancholy for long.

As I walk out onto the dock, it isn't a surprise that Puppy is sitting guard at the very end. He has a powerful connection to the water.

I can empathize with that. In many ways, whether it be a lake or the ocean, water tends to calm my nerves and recharge my batteries.

I'm in desperate need of both today.

Puppy glances over his shoulder as I push out of my sandals. I sit and dangle my feet into the still-warm lake water as I clench my fingers into his thick neck fur.

Squeezing and releasing his fur also calms my nerves. He doesn't seem to mind it, either.

"It's pleasant here today. Calm. Have you seen the catfish today?"

Keeshonds, having originated as guard dogs on Dutch barges, are renowned for loving water. Puppy has his eyes on bigger things since he fancies himself a fisherman, too.

Chase has six pet catfish that congregate around the boat dock. I say pets because they have a symbiotic relationship. Chase feeds them all sorts of nasty garbage, and they let him catch and release them when he's bored and doesn't feel like getting the boat out to go fishing.

Puppy noticed them the first week he came to live with us. Ever since, he's been determined that before he passes into dog Valhalla, he'll catch one of them. My money was on the twenty-pound catfish, to begin with, but now that Puppy is well over sixty pounds, he might have a fighting chance at pulling one out of the lake.

"When we get our new apartment in Atlanta, I'll have to get you a fish tank, so you can keep watching fish. Won't that be fun?"

He looks away, out over the water. We watch as two ducks paddle across the inlet.

"It will be a big adventure. Just me and you finding our way together in the big city. Won't that be fun?"

Puppy turns his head until his snout is level with my chin. He sneezes.

Puppy slobber blows onto my shirt and cheek. "Oh, yuck. Thanks, dude."

I look up from the mess on my shirt to find Puppy has already left my side. I turn to watch his upturned tail saunter up the dock toward the lake house. I might have to do a better job of selling the idea of moving to him.

Oh well, Puppy always has rolled a little on the selfish side. I wish I hadn't pushed so hard, though. I was enjoying his company.

I watch one of our neighbors glide their ski boat out of the boathouse. The air is too cool to go water skiing today, but a boat ride sounds nice.

It wouldn't take but a minute to drop Mama's ski boat into the lake. Yeah, that was a little more work than what I'm prepared to do presently.

I'm not well. The more I think about last night and those last few seconds before Dusty pulled Liza and me out of the play-room... Well, the finality of it is settling in on me.

What bothers me the most or is tearing me up inside is that just before I felt Dusty's hand on my collar, I was at peace with the fact I was going to die.

That's so not like me. And it scares me.

Fighting to the very end has always been a part of my DNA. That is the first time in my life I have come to a point where I truly believed there was nothing left for me to do and nothing left to fight for.

No matter how much I hated the idea initially, I have come to enjoy the paranormal excursions for some weird reason. They are an exciting side diversion to the weekly law work I'm doing.

I hold no illusions that I can continue once I am working for an actual law firm. First, I would be too busy, and second, I would no longer be in the area. But it had been my intention to continue with it until I left in January.

Now I'm not sure that's a good idea. There is way too much at risk.

"Is that seat taken?"

I turn to Dusty's voice. "When did you get home?"

"Just now." He sits, leans back, and braces his arms against the dock. "What a screwed-up day."

"How's Liza?"

"Madder than a wet hen and threatening to quit," he grumbles.

"Is she okay?"

He raises up and runs both hands through his curly red hair. "Physically? Yes, the doctors released her around noon, and I just dropped her off at her apartment."

He shakes his head. "Mentally, she's a wreck. Heck, I'm a wreck. I can't even imagine what would have happened if we had not been able to get you girls out through that hole when we did."

We sit in silence. I can feel the frustration emanating off his skin. It is uncharacteristic of him. I don't feel it helpful to add to his concerns by explaining all the events that took place in the attic—or how they had left me wrecked inside, too.

"Hey, you want to go for a boat ride?" Dusty asks.

"Sure, but Daddy is supposed to be cooking fried chicken tonight."

Dusty looks over his shoulder toward the patio. "He doesn't even have the deep fryer out yet. I just want to run the boat up to the dam and back. I just sort of want to feel the wind on my face, if you know what I mean."

Yeah, I know. Sometimes the air buffeting past your face and the cool mist from the bow breaks against the wakes can strip your cares away.

Something tells me we will need something more like a sandblaster to accomplish that today. Still, a boat ride would be a good start. "Okay. That sounds like a great idea."

Chapter 3

We walk into the boathouse. Dusty boards Mama's ski boat and hooks up the battery.

I go to toggle the switch to lower the boat into the water. Before I can, I have to clear a cobweb off the face of the controller. You would think the spiders would get a hint and build their web somewhere else.

"Looks like we might have to run by the marina, too. Somebody didn't follow the half-tank fill-up rule," Dusty says.

I throw the tie line into the boat and board from the back. "Well, I don't take her out by myself, and if it wasn't you, it would have to be Chase."

"Dang. Chill, girl. I wasn't looking to convict anyone. I was just letting you know why we were going to the marina."

Point taken. I take a seat, determined to keep my mouth shut and enjoy the ride.

Dusty glides the boat smoothly out of the boathouse. Shifting directions, he motors us slowly through the inlet.

Both my brothers are excellent captains. Me? I typically keep it out of the shallows and the lake weed. I'm rarely on the wrong side of the navigational beacons. Still, I'm not comfortable behind the wheel unless it is a necessity.

Leaving our inlet is always one of my favorite parts of the ride. It gives me a chance to inspect all our neighbors' landscape changes and new boats.

"I need to ask a favor of you, April."

"Hmm..."

Dusty's eyes lock with mine. Oh boy, he's got the serious look going. "I'm knee-deep in the write-up for the next book. So, I am limited on time."

"You need me to help with some of the writing?" I ask.

His face draws together as if I said something extremely disagreeable. Considering I all but wrote his last book, that sort of irks me.

"No, it's not that at all. It's just last night—when I wasn't sure we could get to you two—that just can't happen again."

I let a surprised laugh escape. "Darn, Dusty. It's not like Liza and I did anything intentionally to put ourselves in harm's way."

He raises a hand off the steering wheel. "No. You're getting me all wrong, April. I know you girls were as careful as always. That's the whole point. Even though you followed every safety protocol, we almost lost you last night. That's just not acceptable."

"And?" I have no idea where my brother is going with this.

"I know you've already got a lot on you. But I need you to research what sort of weapons might be suitable for the team to carry on excursions."

It's my turn to return the "Have you lost your mind?" look. "Weapons?"

"Yes. What could you two have had last night to help you? To protect you from the monster and ghost."

I think he's joking, but I realize he is serious as I wait for the punchline that never comes with a silly grin on my face.

"I just figured with the studying you're doing with Nana, you might know a lot more about this than I do." His lips tighten. "Before the other night, I just had not given it any serious consideration."

Oh. He really is serious. Considering I have made it this far in life without needing to use a weapon, other than my smart mouth and a well-timed roll of the eye, I can't understand why Dusty would believe I know more about them.

Still, Dusty has that expectant look on his face. I fight back the temptation to make up some nonsense. "I thought Miles was our researcher. Wouldn't he be better suited for the task?"

Dusty shakes his head; he obviously is not happy with my answer. "You can use Miles as a resource. Have him find you whatever obscure text you think you need, but you, and if she is still with us, Liza, need to come up with a game plan on how the team can defend itself against hostiles." His jaw sets hard as he looks out over the water briefly before coming back to me. "If I can't be confident that my team is safe, I'll start writing books about something mundane and harmless like the migration patterns of bats in China."

"Isn't that where bird flu and swine flu get all mixed up together?"

"Yeah. You know what I mean."

"At least give me a guideline here, Dusty. What are your expectations."

"I just told you my expectations, that we are all safe."

Not helpful. "Are you expecting us all to be wearing garlic garlands and have a holy water pistol holstered on our hip?"

"If that's what you find out it takes. Even though that sounds more like we're researching vampires than spirits."

The idea isn't without merit. If I put myself back into the playroom, which I really don't want to, having had some effective weapon against Rollo sure could've helped the situation.

If nothing else, I'm confident I would not have arrived at the point of acceptance of my fate like I did. If I had some means to fight, I must believe that I would've gone down swinging rather than gulping down smoke and praying for salvation.

"Okay. I'll do it. But I will need Miles's help researching some of the historical aspects. I'm not supposed to go by Nana's until Thursday, but seeing as it's Thanksgiving, I'll see if she can see me earlier this week."

"Thank you. You know, while you're at it, you probably will

want to talk to Granny, too."

I choke back a laugh. It's great fun to go by Granny's for some spiked sun tea, pet the goats, and talk about when Grandpa Snow was alive.

One of the first times I visited her when I moved home, she gifted me Puppy. That should be a solid mark in the "reasons not to go to Granny's house" column. I needed a dog like I needed another student loan.

"Why, did she tell you I haven't been out to visit her lately?"

Dusty builds into one of his funny, full-belly laughs. When he looks my way and notices I haven't joined in the laughter, he cuts the laugh short. "Oh wow, you don't know."

"Know what?"

Dusty taps his fingers along the top of the steering wheel. He slows the boat considerably as we enter the marina's no-wake area. "Give me a minute. I might need to touch base with Daddy before I say anything else. I thought you already knew."

I'm not sure if it is the duress from having almost died last night, the stress of the real-world ramifications of being a defense attorney, the reality I can't seem to buy a date with a decent eligible guy, the fact I'm living in an old party room down on the river, or I just haven't had any caffeine today, but my crazy snaps to attention in full-fighting, high-redneck gear.

"Give you a minute?" I slam my hands onto my hips as my shoulders and head sway side to side as I emphasize each syllable. "No! I'm not gonna give you a minute. You know I am sick and tired of trying to help you run your business while you treat me like some second-class citizen. Give you a minute? For what! What is it that you need to think over, Dusty? Are you hiding something from me? Cause it sure seems like you're hiding something from me, Mister."

"April."

"Don't *April* me. I've been helping you identify these ghosts. Most of them, might I remind you, *you* can't even see, not to mention when you got writer's block on the last book, who wrote the book for you, Dusty? Tell me who wrote the book for you?"

"You did, April. That's why I gave you the car."

Sure, he gave me a car, but that's beside the point. "That's right, I wrote the book for you. But now you want to act like you have to decide if you can share pertinent information with me. Really? Really, Dusty?"

I can feel the anger leak from my body. The boil had been lanced, and the bitterness has cleared my bloodstream."

"Are you finished?" Dusty raises a hand. "I just don't want to interrupt."

I exhale loudly. "I suppose."

"I just remembered that you did not know something about our family. I think it's no big deal and something that you certainly should know about. But I don't know if it's my place to tell you. I thought I would give Mama and Dad a call and ask if they thought it best to tell you. I wouldn't intentionally hide something from you, April."

I suck my lower lip into my mouth as I glare at Dusty. I start back in, wagging my finger as I speak in a much more controlled growl. "This is what I'm talking about. I've been back six months now. But it's like here are the Snows, and here's April. I'm sick of it. I'm sick of everybody having little secrets. It's just not right."

"Granny Snow is an exorciser."

"I mean, I feel like I'm an open book with you all. I don't keep any secrets. Bless it, I can't keep a secret in this family. Everybody's always up in my business. Everybody always ... What did you say?"

Dusty kills the engine, and we float the last foot to the marina dock. He catches one of the cleats with his line and pulls us in snugly. "You heard me. I'm going to trust you, that you won't mention to Mama or Dad that I told you just in case they want to tell you."

"You said Granny Snow exercises, right."

Dusty steps onto the dock. "I know you heard me, April. You might be blonde, but you're not slow, so don't even try that act with me."

I feel lightheaded. Like there is suddenly no air to breathe. What air is available feels stagnant and heavy. Which is sort of odd when you consider the fact that I'm outside—and it's autumn.

It probably has much more to do with the significant shift in my perception of my family than it does with the actual air quality.

"Why am I just now finding this out?"

Dusty starts the gas pump. "You know how things work. It's always on a need-to-know basis. You wouldn't know about Nana being an animist if you had never been attacked by the old man in the lake."

"People should tell you these things. People must know where they come from."

Dusty shrugs. "So, you can do what? Besides, when should they have told you? I'm not defending them, mind you, but it's never a good time to find out you're a freak from a family of freaks."

I hate the word "freak." Still, we're from the same parents, and yes … I have always considered myself a freak for the "gifts" I possess.

Still, I have been aware of my condition since I was eight. Two decades seems like plenty of time for my parents to explain the details of my heritage. They obviously have found the right moment to tell Dusty.

It really gets my goat that they don't even realize how they have separated me from the rest of the family. It is now so deeply ingrained in their mindset it doesn't even register with them.

Dusty completes the transaction at the pump and pockets the receipt. He unties the line from the cleat and hops into the boat.

As he pulls us out of the marina, I leave the captain seat next to him and move to the front of the boat. I make sure to strategically place my back to him.

I wish I hadn't decided to stay home this fall. It would have been best if I had found the job I wanted and just moved along so the rest of the family could get along with their lives.

The moisture in the air is thick, and as the sun squats behind the mountains, the temperature drops precipitously. I wouldn't be surprised if we have thunderstorms before midnight.

If I had continued to set up interviews with law firms, I would already have moved. I have to wonder just how dedicated I am to finding my new job. I mean, I have barely interviewed, and I passed the bar in July—the "before September" excuse for not having moved on yet.

"Don't be sore at me," Dusty says.

I thought the whole point of putting your back to someone was to make sure they understood you didn't care to talk to them. Dusty must not have read that instructional booklet. He was probably too busy reading about migration patterns of Chinese vampire bats. Dork.

"April, you got to understand it wasn't my decision."

Don't turn around. Don't acknowledge him. Ah, that won't work. I swivel onto my knees, facing him. "You were complicit, Dusty. I'm your sister. You are obligated to make sure I know."

Dusty starts chuckling. A few violent thoughts cross my mind as I don't think it possible that I could be any more aggravated. He proves me wrong.

"I'm your brother, not your business partner, April. Besides, if Mama or Dad asked you to be quiet about something, you would have."

That's a fair point. "I think at some point I would let you know. See, unlike you, I feel it's important that people be able to have all the information they need to understand themselves."

"Fine. I apologize for not telling you you're a bigger freak than the freak you already thought you were."

I know Dusty thinks he's funny, but I'll make him pay for that. I'm not sure when just yet, but I'm excellent at playing the long game. Plus, there is a lot of truth to the "revenge is a dish best served cold."

We reach the dam. Dusty slows the motor as we cross the face lengthwise. I look over the edge of the boat to see if I can find any of the man-eating catfish. Not really, they don't eat humans, but they're big enough to.

Being by the dam and thinking about catfish reminds me of my young client from the month before. I had to do a lot of quick thinking to keep Jayron Freeman a free man. He had been using pipe bombs his brother made as depth charges to catch catfish.

Some days I wonder how there's a single man over the age of forty in this world. Almost every guy I know can share at least two or three "hey y'all watch this" stories that make me marvel over the fact they are still alive.

"I think I also thought you might've figured it out on your own," Dusty says.

"I'm not talking to you, secret keeper."

"Aw, c'mon, April. Think back to the hotel in Paducah. The chanting, in Latin?"

I said I wasn't gonna talk to him, but I couldn't help it. I turn to face him. "Hello, I read Liza's mind. I simply said what she would have chanted if she had been conscious."

Dusty appears close to bursting out in another fit of laughter. If he does, I might have to hurt him.

"Liza could have given me a double-spaced, typed, and laminated sheet with a prayer on it. After reading it a thousand times, I still would have flubbed the Latin and not been successful in exorcising a demon."

I'm becoming frustrated. Possibly because he makes a lot of sense.

I didn't think about it much the day it happened. Truthfully I was just thankful I was able to rid us of the ghost of Les Blair so we could escape from Paducah alive. Still, I now wonder how the words rolled so easily from my mouth as if I had spoken Latin my entire life. "You don't know that you couldn't have done the same."

"Yes. I do know."

"Well, it didn't work anyway. You seem to forget James nearly drowned in the shower the next weekend. Compliments of Les Blair."

"True, but if you knew how to actually use that skill, you might have been able to figure out more about the demon. Perhaps you would have known to warn James that he wasn't safe."

Man, why is everything that goes wrong in the world have to be my fault? It's exhausting keeping up with everybody's needs.

I return to the other captain's seat for the ride home. It's considerably more comfortable than the bow seating.

I've cooled my temper by the time we pull into the boathouse. I can understand where my parents, or at least my mama, would have thought it better to keep it a secret that Granny has the power to expel.

I cringe at the thought of having to learn another skill set. I'm beginning to enjoy the training sessions with Nana. Still, I can't imagine where I would eke out a few hours every week to sit down with Granny to learn the ins and outs of being an expeller.

More importantly, I don't want or need to know—even though my treasonous curiosity is already itching and formulating questions to lay on Granny the next time I visit her.

"Remember, you promised," Dusty says as the boat comes to a smooth stop.

"Just for the record, I find it highly disturbing that y'all kept this from me all this time. I mean, if *anyone* needed to know about this, I would think it would be me."

"I know that makes sense to you, April. Truthfully, it makes perfect sense to me, too." He looks away from me.

"What? What else aren't you telling me, Dusty."

"I'm not." He pulls at his beard. "At least I don't know. I just always have this feeling that they, our family, knows something they're not sharing with us."

I snort a laugh. "Like what?"

"I don't know." He sighs. "It's just conversations cut short when we enter the room and references to some incident in the past."

"Like when the town was built?" I ask as I cross my arms.

"No. Like when they were our age—or maybe a little younger. Heck, I don't know what I'm talking about, April. It's just some weird vibes I'm picking up on. It's probably nothing."

"Chase could've told you, too."

I'm not sure what to do with Dusty's feelings.

I hop off the boat and tie it off to one of the cleats with plenty of slack.

"I wonder if Dad has started that chicken," Dusty says.

"We've been gone a good bit. I'm sure he has the fryer out," I say as I reverse the toggle switch and watch to ensure the padded forks are securely along the hull.

"I'm gonna go see if they need any help. Do you got this?" Dusty asks.

"I do. Thank you for the boat ride."

I'm not sure which of us is more relieved to escape the uncomfortable conversation. I would reckon it a tie.

Chapter 4

Walking up from the boathouse, I feel a hundred years old again. Being sore, having worked Saturday, and slept most of Sunday to recover, I'm contemplating playing hooky.

The only trouble with that is it's a short week. If you are only working until Wednesday and you lay out Monday, why even go in at all this week?

The issue isn't truly about having to go into the law office in the morning. The problem isn't even the close call Saturday. We survived, and Dusty is actively attempting to determine ways to improve our safety. No, there is a disconcerting thought that continues to distract me. A feeling that I know I need quiet time to process on my own.

I can still plausibly deny it, but some days I speculate I am not cut out for the big-city corporate life. It's such a joy working for Howard, and likewise, there is genuinely no excitement quite like a paranormal research project. It concerns me that I find pleasure in tasks most of my fellow Alabama law graduate friends wouldn't do even if they were starving.

I sometimes worry that no matter how many fancy dresses or too-expensive shoes I put on, in my heart, I'll always be a North Alabama girl. Most of my so-called friends in Tuscaloosa would consider the people I know in Guntersville as low-class commoners. The terrifying fact is, I *get* the folks of Guntersville. I understand their bravado, insecurities, and skepticism. They have zero sense of entitlement, unless it is their entitlement to freedom.

It has also brought to bear the mind-blowing privilege my family has lavished on me. I don't know whether that is because I was the only girl or the "gifts" that afflict me. Still, I now realize it has left me with a severe issue of expected entitlement. At least from where my family is concerned.

If I move away, I won't have to deal with the issue. In a pool of high-powered attorneys, entitlement reigns supreme.

If I were to make my home here, in Guntersville—a preposterous thought, but still, I should plan for all contingencies—I would have to address the issue and be more thoughtful.

True to my word, I didn't mention during dinner that Dusty discussed Granny's particular skill set with me that afternoon. It was less discipline on my part and more distraction by the incredible spread my parents laid out for dinner.

After eating way too much fried chicken and mashed potatoes, I'm too satiated to be angry with my parents' deception. Instead, I call my furry side-kick buddy and wobble off happily toward our boat dock apartment.

Chapter 5

Dusty had assured me he would discuss the need for me to know about Granny's skill with our parents. Hopefully, they won't feel compelled to come to discuss it with me tonight. My plan is to wash my face, brush my teeth, and roll into bed for a solid eight hours.

I walk by my full-length mirror, stop, and turn sideways. "Oh, Puppy. We can't eat anything until Thanksgiving now."

Puppy yawns at me, circles twice on the foot of the bed, and then plops over onto his side. I'm not sure he's really pumped about dieting.

I finish in the bathroom, then slip into my pj's. As I get into bed, I push Puppy out of the middle with my feet under the covers so I can extend my legs. I barely close my eyes when I begin to feel myself float off to sleep.

I know I'm dreaming. At least, I hope I am dreaming. Otherwise, I'm in some panoramic Technicolor movie set with thunderclouds threatening a major storm overhead.

I stand in the middle of acres of freshly turned midnight-black earth. Spinning slowly in a three-sixty, I take in the view as a light mist falls. There is no end in sight to the field. The cloying smell of first rain striking dry, rich soil rises on the breeze.

I complete another slow turn, and the bruised dark skies

open as long silver shafts of light break through to the soil. The clouds retreat quickly as the sun scolds them from the canvas of the sky. The sun's energy caresses the ground beneath my feet, and green sprouts flip their heads up, reaching for the sky.

The sprouts grow at an alarming rate. As they approach knee-high, I walk across the field, feeling the now firmly packed soil beneath my bare feet. The plants continue to shoot up until they are above my waist.

Light, cottony clouds obscure some harshness of the sun now positioned directly overhead as the stalks' tips swell, giving birth to thick heads of golden grain. Without thought, I turn again slowly and take in the endless expanse of gold that sways toward me and then away with each change of the caressing winds. Gold stretches to the horizons in front of me.

With the same suddenness as it appeared, the sun disappears. The bruised clouds roll back, covering the sky. This time they are accompanied by ground-shaking thunder cracking loudly as lightning streaks across the skies. The spectacle causes me to flinch as the smell of ionization floats on the humid, cool wind.

The golden shafts are laid flat as the winds squall across the plains and the rain pounds relentlessly. When the hail begins to fall, I attempt to cover my head with my arms as I search the landscape in vain for any semblance of shelter. The incessant sting of hail strikes forces me to scream out in pain.

When the rain relents, the field has been laid to waste. The golden shafts on their side are now splotched with blight and turning black as they move into decomposition.

As the wheat reverts to the soil, a new sprout appears, pushing up through the wasted field. This one is green like the last but short and squatty in nature. As it grows, it multiplies low to the ground, forming a bush.

I bend over and pull one of the bushes loose from the broken ground. Most of the soil drops from the roots. I give the bush a quick shake to remove the last of the dirt, revealing the root system in full. A multitude of swollen nodes is distributed throughout the root system of the plant.

Peanuts. I stare in wonder at the familiar plant.

As I watch the peanuts begin to swell and glisten. Their shell sparkle as if coated in silver glitters in the filtered sunlight. I reach out and squeeze one of the nodes between my fingers. The shell, soft and damp, tears away easily, exposing the peanut inside.

They're boiled.

My gag reflex kicks in hard, and I lurch as if to vomit. Yuck. I may be Southern, but I never did develop a taste for boiled peanuts.

As if the absurdity of the dream rocked my sensibilities, I wake. I can hear the light rain I earlier predicted would fall. The cloud cover must be blocking out the moon. The apartment is pitch dark.

I hear Puppy's light snoring. I believe I can even hear my own breathing.

I wonder if the dream has any significance or if it is just a function of having overeaten. I could ask Nana. I need to remember to call her tomorrow and ask if I can come by tonight instead of Thursday. I need to discuss Dusty's weapons project with her.

I have that disconcerting feeling again. It feels like the slow creep of kudzu through the forest. You don't notice it daily, but you come back next week, next month, or let's say six months from now, and it has devoured a large swath of the forest. Is Guntersville covering my dream like a run of kudzu?

There is no denying that my desire to leave has lost all urgency. Perhaps the kudzu creep has already attached me to this city, and I will be a prisoner forever.

No. I don't have a kudzu issue. I have a procrastination issue.

That's easy enough to fix. First thing in the morning, I will do what I do best. I'll develop a plan for success and work the plan relentlessly.

Comfortable that I have successfully decoded my situation, I close my eyes and relax. Puppy rolls over onto my feet, but I'm too sleepy to push him over.

Chapter 6

I have a much better attitude in the morning. I feel so cheerful on the way into work I decide to swing by Ms. Bell's and pick up some biscuits for Howard and me.

I'm two blocks away from Ms. Bell's. I see both of Guntersville's firetrucks, our EMT, an ambulance, and several police cars. That would be too many flashing lights even on a Saturday night, much less a Monday morning. My curiosity piqued, I take a right down the street they are on and do a slow roll-by.

It takes me a moment to figure out what I'm looking at. There is a large, blackened chunk of metal surrounded by all of the city's first responders. A dark, round circle surrounds the item as if something the size of a picnic table exploded in the driveway.

The final clue I need is the metal protruding into the air as if torn open by a possessed can opener.

Someone's car caught on fire and exploded. But whose? I don't know who lives in that house.

I turn around at the neighbor's driveway three doors down and slowly roll back by. Maybe ten years older than me, a woman is holding her front door open while she speaks to a police officer taking down notes.

My lucky day, the police officer standing on the slight concrete stoop interviewing whom I presume to be the lady of the house is an awfully familiar face. The sight of Jacob Hurley never fails to bring a grin to my face.

I pull my IROC into a parallel parking space across the street. Manufacturing a plausible reason to interrupt Jacob and find out what has happened proves more difficult than I thought it would be.

Just go to work, April. Mind your own business.

That is sound advice. And if I hadn't seen Jacob, I would listen to my conscience. But all bets are off with Jacob on the scene. There's no way he would keep it a secret from me.

Jacob finishes the interview, putting away his notepad in the front pocket of his uniform as the lady shuts the door.

I hop out of my car and saunter toward him.

Walking up the sidewalk toward the front of the house, I'm drawn to look left. A bout of dizziness hits hard, and I am nauseated as I identify what must be the remains of a human sitting behind the steering wheel.

I turn away from the burnt body, fanning fresh air to my face to no avail.

"April, what are you doing here?"

My equilibrium remains cattywampus. Still, I see Jacob stepping off the stoop walking toward me. He tilts his head in the direction of the human remains as he calls to the EMT, who is without a task. "Kyle, at least cover him until Doc Crowder gets here."

Kyle Musselman shakes into action, sprinting to his ambulance to retrieve a blanket.

"I'm serious, April, why are you here?"

I gather my senses. A job made more difficult due to Jacob's scowl of disapproval. "I figure there's a chance I'm the assigned defense attorney, Jacob. Seeing the scene firsthand rather than photos might be helpful later."

Jacob studies my face intently. I'm pretty sure he isn't buying it. It's not the best story I have ever floated.

"No. Get in your car and go to work." He points to the street.

"But this might *be* my work."

"No, this would be Doc Crowder's today. The last I was aware, defense attorneys don't come in until we have a suspect who has been charged with a crime. We don't even know if this is a crime or an unfortunate accident."

I examine the vehicle, the rear portion of the roof gaping open to the sky. "Really? Seems like a weird place for an engine fire, Jacob."

"April," Jacob says on a sigh.

Squinting my eyes, I ask, "Do they make rear-engine Escalades now?"

"April, stop."

"What?"

"Please go," he says.

I push my lower lip out in a pout. I'm surprised by its impact on Jacob, giving me an unexpected tingle below my waist.

"Please," he pleads again,

"You can't give me a ten-second synopsis?"

"If I promise you I'll come by your office and fill you in after I release the body to Doc Crowder, will you *please* get the heck out of my crime scene?"

"*That* sounds like a fair deal to me, officer." I wink at him.

Jacob shakes his head. Turning, he yells at the ambulance, "Kyle, how about that sheet?"

Chapter 7

I debate going on to Ms. Bell's since I'm now officially late to work. I despise being late to work, even if Howard doesn't seem to care.

The biscuits will have to wait.

I open the door to Snow and Associates. Howard, my uncle, calls out from his office. "April?"

"Yes, sir?"

"I was making sure it was you, dear. I heard across the police channel there was an accident on Fourth Street?"

There wasn't a whole lot that looked accidental to me on Fourth Street. I'll leave the investigation to Doc Crowder and the police force, but that is either a homicide or a suicide. An accident is not one of the multiple choices.

"It looks bad. I think there was a fatality involved."

"On Fourth Street?" He laughs. "You can't get up enough speed on Fourth for more than a fender bender."

I put my purse in the bottom drawer of my desk, "Hmm... It was a little more than a fender bender. And I did see a body."

He laughs again. "Okay. Whatever you say. By the way, I'm taking off early Friday. Christie Brinkley and I are flying to the Canary Islands for the weekend."

I roll my eyes as I sit. The fact will burn across town by lunch. There's no need to argue the point.

My nose twitches. I take note of the small paper bag on the corner of my desk just behind one of my monitors. "What's in the bag?"

"I ran by Ms. Bell's this morning. Jasper came in last night and cooked tenderloin. I got us each two."

My lucky day. "Thank you!"

Tenderloin biscuits are akin to a spiritual event. The crinkle of the bag, the revealing of the golden biscuit top, the spicy scent of lightly peppered meat, and of course, the first bite when I hold it in my mouth as the biscuit dissolves, leaving my tongue lavished in butter with a hint of sugar.

I set the biscuit down to check my Outlook tasks list. First up, review Ronnie Mosley's DUI case. This is his third offense for driving a WaveRunner while intoxicated. Yeah, he's earned some jail time. There's not much I can do to help him if he wants to continue to make poor decisions that can harm someone besides just him.

Truthfully, after reviewing the particulars of the incident, jail may be the safest place for Ronnie. He's getting off light, compared to what might have happened to him. He was jumping the wakes of a ski boat. A ski boat that was pulling a skier who had the presence of mind to lift the ski rope each time Ronnie crossed so as not to strangle or decapitate Ronnie.

Ronnie and I are scheduled to go before Judge Phillips Tuesday morning.

Judge Phillips is a hard man who abhors drunks. For that reason, I consider it improbable there is any defense I can mount that will effectively help Ronnie.

Like Daddy always says, there really is no defense for stupidity.

As I finish reviewing the rest of my cases, I'm horrified to realize I have eaten both biscuits. I planned to only eat one now and put the other in the refrigerator for lunch or a late-night snack tonight.

At this rate, I'll roll from my parents' kitchen to my apartment after Thanksgiving dinner since I will be perfectly round.

Seriously, I was barely able to fit into my Halloween outfit this year. After eating all the chocolate and hard candy leftover from the party, I feel I am approaching the weight of no return.

My pants are tight, and I keep having to tug at my bra since it's suddenly cutting into my shoulders and the cups seem to have shrunk in the wash. If I put on any more weight, I will have to go up a size in everything just to be comfortable during the day.

Why can't I wear pj's all day? I'm always comfortable in them.

Howard comes out of his office, making a beeline for the front door. "I'm going to go check on the Pizza King in Boaz. Do you want me to bring you back a pizza, or maybe a meatball hoagie?"

Back off, you demon of temptation. "No, sir. But thank you."

"Okay, I'll be back in a couple of hours. You'll be alright until then?"

"Yes, sir." Never mind that I can call him on his cell phone if I have any questions.

Howard has been all but an absentee owner of his law office since he acquired his nine Pizza King locations. He's in the middle of a later-life career change. Occasionally I wonder if he hasn't gotten out of the lawyering game yet, so I have a place to work while I'm in Alabama.

There's merit to the thought. Howard is a brilliant lawyer, but he is also passionate about pizza.

I'm happy for him. When he first informed me he purchased the stores, known for cardboard-textured crust and ketchup-like sauce, I believed he had wasted a considerable amount of his retirement money.

Instead, he has thrown himself into the business the last six weeks and made great strides in improving the small chain. For starters, he has revamped the entire menu.

Considering my daddy's prowess in the kitchen, it should not have surprised me that his brother has his own secret marinara sauce. The sauce is already developing a fan base across the Sand Mountain area.

Howard hasn't replaced Torino's as the favorite pizza joint in Guntersville yet. Still, it is not an uncommon occurrence for me to hear someone ask, "Have you tried the new Pizza King? My kids love it."

I'll admit it. It is cool to be related to somebody famous.

Not to mention, as an official taste critic, I can pick up a free medium pizza any time I want. Puppy and I had pizza nearly every night the first week Howard gave me that privilege.

Pizza King isn't just a threat to my aortic passage. It is also a threat to my long-term goals.

It remains a topic he doesn't broach. Still, I get the feeling that once Pizza King is making a suitable profit, Howard wants to transfer ownership of Snow and Associates. Turn it over to the one person who could take over the business without changing the company letterhead.

Leaving Guntersville would be increasingly difficult if I were tied down to this practice.

Sure, I can say no if he were to offer. But who wants that awkward conversation?

As a matter of timing, if I plan to leave Guntersville—I mean when I leave Guntersville—it needs to be before Howard's improvements in Pizza King take off in earnest. That way, there is no uncomfortable discussion between us. He can instead sell the practice to some young country lawyer for a handsome profit.

It's a good plan.

Howard has only been gone for a few seconds. My ears ring from the profound silence. It is a tranquil start to the week, and the office, without Howard, takes on a tomb-like atmosphere.

On the positive, I now have a little time to review the attorney job board. I think something on the East Coast would be good. I'm thinking Boston or D.C.

I know. D.C. isn't really on the coast. You can get to it from the ocean, though.

I smile since I know why it popped into my mind. My friend from law school, Martin Culp, took a position in D.C. after graduation. I'm curious how he is doing with his internship.

I hope things are going better for him than they are for me. Maybe he had the right of it, that D.C. is the place to go, not Atlanta.

I should give him a call and check in. Maybe after Thanksgiving.

I'm startled by the door opening. "Okay nosy, it's a busy day, so I only have a few minutes for you." Jacob braces against the chair in front of my desk. "Did Lane give you the case?"

I really want to know and consider lying. I can't. "Not yet, but the public defenders' office is still shorthanded, and we've gotten almost every defendant's case in the last three months."

Jacob smirks. "Hmm … Okay, just give me a call once he assigns it."

"Wait a minute. You're really not going to tell me?"

"No. There's no reason to. Besides, I can't share details of the case if you're not involved in the defense or the prosecution."

"I bet you shared details with the reporters," I say.

A light blush appears on Jacob's cheeks. "What reporters?"

"I know there had to be reporters for something like this. They hadn't arrived yet because it just happened when I pulled up. It seems like you could tell me the same stuff I'll hear on the TV tonight."

Jacob exhales loudly. "You really are a pain in my side, Snow."

"But you love it."

"Which only proves I'm a masochist."

He takes a seat, which makes me immensely happy.

"The folks that live there are Ben and Lexi Bransford. Formerly of Albertville. Ben owns a body shop in Albertville."

"You can go ahead and get to the good stuff. The SUV that looks like a can opener got a hold of, who was the driver?"

Jacob runs his hand through his short blonde hair. "According to the tag, it should be Ben's. I'm sure you could tell by the marks on the driveway it was some manner of an explosion. It will be a while before we know if it was a fire that ignited the SUV fuel tank or if it was some sort of a device."

"A bomb?" I lean forward.

"I didn't say that."

"What do you think?"

"I think I'm gonna let the people who know how to determine that do their job."

Mr. By-the-Book Jacob. "I saw you talking to the wife. What were your feelings about her?"

Jacob shrugs his shoulders. "Odd?"

"Too much emotion? Not enough emotion?"

His features darken as if he is troubled. "More confused than anything. Like nothing I was telling her was getting through to her. Presumably, her husband is dead in their driveway, and there's no crying, no tears, no nothing."

He looks up, his eyes lock with mine. "You want to know the only thing she told me?"

"Yes?"

"She said she didn't have much time because she had to get the lunches made for their three kids so they wouldn't miss the school bus."

I don't know what to say to that. We just stare at each other as we contemplate just how stunned you must be for that to be your most prominent concern. Or, on the cynical side, I wonder if anyone can be that cold.

"So now what?" I ask.

Jacob stands, putting the chair back in its place. "Now I do my job. I figure out who was in the SUV. Work with the experts to determine if the death was a suicide, accident, or homicide, and if it is the latter, solve the case and bring the murderer to justice."

"Why do you think the Bransfords are living here in Guntersville when their shop is in Albertville?"

"They have three kids. Maybe the school system is better?" Jacob says.

"Seriously?"

Jacob opens the front door. "I don't know, Snow. The investigation is early. If it is of consequence, I'll figure it out."

I believe he will. It's incredible how much my friend has changed in the seven years I was down at the University of Alabama.

If Jacob had claimed something so boldly ten years ago, I would've scoffed and told him he was full of manure. "Thank you for taking the time to fill me in, Jacob."

He flashes a smile. "I didn't do it for you. I did it for me. I don't want to be bothered by you calling and asking layered questions for the next forty-eight hours."

That hurts my feelings. It also makes me laugh because I know it would be true. "You suck."

His smile turns into a laugh. "I'll see you around, Snow."

The office reverts to its tomb-like state. I look at the two items left on my work list: a civil case against Adams Tree Removal and another petition for increased child support by Trina Middlebrooks.

Neither case will move this week. A professional lawyer would go ahead and finish the paperwork on both and prepare for litigation. Neither is sparking my interest at the moment, and I don't feel exceptionally professional.

I have something else on my mind now. Something that is none of my business and way out of my professional training.

I type in auto body shops in Albertville, Alabama, into my search engine. There are only thirty listed in the Sand Mountain area.

I know that number is low. There are at least that many more that are unlisted and only work on a cash basis.

I scan the list for anything that has the words Bransford, Ben, or B&B. Nothing.

Interesting. How do you expect to develop a clientele if you don't advertise?

The quiet in the office is getting on my nerves. More importantly, my curiosity is piqued, and it is as if I have fleas in my brain. I have an itch that's gotta be scratched.

Sometimes it takes one to know one. Chase and Dusty used to do bodywork for side money during high school. Daddy built a small shop off to the side of the lake house that held their welding equipment and a first-class paint booth.

Chase works at the marina on Monday mornings. Taking a pleasant drive down to the marina seems like an excellent idea. I mean, the leaves have colored up nicely, and I bet the temperature is just right to roll down the windows and enjoy some crisp Autumn air.

I gather my purse and hang the *We'll be right back* sign on the front door as I lock up.

Chapter 8

I worked weekends at the family's marina during middle school and my freshman year in high school before making the cheerleading squad. That was back when Mama was still running the marina. Before she became the top-selling real estate broker on the lake.

I always enjoyed working the marina's concession stand. There aren't too many jobs in the world where you can wear flip-flops, shorts, and a bathing suit top. Plus, I like working with my brothers.

While I enjoyed working at the marina, Chase loved it. It didn't matter if he was driving the big tow motor, docking boats for the members, pumping gas, ordering merchandise, or doing the payroll. Chase enjoyed every aspect of the small business. That's why it was no big surprise when Mama entrusted the Marina to Chase.

Mama's tenacious, entrepreneurial spirit was passed on to both my brothers. Me? The jury is still out, but my case is looking weak.

I pass the Cajun Catfish House and the Gunter Lodge. At the end of the road are the two large, steel buildings with the marina office and concession stand in front of them.

Chase's metallic blue '72 Nova Super Sport is parked in front. I'm in luck.

Stepping into the office, I'm assaulted by the smell of burning coffee. I flick off the bottom warmer of the coffee brewer and inspect the tar like substance left inside the glass urn.

That's left a mark. Someone is going to have fun getting that out. I set the urn onto one of the spare cool warmers.

The back door to the office opens. Chase walks in and starts toward the coffee maker.

"I already got it," I say.

Chase pulls up. "I'm going to take Jenny's coffee privileges away if she keeps making tar babies in the urns."

"You can always go to instant coffee."

"That would be a great way to kick the coffee habit." He tilts his head to the right. "Hey, what are you doing out here?"

"Can't a sister visit her brother?"

He sits on top of the desk behind the counter. "Maybe. If it weren't Monday and we didn't live in the same house. What's up with you?"

There isn't any point in carrying on the pretense. "I'm wondering if you have ever heard of a man named Ben Bransford. He's supposed to have an auto shop in Albertville."

Chase crosses his arms, leaning further back. "Uh-huh."

"Well?"

"Tell me why you're asking?"

Man. Chase can be infuriating at times. "I might be working a case he's involved in before too long." It isn't really a lie.

Chase shakes his head and picks up a binder. "Stay away from him. He's bad news."

I know Chase intends that to be a warning to keep me from getting involved in the case. But his warning has precisely the opposite effect as it tickles my curiosity into full bloom. "How so?"

Chase looks up from the binder. I struggle not to take a step back in response to his glowering expression. "Let's just say he keeps bad clientele."

I don't see why someone should be judged by their customer base. "What's the name of his shop?"

"Didn't I just say you don't want anything to do with him?"

"It doesn't work that way, Chase. If it's assigned to me by the DA, I'll have to work on it. Besides, you know I'm not gonna do anything stupid."

Chase scoffs. "Good one, April."

He tries to review the paperwork in the binder. I move closer and squat so I can see his eyes. "Chase," I drawl.

He shakes his head while laughing. "Bless it, April. I'm busy here."

"Me too. Tell me, and I'll be out of your hair."

Chase closes his eyes. His jaw flexes, and I think I've lost.

"The shop's name is J&B. It's in Albertville at Second and Church." He jabs a finger at me. "Do not go alone."

The joy of it. My brothers still can't resist me because they love me so much. "Cool, thank you, Chase." I turn to leave.

"That's it?"

I hold the door open. "How's your day?"

"Good." There is the slightest hint of a smirk on his face. "The steel for the third dry dock came in this morning. It's one of those where the rack can become the beam structure for a new building."

I missed that memo about the family business empire. Mama is tight with the dime. It surprises me she is moving forward with a significant expansion of the marina. "Mama approved that?"

"Well, first off, it's my decision now. I run the marina for her. But yes, I let her know before I ordered the dirt work and the steel. The concrete slab was laid last Thursday."

I know it shouldn't have, and I'm ashamed on some level. Still, I feel a tinge of jealousy. While everyone in the family, for that matter in town, loves Chase Snow, it has always been assumed Chase isn't serious enough to be a businessman. Somewhere along the line, my affable older brother became a skilled business entrepreneur while I was planning sorority parties. All this time, he was honing his business acumen in the real world while I was paying huge dollars for folks to pontificate on the proper methods of litigation. Who looks smart now?

I feel an odd combination of fierce pride for his accomplishment, layered over a core of sheer panic. I need to get my life going in the right direction, too, and quick.

"Wow, three storage buildings. That's pretty big-time for Guntersville."

"There's a little more going on in your hometown than you think, sis. Just the summer clientele alone has doubled. Not to mention with the new data centers nearby, housing is booming. Why do you think Mama's been so busy selling property these last few years?"

I hadn't thought about that, either. It makes perfect sense that all the lake homes Mama has been selling over the last few years weren't all to locals. I assumed it was all big money folks from Huntsville and Birmingham looking for a place to blow off steam on the weekends.

"I get it. You passed your sentence on Guntersville twenty years ago. You have blinders on and can't even see all the changes to the good."

There may be a lot of truth to what Chase says. It irks me to high heaven. "I guess a lot has changed, Chase. I suppose when you move away, you sort of expect everything to stay the same at home. You know what I mean—Oh wait, I guess you don't."

He favors me with a slow smile revealing his perfect, white teeth. "To each their own. But I will tell you I don't have to go traipsing all over the country to figure out I'm already in the place for me. They don't call it God's country for nothing."

Chase taking the high road leaves me feeling like a jerk. Heck, I am a jerk. "You're right. To each their own."

Chase studies my face for a moment. Seemingly satisfied that I'm done with the barbs, he pushes off the desk. "Hey. You want to go see the slab we poured?"

Awkward. I can't even feign interest in concrete. "No, I need to go take care of some things." I point at my shoes. "Besides, I don't have any boots on, and I'm sure it's a mess back there."

"Okay. Maybe next time."

"Yeah. Next time," I agree.

Chapter 9

I scold myself as I open the door to my IROC. My family is not my problem. My problem is that my dreams did not come true as I had anticipated. This precipitated into me being grouchy more often than usual.

I sit and grip the steering wheel as I promise to work at being kinder to my family. They love me, Lord knows why, and they deserve better from me.

I start my car and freeze as Chase runs out of the marina office with a pistol in his right hand. I resist the urge to drive away because it's Chase, and I just promised myself I would be more conscious about how I treat my family. It would be rude to pull away.

God's testing me already. I'm sure he believes I didn't mean it.

Chase taps on my window. I let it down.

His eyes narrow. "Do you still carry that .38 snub nose Dad got you for your eighteenth?"

Crap. I'd forgotten all about that thing. I had packed it away because we weren't allowed to carry guns on campus. "No, why?"

Chase crams the .45 ACP through the window. "I didn't think so. Take this with you."

I wrap my hand around his and push the gun slowly back

out the window. "I don't need that, Chase."

"I hope not. But the way you attract trouble, I'd rather you have it than not."

"I'm not going to take your gun, Chase."

His lips jerk into a smile. "I wouldn't exactly call it my gun."

I arch my brow.

"I mean, it's *my* gun. But I got more just like it inside the office. Besides, you're not taking it; I'm giving it to you."

I know refusing the weapon won't be an option. At least not if I plan to leave the marina parking lot today.

Besides, it's actually a good-looking gun. I lift it from his hand, turning it on its side to check that the safety is on. Of course, it is.

"You remember how to use it?" Chase asks.

"Do you remember how to ride a bike?" I ask.

He laughs as he holds out two clips. "As long as it's motorized."

"That's called a motorcycle, bonehead."

He stands, lifting his arms off my car door. "Thanks for clearing that up for me."

I place the gun and clips into my glove compartment. "Thank you, Chase."

"I still don't want you to go to J&B. But—I know that's where you're headed—"

"I didn't—"

"At least this way, I can tell the police to go looking for you, and I can tell Mama and Dad I warned you and did all I could to protect you."

I laugh as he cracks a grin. "That's awfully big of you."

"Heck, that's what brothers are for."

Chapter 10

Albertville is less than a ten-mile drive from the marina. I take Church Street off of Main. Like Chase said, two blocks off from the town center, I find a squatty mustard and brown building surrounded by a chain-link fence that encompasses an adjacent lot. The gravel area is filled with the skeletal remains of at least fifty cars from the 80s and 90s.

I drive by twice to get a feel for the business, then park next to the chain-link fence. The three bay doors are closed even though I hear work going on inside.

Odd. On a day like today, most shops would have all the doors pulled up to let the fresh air circulate.

I open the smudged glass door to the office. Stepping into the office is like time traveling to the 1950s. The dark wood paneling reeks of oil and stale cigarettes.

A button, covered heavily with oil and Lord knows what else, on top of the front desk is complete with a placard saying *Press for service.* I hesitate as I wonder how bad I want to service my curiosity. I'm dedicated, but everybody has their limits.

My procrastination is rewarded handsomely.

A man, approximately my height with dark hair and a thick mustache, walks into the office. His eyes scan me from my shoes up to my eyes as he wipes his hands on a stained blue rag.

I get a shiver as if I have just been undressed against my will.

"What can I do you for?" he says.

Cute. Like I haven't ever heard that before. "My roommate had an accident last week, and we've been sharing my car. I'm wondering what I need to do to get her an estimate on what it would cost to fix her car."

"We're not taking on any more jobs right now."

I try to look totally defeated. It's not that hard for me to fake these days. "Oh no. My friend said that this was the best place."

Short, dark, and creepy takes the bait. Grinning, he spreads his stance a little wider. "That's true. But I can't help you right now."

"But why?" I whine.

It takes him a minute to come up with a reason. "The owner's gone."

If the mark on the driveway this morning is any indication, that's a doozie of an understatement. "But you look like you're in charge. Like you're the manager. Surely, you can help me. We've just never had to deal with anything like this before and don't know what to do."

"I'm not, and you need to leave. We are busy."

I walk toward the garage door. "Are you? Surely you have to have room for her little car."

Stepping in front of me, he stops my progress. "No. We are full."

"Well then, what am I supposed to do? We can't share a car forever."

He shoves the rag into his back pocket. "Does she have insurance?"

I'm following my gut on this. "She does but not comprehensive. Her car will be out of her pocket."

His mustache lifts. "You don't want to get that done here."

I open the office door. "Well, that's silly. We want to get the car fixed at the best body shop," I complain.

He armbars me from exiting the door. "No. *Muy caro.*"

"How expensive?" I ask.

He places his back against the door and crosses his arms.

"Shops like this, insurance only. It's too expensive to pay out-of-pocket. My cousins and I have a shop on the side. You bring your car by tomorrow. We'll give your friend an estimate. *Mejor trato.*"

"What if the shop owner finds out? Will he be mad at us?"

He waves his hand at me. "No. He won't care. He's real cool."

"Awesome." This is my best opportunity to get a psychic read and consider touching his wrist. I chicken out.

I'm getting all sorts of bad vibes off the man and am afraid of what I might see if I read his memory. "I should ask for you?"

"Yes, Hector Suarez."

"Thank you so much, Hector. I'll see you tomorrow."

"I look forward to seeing you tomorrow." He gives me another full-body x-ray vision scan ending on my shoes rather than my eyes this time. Maybe he has a foot fetish.

Chapter 11

I get back in my car and pull out as soon as possible. I wasn't sure what I hoped to find out. A large part of dropping by was to simply satiate my curiosity about Ben's shop. Still, I learned a lot more than I expected.

I now know that there *is* something illegal going on at the J&B Body Shop. Of course, I can't prove it. But I'm convinced of it because the bay doors were closed and they were not taking on new business.

I am fully convinced that if I had told Hector it was an insurance job, they would be a cash-only shop. Plus, it was abundantly clear, there was no way Hector would let me see the operation.

Just my luck. I make a side trip to Albertville to ease my curiosity, and all I do is get it whipped to a fever pitch.

I should've touched Hector's wrist. That would've been the easiest way to find out.

Now I'll be forced to find out the old-fashioned way. I'll have to research and ask around.

I know exactly whom to ask. Somebody who knows enough to tell me to be cautious. I just need to think up the best way to bribe, extort, or blackmail Chase into giving me the lowdown on J&B.

Bless it. I forgot to call Nana and ask if she can see me tonight. I press her speed dial number on my phone.

"Hello?" She sounds preoccupied.

"Hey, Nana. What are you doing?"

"Trying to fill all these orders. Ever since I started advertising on the internet, I have had a tough time keeping up. When this began, I aspired to be in the one percent those kids complain about. Now I think it's too much work."

"Nana, I'm sure the one percent would have somebody else fill their orders."

"True, but I think the shipping charges from a foreign country would really cut into my profits."

I shake my head. Mama says all the time you shouldn't argue with crazy. I consider that to be sage advice and realize she probably learned it firsthand while being raised by Nana. "I was wondering if it would be okay if I swing by this evening. I could help you finish your orders."

"Are you sure?"

"Yeah. It will be fun."

"Fun? It must be a hundred and thirty degrees in this kitchen. Not to mention the wrinkle remover that I make smells like boiled broccoli and cabbage—wait a minute. What's up, April?"

Busted. I was hoping Nana would be too distracted to catch on. "Dusty has asked me to do research on weapons. Paranormal weapons to be precise. I thought I would start by asking you what you know."

Nana laughs. "I don't know anything about weapons to use against the supernatural. As far as a ghost, the best advice I can give you is that a twelve-gauge will turn a man into a ghost every time."

"Stop it, Nana."

"What? That was funny."

"What time can I come over?" I ask.

"You can come over right now. I'm not sure what I'll scare up for dinner, but we'll figure it out."

I pull my phone from my ear, checking the time. It is already four. Where did this day go? "Would you like me to stop and get a box of chicken?"

"Well, I wouldn't turn it down. I'm not particularly fond of store-bought chicken, but I know this skillet of mine is not going to get warmed up tonight, and it's better than starving."

"I'll see you in about half an hour."

Wrinkle remover. Huh. I wonder if it actually works.

Some of Nana's potions and lotions are highly effective. Others are right down dangerous. I'll let her demonstrate the wrinkle remover before I give it a try.

I stop by Kocky Cluckers on the way out of Guntersville. Kocky Cluckers is a regional chain known for its extra crunchy chicken. Because of the double battering and high salt content, a single drumstick easily covers half the recommended daily caloric intake and twice the day's sodium allowance for a healthy diet.

So much for my pre-Thanksgiving slim-down. Maybe I should try reverse psychology and tell myself to add on fifteen pounds.

Turning onto County Road 13, I realize I totally forgot about my paranormal nemesis. I cringe as the old Willoughby covered bridge comes into sight. I keep meaning to take the time and locate an alternate route to Nana's home.

There is a paranormal spirit that appears as a full apparition to me at the bridge. A nine-year-old girl dressed in nineteenth-century clothes.

We have a running dispute. The last few times, she has taken to flinging odd things at my car as I pass. So far, she has flung leeches, green slimeballs, and dark mud that smells oddly like excrement.

Despite needing to wash my car Friday mornings after the Thursday visits to Nana's, the ghost throwing stuff is an improvement from what she used to do.

The first few times I came through the bridge, I tried to drive through her only for her to reappear in my rear seat. You know you're made of strong stuff if you can cross a three-hundred-year-old covered bridge while you watch a dead girl scream at you in your rearview mirror.

Just like clockwork, she waits on me. I can make out her diminutive form on the left side of the entrance. Her doll hangs limply in her left hand.

Bad omen. She is tossing something repeatedly in the air and catching it in her right hand.

I pull my car within fifty feet of the covered bridge entrance. No particular reason. I just want to get my nerve up before I deal with her.

I can see the red glare of her eyes through the lank, wet bangs that hang over her face. The baby doll in her left hand has an identical hairstyle. A puddle of water collects under them as they drip dry.

The item she is tossing in the air barely fits into her fist. I'm horrified. It's a frog she holds in her hand. The drowned girl is playing catch with a frog.

No, that's not disturbing in the least.

Taking my time is not increasing my intestinal fortitude. Instead, it turns me into more of a chicken than what I just purchased at Kocky Cluckers.

I slam my foot down on the accelerator. My rear tires spin as my IROC inches forward the first ten feet. The drowned girl throws the frog in the air, then shoots me a bird before catching the frog in the same hand.

I return the symbol of our mutually respectful friendship a millisecond before the rear wheels catch purchase and fling my car onto the covered bridge. The acceleration slams my head firmly into the headrest.

With only one hand on the steering wheel at takeoff, my car fishtails hard to the left. I overcorrect to the right.

The process of correcting and then over correcting continues through the forty-foot span of the bridge. Each time I'm sure the rear end of the car will strike the bridge wall, crash through, and send me tumbling to my death in a fiery car crash.

My car jerks straight as it grips dry pavement. I breathe once again and catch sight of the drowned girl throwing the frog at my vehicle. *Thump. Thump. Thump.*

It is literally raining frogs. I wince as I listen to the tiny amphibians' bodies strike my car. There's something seriously wrong with that ghost girl, and I can't fix her.

Chapter 12

Nana isn't kidding about the smell. When I open the door to her trailer, I gag. The stench of broccoli and cabbage is so pungent I believe it may take up permanent residence in my nostrils.

"I'm here."

"In the kitchen," Nana says as if I wouldn't think she was in the kitchen considering the gosh-awful smell.

"I don't see how you're standing that smell, Nana."

She lays a wooden spoon down as she looks over her shoulder. "It grows on you. Give it a few minutes, and you won't even notice it."

I lift the box of chicken I brought. "I've got the chicken. Do you want to eat outside at the picnic table?"

"Whatever for?"

I don't know, maybe because it smells like butt in here. "It's a beautiful night. We don't get that many fall days. We might as well enjoy it."

Nana turns again, this time studying my expression. "Are you feeling okay?"

"Sure. Why?"

She grins. "That's just the closest thing to 'stop and smell the roses' I have ever heard you say. It surprised me, is all."

I'm getting that sudden antsy, frustrated feeling. "Do you

want to eat outside or not, Nana?"

She turns the stovetop off. "Sure, this needs to set a bit before I jar it up anyway."

Nana reaches into the fridge, pulling out two sodas. She grabs a couple of paper plates and leads the way out of the trailer.

"Oh. It is pleasant out here. I don't remember being outside once today."

"So, I have to ask. The stuff you're cooking up right now..."

"Wrinkle remover."

"Right. Does it really work, or is it just like regular hand lotion?"

Nana smiles, revealing her tiny bright-white teeth. "It works. At least as well as any of the lotions you get at the big box stores."

"Is it the active ingredient that makes it smell so atrocious?"

Nana's eyebrows knit. "No. Retin-A and glycerin, as far as I know, don't have a smell."

"What is causing the cabbage and broccoli scent?"

"Cabbage and broccoli, of course. I put a little of the leftover water from boiling the vegetables into the lotion. To make it smell bad. You know how folks are. They only take cures seriously if they taste or smell bad."

That is so seriously messed up. What really concerns me is that it also makes perfect sense to me.

"Between the wrinkle remover and the hair remover, I can barely keep up with orders," Nana says.

"Did you ever perfect the hair growth tonic you were working on when you found the hair remover?"

Nana opens her soda. "I haven't had time."

"Well, if you ever get back to it and get it right, I'll probably be your first customer."

"How do you figure that?"

I point to the portion of my eyebrow missing.

Nana laughs. "I wasn't going to ask."

"Yeah. You and everyone else. I see everyone's eyes go to it and then look away. Seriously, though, I keep seeing extra hair in my hairbrush. I think all the stress of my jobs is gonna make me bald before the end of next year."

Nana twirls her finger. "Turn around, let me see."

I oblige. "Much more and I will have to get extensions."

"That's a thought. I love Dolly Parton's hair. Of course, I would never be able to pull that hairstyle off."

"I think that would be more like a wig than extensions, Nana."

"Nope. There's nothing wrong with the volume of your hair. Most women would kill to have hair that thick, April."

"But it's getting thinner."

"I've known you your entire life, child. I think your Nana knows how thick your hair has been, and it is as thick as ever. You're just having one of your overly dramatic moments."

I dig into the box of Kocky Cluckers for a breast. "I'm the least dramatic person I know. I'm like the anti-drama queen."

"Honey, you just don't know enough people, then," Nana says.

Whatever. Nana is obviously having one of *those* days. Mama always said she can be a ball-buster when she gets in one of her moods. I rarely have had the pleasure of experiencing one.

"Tell me about all the stress you've got going on," Nana says as she throws a wing bone toward the woods.

"On the working for my uncle side, most my clients seem to have a death wish for themselves. Sometimes I think they're incapable of making a correct decision.

"I'll be sitting there listening to them, taking notes. It's like, *okay, so you made this bad decision, followed by this bad decision. Then you topped it off with this horribly bad decision—So, how did you really think it would work out for you?*

"I hate to think like that, Nana. It makes me feel condescending. But, bless it. It's exhausting defending people because they don't think before they act."

Nana has stopped eating her chicken. She's grinning at me. Her lips, glistening with grease, and her tiny, white, sort-of-sharp-looking teeth make me pause.

"What?" I ask.

"April. You're talking about when you're acting as a public defender. Why do you think these folks have no money to hire a lawyer on their own?"

"I don't know."

"Not to be mean, but because many have made a lifestyle out of making bad decisions."

"So why don't they stop!" I feel my blood pressure working its way up the scale from the stupidity of it.

"Pot meet kettle," Nana says as she fishes another wing out of the box.

"What's that supposed to mean?" I ask.

"It means none of us are immune from bad decisions. Remember that man you liked? The one with the little boy?"

"Patrick." I feel like a loser just mentioning his name.

"I know you would like to have a redo on the night you freaked and skipped the dinner they had prepared. Not to say you wouldn't have stopped the relationship anyway—but you could have saved yourself a bunch of time for having been rude."

"I didn't mean to. It just happened," I grumble.

"Yep. Bad decisions can just happen. Often because they are easy decisions. The ones that don't require any work or sacrifice. You were raised to do the tough thing, April. You've been given enough advantage to see past the next five minutes and instant gratification. Sadly, there's a lot of folks who haven't had that advantage."

Nana reminding me of my privilege has killed my appetite. I push my paper plate away. "So, there's this guy. He owns a body shop over in Albertville. He has a wife, three kids. Guy gets in his car to go to work this morning, and *BLAM*! His car blows up. Nothing left of him except the skeleton with just a bit of charred flesh shriveled to it."

Nana grimaces. "Oh, honey. I know that was tough to see."

"You would think with what I've seen already, it would just

get easier."

"Let's hope it doesn't. For your sake."

I feel my face contort. "Why would you say that?"

"Because if you get numb to seeing stuff like that, you have lost a part of your humanity. I would never want that for you."

"I'd say the world has lost its humanity, and I'm just joining the crowd."

"There is my little drama queen again, with her full head of hair."

"Hush," I say with a laugh.

"The truth can cause more pain than any weapon," she says with a smile.

Fudge biscuit. I'd almost forgotten. "I need to ask you again about the paranormal weapons. I'm hoping if you don't know anything, perhaps you know somebody who can help."

"I've been thinking about that ever since you asked on the phone, April. Are you talking about like a ghost gun?"

"Is there such a thing?" I ask hopefully.

"Not that I'm aware of. Why does Dusty think you'll need something like that?"

And so, the conversation turns down the one road I don't want to go. I can try to cook up a lie that I'm sure she will see through, or cowgirl up and just spill the beans. I guess I will follow her advice and make the difficult decision.

"We've found ourselves in some nasty situations over the past few months. Almost everything we researched was a full apparition with the ability to move objects."

"Excuse me?" Nana's face twists.

The shock registering on her face tells me this might have been a better time to opt for the lie. I now wonder if this news might get back to Mama. That wouldn't be good for Dusty or me.

"I mean, we've handled it. Look, here I am."

"Moving inanimate objects?" Nana asks.

"Yeah. Majorly not cool. Right?" I gesture as if I'm wiping sweat off my brow.

"More like majorly not safe." Nana's eyes narrow. "Where have you kids been hanging out. The old Bryce Insane Asylum?"

"I don't think it is proper to call mental health institutes that anymore, Nana."

"Girl, don't sass me! Do you hear yourself?"

I must've lost track of the conversation because I don't know if Nana is upset because I sassed her or because of the powerful ghosts we have been dealing with of late. Still, I'm feeling mightily uncomfortable with the way she looks at me as if I have three heads.

"I've been dealing in animism and witchcraft for sixty years. Do you know how many full apparitions with the ability to move objects I have come across, April?"

I shrug my shoulders noncommittally. "No, ma'am?"

"Zero. Exactly zero."

"What about the drowned girl at the bridge. You have to see her every time you go to the grocery store."

"I've seen a partial outline of her twice. Not once has she moved an object."

The hair on the back of my neck stands up. "Seriously? Never?"

Nana's head ticks slowly from side to side. "No. I have never seen a ghost move an object. Never."

That makes no sense to me. I know it is Miles's job to find the most spectacular paranormal stories to research. But how can it be possible that Nana has never seen a spirit powerful enough to move objects? We can't seem to go on a research excursion without running into one.

Nana crosses her arms. "It's such a rare event that animists think the idea a bunch of bull malarkey."

"Oh, I assure you it's real," I say.

"And I do not doubt you. I'm just saying people don't waste their time designing weapons against something that doesn't exist, April."

"Well, darn. I just knew you would be able to help." Here I

thought this might be a project I could quickly tick off my list to help Dusty and the team before I left town.

"I'm sorry. There are certain things as a witch you might be able to create—dispersion spells, protective shields—but nothing your team could carry. What have you been doing to date?"

"Shields mostly, but this last entity was too strong for anything I could generate," I say.

Nana raises her eyebrows to signal I should finish the story.

I don't want to tell her, but I feel it best to get it over with. "Without thinking, I tried a fire cast."

Nana wrinkles her nose. "On a ghost?"

"It was an exceptionally real-looking, twelve-foot-tall ghost. I thought it might be worth a try."

Nana hangs her head. "You're killing me, child. Is it too much to ask that you keep safe, so your Mama doesn't skin us both?"

"What?" I huff. "I didn't go looking to be attacked by a gargantuan maniac clown ghost. You make it sound like this was my fault."

"I can't speak to the clown part." She wags her finger at me. "But I know I specifically told you not to use your fire cast spell until you developed better control over it. So, tell me. How did that work out for you?"

"Real good, until the house caught on fire."

"I told you, you didn't have good enough control to use that yet."

"Actually, my aim was solid. I hit the clown right in the chest, and the next thing I knew, everything from his waist up was on fire.

What I didn't account for was that he was taller than the ceiling. By the time his head was on fire, the entire attic had gone up like a tinderbox."

"Please tell me you're just pulling my leg," Nana whispers.

"No, ma'am. True story."

"Goodness. I guess I should just be happy that you were able to get out uninjured."

I thought I had gotten past that brush with death. But seeing the concern in Nana's eyes brings my emotions back as well.

It makes me more determined to find answers about how the team can protect itself in the future. Unfortunately, if Nana is correct, that sort of weapon may not exist.

Still, I'm not prepared to give up so easily. If there is a source for effective paranormal weapons on this earth to protect us from spirits with a masochistic attitude, by gosh, I'll find them.

"I would strongly urge you not to discuss the fire with your mother. I'm not big on children keeping secrets, but I promise you she would find some way to blame the fact you and I are working together on your skill set for the mishap."

"I won't."

"We'd never hear the end of it if Loretta ever found out."

That reminds me. "Speaking of Granny Snow. The other day, Dusty claimed she was an expeller. Is there any truth to that?"

Nana quickly begins to tidy the picnic table as she looks away from me. "I think that's a better question for your granny."

"But I'm asking you."

With the dirty paper plates in one hand and the remainder of the chicken box in the other, Nana walks toward the trailer door. I'm quick on her heels.

"Come on, you can at least give me a yes or no."

She struggles with the screen door. "No. I really don't think it's my place. You need to ask your father or your granny."

I can't believe this. "You're as bad as Dusty. Why is everybody so concerned about keeping this a secret from me?"

"You do realize there is a difference."

"In what?"

Nana drops the paper plates in the garbage. "Animism and witchcraft are about energy fields, potions, and spells. Almost everything we do is by choice. We then choose if we want to do good magic or evil magic. The stuff your granny used to mess with—there is no choice there. It's ordinary people being in the wrong place at the wrong time and a demon hijacking their bodies.

"Yes, April. She is or was an expeller. From what I understand, she was a highly skilled one at that. But I want to ask you. When an expeller drives a demon from the host's body, where does it go?"

I have a goofy grin on my face. I have never considered the question.

"It either returns to hell to be tormented for its failure or finds a new host. It's not uncommon for a demon to attempt to take the expeller's soul as retribution."

Okay, maybe there are a few details about being an expeller that I didn't thoroughly think through. I thought it might be handy to have some of Liza's skills. And if granny has the talent, maybe I could develop it as a kind of backup for Liza.

Now I'm thinking maybe not.

"Do you understand?" Nana asks.

"Dusty thinks I have the skill set," I blurt.

"It is strong in you. I knew this could happen. That's why I warned Vivian against dating your father. The Snows and Hirsches never should have mixed. This was always a possibility."

Nana is so agitated I'm becoming worried. "It's alright, Nana. With your help and Granny's, I'll get a handle on both, and everything will be okay."

Nana leans against the wall. She appears to age twenty years at that moment. "April, you do not see full apparitions because of the strength of your "gifts." It's the other way around. They are coming to you because they want to feel your power and be near the source. To develop the expeller skill would just magnify that power exponentially. I worry what that might do."

I don't know how to respond to that revelation as I watch Nana go to the pot on the stovetop and stir it with the wooden spoon. Liza and Dusty both believe I hold the skill of an expeller. Neither could know the ramifications that Nana just laid out.

"Why have you kept it a secret from me?" I whisper.

"It was really Loretta's choice. Well, all of our choice. Loretta, mostly, because she knew the real dangers and costs of utilizing the skill.

"She didn't want that lifestyle for any of her grandchildren." Nana pulls a funnel out of the cupboard. "Who am I to tell her differently? I don't know the pain or fear that afflicts her."

I attempt to square this dark, cryptic explanation from Nana with the diminutive widow who always has a ready smile on her face and appears to spend the majority of her time half-lit by Long Island iced tea on her front porch while she looks over pastures dotted with goats and cows.

"Granny doesn't seem to have a troubled bone in her body."

"Hmm," Nana responds as she ladles the bright green liquid into the quart mason jar. "Loretta and I disagree on a few things—most things. But she's a powerful woman, and I respect her for that. She would never let on about her troubles to you children."

"What's wrong with her?"

Nana locks eyes with me. "Sadness. Profound sadness." Nana shakes her head and returns to ladling the wrinkle remover. "I've already said too much. It's Loretta's story to tell—or not."

Chapter 13

The drive home from Nana's is a somber affair for me. I know there are times I am frustrated, scared, or even profoundly sad. Still, I don't know that I ever considered my parents and grandparents could experience the same emotions.

I know. It sounds silly. Still, they're the adults. They have all the answers—except I'm supposed to be an adult too now.

I forgot to move the adults in my life from superhero status to human beings somewhere along the line. Human beings who have real fears and disappointments like their offspring and grandchildren.

I'm disappointed in myself, and yes, even a bit ashamed that this has not occurred to me before now. That Granny might be putting on a brave face for me, literally.

The bridge looms in the distance, its roofline silhouetted against the half-moon. There is no sign of the drowned girl. It must be past her bedtime. As I enter the covered bridge, a loud ring makes me nearly pee myself.

I exhale in relief as I realize it's only my phone. I peek at the screen. Then I pick up.

"What?" I say with more edge than I intend. The *clack-clack* sound of the bridge below me can't end quickly enough.

"April? Is everything okay? You sound tense," Jacob says.

"Yeah. I'm just crossing that old wooden bridge. It gives me the heebie-jeebies."

"Do you need me to call you back?"

"No. It's fine. What's up?"

"Can I swing by tonight?"

I get that slight tingle below my waistline again and frown. *Inappropriate much?* "I guess so. Why?"

There is an awkward pause. Jacob clears his throat. "I need to talk to you about something."

I guess because we can't talk on the phone? "Well, just tell me."

"Umm... I really need to tell you in person. When are you going to be home?"

Let's see, the drowned girl threw frogs on my car, Nana told me I'm more of a freak than I ever imagined, and I have come to the realization that I am a self-absorbed brat. Why do I not feel like any more human interaction tonight? "Jacob, I really need to get some sleep. How about you stop by my work tomorrow if you can't tell me over the phone?"

"Yeah, okay. I understand."

"Okay. Thank you, Jacob. You're the best."

I hang up and spend the next few minutes wondering what Jacob could possibly have to tell me that he can't say over the phone. If it's about the Bransford case, I don't know why he couldn't tell me over the phone. It's not like the FBI can be tapping *our* phones.

The more I think about Jacob's call, the odder it seems to me. Almost bordering on sketchy. Who knows with guys? Maybe Jacob opted for something stronger than beer tonight, and the call is his version of a drunk dial.

It's ten thirty when I pull up my parents' driveway. Both their cars are in the drive. Both my brothers' are gone.

All the lights are out at the lake house. So much for bumming a soda from my parents. The last thing I need tonight is to accidentally walk in on sexy time.

As I approach my door, a growl emanates from behind it. Puppy shoves his snout out the doggie door, letting out a single whine as he recognizes me and comes out to greet me."

Leaning over, I scratch behind his ears—roughly. "Did you miss me?"

Satisfied that he has been acknowledged, Puppy turns and goes back through his door. I'm left on my own, fumbling with my key in the shadows.

I open the door finding he wasted no time and is already curled up on the bed watching me.

Yeah, I want to crash on the bed too, but Nana said to keep the jar of wrinkle remover refrigerated. I won't breathe easy until the neon green quart-sized mason jar is safely stored in the fridge.

After pushing the jar to the back of my near-empty refrigerator, I stand in front of the open door debating if I need a snack. I'm left wondering just how old the leftover nacho dip is in the fridge.

What is the lifetime limit on nacho cheese anyway? Is it actually cheese?

These are all questions I do not have the energy to research tonight. I opt to brush my teeth, slip into an oversized T-shirt, and push Puppy out of the middle of the bed.

Chapter 14

Tuesday morning is a complete drag. On the way into the law office, I receive a message from Howard informing me he won't make it in today. I get it. Some days the idea of cooking a pizza sounds more energizing and satisfying than filling in one more legal document template.

Like a good girl who tackles the tough jobs first, I complete the two most pressing contracts first. Setting them to the side, I check the intercompany emails.

As I finish answering the last of them, the door to the office opens. Lane Jameson, our local DA, enters the office, craning his neck toward Howard's office.

"Is he in?" His tone is uncharacteristically harsh.

"No, sir. He's working at Pizza King today."

"Why couldn't he have worked at a pizza joint and gotten it out of his system when he was eighteen like the rest of us?"

I'm pretty sure that is a rhetorical question from Lane, and I decide to keep quiet.

"I'm sorry I shouldn't have said that." He frowns

"Are you okay?"

He shoves his hands into the pockets of his slacks. "This too shall pass. In the meantime, the state attorney general is all over me about keeping the Bransford case off the radar. But the town is already crawling with reporters."

I was so deep in my thoughts about Howard not coming in and how unfair it is I must run the law firm alone so he can bake pizzas, all the media vans on the town square did not register in my mind this morning. Come to think of it. I hadn't seen that many since this summer.

"AG Pinegar can't hold you responsible for criminals committing crimes and reporters reporting the news."

Lane favors me with a rueful smile. "Heidi Pinegar doesn't hold me responsible for that. She does expect me to make sure the general population has the perception crime has dropped precipitously since she took over the position of attorney general from Owens."

Heidi Pinegar is a hard-driving, forty-something professional. She has harsh features, a merciless tongue, and a quick temper. She is also extremely ambitious, with higher offices in mind for her future. It is well known in the political circles that Heidi Pinegar intends to be the next female governor of Alabama.

In the same political circles, it is also known that if you impede Heidi's progress toward her goals, you won't be working for the state any longer. Last month she replaced the DA of Montgomery County over an allegation of bribery. No trial; just the allegation was enough for her to remove him.

When your name officially appears on the ballot as Heidi "Lock 'em Up" Pinegar, you build a specific expectation within your political base. It also means the perception of your base can be more important than justice if it is the political power you seek.

"Police Chief Kline has brought in a person of interest in the Bransford case. Unfortunately, she's already requested an attorney before talking with the investigators," Lane explains. "I need to get this wrapped up as quickly as possible to get the reporters out of town and get everything quieted down.

"The trouble being, Lesley is still out on maternity leave, and several of the other attorneys have done work for Ben in the past." He shrugs. "Conflict of interest," he offers as an explanation.

I nod my head. "And…"

"I was hoping Howard might actually be playing lawyer today."

"Well, he's not, but I am." My head is swirling with questions. This is precisely the opportunity I hoped for. I can learn even more details about the case. I'm so invested in the case now I would almost waive our fee to take it on. Almost.

Lane shifts his weight. "Yes. And don't get me wrong, April. You do excellent work. But I really don't want you getting involved in this if you don't have to. I can't guarantee your safety."

Safety? "What do you mean, safety?"

"There's been an ongoing FBI investigation into the Bransford business for the last two years. The FBI was getting close to blowing the whole case open, and then something else blew up. The thinking being that possibly someone close in the business, but not one of the Bransfords got word of the impending FBI bust, got nervous and offed Mr. Bransford."

"Car bomb." This is getting more exciting by the second. It's not every day you get a car bombing in your hometown.

Lane crosses his arms and studies me. "Yes. But that wasn't official until an hour ago when the expedited tests came back from the lab. How could you know?"

"I heard Howard talking about it. He heard about it on the police scanner." I tap my head. "I can figure stuff like that out."

Lane nods. "Right."

I stand up, moving closer to Lane. "Who did the sheriff bring in? Who is my client?"

Lane shakes his head. "Not your client, and you're beginning to sound like the reporters outside, April."

I change my body language and cross my arms. "Hey. Inquiring minds want to know."

"Tell me about it. But that's part of the problem. Sheriff Klein brought in Ms. Bransford for questioning, but the FBI swears up and down that he has it wrong. The FBI is standing firm on the silent business partner theory. Trouble being, if Ben had a silent partner, nobody, including the FBI, has a clue as to their identity."

"Geez, I never realized operating a body shop could be so filled with intrigue and danger."

Lane frowns. "Typically, it wouldn't be the case. But then again, this isn't necessarily a typical body shop from what I've been able to piece together. Do me a favor and have Howard call me as soon as he gets in."

Lane walks toward the door, and I follow him. "You need to let me handle this case for you."

Lane's jaw flexes. "No. This one's not for you, April."

I put my hands on my hips and give Lane my best "are you kidding me" look. "Wasn't that you just last month at the Alabama game telling me about all the great opportunities in Guntersville? That I should stay and use my skills in my hometown? Sort of the legal version of giving back to my community. You made a relatively compelling case. So here I am. I want to take care of this case for my community, Lane."

"Not happening," Lane says with a note of finality.

"I don't get this. You tell me you have an immediate need, and I tell you here I am. You tell me to seriously consider staying in this community and working in the legal field. Then you withhold a case from me that I'm interested in. What am I missing here, Lane?"

Lane's eyebrows shift up. "The fact we might be dealing with some seriously evil people. The type of people who don't have any issues eliminating a defense attorney who threatens their organization. Not to mention your one run-in with the FBI wasn't exactly the smoothest bit of teamwork I've ever seen."

Agent Taggart, from the FBI's Gadsden Bureau, and I got a little sideways during the Freeman case. It was Taggart's fault. He's sort of a know-it-all, but we got it sorted out and took care of business in the end. It wasn't fair for Lane to bring that up as a negative.

"I'm not even going to justify that with a response. I'm a

good team player. And you need a defense attorney who hasn't already done work for the body shop. So, I need to know. Are you serious about the opportunities here in Guntersville, or is that just lip service?" I wave my hand toward my laptop. "I mean, I specifically slowed down my employment search since you and I discussed this. I need to know if I should start scheduling interviews again."

"God bless, woman. Why is everything a negotiation with you? I'm trying to keep you safe."

"And who asked you to? You're not my daddy."

The left side of Lane's lip tugs up into a sardonic smile. "No. I just know your daddy and his brother. I know them well enough that if something were to happen to you from a case I assigned you, they would blame it all on me."

I drop my arms and stomp back toward my desk. "Wrong answer. But I guess it's good that I know so I can take care of what I need to do." I sit and make a bunch of keystrokes, not actually typing anything.

"What are you doing?"

"Applying for another job. I mean, you can't expect me to stay here where anytime I might be dealing with a hardened criminal, you're going to pull me off the case."

Lane drifts back toward me. "This isn't an every time thing. Just this case. You do understand that?"

"Oh, I understand perfectly." I try not to grin as I watch him shuffle from left foot to right as he contemplates the situation.

"Get Howard to call me. I'll discuss it with him. If he gives you the green light, we'll see what we can do."

I lock eyes with Lane. "I don't want to be perceived as bending your arm."

Lane scoffs, turning toward the door. "There's no 'perceived' about it, April."

I'm proud of my professionalism. Even though I want to stand up and do a victory dance after Lane leaves, I contain myself.

I have no idea why the Bransford case intrigues me this

much. However, once my curiosity latches onto something, I know that you have a better chance of getting a pit bull to turn loose of a meaty soup bone.

Being I'm on a roll, I decide to call Granny. After discussing the matter with Nana last night, it appears Granny may be the key to solving the paranormal-weapon conundrum.

"Hello?"

"Hi, Granny. This is April. How are you today?"

"Fine." She drawls the single syllable out considerably.

"Can I come by this afternoon?"

"I play bridge on Tuesday nights. I leave at five thirty. If you can come by before then, I would love to see you."

That means without Howard available, I would have to close the office early. Still, given the importance of what I need to do, closing early is warranted. "Yes, ma'am. That will work out great. Say about four o'clock?"

"Yes. That'll work well. I'll see you then, love."

"Yes, ma'am."

No sooner do I hang up with Granny than my stomach rumbles. I check my phone. Quarter to eleven is close enough to lunchtime. I can buy a turkey sandwich at Jerry's sub shop. That won't be a diet destroyer. I'll even order it on wheat bread.

I collect my purse and lock the door on the way out. It is still beautiful weather, and I opt to walk the three blocks to Jerry's.

Lane trying to keep the case from me still stings. I know he's old school, but it still feels like he thinks I can't handle myself.

There's nothing I've done that should give him that notion—well, besides the fact that I'm a female. In his world, breaking a nail is still a crisis for females. Well, it kind of is, but today's women can prioritize crises much better than their mothers and grandmothers. We incapacitate the criminal and *then* worry about our manicure.

It would be possible for me to dismiss Lane and Howard as the dinosaurs of a chivalrous state long gone and buried. What does that say about my future in Guntersville if I have a change of heart and stick around? Wouldn't I always be fighting the gender gap that is all but nonexistent in the big cities?

Still, if the vestiges of sexism remain here, how do I explain Judge Rossi? She is female and a minority—how has she navigated the good ole boy system to become a judge?

I pull out my phone and hit "tasks." "Talk to Judge Rossi about good ole boy syndrome and how to overcome it." Yeah, I definitely need to talk to Judge Rossi.

I beat the lunch rush at Jerry's. There are only two people in front of me. Immediately, I begin comparing the turkey light sub versus the double meat Italian. How is it both of them can be six inches long, and the Italian sub has twice the calories?

How is that even physically possible?

"April?"

Turning, I see a familiar face. Well, mostly familiar. She is happy, virtually luminous, and looks full of energy and life.

The last time I saw Charlotte King, she had raccoon eyes, gray skin, and was twenty pounds lighter—not in a good way.

"Hi, Charlotte. You look fabulous. How have you been?"

Her eyes nearly close from how hard she is smiling. "You'll never believe it. It's like all my prayers have been answered lately."

Her optimism is so contagious, I begin to smile as well. "That's awesome, Charlotte."

She grabs my wrist. Her joyful energy flows up my arm, and I feel as if I'm about to float.

"You don't know the half of it. It was hard at first. I mean, after you got me out of jail. The insurance money gave me a little peace of mind, but I knew that wasn't going to last forever. The kids, they were trying to be good. Still, they were sad. They missed their daddy. You don't realize just what having an extra pair of hands to help out at bath time means when you have four little ones to take care of."

"I can't even imagine." Truer words have never been spoken.

"I was trying to hold it together for everyone. I even had Alan's team finishing up the last of our contracts. His guys were so supportive." Her voice falters. She releases me, placing her hand on her heart as she tears up. "But you know, nobody could help me with the grief. How could they? Most people haven't had to deal with anything like that."

"Isn't there like a survivor's group or something?" I ask.

"Oh. I'm sure there is in Huntsville or Birmingham. But I don't have time for that, and Rachel would be the only one who could watch my babies. I would hate to put her out after she kept them while I was in jail."

"I'm sure she would have understood," I say.

"Maybe, but she is dealing with her own grief, having lost her brother."

It seems counterintuitive to me. Alan's death affected both women, and it looks like they could help each other heal. I decide not to say anything since I have been fortunate never to be in her situation.

"Then two months ago, it was actually Labor Day, I had a complete meltdown. I was buying new school shoes for Jason and Justin when it occurred to me. I had already burned through half of the fifty-thousand-dollar insurance money between the funeral cost and everything else. My security blanket was half gone. The last of the projects Alan's team contracted on was complete, and I didn't know how to make a living to support my children. I went home that evening, put the kids to bed, and really, really wondered if I wanted to get up in the morning."

Her candor shocks all my sensibilities. "Oh, Charlotte. I wish you had called me." I also wish I had thought to call her. Why would it not have occurred to me to check up on her progress?

She waves her hand dismissively in front of her face. "No, wait. That's what I want to tell you. I was lying there crying, feeling trapped, and most of all feeling alone.

"Just a deep, hollow feeling in my gut. I wasn't alone. I know that. I had my children but just missed my partner, my rock. I was missing Alan's sureness. I wanted to lay my head on his chest and listen to him tell me it would all work out as he combed his fingers through my hair."

Charlotte never shared this level of intimacy about her relationship with her husband Alan when I represented her. Still, the scene she describes is indicative of the intense energy imprint Alan left in his home. The imprint was passionate, sincere, and full of adoration for his wife.

"Then I saw the stack of composition books he kept on his dresser. They had been there the whole time. I just had not paid them any attention. It was as if they weren't even there.

Suddenly, I had this overwhelming urge to hold them, touch them, to be close to him, his thoughts and dreams. Alan loved to design furniture. The composition books held all the designs he had dreamed up over his lifetime."

I understand how Charlotte would have found comfort in holding the composition books of her late husband. The passion of creativity leaves the most vital electrical impulses after all. She would have felt that even if she were not aware of it.

"I opened the books and began to go through them—page after page, book after book. Alan always showed me his designs, and I would be like, 'Oh, that's really pretty, baby.' But that night, as I looked at the designs through my tears, it was like I was looking at them with fresh eyes.

"Maybe I was seeing them through Alan's eyes. Then it came to me, and I knew everything was going to be alright."

I seem to have missed part of the story. Mainly how everything was going to be alright for a mother of four without gainful employment. "How so?"

"The designs are beautiful originals. The best I can describe it is a refined old country house style—lots of leaded glass and lots of ingenious cubby holes for specific storage. Servers, sideboards, china cabinets, dining tables, and even some bedroom furniture pieces.

"I asked Iker, he was Alan's lead man on his crew, if he thought we could possibly make the pieces. He thought we could, and we began to make them.

Two weeks later, I put the first pieces out on the internet and took a gamble with the last of Alan's insurance money, it only seemed fitting, on advertisements."

She raises her hands upward. "Praise Jesus. Two months later, we had the whole crew back to work, and we are going to have to add on to Alan's workshop to keep up with the demand."

"That's awesome, Charlotte!"

"I know, right. It is so incredible. Not just the money coming in, but getting to bring Alan's pieces to life." She taps her heart. "It helps. It helps a lot."

I'm reciprocating in the tearing-up process. I'm thrilled for Charlotte.

"But I want to tell you thank you. I had all but given up hope when you came to me in the jail back in June. But as soon as I saw you, I was like, 'April Snow will be defending me. If she can't get me out of jail, nobody can.' Then you did it. You got me out of jail and made sure I got the insurance money that was due me. The money I used to start this business. To bring a part of Alan back to life and build a legacy for his children."

Charlotte is giving me way too much credit. "Thank you, Charlotte," I croak.

"No, thank you." She pulls me into a hug I wasn't expecting. "I always thought you were a special person, and you are definitely an angel in my life."

"I'm so happy for you, Charlotte."

"I keep hearing that you're moving away. As soon as you get your new fancy apartment, I'm going to make you a special kitchen table. You'll let me do that?"

I don't really see how I could say no and not be rude. "I would love that."

Her smile stretches across her face. "Good. Don't you forget."

Having Charlotte there makes it easier for me to pass on the Italian sub and be a good girl ordering the turkey. Who says accountability doesn't work?

Chapter 15

Wanting to maximize my enjoyment of the beautiful fall weather, I decide to walk over to the courthouse square. I select one of the stone benches between the annex and the courthouse shaded by the three ancient oaks in the courtyard. The light breeze chills my skin giving me a light case of goosebumps.

Perhaps my stint in Guntersville isn't a complete washout. Charlotte was staring down at least a twenty-year sentence, and her sister-in-law would've had to raise her four children.

Suppose I had not been assigned the case. In that case, I am sure that Charlotte would've either been found guilty during a trial or finally relented to the plea offer of a thirteen-year sentence Lane offered. Thirteen or twenty years for a mother—it doesn't much make a difference. Either way, she misses her children's lives.

I think about calling Howard to ask how things are going at Pizza King. But I still have a bit of a petulant streak in me that keeps my phone at my side. He's the boss. Howard should be calling me and checking up on the law office.

Yeah, but I am curious how things are progressing for him. I can swing by the Pizza King on the east side on my way out to see Granny. That'll take care of two things at once. I can pick up a pizza to see if they are still improving and take Granny dinner.

She may be going to play bridge, but she still has to eat dinner, and Long Island iced teas don't count.

My phone vibrates next to my thigh. The screen reads "Jacob." "Mandy's massage parlor."

"Have y'all relocated?"

"No, sir. We're still on happy endings trail like we have always been."

"That's odd. Because I'm standing in front of your door because you told me to come by this afternoon, and you're not here."

A brief laugh escaped me. "Bless it, Jacob. I didn't know it was like an appointment, appointment."

He pauses before answering. "I thought I told you that I needed to talk to you face to face."

"Well, yeah. But I was hungry, so I went to get a sandwich."

"Where are you at?"

"Up on the square. Against that tree Billy Randall broke his arm on back in third grade."

"I'll be up there in a minute."

"Well, I—" He hangs up. "Suit yourself, dude."

I wonder if it is a full moon. I need something to explain away Jacob's sudden odd behavior.

One of the reasons Jacob and I have been best friends all these years is his predictability. I'm supposed to be the unpredictable one in the relationship.

I rack my brain but can't think of a single time he had explicitly requested to talk to me face to face. As if he has something essential to tell me. Oh my gosh. Oh no—Jacob's getting married. I didn't even think he was seeing anyone right now.

Last month he embarrassed me when he finally told me he had been dating Dominique Rodriguez for a month. That was my first indication I was a really crappy best friend because a good friend would have known immediately.

He isn't dating her anymore. Is he? Did he get back together with her?

This "being a friend" thing requires a lot more work than people let on. Most of the time, it leaves me feeling guilty.

I hear the big motorbike before I see it. Jacob pulls alongside the curb, sets the kickstand, and pulls his helmet off.

He's wearing riding boots, jeans that have been washed enough to form to his body, and a black T-shirt that might rip in half if he coughs too hard. He looks hot and dangerous—basically, he looks like he usually does.

"I don't have my massage oil out here," I tease as he approaches.

He plops down on the concrete bench next to me, extending his legs out to full length. "I suppose we'll have to improvise."

"What's so important that you have to interrupt my lunch anyway?"

Jacob examines the sandwich in my lap. His eyebrows knit. Reaching out, he lifts the top piece of bread. "Turkey?"

I roll my eyes. "I'm trying to be a good girl until the big Snow feast."

"But aren't you having turkey on Thursday?"

Darn it. I should have thought of that. "What? Do they set limits on turkey consumption now?"

"I just didn't think you liked turkey that much."

I don't. "Sure. Everybody likes turkey sandwiches."

Jacob leans back against the oak tree. "I need to ask you something. But you have to promise not to get weirded out, and you can't get mad."

"Okay … of course, you starting the conversation that way really puts me at ease, mister."

"Sorry."

I wrap the last of my sandwich. My appetite is gone, and Jacob is right—I don't really like turkey sandwiches. They are way too dry.

Looking up, I see Chuck Grassley from Gadsden News Station 3 marching toward us. I tense momentarily, then realize he must be coming over to ask Jacob, the first officer on the scene, about the Bransford car bombing.

"I just need you to know—"

"Bogey, three-o'clock," I say.

"What?"

I gesture toward the opposite side of the park. "Channel 3 is coming to get the truth out of you. They even sent their best, Greasy Chuck Grassley."

"Man. I can't stand that dude," Jacob grouses.

Chuck Grassley has had enough plastic surgery and Botox to last five lifetimes. Consequently, his face resembles a mannequin more than a human. Coupled with his incredibly white teeth, all the same height, that appear too large for his mouth, nothing on the man is the original model.

Chuck is to reporting what ambulance-chasing lawyers are to the law profession. If there is blood or shame involved, you can count on Chuck spending his time on the story.

Chuck shoves a tape recorder toward Jacob's face. "Officer Hurley, I understand you were the first on the car bomb case yesterday morning."

"I'm sorry, sir. I can't comment on an ongoing investigation."

I know I don't want to get into this scene. "Jacob, I gotta get back to the office. Howard's out today," I say as I stand.

"Wait." Jacob stands. "I didn't get to tell you what I need to talk to you about."

"There are reports that the hit was from the Perez cartel. Can you confirm that?"

Jacob swings on the older man. "What part of 'I can't comment' are you not understanding, sir?"

Chuck stands up straight, maximizing his five-foot-seven frame. "Do you have a problem with the First Amendment, Officer?"

That really is my cue to leave. I start back toward the office.

I hear Jacob say, "No. But I have a problem with pipsqueaks interfering in my day off."

Chapter 16

The following two hours are productive as I clear most of the contract work from my desk. When three o'clock comes around, I spend half an hour googling supernatural weapons. I'm not sure what I thought I would find, but it is *not* helpful.

I lock the door and drive toward Granny's farm.

Downtown is still in my rearview mirror when my phone rings. "Hello?"

"Hey, I was just investigating a disturbance here locally, and the owners of the home told me they know you," Dusty says.

"Really? Who are they?"

"Vance and Leslie Wagner."

The Wagners are a young couple I helped this past summer. Vance is in construction, and one of his contemporaries hired some thugs to rough Leslie up in an attempt to drive them out of business.

Vance is a bit of a hothead. Consequently, it didn't go so well for the hired thugs.

When I met Vance, he was facing two charges of manslaughter. I'm not allowed to say so out loud, but I thought he did the world a favor by taking the two criminals out.

"Yeah, I know them. What's going on?"

"Nothing much. Just the standard spook items. Odd noises and an occasional draft."

"I visited that house. I didn't even get a blip on the radar."

"I'm not sure. This might be a different house. Leslie said they moved in a month ago after Vance got the remodeling done."

"What does the house look like?"

"It's an older, three-story Victorian."

"Nope. That's not the house I visited. I guess the drywalling business is excellent right now."

"Do you think it would be possible for us to get out there tonight?"

I feel my stomach jump. "I can't. I'm with Granny tonight about the weapons you are looking for."

"Oh yeah. We don't want to delay that. How about Saturday?"

"I don't know, Dusty. I think I might need to take a little bit of a break since the last event."

"Saturday it is. It's not like you have anything else to do in the evenings."

My face flushes hot. "What do you mean by that?"

"Just that you're not eating much?"

"I guess you think you're funny."

"Aww, cool down. I'll send you an itinerary."

"I said no."

"You're really going to turn down an extra forty dollars an hour?"

I wonder if Dusty is getting a bit careless. After our last excursion, I believe he was correct for requesting we study how to protect ourselves. Now, here we are leaving for another outing before a whole week goes by—still without any means of protection. That doesn't make any sense to me.

His love for the excursions and figuring out each case is becoming an addictive part of his personality. It isn't enough to have identified a few ghosts, actual ghosts, along the way. Dusty has a need to educate everyone about what is beyond the veil. Even if they don't believe him.

Often these leads will end up being a four-hour excursion

with no sign of paranormal. Typically, just a snooze fest. Occasionally they become a life-or-death event.

Chapter 17

I pull up close to the gate at Granny's, open it, drive through, and re-close it before any of the goats can escape. I know they wouldn't go far. Still, herding escaped goats is only one degree easier than herding cats.

With pizza in hand, I knock on the front door. Gospel music spills out onto the porch. No Granny.

I ring the doorbell in three quick successions. I consider tapping on the window, and the door finally opens.

"I thought I heard something," Granny declares as she throws the door open. "Come on in."

"I won't stay long. I know you said you have a bridge game." I hold the pizza up. "Compliments of your son."

"Wonderful. Let me get us plates."

A paper towel would work, but she's already shot out of the living room to the kitchen. Granny can be deceptively fast.

"What flavor did he send us?" she asks as she reappears.

"Pepperoni and mushroom."

"My favorite."

I strategically wait for Granny to settle in before I ask her my question. "Were you able to find out anything for me on the paranormal weapons?"

She frowns. "Now, understand I don't run in those social circles. Most of my protection is derived from religious symbols and specific prayers."

"Oh." This mission Dusty sent me on continues to be a goose chase.

"However, I was able to locate a diary from my great-great-grandmother who did detail several old-world weapons that were supposed to work against spirits. There are actually a few modern weapons as well."

"Defensive weapons that work against demons as well as a ghost?"

"No, dear. Those are two different animals altogether. You should know that."

I suppose, instinctually, I do know that. It only makes sense, just like there are expellers and witches. But it sure would be nice if there was something that could affect both hazards of the paranormal investigations at the same time.

Granny gestures for me to follow her. I follow her past the formal dining room and parlor toward the back library. Two decades have passed since Grandpa Snow went to meet his maker. I can still smell Sir Walter Raleigh tobacco and his cologne, a mix of leather and musk.

An ancient-looking, maroon-and-orange-bound book sits on the table next to Grandpa's recliner. Granny lifts the book, carrying it over to the long study table where my brothers and I were allowed to read books as kids.

"Now, you understand I can't vouch for anything in this book. For all I know, it's complete fiction," she says while setting it down.

I take in the richly colored fabric cover. I run my finger along the edge where parchment sheets are beginning to escape the binding. The energy of the book leaps from the page and shoots up my arm.

There is nothing fictional about the book. This is the genuine article.

"When you said diary, I was expecting a composition book."

Granny leans over and opens the book. The two pages are completely filled with flowing calligraphy and several full-color illustrations of what appear to be old-fashioned maces.

"Good Lord. Look at the detail," I marvel.

"That's why the larger book. The illustrations wouldn't fit in a composition book."

I flip a page. It is an extended entry with no illustration. I scan the writing. It takes a few lines for me to become accustomed to the handwriting.

I look over to Granny. "These are detailed accounts about an exorcism?"

"Yes."

"Have you read these?"

"A couple of times."

I flip another page, and this time there is a drawing of a necklace. "Where are these items? Do you have them?"

Granny sits down at one of the long table's chairs. "No. I have several diaries. But none of the artifacts."

"What happened to them?"

"I don't know." Granny pulls her necklace from under her collar and strokes the crucifix. "I suppose they might be items that other people owned, and she just recorded. I'm sorry, April. I just don't really have any answers."

As exciting and beautiful as my fourth-great-grandmother's diary is, I don't see how it can possibly help me. It is the equivalent of reading a book saying unicorns exist, but I'm sorry I can't tell you where to get one.

I sit down in the chair next to her. "So, what should I know?"

"About your gift?"

"Well, I'm not interested in playing bridge," I joke.

"I just wish." Granny's lips disappear on a tight frown. "Neither of the boys had the gift. I was hoping it had petered out. With my great-grandmother, it was powerful, my mother less so, and me even less. Then neither of my boys had the skill. I hoped it was over."

"See, that's something I don't understand. What was with all the top-secret business? Why didn't y'all share?"

"Safety. Who wants their daughter or granddaughter always

in jeopardy of being possessed by a demon?"

"Aren't I in more danger if I have the gift and don't know how to use it?"

Granny waves her hand at me. "You're thinking of animism. Yes, spirits are attracted to anybody that can acknowledge them and validate their existence. Demons are totally different. Demons would prefer not to be identified. They would love to possess and live within a person for twenty or thirty years, and often do. The only time a demon will attack you is when you're trying to rip them from their host. It has a tendency to agitate them."

I scan the library. The birch shelf and paneling are fourteen feet tall and encase the entire room. Thousands of volumes grace the shelves, accompanied by small angel figurines and praying couples.

Reconciling my granny, keeper of the cute porcelain figurines, with an accomplished expeller doing battle with demons in service of Satan is not easy.

It would help if she looked the part. A five-foot-tall septuagenarian with white, cotton candy hair does not seem like the most formidable hero.

"When can you start teaching me?"

Granny laughs. "Teach you what?"

"How to expel."

"No. Absolutely not."

"You have to," I insist. "I need to learn."

"You need to let it be."

"Why will you not teach me?"

"Because I want something better for you. Because you're a lawyer, not some ancient clerical warrior."

"I could be when I'm traveling with Dusty."

"That's easy enough to fix," she grumbles. "Quit traveling with Dusty."

There absolutely is merit to that. But I know I will have to try, now that I know I can expel demons. I figure it would be better if Granny would teach me rather than learning in the field.

Granny looks at her watch and pushes the book toward me. "Listen, I really do have to leave for my bridge game. Feel free to keep the book for now. I wish I could tell you more about where you might be able to find some of these weapons. I worry every time I hear that you and your brother are headed out for one of those cockamamie excursions. You know what they say about poking bears."

"Then teach me."

Granny shakes her head. "No, honey. You don't know what the true cost is. I will make you a promise. There is a skill I believe I can teach you that will be far more useful to you. Plus, it will be much safer."

"It's not safe being around demons with no way of expelling them," I continue.

She points to the book then gestures for me to leave with her. "I'm running late."

Reluctantly, I pick up the ancient text and tuck it under my arm. The energy surges from the book. I know then everything I need to learn is in the diary.

Chapter 18

The ancient diary practically hums with energy. The entire drive home, I keep glancing at the book in the passenger seat. Several times it appears to even glow.

I pick up my phone and call Liza. "Hey. I was wondering if you are going to go home or play the sick victim for a few more days."

"The concussion is gone, but I'm still a little unsteady."

"Sorry I haven't been able to get by to see you just yet."

"Aw, it's not like I really expected you to."

Ouch. Sure, you know things are true, but it's better when your friends just let it roll rather than point it out to you. "I've got some interesting news."

"What's that?"

"Guess who also is an expeller."

"If you're planning on telling me it's you, I'll act all excited if it makes you feel good, but I knew that from the first weekend we worked together."

Well, that is a little anti-climactic. "Really?"

"Yup. When is your granny going to teach you?"

"Not a thing. She says it's too dangerous, and she doesn't want me to get involved with it."

"That's like someone saying they're concerned about teaching you how to use a gun because you might get eaten by an alligator, but you're already waist-deep in the swamp."

"That's what I was thinking. Right?"

"She's just being overprotective. That's a grandmother's prerogative."

"At least my nana's not like that," I say.

"Uh-huh, I'm sure you agree they're polar opposites."

That is true. They're so opposite they have a hard time being in the same room and remaining civil. That always makes Thanksgiving fun if you are into family drama.

"I'll teach you some of the basics," Liza says.

"Good, I'll enjoy being a backup to you. Oh, are you going with us tomorrow?"

"I think so. I'm still a little fuzzy. Hopefully, by then, it will clear up."

"Are you sure you're okay, Liza?" I ask.

"I just said I was getting over a concussion. I have a couple of loose teeth, and my left wrist is swelled up," Liza says.

"I was actually talking about—are you sleeping alright," I whisper.

"Good. Actually, really good."

It makes me uncomfortable that I'm the only one having an issue with spaced-out dreams. "I'm not good. When Dusty mentioned we were going back out, I had a mini terror attack."

"In all fairness, I was unconscious for a good bit of it. So, I probably didn't experience the same emotions you did."

"You know a good portion of it is fear, but there's a portion of me that's also angry. Angry because when we were being attacked by Rollo the loco clown, there was nothing effective I could do to protect us."

"April."

"Yes."

"There isn't anything anybody could have done in that situation. You burning the house down probably was as good as any other cure for the situation," Liza says.

I'm not sure if she is just saying that to make me feel better. But if she is, it is working. "Thank you, Liza."

"There's no need to thank me. And the next time we work together, I'll make sure to give you a beginner's tutorial on expelling."

"I'll hold you to that."

It is five o'clock, and I don't see a good reason to head into town. I pick up old County 31 and go the back way to my parents' house.

As I pull into the driveway, I see there is a family party going on the patio. A family party that obviously I had not gotten my invitation to.

I pull my gear out of my car and walk toward my apartment without looking to the patio. If they aren't going to invite me, I'm not going to invite myself.

I open my apartment door and close it behind me. A quick scan of the room tells me Puppy, a.k.a. Benedict Arnold, has traded sides again. It seems everybody *does* have their price. Puppy's price appears to be a meat lover's pizza.

There is a knock at my door. I'm positive it is either Dusty or Chase. "What?" I whine irritably as I pull the door open.

Uncle Howard is standing in front of my door with a beer in each hand. "You want a beer?" My stomach roils again, just like this morning.

"Thanks, but no. I'm trying to cut back during the week."

"Yeah. I know I should lay off, myself. But they're about all I have left to calm my brain."

There is an awkward silence that ensues. I consider washing my makeup off and lounging in bed for the rest of the day, but also consider accepting the beer and joining the family party.

"Lane came and talked to me about the Bransford case. He told me you had an interest in defending Ms. Bransford?"

"That's true. I've already done some research on the side."

"When you're going there, make sure to let me know. I want to keep up with you while you're doing this research by yourself."

It strikes me odd that suddenly, everybody is worried about my safety. Both Lane and Howard are overly concerned I might get hurt helping Ms. Bransford on this case. Then Granny refuses to help me hone my skills.

"Are you going to let me have the case?"

"I'm thinking about it." Howard leans against the door jamb. "It's just with all the work you already have, and we're coming up on the holiday season for the next six weeks—I'm tempted to tell Lane to find somebody else."

"Don't do that. I'm sure if you'll give me the opportunity, I can do a good job with this case."

"I know you would. But, are you sure you can handle it? I mean, you've got a lot of moving balls in the air."

Howard just qualified for understatement of the year. But I figure with this many projects, what's one more?

"I can handle it."

He studies my face carefully before responding. "I'll call Lane and discuss it further. For the time being, I'm lead, but you can gather the information as long as you keep me in the loop about where you are going at all times. Lexi Bransford is in the city jail pending her bail hearing. I'll also need to get you hooked up with Agent Thomas Clifton. He's the FBI agent assigned."

"What happened to Agent Taggert?"

"Huntsville office. Taggert works for the Gadsden office."

It's odd. There's no love lost between Agent Taggart and me. But the idea of having to meet a new FBI agent doesn't exactly thrill me.

Howard notices my expression. "Agent Clifton is pretty chill. You will definitely want to be candid with him at all times, but other than being strictly by the book, he's a good man to work with."

"And Lexi?"

"Lexi's a little—" He measures his words. "Let's just say she's used to getting what she wants. At the moment, this is all looking more like an inconvenience to her than a tragedy."

That is a harsh judgment. Especially coming from Howard, who usually extends everybody the benefit of the doubt. It also does not square with the dazed woman I saw on her front porch talking to a police officer while her husband sat fried in his SUV.

That's precisely why Lexi needs me.

"Are you not hungry? Your daddy grilled a couple of pork loins, and Chase cooked mac and cheese and baked beans."

I want to say no. I should say no. "Yeah, that actually sounds delicious."

Howard pats his stomach. "It is delicious."

I spend the next hour catching up with my family and taking in five thousand calories that I don't need to deal with. Thanksgiving is in two days, and I am already more stuffed than the turkey.

Come to find out, it wasn't a planned party. Mama sold the Trinity home that sits on the furthest point of the peninsula into the lake from the west bank.

The home once belonged to the old Martin clan. They were Guntersville's version of the robber barons. At one time, they owned the textile mills around Sand Mountain.

Mama mentioned the buyer was connected to sports somehow. But she was short on details.

The buyer also asked her to have the house furnished for him. He didn't have any females in his life and said he didn't want the place to have a "man cave" feel about it when folks came to visit. He told her to make it classy.

He's probably some sportscaster or maybe one of the general managers. That sort of money has an appreciation for the finer things.

Well, Mr. Sports Dude is now the proud owner of a white elephant with really nice furniture. Not to mention expensive, at the 3.5 million dollar "reduced" price of the listing.

It works out well for Mama, if not him. It will be a nice commission. More importantly, she has finally sold the most challenging house she had listed.

After dinner, I gather up my treasonous puppy and walk down to the dock. The porch lights are off, but the silver moon offers enough illumination to find my way. Looking up, I admire the stars so prominent in the autumn sky.

I sit on the edge of the dock, contemplating the different items I need to complete.

In the morning, I'll have to meet with Lexi and introduce myself to agent Clifton. There's a chance that Jacob may have some more information on the case. I'll want to call him for sure now that I have cleared his hurdle of need-to-know.

Reciprocation is a good thing. That gives me an excuse to take another field trip to J&B. Not that I'm looking for or expecting to find anything specific. Still, you can't catch anything if you don't drop a few lines in the water. The more lines in the water, the better your chances.

I trail my big toe through the warm lake water. I'm beginning to think there's something significant going on in our small community. Something not on the up-and-up.

A shock travels up my leg, forcing me to leap to my feet, cat-quick. Taking a step back, I look down at the black mirrored water, catching a momentary glimpse of a gray hand before the water's surface returns to pitch black.

Him.

A chill runs down my spine as my chest constricts. I want to run, but my feet won't abide.

"Mama! Dusty!" I have no idea why I'm calling out to them. They can't help me.

The old branding on my ankle he gave me when I was eight burns incessantly. The feeling of a thousand ants biting at once.

I'm not afraid of him. Not anymore. Whatever he is, he holds no power over me now. He only startled me.

If he does hold any power over me, it is only mindshare. I spend a little time each week thinking about him. The day he almost killed me.

My brothers called the spirit "the old man of the lake" from how I described to them what I saw in the murky depths of the lake water that day. Over the years, on the rare occasions we

FOOLISH EXPECTATIONS; APRIL MAY SNOW NOVEL #5

bring up the incident, we have come to refer to the malevolent spirit simply as "Him."

He is one of the reasons I need to leave Guntersville. Something about the day he pulled me by the ankle to the bottom of the lake, and every other time he has haunted me, seemed personal. I can't explain it, but it is as if he has a vendetta, and I am the target he obsesses over.

Despite Dusty's "gifts," he's never seen Him.

No one else in the family has been attacked by Him.

With me, he tried to kill me and would have succeeded if not for my brave brother. When I'm in Guntersville, he makes impromptu appearances reminding me he's still around, lurking, watching me.

Most often on nights that I am tired. When the world has worn me down, and I am sad, he comes to me in my mind and whispers my name repeatedly like a lullaby with the promise of death.

All spirits are attracted to my ability to listen and acknowledge them. It is most unfortunate for me the very first spirit I came into contact with was Him. A fully animated apparition with a homicidal streak.

If not for Him, I might make peace with my "gifts" and even come to enjoy them. If not for Him, Guntersville might be safe for me.

Dusty hit the dock at a full run. Mama is shuffling behind him, wrestling with the sash of her robe.

"What's the matter?" Dusty asks as he puts his left arm around me and scans the dock.

I feel silly for calling them now. What is Dusty going to do? With his limited abilities, all he can ever do is offer moral support.

It helps me realize something as I lean into his protective embrace. I'm the only one who could stop the evil spirit. If I ever want to vanquish him from Guntersville, it will be solely on me and my "gifts."

It's a sobering thought to realize I'm the one with the power.

Nobody else can fix this for me.

"Him." I point over the end of the dock. For the first time, I notice Puppy's stance. His legs are set wide, and the hair on his back stands on end as he emits a long, low, rumbling growl.

Dusty leans over the edge and examines the water. "Where? How do you know?"

"How do I know?" I'm about to describe what appeared out of the lake when Mama arrives next to us.

"What's the matter, April?"

I reconsider how many people I want to involve in the reappearance of Him. Now, understanding that I'm the only person who can affect change, I decide the fewer, the better.

"I'm sorry, Mama. I had my toes in the water, and all of a sudden, something ate my toes." I laugh, but it sounds hollow and fake. "I screamed out for help before I thought about it."

Dusty clears his throat. "I bet it was just one of Chase's catfish."

I'm eager for my brother's help, as I am wilting under Mama's incredulous frown. "Exactly. It was. I realized it right after I yelled for help. I feel so foolish now."

"Chase needs to do a better job of feeding them if he's going to keep them around as pets. I'll give him a stern talking-to in the morning."

I bump Dusty with my hip. *Too many details, dude.*

I give Dusty a sharp look before I cut loose with a doozie. "I was just telling Dusty that he and Chase need to do a better job of washing the boat when they use it."

Mama looked from me to the covered boathouse where the family boat resides and then back to me.

The extended silence between us as Mama looks to the dock, our faces, and finally my toes, feels like an eternity.

Mama sigh. "Honestly, April. I thought you had seen a ghost or something."

I relax and take in a deep breath as Mama turns toward the lake house. Dusty and I remain silent as she steps up to the porch.

"I thought you said it was Him?"

"It was. But what is Mama going to do about it, Dusty? I don't want her worrying about me, especially since she doesn't believe in Him."

Dusty's eyes narrow. "She's your mama. Worrying is part of the job description—even if she thinks you're nuts."

I pull over one of the wrought-iron chairs and sit. "I know. Still, if she thinks I've gone crazy, she might do something drastic like insist I move into the house so she can keep a closer eye on me."

"I thought you hated being in the boathouse."

True, I have said that on numerous occasions. "I know. But I think it's grown on me. It's sort of like having all the comforts of living at home, meals, laundry, no rent, advice when you ask for it, and not having a curfew or having to worry about waking someone up if I come home late."

"I understand that." Dusty points toward the lake. "And Old Man in the lake? How long has that been going on?"

"Pretty much ever since I moved back?"

Dusty pulls up a chair. I watch his face light as his interest is piqued. "Really? In what form."

"Forget it, Dusty. I'm not going to be your research rat—or for that matter, bait."

He places his hand on his chest. "I just want to understand how I can help. Knowledge is power."

Knowledge my butt. He just can't stand to leave a mystery unsolved—it probably aggravates him even more since it's in his own backyard.

"I thought you learned how to block him with the techniques you learned from Nana."

"I did. Or at least they worked until I came back home. Ever since then, it's like I'm an open conduit for all sorts of spirits. Most of them I can ignore. It's more like a low whisper. He seems to have a direct intercom to my brain."

Dusty leans back in his chair. "That's messed up. How do you keep from going crazy? Oh, never mind—my bad."

"Funny, jerk. I'm glad you're having such a great laugh at my expense."

"I'm sorry. It was just too good to resist."

"The point is I'll be leaving before too long, and I would rather Mama not know that He has raised His game to a full poltergeist."

"Wait," Dusty drawls the word out. "I knew you heard His voice—and of course, the first day the Old Man pulled you under the water—but you've never mentioned seeing him since that day."

I lean forward, cradling my head in my hands. "Like I said. He's upped his game. When I called out a minute ago, two grey hands were rising out of the water, and they touched my leg."

"And that's never happened—"

"Never," I insist.

Dusty leans back. "Wow. We may have a situation here."

"Tell me about it."

Chapter 19

Dusty convinces me to sleep on the den sofa. It doesn't take much convincing.

Puppy doesn't mind. He is cool sleeping just about anywhere.

It's different for me, especially after my unwanted visitor.

Every creak of the house has me jumping. All the LED lights from the electronic equipment light the room in an eerie blue and red, just enough light to make shadows resemble ten-foot-tall humanoid shapes lurking in the corners.

I stare at Daddy's circa 1990 stereo system. I watch it turn from 3:32 a.m. to 3:33 a.m.—the next thing I know, my alarm is going off at 5:30. I take inventory of my condition.

Yep. I feel like I've been ridden hard and put up wet.

I want to roll over to see if I can catch another half-hour of sleep when the ruckus of pans rattling in the kitchen drills into my mind. I pull my pillow tightly around my ears. How annoying.

The smell of bacon wafts into the den. Puppy whines. I push against his side with my foot. "Hush."

He considers that tacit permission to take his leave. He jumps from the sofa. I look out from my pillow cocoon and watch him with his tail high in the air as he disappears around the corner into the kitchen.

Fine. What do I care? At least I won't have to deal with his whining.

My stomach rumbles. Bless it. The treachery of my stomach is only slightly below that of my dog.

Throwing back the comforter, I rise like an extra from a zombie apocalypse movie. I make a slow shuffling track toward the kitchen.

Bacon ... bacon ... I must eat bacon.

Chase is cooking an omelet with expert wrist action as I trudge around the corner into the kitchen. He pauses, takes in all my morning glory, and asks the obvious. "Hey. Did you sleep here last night?"

"Sleep is a relative term," I reply as I take a seat at the counter. "That looks good."

Chase smiles, exposing his dimples. "Fang likes his omelets with extra cheese and the eggs runny—no mushrooms." He slides the omelet onto a paper plate, tosses two bacon pieces onto it, and sets it in front of Puppy.

Seriously? That dog eats better than me. "You're going to give him diabetes."

Chase looks at me as if I have lost my mind. "That's impossible. That's all protein. I don't even give him jelly toast. You know how much he likes his blackberry jam on toast."

Actually, no. I don't know Puppy's favorite jam.

"Any chance I can get one of those?"

Chase pauses. "Sure. I didn't think you were interested in cooking—but omelets are easy once you get the hang of it. You might get them a little too brown your first attempts, but that's about keeping the eggs moving evenly."

I must be giving him the "eye of death." He stops demonstrating the requisite wrist rotation and tilts his head. "Oh. You mean, I cook you one."

"Please."

"Yeah, no problem. What do you want on it?"

"Surprise me."

He chuckles. "You should know better than to say that in

this house."

True that. Seven years away from home has me forgetting some fundamental rules of life with two older brothers. "Onion, mushroom, and cheese—none of those tomatoes," I say.

"Granny would be hurt. She brought these over the other night from the farm. She said they were the last from the season."

"I went to talk to her last night about her past experience as an expeller. When did she have time to bring these over?"

Chase shakes his head. "The tomatoes are from the grocery store. Peru, more accurately. I was trying to shame you into letting me put tomato on your omelet, and then you have to go all expeller mumbo-jumbo on me."

"It's not mumbo-jumbo. It's serious stuff, Chase."

Chase slides the omelet onto my plate. "Listen, I think it is great Dusty has been able to make a killing with his ghost stories—I mean, I get it. Some folks like to be scared. I'm not sure why but to each his own.

But that stuff with Granny and Nana, sometimes I think they really believe all that vampire and werewolf stuff they've been spewing since we were kids."

"I don't think anyone is talking about vampires and werewolves. Most of what we are talking about are ghosts and, even worse, demons."

Chase points his spatula at me. "See, that's messed up. If there were real demons, that would be like the end-of-the-world stuff. If there really were demons, there would be no way to stop them. But lucky for us, there is no such thing as demons."

This is why I am most confident Chase will never see anything supernatural. Beelzebub himself could be standing in front of him, and he wouldn't see him.

"I get why Dusty keeps it stirred up, but Granny and Nana, it's just silly. Nobody really buys into that crud."

Chase starts an omelet of his own. I decide to change the

subject.

"How's the new dry dock coming?"

He looks up, favoring me a smile. "Great, we should have it done before Christmas at the rate we're going."

"Do you have any new customers for it yet?"

Chase's expression turns more serious. "It's seventy percent committed already. I wouldn't have pressed Mama for the investment if we didn't have a high demand and the first quarter's deposit from them."

"That's impressive."

"Thanks, you can't ever have too many committed customers." He takes a bite of his omelet as he reaches for the hot sauce. "Or too much hot sauce."

I know better, but I can't seem to help myself. "You do know that there really are ghosts and demons. Right?"

"Sure, and Santa Claus, the Easter Bunny and a perfect soul mate just waiting for me to find her at Piggly Wiggly."

"You found your soul mate. You two just went all weird about it."

Uh-oh. That strikes a nerve. As Chase's jaw clamps shut, the small vein on the side of his forehead becomes a visible warning of his displeasure, and I wish I could take back my quip.

"I love you, April. But you really need to stop talking about things you know nothing about."

"You're right," I say cautiously. "So, enlighten me."

Chase lays his fork down. "Okay, I'll enlighten you. April, Barbara and my relationship are none of your business. How's that for enlightenment?"

"Pretty disappointing, actually."

Chase and Barbara Elliott were the perfect couple in high school. Chase was the multi-sport athlete. Barbara was the whip-smart cheerleader everyone loved to be around. The entire town, including the two of them, assumed it was a foregone conclusion they would marry one day.

Then, *poof*. A few weeks before graduation, it was over. Neither of them has ever shared the details with any of us.

"Barbara spent so much time over here when I was a kid it was like losing a big sister when she dropped out of our lives."

"Well, it wasn't exactly easy on me, either."

"I know that," I say. "I just don't understand."

"Yeah, well, that's how I go through a lot of my life. But believe me, there's a lot of things you don't have to try to understand because they don't pertain to you."

Touché. Blame it on my incessant curiosity. If he wants his space on the topic—*still*—I should honor it. Besides, the man made me an omelet. "Sorry. I shouldn't have pried."

The scent of sulfur rises in the air. I lift a bit of egg from my plate and sniff. My eggs smell fine, but the smell of sulfur becomes even stronger in the air.

"Are you sure your eggs are okay?" I ask Chase.

"Sure, I'm sure." Chase's face pinches together. "Oh, man." He comes around the corner of the kitchen island and moves toward the glass door.

Puppy is standing at the door, his tail uncharacteristically tucked between his legs. Chase slides the door open. Puppy shoots out like a furry cannonball.

"Man, April. You need to get him checked out. Your dog has issues!"

Chapter 20

I'm reviewing the deposition notes on the Stevenson divorce, and Lane comes into Snow and Associates. I get a heady adrenaline rush, thinking this will be our first conversation about the Bransford case.

Lane gestures with a nod of his head. "Is he in?"

"He's playing pizza franchise king again."

"You have got to be kidding me," Lane complains.

The petulant little boy look on Lane's face almost forces me to laugh. "I'm afraid so. What can I help you with?"

"You know, if he's going to make you run this place, he might as well make you a partner."

That's what I was thinking. Wait. That would mean I'm staying in Guntersville. "He takes care of me. You know that."

Lane runs his hands through his salt-and-pepper hair, leaving it spiked. "I hate to ask. We just got in a simple theft case, and the judges will be on break until Monday for the Thanksgiving holiday. Is there any way you can break away and take care of this one for me on the afternoon docket?"

I'm about to agree, then see my perfect point of leverage. "So, how is the Bransford case coming?"

Lane eyes me as if he is confused by the question and then smiles. "That's Howard's decision. If he wants to absolve me of anything that befalls his lovely—uhm—well, somebody from

Snow and Associates will be defending Ms. Bransford."

"I'm building the case file for him."

Lane's eyes narrow. "He hasn't mentioned a word to me yet. Now that you mention it, Ms. Bransford will be staying in jail for the holidays, too."

The vision of Ms. Bransford at the door talking to Jacob comes into my mind. Jacob said all she was concerned about that morning was getting her three kids to school.

"Lane, she has three kids. Where are they?"

"They're with her mother-in-law in Oxford."

"You're going to keep her locked up away from her kids during Thanksgiving? That's brutal."

"No." His expression hardens. "Blowing up your husband while your kids are in the house is brutal."

That's the thing about Lane. Mostly, I enjoy having him as a mentor.

He is intelligent, experienced, and a good teacher when he has time. He also has this metro-sugar-daddy vibe that tickles my sense of humor. Still, every so often, he says something that is so void of basic empathy I want to throttle the smugness of his "high-end retail ad model" face.

"You need to ask Judge Rossi to put her on the afternoon docket and let me try to secure her bail."

"No."

His word feels more like a slap in the face. "Why not?"

"Because I make those decisions. Not you. I'm in no hurry to let the motor bombing mama out on civilized society just yet."

I can't believe what I hear. "You're serious."

"Darn right, I'm serious. I'll have her on the Monday morning docket, but I'm not going to hurry up the process for a murderer."

"You do remember she hasn't had her day in court yet."

He crosses his arms. "I also remember a preponderance of evidence proving her guilt and a large insurance policy with Lexi listed as the beneficiary."

"Fine. You do what you need to do." I see him toward the

door. "I'll let Howard know you are looking for him if he ever shows up. Now, if you don't mind, I've got work to do."

"What about the theft case?"

"What about it?" I ask in an overly innocent voice.

"Can you help me out?"

"No. But I'm sure Howard can get to that one Monday, too."

Lane's neck flushes pink whenever he is getting angry. His neck turns the color of pickled beets. "That's blackmail."

"Technically, no. It's more along the lines of negotiation. So, do we both win, or both lose? The choice is yours."

"Fine." Lane shudders involuntarily as his ears turn red as well. "One of these days, you're going to bite off more than you can chew, April. When you do, you'll have nobody to blame but yourself."

Yeah, yeah. I've heard that my entire life.

"Careful what you ask for" is definitely the theme of the day now. I text Howard to let him know that he might have to trade in his apron for a sports jacket to come babysit the office. Because I'll be busier than a cat covering crap on a marble floor this afternoon. I will either be a hero and get two people out for the holidays or come up a zero.

Chapter 21

Lane arranges the meetings with Sylvester Langham, the petty thief, and Lexi Bransford, aka the motor bombing mama. Theresa Graham, Lane's newest intern, meets me inside the city jail to hand me the case files.

"Lane wanted me to tell you that he has arranged for Ms. Bransford to be on Judge Rossi's one p.m. docket. Mr. Langham is on that one already."

I check the time on my phone. Nine thirty—I'm an idiot—there is barely time for the interviews, much less time to think up a plausible argument.

"Thank you, Theresa."

My prison guard friend, Jade Woodson, meets me at the entrance to the interrogation rooms. "I knew you'd end up in here sooner or later," she jokes as she opens the office door for me.

"Not yet. They still haven't found his body." I add a mischievous lift of the eyebrows.

Jade laugh. "Girl, you are all kinds of wrong."

"Yeah, I get that a lot. How's Ms. Bransford holding up?"

Jade clicks her tongue. "Truth is, I'm worried about her. She won't eat and just stares at the wall mostly. She's awfully sad."

"Well, maybe I can get her out for the holidays. That should cheer her up."

"I don't know." Jade shrugs her massive shoulders. "I'm sort of torn on the subject. It's hard enough to find a guy nowadays. Then you got women like her blowing them up. If she was done with him, I might have found some use for him."

I take in all six feet and three hundred pounds of Jade and decide I don't have anything to say about that to my sweet friend. Besides, given my recent track record, she might be making a very valid point.

Sylvester Langham stands as I enter the room. Judging by the gray in his hair, I would put him in his mid-forties. Still, his athletic build could place him in his late twenty-somethings with an early case of graying.

"Hey. Are you my attorney?" Sylvester asks.

"It would appear so." I extend my hand. "April Snow of Snow and Associates."

"Can you get me out today? My mom is cooking Thanksgiving dinner tomorrow, and I can't be late."

I can empathize with the thought. Missing Mama's Thanksgiving feast is always taking matters into your own hands. Regardless of what is on your agenda, you're expected to attend. Of course, it isn't that hard of a call to duty. Where else do you get fed like royalty for free?

"Well, I'm sure going to try. We go before Judge Rossi this afternoon. I'll need you to bring me up to date on everything before then."

Sylvester holds his hands together in front of him. "The thing of it is, I was framed. It was like one of those sting operations. Someone dropped that wallet in my pocket."

I now realize that when I came through the door, I entered the stupid zone. I don't want to hear any more of Sylvester's story before I read the report. As I scan his arrest record, it is obvious Sylvester is no stranger to the law. In fact, he's probably on a first-name basis with a few of the officers.

All of his convictions are of small-time crimes, with shoplifting being the preponderance of charges. There was one physical assault charge that was dropped that made me note Sylvester is not wearing handcuffs.

The police arrested him last for theft of a wallet. It should've been a thirty-minute case, except he is pleading his innocence.

"Tell me about this wallet they say you stole."

"I didn't steal nothing." The stoic look on Sylvester's face dares me to call him a liar.

"Okay. Why don't you tell me how someone else's wallet ended up in your back pocket?"

"I was framed. Somebody has it out for me, and they won't be happy until I'm in jail for good."

If I'm going to mount any defense for Lexi Bransford, I need to quickly wrap up Sylvester's interview.

"Sylvester, listen. According to this report, you've been caught red-handed, and now it's time to pay."

"You can't believe everything you read."

I can't help it. The dramatic eye roll is automatic. "Alright, tell me your version of the events."

He hesitates before beginning. "I was at the VFW, and there is this big fellow there that I seen before. I think his name is Twinkie."

I nod my head to affirm I'm still listening.

"This Twinkie and I strike up a conversation, and then all of a sudden, he bumps into me. Hard."

"Okay."

"That's when it happened."

I must have dozed off. "When what happened?"

"When he slipped his wallet in my pocket." Sylvester looks at me as if I'm daft.

"Explain to me why he would stick *his* wallet in *your* pocket."

Sylvester's jaw drops open. "Aren't you listening? To frame me, of course."

"Why would Twinkie set you up?"

"Well, it's obvious he doesn't like me. Probably because I'm Army, and he's Marines."

This is the last thing I need. I must get with Lexi as quickly as possible. It's the only way I'll be able to mount a defense before we go before Judge Rossi.

Instead, I'm stuck with this yahoo who is lying to me about some mythical man dropping his wallet into his pocket to frame him. I'll suffer a little bit of foolishness, given the job, but this is beyond the pale.

"Sylvester, it doesn't do you any good to lie to me. I'm your attorney. Even if you tell me you committed the crime, I still have to defend you."

"I'm telling you the truth."

"Okay, if you're telling me the truth, then explain what makes you think it was a setup."

"Easy, the same person who dropped the wallet in my pocket was the guy who called the cops on me."

I rifle back through the file. There is no mention of who called the cops on Sylvester. "Explain yourself."

"This guy, Twinkie, he thinks he's all that. He just came back from Afghanistan. Those boys had it bad, but we all came down with illnesses from the Iraqis burning off the Kuwaiti oilfields in the first Iraq war. But he did buy everybody around beer, which was cool."

"Sylvester, is there a point to the story?"

"Yes. I'm getting to that. Come to find out, this guy, Twinkie, owns a bar in town. Being we're both ex-military, I figure I can get a drink or two on goodwill. But *no.* He decides he's going to charge me full price for their watered-down drinks."

"Wait a minute. Do you mean Winky Warner?"

Sylvester's brow wrinkles. He shakes his finger at me. "That's it. That's the dude's name."

I know Winky Warner from grade school. He runs his father's bar, Jester's, on the south side of town.

"Sylvester, did you have Winky's wallet in your possession?"

"Lord, no. He took it from me when I went to pay."

"You gave Winky the wallet, *his* wallet?"

"Yeah, the dude got seriously bent about it, and then he called a small army to arrest me. I mean, he's the one who put the wallet in my pocket. He should be on trial for a false report. That's what I think. Instead, here I am."

"Sylvester, look at me."

He makes eye contact with me.

"Get this through your head. I can't get a single juror to believe that story, much less a judge. Are you really wanting to base your freedom on that position?"

Sylvester crosses his arms. "But if it's the truth…"

"It's not the truth, Sylvester. You and I know that for a fact. I'll go to Winky and get his story. I know him. We go way back."

Sylvester pushes out his lower lip as he contemplates the situation. "I need another lawyer, then. This is all just a witch hunt. I won't be railroaded into doing time for a crime I didn't commit."

"Guess what. The county is fresh out of lawyers. You either deal with me or miss your mama's Thanksgiving dinner. Hey, but I bet they'll be nice enough to let you call her and tell her you won't be able to be there—because you're a bonehead."

Sylvester's eyes pop open wide. "Dang, that's just harsh. Anyone ever tell you you're just plain mean."

"All the time. Now, are we going to deal or what?"

"Man." His shoulders slump. "I guess so. What are my options?"

"First option is to tell me the truth, or I'm walking out the door. I've got other clients to tend to, and they don't cook up big lies to feed me."

"Yeah. Okay, I get it." He rubs his eyes with the base of his palms. "So Twinkie—"

"Winky," I correct.

"Yeah, Winky. Like I said, he's a regular at the VFW. Monday night is spaghetti night at the hall, and many of the guys make it on that night. Most of us don't have wives or girlfriends to cook for us, so any meal we don't have to cook is good. Plus, there's beer and other folks to talk to—folks who have been in the real world, if you know what I mean."

"I can understand."

He smiles, seemingly encouraged that I am listening to him. "I didn't mean to, or I guess it would be better to say I didn't plan to steal Winky's wallet. I mean, he's a good guy, and he's always generous with the rest of us."

Sylvester's eyes narrow. "But he has this odd habit. In his wallet, he carries a bunch of receipts and cards. It makes his wallet too thick for him to sit on. It would be like sitting on a short brick. So, whenever he sits down, he lays the wallet in front of him."

"And you thought it would be a good idea to steal it?"

"I don't know that I thought about it at all. It's like I saw the wallet, and the next thing I know, I had it in my back pocket. It was like magic."

I can't believe the proud smile on Sylvester's face. "It wasn't magic. It was theft."

"Yeah. It was that, too. I felt awful afterward. Like I said, I like Winky. But I had to get out of there. The guilt was eating me up. I didn't even get a plate of spaghetti that night."

I remain professional and don't mock the hardship of missing a plate of spaghetti when you committed theft. "Tell me about how you got caught."

"Well, that was just stupid on my part. I got back to my lean-to at the park, and no matter what I did, I couldn't fall asleep. Some nights, it can be hard when you are sleeping in the park to fall asleep, but this was guilt eating at me all night. I knew in the morning I would have to return the wallet."

I missed the part in the report about Sylvester being homeless. I'm glad I skipped the sarcasm about the plate of spaghetti. "How did you know where Jester's was located?"

"I didn't. But there were a couple of guys at the VFW yesterday morning, and when I asked them where Winky worked, they told me. I thought this was great. I could return the wallet and get something to drink. It seemed like a great plan to me."

I'm getting a feel for Sylvester Langham. Not with my animism or clairvoyance skills, just human-to-human interaction. He is a primarily good man with a drinking issue and nothing to live for in his life. He is full of regrets and holds a profound sadness.

His face darkens as he continues his tale. "I walked out to Jester's, and Winky was tending the bar.

He greeted me all nice, like he usually does, and I realized he didn't even suspect that I might have been the one to steal his wallet. I'm used to people assuming that sort of thing about me."

He stops talking. Sylvester scans the floor. When he looks up, he wipes a tear from the corner of his eye. "I'm sitting there with the man's wallet, and he's all nice to me, not knowing what I done did to him. I feel ashamed. Dirty. You know what I mean?"

"I can understand that, too," I agree.

"It was wearing on me something fierce. The guilt, that is." He exhales. "So, I do what I do when I get bothered. I ordered a whisky. Then I ordered another."

"But you finally told Winky what you had done—after you got up your courage. Right?"

Sylvester shakes his head slowly from side to side. "No, ma'am. I wish I had. After a few drinks and a couple of conversations with Winky, I lost my nerve. I handed him a credit card to pay for the drinks, and when it came back declined, he recognized the last four digits of the card and put two and two together right quick. He's a sharp one, he is."

"I bet he was angry once he realized what you had done. I know Winky. That would have really hurt his feelings since he knows you."

"That's the worst of it. He wasn't mad. It's like you say, he was hurt. He was all, 'I'm sorry, Sylvester, but you know I will have to call the law.'" Sylvester gives an exaggerated shrug. "And now I'm here and about to miss Thanksgiving dinner on account of a wallet."

"On account of making a stupid decision," I correct.

He stares at the top of the table. "Yeah. It wasn't my greatest decision."

There is probably enough from Sylvester's story to earn him an opportunity for bail until Lane and I can negotiate a plea and get the paperwork filed. Fortunately, we have Judge Rossi. Judge Phillips would have wanted Sylvester to stay in during the holidays just to inconvenience him.

My curiosity is piqued, and even though I'm short on time, I must ask a question unrelated to the case.

"Sylvester, you're supposed to be going to your mom's for Thanksgiving?"

"Yes, ma'am."

"Why do you stay in the park instead of living with your mom."

"Well, you know. I'm a grown man and all." He looks away from me.

"I live with my parents right now. It's just temporary, but that's what parents do when you need a little help through a rough patch."

"Hmph ... maybe that's how it works for rich, white girls." His eyes steal a look at me. "No offense. But not for me."

I'm not buying that. If his mom would cook for him during the holidays, she is probably worried sick about her son being on the street. "You can quit with the racial and money stuff. Mamas are always worried about their children. That doesn't have anything to do with what color you are or how much money the family has."

Sylvester lets out a short laugh. "Man, did you go to ball bustin' school or something, girl?"

"Yeah. I majored in it."

He leans back loosely in his chair. "You're as tough as my mom."

"It sounds like she might have to work to get the truth out of you, too. So how about it? Why don't you lay the real reason on me? You don't know me. Why would you even care what I think of the truth."

Sylvester's eyebrows dip as my words rub him the wrong way. He crosses his arms. "She just has so many rules. I got out of the Army because they have too many rules, and then when I get home, my mom was a drill sergeant in a cotton dress."

Still not buying it. "You mean she won't let you drink in the house."

"It's not that—" He reconsiders. "Well, it is. But, it's not the only reason."

"But she still cooks for you on the holidays."

"She wants all her kids home for the big three holidays. She likes to cook." He sits up straight in his chair. "But no alcohol, except for that weak red wine she'll serve with dinner on Christmas Eve."

I watch his outrage in calm silence. I suddenly feel sorry for all the times I have bucked my parents' rules.

Sylvester has it all wrong. When it is done with love, rules are only a parent's attempt to keep their children safe, even when they have become adults.

"They'll bring you over a little before one this afternoon. Please remain silent unless the judge asks you something directly. Are we clear?"

"Yeah, I'm clear." He waves a hand. "So that's it?"

I gather my folders and slip them into my backpack. I favor him with my sweetest smile. "Until this afternoon. See you then."

I tap on the door and Jade lets me out. "That was quick," she comments.

Gesturing over my shoulder with my thumb, I roll my eyes. "I'm not worried about getting Mr. Langham out with bail. Judge Rossi has a sweet spot for hard-luck men, and especially military. Ms. Bransford will be a coin toss. So, I need to spend as much time as possible with her before the hearing."

"Well, good luck. Let me know if you need anything."

"Thank you, Jade."

Chapter 22

I'm forced to do a double-take as I enter the room. It is impressive what makeup and a nice outfit can do to change a woman's appearance.

Lexi Bransford sits chained to the table in the center of the room. Her ankles are manacled through a steel loop on the floor. Her hair, which appeared not to have been brushed since her husband's death, hangs in straggly, tangled clumps around her ashen face.

Orange is definitely not her best color.

"Hi, Ms. Bransford," I begin as I take the seat across from her. "I am your court-appointed attorney. I have gotten your bail hearing expedited to today to try and get you out of here for the holidays."

"Do you know where my children are?"

"Yes. They're with your mother-in-law."

"I want to see them."

That could be awkward. A fact I hadn't considered before now. Depending on if Ben's family believes she is capable of killing him. "That's what we will be working toward. But I will need to ask you a few questions first."

"Now. I want to see them *now*."

Leaning back in my chair, I study Lexi. The intensity of her brow drawn together, the slight curl of her lip, and the tone of her voice. Something isn't quite right—or maybe Lexi is one of the few women who can get under my skin the moment they open their mouth. I can't be sure which it is.

"If you want to see them, you need to help me get you out on bond. To do that, I'll need your complete story as quickly as possible. If you cooperate, there is the outside chance I can have you home for Thanksgiving tomorrow."

Lexi's body language doesn't change. "What must you know?"

Everything. "Since we don't have much time, let's not beat around the bush. Did you kill your husband?"

Her face wrinkles violently. "No. I would never hurt Ben."

"Sure," I say as I jot notes down in my notebook.

"Don't patronize me like that. He was our sole income earner, and we have children. Why would I kill him?"

"I don't know, why would you? Or why would someone else kill him?"

Her neck flushes red. She regains her composure quickly. "I don't know. Ben had some rough business partners. Maybe it was one of them."

"Or maybe someone closer? Closer to you?" I'm only fishing. Still, my question elicits an even darker shade of red on Lexi's neck.

"What's that supposed to mean?"

I tap my pen against my notepad. "It means you need to tell your lawyer everything, and quick, if you want her to have a decent chance of getting you out for the holidays."

There is an odd transformation in her. She leans forward as if to engage in the interview process. Before she says a word, she slouches back in her chair, her eyes glazing over.

"Are you not going to tell me?" I prod. "Silence is not usually the best defense."

The color has drained from her neck, and her ashen color returns fully. It is as if she has shut down. I do not understand her peculiar behavior in the least.

"Lexi. Answer me."

"There's no point in any of this. My life is over now."

I'm not prepared for her declaration. "Why would you say such a thing—unless you did kill Ben? If you did, I'm sure there were some sort of extenuating circumstances."

"No. I didn't kill Ben. At least not directly. I would never want to hurt Ben. I know he hung with some rough people, but I don't believe any of them would have done something like this to him, either."

I'm locked in on her every word now. "What do you mean not kill him directly?"

She again appears as if she will actively join the conversation. She laughs and looks away as her moment of possible candor disappears. "Let's just say I've made a few mistakes recently."

"I feel you there." I laugh in hopes of building some sort of bond and to lighten her mood.

She winces. "No. No, you don't."

"Then tell me. What sort of bad decisions have you made lately?"

"I can't! I just can't." She buries her face in her hands. The chain clicks taut along the retaining ring. Her cries echo in the small room.

Daddy tells me I can be sort of harsh at times. I suppose he's right, but certain things set me off. One is when I feel someone is faking an emotional outburst. Lexi's "woe is me" outpouring has all the makings of a phony display for sympathy. Bless her heart. The poor girl doesn't realize I'm fresh out of pity but within an inch of jerking a knot in her tail.

"Lexi, you're going to have to share with me so I can rule it as immaterial to your case."

"It's too awful. I am so ashamed!"

Was it Lane who said, "Careful what you wish for"? I can't remember, but I do recall someone warned me against taking this case.

I should have listened to them.

"Lexi, think of your children. They need their mama."

FOOLISH EXPECTATIONS; APRIL MAY SNOW NOVEL #5

"I am thinking of my children. That's why it horrifies me."

"Okay, you know what. If you don't want to help me defend you, this is going to go badly. Either tell me right now what you are talking about, or we'll just have to agree that we can't work together."

She appears to sober. "Can you promise me that it will never get out? That nobody will ever know?"

"No. I can't promise that. I'll do my best to keep it out of the case, but if it is valuable to your defense and I need to use it, trust me, I will use it."

She takes her time evaluating her predicament. She begins to explain herself. "There's this guy, Tad Sapp, who has begun to lavish me with attention when the kids and I visit the park."

Oh boy. Here we go. "Did you know Tad before?"

She shakes her tangled hair. "No. He just moved here. Two years ago."

"And he has children, too?" I ask.

"No. He has a basset hound he walks at the park. My kids think he is cute, the dog, and like to pet him."

I'm guessing she finds Tad cute and likes to pet him. "How long have you two been an item?"

"Like I said, two years."

Silly me. It is surprising how easily she shifts into normalcy about her affair once it is in the open.

"Did Ben know about Tad?"

The look of horror on Lexi's face is comical. "Good Lord, no."

"Did anyone else know about your affair, a sibling, or maybe a girlfriend?"

"It isn't an affair. It is a simple, harmless fling."

I don't have time to argue the definition of having sex outside your matrimonial vows. "Did anyone else know about your fling?" I repeat.

"No. Nobody. I kept it very discreet."

Maybe I need lessons from Lexi. I can't date a new guy for a day without my entire family running a background check on the poor guy. There is no way I believe Lexi could keep it away from her friends and family for two years.

"And he felt the same way—Tad—that it was just a fling."

"He knows how I feel about it, but he would pressure me every so often to leave Ben. But I never would. I can't break up my home like that."

My opinion of Lexi is nose-diving. On the positive, we do have another plausible suspect now. Part-time boyfriends in love can do some crazy things if they feel like their booty call is in jeopardy.

"We'll need to question Tad as soon as possible. Can you give me his number and address?"

"Why in the world would you need to question Tad? He didn't even know Ben."

I can't believe I have to answer that. "Because he would be a person of interest in your husband's murder for the police once they know about his role in your life."

She becomes agitated. "No! Don't do that. You don't understand. The only reason I told you about Tad was that I have tried to call him to let him know I may need his help to post bond.

"But the three times the guards let me call him, he didn't pick up. I'm afraid he's cut me loose. If I've lost both men in my life, I might as well kill myself."

I've known women and men to give the person they love every benefit of the doubt—even when it's evident to everyone else that their lover is using them only for sex. Lexi wins the award for the most gullible lover of the decade.

"You do realize that Tad may have skipped town because he killed your husband?"

Lexi grits her teeth and growls. "I told you he didn't know Ben."

"He knew of Ben. He knew Ben stood in the way of you two getting together without having to look over his shoulder all the time."

"You haven't had many relationships with men, have you?"

"I've had my fair share," I stutter at the personal attack.

"Uh-huh. Listen. Let me explain something to you. A fling is just that. Both parties know the rules going into it. It is a fling, temporary—no jealousy, no love, just sex. Period. Second, let's say your theory is correct. It's not, but for the sake of argument, let's say Tad wanted to break the rules and wanted to be with me full time and raise another man's children. So, he kills my husband and then has to run from the law for the rest of his life? That's just stupid. How does that get him in my bed permanently?"

She makes a pretty fair point. But Tad is still too good of a lead to ignore. "Perhaps he thought it was over and decided to take out his competition. Sort of an 'if I can't have her, he can't either' scenario."

"I never gave him that indication. If he thought it was over, it was his own doing. I assure you there weren't any mixed messages from me. The arrangement was working out great."

She gestures to my notebook and gives me Tad's phone number and address.

I know the apartment complex. It is a dive of an old motel where you pay by the week, frequented by folks who are one step from living in their cars—if they own a car.

"What about Ben's business partners?"

"What about them?"

"Can you tell me their names or numbers?"

Lexi shakes her head and looks disinterested once again. "No. They're what Ben called silent business partners. I never met them. I don't even know how many of them there are or where they are located."

"Do you think they are out of state?" I ask.

"I didn't say that. I just don't know anything about them."

"But he had regular contact with them?"

Lexi turns her hands over. "No clue. Ben's job was taking care of the body shop, and my job was taking care of the kids and the house."

And Tad's body. "Is there anything else you can tell me about that morning that might be helpful?"

"Ben and I had sex that morning."

"Okay." I really am not sure how I'll weave that into her defense or why it would be helpful.

"I just say that because we hadn't had sex in a few months. It was just odd—you know, we finally have sex like maybe we are turning the corner to better times, and then boom. He's gone."

"Why do you think your relationship had cooled?"

She chews her right thumbnail. "I don't know. He always seemed agitated. Like something was bothering him at work. I would ask if he wanted to talk about it, but he said he would talk to me once he had it worked out in his head. He was sort of that way. Secretive."

I make the last notations in my notebook as I deem Ben and Lexi are two peas in a pod with their secrets. Still, I'm trying to cut back on my judgment of other folks these days. I close my notebook and try something more helpful.

"Lexi, there are a lot of loose ends that need to be tied up in the investigation of Ben's death. I believe the detectives should have finished investigating all their leads before arresting you.

"I'm telling you this because I believe we can cast enough doubt on the case to get you released on bail for the holidays so you can spend it with your children."

"Really?" She visibly perks up.

"Yes. But I need you to do me a favor and get cleaned up. You don't have to have makeup on, but you need to get the tangles out of your hair, take a shower, and when we get in front of Judge Rossi, at least look interested in the process."

"I am interested in the process. I want out."

"I hear you, but your body language is all wrong. Judge Rossi is a good judge and a kind woman, but she doesn't curry favor to folks that act put upon." I finish forcibly. "Understand?"

"Yes. I think I do."

"Okay. I'll see you at one at the courthouse." I stand as I remember one last question. "Did Ben have any life insurance policies?"

"He has one for the business."

"But no insurance for the family?"

Lexi dips her chin. "I know I should probably know that for sure, but Ben handled all that stuff. I only know about the business insurance because I heard him complain about how expensive it was on a few occasions."

"Okay. I'll see what I can find out for us a little later. We'll have to let it slide for now and hope it doesn't come up."

It is difficult for me to empathize with Lexi. We are different on so many levels. I can't imagine cheating on the man I have children with, and I can't see myself purposely keeping my head in the sand about my husband's business.

Silent partners my butt. Odds are, when there are partners nobody has ever seen or can identify, there is bound to be a solid criminal element.

That probably explains the significant life insurance policy as well. If anything "happened" to Ben, there would be a need for a cash infusion. Then the silent partners could step away with their money after selling at a deep discount.

As for Lexi, she is way too smart to pass herself off as the clueless trophy wife. Besides, she is no trophy wife. True, even with a rat's nest hairdo and in desperate need of a shower, her high level of sexuality is apparent. It is impossible to ignore. Still, she is no beauty queen. Men are drawn to the power of her sensuality and what it promises, not her good looks.

That leaves me wondering, why the act?

Or am I being too hard on the woman? How are you supposed to act when you find your husband burned to a crisp in your driveway?

I'm not exactly sure, but I know something tells me in my gut not to trust Lexi. One thing is sure—I won't tell her what type of car I drive. Just in case she does post bail.

What? There's no harm in being safe.

Chapter 23

It isn't quite noon, but I'm famished. I wrestle with the idea of getting in my car and driving over to Rex's for some chicken and rice soup or if I should just walk down to Jerry's for a small sub.

My phone rings. "Hello?"

I hear heavy breathing, followed by Jacob's deep voice. "What color panties are you wearing?"

It annoys me that I feel a quick hitch below my belly button. "I was in too much of a hurry to put any on today."

There is a short cough on the other line. "How do you always get me?"

"I don't always get you. I am serious, though. I'm as busy as a water bailer on the Titanic."

"Darn it. I wanted to see you and talk to you—about what I started to tell you yesterday."

"Not going to happen today, buddy," I announce. "I have two bond hearings at one and two this afternoon, and then I'm going home to help Mama get the house ready for Thanksgiving.

"You can come by tonight if you don't mind my family eavesdropping in on the conversation."

"Nah. I'll pass."

The disappointment in his tone is hard to ignore. I don't like to disappoint Jacob if it is possible to avoid. "Hey. How about you come over for Thanksgiving dinner tomorrow. We're serving at three."

"Can't. Granny Hurley is serving at that time."

"I thought she hated to cook."

"She does. But she worked a deal with Cheese Barrell. They are delivering the meal."

I can't help but laugh. "Your Granny is whacked. I mean that in the most respectful and complimentary manner."

"I know someone else who is whacked—and you can take that however you want to."

"Alright, Mr. Mean. I guess I'll let you go."

"Sure. I'll catch you later."

He hangs up. I shove my phone into my purse. I swear Jacob Hurley has become so very odd lately. It is so out of character for him.

Once everything slows down after the holidays, I guess I'll need to carve out some time for him to tell me whatever he thinks is so darn important. Whatever it is, it better be good considering the level of drama he has created.

As much as I would like a bowl of Rex's chicken and rice soup, I decide I'm too pressed for time. I needed to review the Bransford case and outline my defense. With the new information about a boyfriend being in the picture, things are looking more optimistic that I can secure a bond for Lexi. I just need to keep my fingers crossed that there isn't a huge life insurance—motive—sitting out there to torpedo our case.

Chapter 24

I'm proud of myself as I walk out of Jerry's with my Cobb salad. Jerry told me he added a couple of salad options to the menu two years ago, and I'm the first customer to order a Cobb salad from him.

I'm not sure if that makes me a trendsetter or stupid.

I dump the second packet of ranch dressing onto my salad when I see a familiar face with an unfamiliar haircut. "Jayron Freeman, are you staying out of trouble?" I holler.

The young man shoots me a stern look. It evolves into a full smile as he recognizes me. He trots to my park bench. "You caught me deep in thought, Ms. April."

In Jayron's case, catching him deep in thought is like a one-in-a-million chance. "What have you been up to?"

"Training," he declares full of pride.

"Training?"

"Yes, ma'am. I head to basic training next month, and I want to be a squad leader."

"That's some wonderful news. Which branch?"

Jayron puffs out his bony chest. "Army, of course."

"Of course. I wouldn't suppose the Colonel had anything to do with that choice."

"Well, he might have let me in on a few reasons why the Army is the best arm of the service."

With some folks, you worry about them when you hear they have joined the service. I don't worry about Jayron Freeman. The young man is a crack shot, likes to handle explosives, fearless, loyal to a fault, and will consider the guaranteed three meals a day offered by the Army a huge fringe benefit. In short, he is a survivor and a good kid who will do well with some structure in his life and could use some exposure to the world outside of the county he was born in.

"I want to thank you, Ms. April. For what you did." He dips his head. "Helping me with the law."

"Just doing my job, Jayron."

Fierce determination flashes across his face. "No, ma'am. Don't you do that. You didn't have to do what you did to get me out of trouble. You didn't have to put me in touch with the Colonel, and you didn't have to find out about the internship at Redstone for Kenny. It was special what you did for my family. We won't ever forget it."

I really was just doing my job on the Freeman case, or doing what I thought needed to be done. It had only been a month earlier when Jayron was looking at terrorism charges, and the FBI had painted a target on his back. Maybe I had fought a little harder than another court-appointed attorney would have to keep his record clean of a felony so he could join the service. Perhaps, it wasn't my place to search for scholarship opportunities for his brother. But I did—someone had to.

"I can't tell you how happy I am that everything worked out for you, Jayron."

"Just like you said it would, Ms. April."

"I did?"

"Yes, ma'am. I was sitting in jail, lower than I've ever been, and you said, 'Jayron, I know things look tough, but it will all work out for the good.' I hadn't known you but for a few minutes. Still, I knew you were smart, and if you believed it was going to be alright—well, I needed to believe it, too. And now look where we are."

Note to self, pay more attention to what you say to clients. I have no recollection of the conversation Jayron is alluding to.

"I'm so happy for you."

The intensity comes back to his eyes. "I'm going to make you proud, Ms. April. Mark my word, I am."

"I already am Jayron, and more importantly, I know your mother is too."

Glancing at his watch, he says, "I guess I better get back over to the gym. I'm glad I got to see you."

"Likewise, Jayron."

He grins and turns to walk away.

"Jayron?"

Looking over his shoulder. "Yes'm?"

"You be safe. You understand?"

He doesn't answer me. He just flashes his crooked-toothed smile, turns, and begins to jog.

The Freeman family's predicament may have been changed for good. It appears the trajectory of the family's fortunes is going to the positive, where they were hanging on by a thread a month earlier.

I can't lie about it. It does put a glow on my attitude when I consider I may have helped improve their situation. I hope that's not prideful. If it is, I hope the Lord will cut me a little slack on it this once.

I look back to the salad in my lap. The most gigantic horse fly I believe I have ever seen is stuck in the ranch dressing. His bulging red eyes, metallic green thorax, and bulbous black rear end are firmly encased in the thick, white salad dressing. I watch as his wings beat furiously, motor boating him into one of the hard-boiled eggs.

Yeah. I knew the salad was a bad idea. I think I'll get a candy bar and a soda from the gas station.

Chapter 25

As I enter Judge Rossi's courtroom, I'm the only person present. I pull out my two clients' folders from my backpack and consider my odds of success. Sylvester is a slam dunk for bail. He is male, ex-military, and a man on hard times. All things that strum the strings of compassion for Judge Rossi. It also does not hurt that his crime is nonviolent.

Bail is a near certainty. But we don't stand a chance of avoiding a conviction. Unless Lane wants to offer a plea. Which given the preponderance of the evidence, Lane has no motivation to do.

Lexi is a crapshoot. Judge Rossi is apt to trust her even less than I do. Plus, she may have blown up her husband. That's pretty cold by anyone's standards.

The revelations about a jealous boyfriend do appear to be the ace up my sleeve. I only wish I had known sooner so I could have interviewed him and gotten a feel for the man. I also wish there were time to investigate the possibility of a life insurance policy with Lexi as the benefactor.

Oh well, as Howard says, wishing is the precursor for the excuse of your perceived future failures.

I hear the courtroom door open. Lane enters with a tall, older man with tightly curled graying hair. The tall man might as well have "Accomplished FBI Prosecuting Attorney" monogrammed on the lapel of his trim, navy-blue suit coat. For the first time in a long time, I'm a little intimidated by my competition in the courtroom.

"You're eager today, Counselor Snow."

"I'm always eager, DA Jameson," I retort.

That brings a smile to the tall man's face. At least he may have a sense of humor.

"I would like you to meet Prosecutor King Casey from the Huntsville FBI office."

King extends his hand. I'm surprised that he has callouses on his palm and the pads of his long fingertips. A vision of a scroll saw and a rip saw flash through my mind before releasing his hand.

So, Prosecutor Casey keeps it real and burns off steam from his high-level cases by refurbishing antique furniture. That's sort of cool. I think I might end up liking him.

"Pleasure to meet you, Counselor Snow. Lane has told me about all the good work you have done this year."

The thought of Lane mentioning my work, and in a positive light, is gratifying. Also, awkward. "Thank you."

King places his briefcase on the prosecution's table. "If you ever have the mind to, the FBI is always looking for new prosecutorial talent." He points to Lane's shoes. "We might not be able to afford the latest Italian loafers, but we do alright for ourselves. Besides, there are other intrinsic values when you serve the public."

Yeah. I like King a lot. He is incredibly smooth and confident in an unassuming manner. "I'll keep that in mind."

"You do that."

"Here I bare my soul over how difficult it is to attract talent to a small town, and then you go poaching the only new talent in town, King. You ought to be ashamed of yourself." Lane says it jokingly, but it comes out more like a mini hissy fit.

"Just making sure the young lady is aware of all her options." King pulls a large folder from his brief.

Moments later, Jade and another prison guard bring in Sylvester and Lexi. Sylvester sits beside me while Lexi stays in the second row behind me, bracketed by the guards.

I'm about to remind Sylvester to let me do the talking unless asked a specific question when Hal Joiner, the bailiff, enters the courtroom announcing Judge Rossi.

It is always best to rise in Judge Rossi's court. Otherwise, you wouldn't be able to see her diminutive form as she makes her way to the bench. She sits on the vast leather seat that dwarfs her as she slides her wire glasses up from the tip of her nose.

Hal calls the court to session.

Judge Rossi lays a folder she is reading down and looks to Lane.

"Good afternoon, DA. Jameson. Do you care to tell me about the case you are bringing against Sylvester Langham?"

"Yes, your honor."

Lane explains to Judge Rossi about the stolen wallet and subsequent reappearance at Jester's the next day. Lane's story is almost identical to Sylvester's, save for Sylvester's continued claim that he was set up.

"Counselor Snow, how does your client plead?"

I nearly choke on the words. "Not guilty, your honor."

Judge Rossi removes her glasses. "Pray tell, Counselor."

"My client was framed, your honor. Someone placed the wallet in question in plain view, and my client picked it up with the intent of returning it to its rightful owner."

I see a smirk flash across the judge's face, or possibly she has gas from eating something disagreeable at lunch. She picks up the folder and flips to a different page.

Lane and I exchange a look. He shrugs.

Judge Rossi taps her pen against the folder. "Langham. I used to know some Langhams. Reverend Richard Langham, he used to have the revivals up on Freedom Hill back in the eighties. Would you happen to be kin to him?"

Sylvester looks to me as if asking what he should do. I gesture toward the judge, suggesting he should answer her question.

"Yes, your honor. He's my daddy."

Judge Rossi makes a *tsk*ing sound as she shakes her head. "I bet your daddy would roll over in his grave if he knew his own flesh and blood was acting out like this."

"He's still alive, Judge."

"I bet not for too long if he knew this. Maybe I should call him and let him know what his son is up to."

"There's no call for that, Judge."

"I think there is plenty of call. I'm sure he would want to know if one of his own had strayed off the straight and narrow."

Sylvester's body stiffens. "You can't understand what it's like to be raised by a preacher. It's impossible."

Judge Rossi rolls her eyes. "Please. I see impossible every day of the week, son. Young men coming into my court having done something that will take their freedom and the best years of their life away from them. Often it's because they never had someone show them the right path. They never had a daddy to whack them upside the head when they're *boy* dumb.

"Don't come into my courtroom and tell me about impossible, son. I've seen impossible, and you have no claim to it."

She falls quiet as she scans the folder some more. "Says here you were in the Army. Is that correct?"

"Yes, Judge."

"What did you do? Infantry?"

He stands a little straighter. "Medic."

She pulls her glasses off her nose. "Come a long way from being a medic, haven't we, Mr. Langham?"

"I suppose, ma'am."

"I suppose," she mocks. "You're not a tweaker, are you, Mr. Langham? You know, be a medic to stay close to a steady supply? You don't do drugs, do you?"

"No, your honor—well, besides alcohol."

"I'm trying to figure you out, Mr. Langham. If you were a medic, there are hospitals all over this county begging for additional staff and nobody to fill the positions. Why would you steal rather than get a job?"

"First, I didn't steal your honor. I was set up. As for a job, I'm not particularly fond of getting up and going to work every morning."

Judge Rossi laughs. "You don't like to get up and go to work? That's ninety percent of the population, son. Heck, I'm seventy-six years old, my feet hurt, my teeth don't fit right anymore, and I'm tired of listening to people telling me fibs all the time. But I figure if the good Lord gave me today to live, I might as well get out of bed and do what he has given me the skill to do. Not particularly fond—please."

She writes something down in the folder and speaks. "The defendant has been a resident of this county most his life and has limited resources. I do not consider him a flight risk. I am setting bail at five hundred dollars." She strikes the gavel to signify we are done.

"Does that mean I'm out?"

"Yes, but we'll need to find someone to bail you out. Do you have anyone you can call to help you?"

"I think my mom might. As long as nobody tells my dad."

"Good." I lay my hand on his shoulder, directing him toward Jade. "Now go sit with Sergeant Woodson until I am finished with my second case."

Sylvester is ecstatic he will be able to go home for the holidays, as he should be. But knowing Judge Rossi and considering the tone she took with him, I have a suspicion it may only be a concession due to her knowing his family.

I'm positive unless Lane offers a deal, the next time we see Judge Rossi, she'll give Sylvester free room and board with a view of the guard tower for as long as the law will permit.

That will have to wait. A murder charge trumps theft in any lawyer's hierarchy of priorities. Lexi is the focal point now.

Lexi quietly slips into the seat vacated by Sylvester. She has showered and pinned her hair back neatly with bobby pins. She looks the part of a docile mother of three, mistakenly accused of her husband's murder.

"Prosecutor Casey, it is a pleasure to see you again today," Judge Rossi says.

"Thank you, your honor. The pleasure is all mine. I wish it were under happier circumstances."

Judge Rossi looks from Lexi back to King. "Yes. An unfortunate set of events, to say the least. Please begin."

King buttons his jacket and proceeds to lay out the bureau's evidence against Lexi. The first thing out is the existence of a hundred-thousand-dollar motive in the form of a life insurance policy.

The second fact Lexi failed to mention to me is the couple separating three years earlier when Ben had an extra-marital affair. Lexi had been pregnant with their third child. Originally he planned to divorce Lexi and marry the other woman. In the end, he changed his mind and begged Lexi to forgive him, which she did for the children's sake.

Recent rumors were that the other woman might be back in Ben's life. It was also rumored Lexi had become afraid Ben would divorce her, leaving her and the children to fend for themselves.

I lean over and whisper into Lexi's ear, "Why didn't you tell me about this?"

"I didn't think it was important. I didn't realize Ben's lack of morality was on trial."

"It is when it would give a wife *reason* to kill him."

"He wouldn't have left us. Besides, I can't rightly call him out on it when I was doing the same thing with Tad Sapp."

Wow, that is stunningly insightful coming from Lexi. Maybe I underestimated her.

I had been wrestling with my strategy for the last hour. The safe play is to show that with three children and a business left to be liquidated, Lexi is not a flight risk, then attempt to secure the lowest bond possible for her.

Then there is the big play. The "all-in" play is calling to me.

As a rule, I'm conservative regarding other people's situations. Still, the fairness in what Lexi said about her husband having an affair makes me decide she deserves better than the safe play.

She needs someone to fight for her.

Judge Rossi removes her glasses. "Counselor Snow, how does your client plead?"

My stomach rolls as if I'll be sick. Still, I force the words out with incredible difficulty. "Not guilty, your honor, and we petition the court for dismissal."

I catch King's head whip from the Judge to me in my periphery.

Judge Rossi raises her eyebrows thoughtfully. "On what grounds, Counselor Snow?"

"The arrest of my client was premature. There is a minimum of two other parties of interest that are not even listed as having been interviewed in the prosecutor's discovery notes."

Judge Rossi slips her glasses back on and sorts through the Lexi Bransford file before her. "Ms. Bransford has always been the primary person of interest as I see it, Counselor."

"Correct, your honor. But J&B has a silent partner."

"Your honor." King is shaking his head dismissively. "There is no reason to believe this silent partner has anything to do with the murder of Ben Bransford."

"Business partners kill each other over disagreements from time to time. It's a fact," I counter.

Judge Rossi talks into the papers as she shuffles through them. "I don't even see where the partner was interviewed, Prosecutor Casey."

"Uh, no, your honor."

She looks up. Her forehead creases. "Why not?"

"We haven't identified or even confirmed that the partner exists."

The judge's lips thin as she eyes King. She looks unhappy with what she is hearing from the prosecutor.

I feel it an excellent time to lob a stick of dynamite into the fire.

"In addition, Ms. Bransford had a two-year affair with a man who has been pressuring her to leave her husband for him. She recently made it clear to the individual that she would not leave Mr. Bransford."

The Judge rifles through the folder again. "Prosecutor Casey, why do I not—"

King turns to me. "Is that true?"

I give a quick shrug. "I'm afraid so."

King exhales loudly and directs his attention to Judge Rossi. For her part, the judge looks fit to be tied.

"Judge, if we can get assurances that Ms. Bransford will not leave the county and keeps in contact with the bureau, I would be agreeable to a temporary stay. That would give us time to complete a thorough investigation."

"I would say so, Prosecutor Casey," Judge Rossi says. "If I could get the bureau's assurances of completing a proper investigation before charging someone the next time, that would be welcomed, too."

King packs his brief. "Point taken, your honor."

"Very well then—the defendant is released into her own custody with strict instructions not to leave the county until the investigation is complete."

Judge Rossi removes her glasses. "I want to wish each of you a joyous Thanksgiving holiday. Please take the time to reflect on the blessings in your life and show true gratitude for them. I'll see you next Tuesday. Court adjourned."

Rossi strikes the gavel. She disappears through the door to her office.

"I can go home?" Lexi asks.

"Yes. But you have to stay close."

"What about my children?"

"They're going to have to stay with your mother-in-law until your name is cleared."

The hope fades from her eyes. "I should have just stayed in jail, then."

"No. Don't say that. I'm sure your mother-in-law will bring them by to visit."

"She thinks I killed her son. I don't think she is going to be that forgiving."

I turn to a tap on my shoulder. King Casey has a bemused smile. "You are wasting your talents here, counselor. Give me a call when you're ready to serve your country."

"Yes, sir. Thank you."

"Alright then. Have a good holiday."

"You too, sir."

Sylvester tucks in behind King. "I need to call my mom."

Nobody warned me in law school that I would have to be a part-time babysitter, too. I gesture for Jade. "Can you take Sylvester back and let him call his mother?"

"You said I was getting out." Panic glints in Sylvester's eyes.

"You are, as long as your mother or someone else bails you out. But you have to stay at the jail until then."

Jade lays a hand on his shoulder. "Come on with me, Sylvester. The quicker we get back, the quicker your mom can come to get you out."

His shoulders slump, but he does as she asks. He walks outside side by side with Jade.

"Let me give you a ride home," I say to Lexi.

"Why?"

I get it. It sucks. She's innocent, her husband is dead, and her mother-in-law, who thinks she murdered her son, has custody of Lexi's children—it couldn't get any worse. Oh wait, there's a big family holiday tomorrow, it just got worse.

Daddy was probably righter than he knew when he teased me that my empathy button sometimes doesn't work. At the moment, I want to slap Lexi and scream, "Snap out of it!" She has been given a "get out of jail free" card and is sulking.

"Either way, you have to go home. You might as well take a ride with me. How about I call your mother-in-law—what's her name?"

"Delila," Lexi grumbles.

"Call Delila and see if we can get her to bring the children over for a visit tomorrow. Doesn't that sound like a good idea?"

"Don't waste your time."

I don't waste my time. I get what I want through sheer will-power if necessary. "Well, it's my time to waste now, isn't it?"

Once I have Lexi in my car and am on Highway 79, I dial Delila's number. I pin my phone against my right shoulder.

"Hello?"

"Hi, Delila? This is April Snow, your daughter-in-law's attorney."

"That must be a crap job? How do you live with yourself? Are your parents proud of you?"

I'm disoriented and nearly drop my phone when it slides under my ear. "Excuse me?"

"There's no excuse for you. If you are trying to get that evil woman off, you deserve to burn for all eternity just like she does."

"I'm sorry you feel that way, but on other topics, Lexi has been released, and she would like to see her children tomorrow."

"What? They're in the habit of releasing murderers now? You want to bring my son's children to her so she can kill them, too?"

I would think Delila was only being dramatic, but there is a definite hint of fear in her voice.

"I'm sure it would be good for the children to see their mother, don't you agree?" I ask.

"No. That's not happening. You need to let her know she's not welcomed here no matter what the judge does. Do you hear me?" she yells.

"Yes, I do." Before I can explain the importance of the children spending time with their mom, the line goes dead. I pull my phone away from my shoulder.

"How did that work out for you?" Lexi asks with a smirk.

"Not as well as I hoped."

Chapter 26

After running Lexi to the grocery store and dropping her off at her home, I didn't get home until six. Mama is busy mopping the kitchen floor.

She looks up as I enter through the glass door. "I thought you were going to leave early so you could help me get the house ready."

"I had a horrible day," I whine as I walk toward the refrigerator. I open it in search of a beer, wine—anything to stop my mind from whirling.

"It won't get much better. You've got the bathrooms."

I collapse against the open fridge door. "No, Mama. I hate bathrooms. Make one of the boys do it."

"Chase is cleaning out the boathouse and washing the boat in case it is nice enough to go for a ride after dinner. Dusty has already mowed the lawn and took the trailer to get some more mulch from Ralph Bates. Your daddy did the hardwood floors today and is at the grocery store for me. That leaves you, little girl, and three nasty bathrooms in need of a scrubbing."

I need something stronger than beer. "Do we have anything to drink?"

"There's some lemonade right in the front there."

I had seen that. "I meant stronger. I think I need a drink."

Mama stops mopping and places a hand on her hip. "Please

do. If it will help with the whining." She gestures toward the farthest cabinet. "Your Daddy keeps the liquor up there now."

Good to know.

I located a bottle of tequila and make a quickie margarita imposter. That is two parts lemonade to one part tequila. I take a sip, smack my lips, and add one more shot of tequila to the large plastic cup before screwing the top back on.

On my way to the guest bathroom, I gather the cleaning tote complete with three types of brushes, five types of cleaners, and rags.

Entering the guest bathroom, my nose turns up involuntarily. Yuck. The place is a pigsty. Which, considering I used it twice yesterday when I camped out in my parents' den, is sort of amazing. I'm just now taking notice of it.

Putting the cleaning tote on the counter, I take another long draw on my quickie margarita. Man, that is very refreshing. I'm going to need to remember how I made that.

Scanning the bathroom, I look for the quickest project to tackle first. They are all on an equal level of disgusting.

Grandpa Snow used to say mucking out the stables smelled terrible and was a dirty job no matter if you started on the near side or the far side of the stables. That is to say, it is more important to just start and focus on more pleasant things while you finish a distasteful job.

I kick off my sandals and climb into the tub. The formerly chrome spigot looks like a horizontal stalactite with the crusty calcification encasing it.

Selecting a green spray bottle with a smiling soap brush, I liberally apply the liquid. The air in the bathroom immediately smells of chlorine, and the white crust begins to bubble rapidly. Hmm ... that stuff seems to work pretty well.

That's very satisfying. I take a moment to watch the cleaner do its magic.

It becomes necessary to get out of the tub to turn on the exhaust fan. My lungs are burning a little. Plus, my drink is on that side of the bathroom, and I need another tiny sip.

King Casey was one smooth dude today. It was incredibly cool once he became aware his team had not completed their investigation thoroughly. He was so chill as he immediately sought to stay the arrest.

Once they realized their team had not done a good job, most folks would have pressed ahead at full speed and tried to force the situation. Not him. He was under control like he had all the time in the world.

How do you get to that level of confidence? Where you don't sweat the details, and you don't get frustrated—or at least show your frustrations.

Oh. I'm sure a couple of field agents who did lazy investigative work are going to get a dressing down when he talks to them Monday. Still, he didn't throw them under the bus during the hearing. He just took responsibility for the issue as if it wasn't any bother and moved forward.

I have no delusional thoughts that this changes his attitude toward Lexi in the least. Suppose the investigation is completed to his specifications, and it comes back that Lexi is their most probable suspect. In that case, he will do what he can to put her away for life.

Am I prepared to go against an opponent as formidable as King? I have my doubts.

It would be fantastic to work with someone as talented as King. Someone who could really teach me not just the mechanics of being an effective litigator but the body language and nuances.

Heck. I could work for him. He practically offered me a job today, didn't he?

Yeah, he did. But public attorneys don't make the kind of scratch private firm attorneys make. Not even close, and wasn't the plan to put in a lot of hard hours in school to make some *insane* money?

The plan was never to put in a lot of hard hours to put in even more insane hours to serve my country.

Don't get me wrong. I'm a patriotic girl, but I think I might be a capitalist first.

A laugh escapes me. Poor old Sylvester, he was screwed six ways to Sunday. It was nice of the judge to let him out for the holidays. My bet is the local school kids will all be heading down to the beach for summer break the next time Sylvester gets to eat dinner at his mom's.

Winky Warner is definitely on my need-to-talk-to list. The bar will probably be open Friday. I'll need to make it a point to get by to see him.

I nearly puke when I lift the commode lid to clean the bowl. My word, what in tarnation is that growing under the rim? It looks like the beginning of some sort of cheesy sci-fi blob monster movie. I spray some more of the magical concoction from the green bottle with the smiling brush on it.

Saturday is supposed to be the day the paranormal team checks out Vance & Leslie Wagner's home. Dusty is going to be disappointed that I have not been able to locate defensive weapons. After tall, long, and creepy clown, I, too, am disappointed.

It is still difficult for me to believe Granny was so little help on the subject. I suppose I shouldn't have put all my hopes in one contact.

There's bound to be other people with that sort of specialized knowledge. I'm not sure they exactly advertise it to the world, though.

Either way, it is going to be nice to see the Wagners. I like the fact they were able to get a larger home—even if it is haunted. I'm surprised I haven't run into them in town over the last few months. But they do live a good way out of town.

But hey, they must come in town for groceries. Right? How would I know. I do most of my grocery shopping in my mama's pantry.

I giggle as I chomp a few ice cubes. This was a tasty mix on the fly, but next time it needs more tequila. It doesn't seem like there is hardly any alcohol in it.

The grout of the bathroom tile is in bad shape. The majority of it around the commode is discolored yellow. I have a pretty good idea what caused that, and I opt to pour bleach directly on the tile around the commode.

All the paper targets in the world won't improve some little boys' aim. You'd think after thirty years their aim would improve—but what do I know?

Sometime soon, I need to do some more snooping around at J&B. Something is *wrong* with that place. I need to figure it out. I don't know why, just a gut feeling, that the key to why Ben was killed is to be found there.

Lord, I wish Vander was available. He could do all that research for me in a tenth of the time it will take me.

With his connections and tenacity, Vander would know the partner's name, current location, and favorite flavor of ice cream before the FBI completes their paperwork.

Michael and I aren't and never have been an item; I mean, I would— *Where did that come from?*

Oh, Lord. Me and Michael? How weird would that be?

Not so weird. I mean, he has never been anything but a perfect gentleman to me, not to mention he is incredibly hot. He's smart, engaging, and a good listener. He's also secret-agent-level secretive and has a habit of disappearing for weeks at a time.

No. Michael Vander is definitely not dating material. Still, he is hot.

I wonder what it would be like to kiss his full lips the next time I see him. Would it be as electrifying as I think it would be?

It would have to be. I'm getting little tingles just thinking about it.

"Looks great, baby."

Mama's voice startles me enough to get at least the most risqué thoughts of Michael Vander out of my mind. "Thanks."

"I didn't expect you to clean the grout, but thank you. I'm sure it needed it. I'm making some avocado-spinach wraps if you're hungry. Your daddy just made it back from the store. Get those gloves off and wash your hands."

Mama looks fuzzy. She has a halo around her heads, both of them, as I look up from my crouching position. "Sounds good."

Chapter 27

Daddy is already sitting at the kitchen counter eating a veg-gie wrap by the time I clean up. He seems genuinely happy to see me.

"There's our busy career girl. I was starting to wonder if you had moved out a few weeks ago and forgotten to tell us."

I roll my eyes. "We had pizza with the boys last Tuesday night."

"Oh yeah. Seems like a month ago already."

Mama places a wrap in front of me and then the salt shaker. "You'll probably want to put some salt on it, but it doesn't need it."

"Thank you." Mama gave up on preaching about salt a few years back. Mama now specializes strictly in passive-aggres-sive coaching. It isn't working, either. I unroll the wrap and apply a liberal dusting of salt to the veggies.

"April did a stellar job on the bathroom, Ralph. It shines when you walk in. You could eat off the floor," Mama says.

"Your mama is going to make a housewife out of you if you're not careful, April."

"Fat chance of that." Eating off floors prompts something in my mind. "Have y'all seen my dog?"

"Bear went with Dusty to get the last load of mulch to spread in the yard."

I know it's silly, but that rubs my fur the wrong way. "It would be nice if someone could at least call or text me before they let my dog go traipsing all about the country in a pickup truck."

Daddy's brow furrows. "I don't think any of us thought you would mind."

"Well, I do. He's my responsibility. How am I supposed to keep him safe if I don't know where he's at?"

"Please, April. Fabio hopped up in the truck before Dusty knew what had happened. When he tried to shoo him out of the truck, Fabio just growled at him. You know how hard-headed that dog is."

"His name is Puppy."

Mama shakes her head. "Whatever his name, he called shotgun, and your brother wasn't going to wrestle with the Tasmanian devil to get him out of the truck."

I know she is right, but it still irks me. My dog is a typical male. He thinks everybody loves him just the way he is, he can handle himself in any situation, and he doesn't have to tell anybody where he is going—which is pretty much the truth—but that is beside the point. It is just infuriating.

"Just fair warning, April. The Neals and the Rainses will be eating with us tomorrow. I think Jackie might be coming with the Rainses."

"Mama, no," I cry.

"Hush now. I don't know what has gotten between you two, but it's high time you two worked through it."

"Now, Viv, you know it's that Randy boy," Daddy tries to add helpfully.

"That's just silly," Mama says. "Jackie is engaged to him, and April hasn't cared for that boy in seven years."

"It's just awkward, Mama," I continue to whine.

"So is living in the same town as your high-school best friend and never talking to her."

Touché.

Mama turns her back, walking toward the refrigerator. "It

seems to me Jackie did you a favor by taking that boy off your hands after you kicked him to the curb."

I know it is rude, but I can't help myself. I mock mama's "It seems to me" with her same exaggerated shoulder swing while her back is turned.

"You know I just cleaned the refrigerator, April." She opens the fridge door and pulls out a pitcher of tea. "I can see you as clearly as if I'm looking in a mirror."

I freeze in terror. Daddy covers his mouth. He's laughing now, but will he be after Mama knocks me into next week?

She shuts the refrigerator door. "That goes for you too, Ralph."

"I just don't know why we can't just have family over, Mama. Our family's big enough without inviting over everyone we know."

"Diane and Wanda are family to me. They are my sisters."

"But they're not, Mama. They're just high-school friends of yours."

When Mama's "look of death" frosts over the top of her tea glass, I know I should have held my tongue on the last comment. "I'm sorry, Mama." I try desperately to retract my careless statement.

"Just because you have the need to throw away every relationship that is over ten minutes old doesn't mean I have to."

Wow. I can't remember my Mama ever saying anything quite that mean to me. All I can manage to do is gape at her. She has all but destroyed my buzz.

"Now, Viv."

"No, I'm sorry, Ralph. But someone needs to let her know." She turns back to me. "Relationships are something that should be nurtured and coaxed to a bloom. They are not always perfect, and some of them are a lot of work. Now, if you want to drop all your relationships as soon as they do not suit your need, or you have some petty perceived slight, that's your business. But you will not sit in judgment of my relationships."

"Geez, I was just saying it would be awkward for me and

Jackie, Mama."

"Who made it awkward, April? I can tell Jackie has moved on from it. There's not a time I see her that she doesn't ask me how you are doing."

Well, Mama wasn't at Jackie's veterinarian office when Puppy got his last shots. Nobody ended up in the hospital—thanks to a well-aimed urine stream from Puppy. But that was all that prevented Jackie and me from getting into a kick-and-scratch match.

I poke my wrap around on my plate. I know I am sulking, but I feel like I have earned the right after that full-frontal assault. My buzz is *completely* gone now. Thanks, Mama.

"Your Mama's just concerned that you keep isolating yourself from your friends. You're too young for that. This is the time in your life you should be doing wild and crazy things with folks your own age.

"You spend all your days working with a bunch of older folks, and then what free time you have you spend with your brothers. How are you supposed to meet new folks like that? Maybe if you spent time with your friends like Jackie, you would have a better chance of meeting new folks. Your own age."

I look from Mama to Daddy. "What's this all about?"

"We're just concerned about you. You've been keeping yourself cooped up in that boathouse too much these past few months. I know you've had a couple of tough breaks recently, but you can't just quit." Daddy seems to realize he said too much, and his eyes widen.

"Wait just a minute. What are you two up to?"

"Nothing." Daddy looks down at his plate.

"I don't know what you're talking about." Mama takes a sip of her tea.

They are both lying. But why and what about?

"For Pete's sake, you two. You're so juvenile. Just tell me."

"Well, at the risk of you standing in judgment of my decision, I invited someone else to dinner tomorrow night," Mama

FOOLISH EXPECTATIONS; APRIL MAY SNOW NOVEL #5

announces with her brows held high.

"Of course, you did," I say with a roll of my eyes.

"He's a ballplayer," Daddy adds as if that makes it all better.

"I guess one more jock at the table can't hurt. I'm sure Chase can keep him company," I say dismissively as I take a huge bite of my wrap to end the conversation. After all, it is their house and their party. I can complain about it all I want, but it is theirs to do with as they please.

"It's the young man who bought the Trinity home from me," Mama adds, as if the guy having money would impress me.

I twirl my finger in the air as I labor to chew the enormous bite. I may have bitten off more than I can chew. Literally.

"His name is Lee Darby. He says he remembers you from school," Mama says.

I draw in a breath in surprise and begin to choke on my wrap. As I reach for my water to help wash my food down my now-closed throat, Daddy comes around the bar and pats me on my back.

"Are you okay?"

I clear my throat. "Yes."

Lee Darby and I certainly know each other. We went through middle school and high school together.

My brother Chase played ball with Lee's older brother, and he always told me the whole Darby family was trouble. He knew Lee and I had homeroom together my junior year and told me he would take Lee *night fishing* if he ever asked me out. Lee didn't fish, so I took that as a warning against any romantic involvement with Lee.

We dated later that year in secret for two months. Warning or no warning, or maybe because of the warning, I couldn't resist. He was tall, lean, and athletic, with a killer smile and devasting gray eyes.

Lee was considered a baseball diamond stud. I was less than impressed by his athletic skill; it was a constant sore spot in our brief relationship.

I was impressed with his Daddy's '67 GTO. So much so that

Lee was the first boy I ever let get to second base.

I broke the whole thing off the following day. I knew if I kept dating him, I would give in to his constant urgings and be a teenage mom of two brats before long, and my dreams of college and law school would be just that, dreams.

My body still leaps to the thought of him. I hate myself for that.

Now I'm going to have Thanksgiving dinner with him, what, nine years later? Oh, that won't be awkward with a capital "A."

Get over yourself, April.

I was just some girl he made out within the back of his daddy's car at the age everyone is trying to figure out what it is all about. It's not like he's an ex-husband or something. He probably hasn't even thought about me since he left high school. That is before Mama showed him the lake house—mansion—he bought.

"Are you sure you're alright?" Mama asks, a few inches from my face.

I tap my chest again. "Yes, ma'am. Just had a piece of spinach go down the wrong hatch."

"For heaven's sake, April, be careful. You scared the daylights out of me." Daddy retreats to his stool.

"Do you remember him?"

"Who?" I ask, hoping I appear casual.

"Lee Darby. The baseball player."

I give a noncommittal shrug, "I don't know. It seems like we might have had a class or two together, but I'm not sure."

"I want you to be nice to him tomorrow night."

"I'm nice to everyone, Mama." It is worth saying just to watch her face twitch.

Chapter 28

It is chilly this evening. I have to grab a hoodie before I go down to the dock to sit and think. The days of hanging my feet over the edge into the water are over, at least for now. Playing footsie with Him is the last thing I need.

Pulling one of the wrought iron chairs to the edge, I sit and peer out onto the dark surface. "I dare you," I grumble toward the water. "I promise you I'll boil you with a fireball."

My challenge goes unaccepted. I figured it would. That poltergeist has always been more of the sneak-attack kind.

Relaxing, I slouch back in the chair and jam my fist into the pocket of my hoodie.

I missed this when I was in Tuscaloosa. The tranquil of the night. The water laps at the edge of the boathouse.

Just seeing the stars in their full brilliance, unhindered by a barrage of street lights, is remarkable. I had forgotten how bright they could be, how vast the heavens are, how small I am.

So, Lee Darby is a professional ballplayer. Wow. Good for him.

I love the fact he chased his dream and brought it to fruition. It gives me hope that I will one day be able to attain my ambitious goals, too. In a way, it is as if I have been in the minor leagues waiting to be called up for the last six months.

Didn't the FBI make a trade offer just this morning?

I'm looking forward to hearing Lee's story about his journey to the top. There is something to be excited about besides some excellent casseroles tomorrow.

Something warm and furry brushes across my leg. I look down in time to watch Puppy collapse on his side, pinning my foot to the dock. He lets out a long huff as if emptying the last of his lungs.

"Long day? Serves you right wandering off with your uncle while not letting me know where you were." He doesn't even bother to look chagrined. "We'll talk about this in the morning, young man. Mark my word."

Chapter 29

Is there anything as sweet as waking up in the morning without an alarm clock and realizing you don't have to go to work? I mean, the most challenging decision is do you want to get up and do something fun or do you want to lounge in bed another hour.

My right foot is asleep because someone decided they wanted to sleep across my leg last night. I push him to the side and stretch my leg.

My phone rings. *Mama.* That's odd.

"Hi, Mama."

"Are you dressed?"

"No, ma'am. I just got up."

"I need a favor if you can. Granny called and needs a block of cheese for her broccoli casserole. She has two pies in the oven and was wondering if you could bring her the cheese, so she doesn't have to stop baking."

"Why can't the boys—" I catch myself. There is no need to draw attention to the fact that I'm the moocher, leach, Freddie freeloader of the holiday dinners. The boys can't run Granny the cheese because they are cooking their own signature dishes for the festivities.

Dusty will be finishing up on his double-stuffed sweet potatoes. A sugary concoction that is a twist on the sweet potato rituals. A half-skin of one of those delicacies makes a double cheeseburger, large fry, and a jumbo chocolate milkshake look like a low-calorie menu option. I can gain weight by smelling them when they come out of the oven.

Chase will be providing the appetizer, Thanksgiving gumbo. I know it sounds a little out of season. He covers that by adding turkey into the fish and shrimp gumbo. It is definitely one of those "don't knock it until you try it" type things. It honestly grows on you.

And April will be bringing the what this year? Wait for it, wait for it, oh yeah … nothing.

"I don't know where they keep those blocks of cheese at the grocery store." Sad but true.

"I have a couple extra in the refrigerator," Mama says.

Of course, she does. Mama is prepared for everything.

"Just get dressed as soon as you can and run it over to her."

"Yes, ma'am."

"C'mon, Puppy. We have an errand to run. You want to go visit Granny?"

He appears to be game enough to tag along and follows me out as I pull on my hoodie.

As I open the sliding glass door to my parents' kitchen, he changes his mind. Puppy whines as the delicious smell of frying bacon surrounds us.

Heck, I almost whine. My dog and I apparently have the same DNA composition when it comes to bacon.

"You didn't tell me you were making breakfast," I complain to Chase, who is manning Mama's old fourteen-inch cast iron skillet.

"You didn't tell me you were up," Chase says.

Dusty stands next to him, turning some incredibly fluffy-looking scrambled eggs. "We figured you needed all the beauty sleep you could get." He takes an exaggerated look at me. "Hmm … looks like you need about twelve more hours."

"Dusty Snow, I'm warning you. You do not want to mess with me this morning."

"Why would this morning be any different than any other." Chase tosses Puppy a piece of bacon. Puppy snatches it out of the air.

"Chase, don't give him any bacon. It gives him gas," I say.

"Everything gives that dog gas," my brothers say in unison. True that.

Mama walks into the kitchen. "Good morning, Sunshine." She goes to the refrigerator and pulls out a block of the melting cheese. "Granny will probably want to get a ride over with you. You know how particular she is about somebody holding the pies."

"It's cause of those craters out there on County Road 17. They never fixed them after last winter," Dusty says.

"Granny said old man Brate lost a tractor to one last month," Chase says as he jerks back from a grease pop in the skillet.

"Your Granny makes up stuff. You two know better than to believe everything she says."

"I want to eat breakfast first." My stomach has decided it is on empty.

Mama frowns. "Granny said she needed that right away. I tell you what, I'll make you a breakfast burrito to go."

I don't want a burrito. I want a plate of scrambled eggs, bacon, and toast with hot coffee and sweet blackberry jam on the side. A burrito while driving in my car isn't even in the same league.

Mama puts a burrito wrapped in a paper towel in my left hand while pushing the block of cheese into my right. "Now, don't be late. And do mind those potholes on the way back."

My life sucks. Everyone else gets to hang out in the kitchen and eat a leisurely paced breakfast. At the same time, I have to scarf down a burrito on the go and hope the stuffing doesn't fall out of the bottom, ending up in my lap. I'm just the errand girl around here.

True, I could take the time to learn to cook something. Nah, that sounds like real work.

I knew as soon as I entered the kitchen that I had lost

my shotgun rider. Considering what bacon usually does to his stomach, they are welcome to all his company they can stand.

My stomach is a voracious black hole this morning. The burrito was delicious, but when I finished, it somehow left me even hungrier than when I started. That isn't possible.

I pull up to the gate of Granny's farm and complete the routine of opening the gate, driving through, and then closing the gate. I can see Maleficent standing on a small knoll, eyeing my progress. She appears to be sizing up if she has time to escape. Sometimes she seems more human than goat to me.

The American flag is whipping in the breeze as I park. Dusty told me he fixed a bank of lights to come on whenever it gets dark so Granny wouldn't have to retire the flag each night. The flag had been Grandpa's responsibility. Granny likes to keep it up. She claims it reminds her of him, but she doesn't care for the upkeep.

I knock on the front door. She doesn't answer, and I ease the door open. "Granny?"

"In here, Sweetie."

I expected her to be in the kitchen, two pies going and a casserole missing one of the two main ingredients and all. Instead, she is in the back library.

I poke my head into the library. "Hey. What are you doing in here? What about your pies? Your casserole?"

She waves her hand. "I finished all that stuff last night. When you get to my age, you can't afford to wait to the last minute."

I want to ask her why the heck I was at her house if she didn't need cheese for the casserole, then decide to hold my tongue until I can determine what she is up to.

She waves me in. "Mercy, don't stand there like a doorstop."

Her face is flushed to bright pink. She is excited about something.

"You remember our talk the other day?"

Of course, I do. "Yes, ma'am."

"I know it was disappointing for you. You know I don't like

disappointing any of my grandchildren."

I sit on the arm of the old leather loveseat to the left of the door. "Yes, ma'am."

"I have been racking my brain ever since you left. I was just trying to remember any contacts I might have had over the years that might be of use to you." She gives a violent shake of her head. Her powder-puff white hairdo does not move in the slightest. "And I can't believe that my memory is so bad."

She crosses the room, a book clutched to her bosom. She extends the book to me. "This is what you were looking for."

Reading the title, my face contorts into a frown before I can catch myself. *Genocide in Middle Ages Latin America.* How is that supposed to help me with expulsions or provide me with a reliable weapon against apparitions? "I don't understand how this helps, Granny."

"Isn't it obvious?" she asks.

"Uh, no, ma'am. *Genocide in Middle Ages Latin America*—how does that help me?"

Granny laughs as she pulls the book back toward her. "Not this book, silly, the author. Dr. David Deveraux is who you are looking for."

"I am?"

"Yes. Dr. Deveraux's early work had to do with the prominence of genocides throughout the ages." Granny holds up a finger. "But from what I understand, after successfully chronicling almost every known occurrence, major and minor, he moved onto unconventional weapons."

I don't see how some professor's research on slingshots and bolo balls will help me defend myself against ghosts and demons, but I don't have any other leads. I might as well tug on this thread and see what happens.

"Did you work with Dr. Deveraux, Granny?"

Her cheeks turn pink. "Oh, no. I had my boys and was out of the paranormal way before I met David."

I didn't have to be a clairvoyant to see the obvious. "Granny! You were sweet on him."

"Oh. It wasn't like that. He's an extremely handsome man, but it was his mind that was always so intriguing to me."

Uh-huh. If it was his mind that was so intriguing, why is her neck flushing red?

It's funny to me; I don't have a choice but to occasionally think of my parents as sexual beings. They constantly give each other kisses, hold hands, or slap one another affectionately on the butt. Awkward. But Granny? That isn't awkward to me; it is frickin' hilarious for some reason.

"Were you and David," I mimic how she had said his first name, "like a thing?"

"You are an incorrigible child."

I thought it was a fair question, but I had obviously crossed some invisible line. "Do you have his contact info?"

Granny pulls a slip of paper from her polyester slacks. "He is a professor at the University of Sewanee."

Now that is good news. The University is a two hour's drive. "That's awesome, Granny."

"I was even able to get you an appointment to see him tomorrow."

"Tomorrow?"

Granny's brow furrows. "You sounded like this was an immediate need."

"Sure, you're right. I just need to move my schedule around. I'll make it work."

Granny motions toward one of the tables, and I dutifully take a seat. "I owe you an apology," she begins.

I don't answer her. I just lean forward in case she wants to reveal some deep-seated dark trait.

"You caught me off guard the other day, and I wasn't particularly truthful."

Okay, so she has my *full* attention.

"The problem with using expulsion is that you have to be very pure of heart and extremely focused. If you fail in either of these, you can have your body hijacked by an evil spirit."

I hate to ask the question, but everyone wants to know.

"Pure of heart?"

"I have a close personal relationship with God, and I can recite the entire King James Version."

If Granny is going to be that strict about a pure heart, I might as well not even bother with learning the art of expulsion. "Yeah, I think I can recite a few Psalms."

"That's just it," Granny pleads. "It's so dangerous and your faith—it's good, but not expulsion type of good. If something were ever to happen to you, I would never forgive myself."

"With all due respect, Granny. Isn't that my choice? I am an adult."

"And the government won't let you run around your yard with a lit stick of dynamite, either, even if you're an adult, because they don't want you to get hurt."

It's not logical, but what Granny is saying actually hurts my feelings. I believe in the holy trinity. Just because I don't go to church twice every Sunday doesn't make me a heathen—I just might need as much instruction as Granny needs.

My mind wanders back to the first paranormal excursion Dusty hired me to work on. So much for easy introductions. The team had relied on me heavily the entire day, but when all the chips were down, it was Liza who saved us, saved me.

It took my mind several months to accept what I had seen her perform. People pulling crucifixes out of elaborate tattoos is not supposed to happen. But I am eternally grateful she was able to.

I can still feel the cold, oily tendrils of the spirit that sought to enslave my mind and take free reign over my body. If Liza had not been there for me, it would have gone very differently that day.

"You have to understand," Granny is still talking, "I became possessed once, and your grandpa gave me an ultimatum. Quit trying to help folks with expulsions or give up on being around my family."

"That doesn't sound like Grandpa to give an ultimatum like that," I comment. Grandpa was more of the "I'll let you figure out on your own that's a bad idea" sort of man.

"No, but if—I didn't leave him much choice. It began with me not feeling right a lot of the time. I felt sort of spacey—I couldn't follow conversations like I used to. Then when I would eat, all I could eat was meat. The rarer the meat, the better, and I avoided vegetables like the plague."

If that diet habit is the threshold for being possessed, I must have dated a good number of possessed men.

"The kicker was when your daddy had to tackle me and take a knife out of my hand to save Uncle Howard. They might have been fifteen and thirteen at the time."

"What were you going to do to him?"

"I think I planned to carve him up like a little piglet."

My mouth gapes open as my head shakes involuntarily.

Granny notices my reaction. "Scary stuff. Of course, it wasn't me. It was the demon that had possessed me. It wouldn't have made any difference if Ralph hadn't stopped me. I know I could never have forgiven myself for hurting Howard even if I had been possessed."

"How did you get rid of it? The demon."

"If I tell you, can you keep it a secret?"

"Sure."

"It's imperative. There is still this stigma folks attach to those of us who have abilities that fall into the religious supernatural. It's bad enough that we didn't ask for the gift, but people can treat you like you have a contagious disease. When mostly, we would prefer just to be normal."

I think about the random voices I hear when I forget to block them properly. "I can understand that."

"Do you know who Felicity Bell is?"

I can't precisely place having heard the first name before, but I know the last name. "I would assume related to Jasper and Ms. Bell."

"That's right, Jayla's mama, Felicity. She was the one who actually started the diner."

"I always thought Jasper's mom ran it."

Granny sits in one of the leather chairs. I take the hint and sit, too. "I could see where you thought that. Felicity opened it up in the fifties, and Jayla took over running it when you were very young. Felicity continued to work in the kitchen when she could. Still, after being as healthy as a horse her entire life, one Thursday night while brining ribs in preparation for the ever-popular Rib Friday, she dropped dead of a massive stroke. Doc Tanner said she was dead before she hit the floor."

"That's awful."

Granny shrugs. "Beats having one of those long-protracted illnesses. Where you watch yourself die a little bit more each day, but your body continues to hold on while you take on the appearance of an emaciated zombie."

"That had to be a shock for Ms. Bell."

"It was. Jayla is a strong woman like her mother, but she was sad. Real sad for a long time."

Mama and I have our differences from time to time, but I couldn't even imagine what it would be like to lose my mama. To lose the opportunity to talk to the one person who can stabilize me when my whole world goes sideways is a hard one to get my head around.

"Felicity had approached me a year earlier when I was in the restaurant. She told me that she could sense the skill when I came into the diner. She wanted to warn me against using the skill. She said I didn't have the prerequisite power to control it."

"Why didn't you listen to her?"

Granny flashes a quick smile. "I suppose because I was in my early thirties, knew everything, and wasn't about to have some old lady tell me I couldn't use one of my hard-earned skills."

She looks over my head as she pauses. She starts back, sounding markedly more tired.

"We had a family come in and buy the old Conroy land. Most of that land is nothing more than rock. At the time, there was a cedar forest covering most of the property.

"Blake Simmons was the name of the owner. He had a pretty, young wife, I forget her name now, and a baby boy. Blake was determined to turn that old forest land into pasture land. He worked all hours clearing that land over the first three months he owned it."

She shifts in her seat. It is obvious she would rather not tell the story.

"It's okay, Granny. You don't have to tell me if you don't want to."

She reaches out and grasps my hand. "It has not so much to do with what I want to do as it does with what you need to know to be safe. When you attempt to expel a demon from a possessed individual, you open two paths. One path directly back to you and a second which is wherever you want the demon to go. The demon will always traverse to the path of least resistance. But I'm getting ahead of myself.

"Blake got his land cleared. I'm not partial to cedar trees, but he had hundreds of them that were probably three hundred years old if they were a day.

"These trees had bases so wide you would need three or four people holding hands to encircle the tree. Well, he made a mess of the land. It was scarred and pocked from where he had attempted to pull up stumps. But he just kept working his plan and bought about fifty head of cattle."

"That must be hard to watch someone tear up their land."

"It was, but understand it was his to do with as he saw fit. That is the law of the courts. That is not the law of the forest."

A chill runs up my spine. "Law of the forest?"

"That forest at least. When Blake cleared the land, he woke a demon, an ancient and powerful demon.

"Neighbors began reporting an unusually tall man skulking around the Simmons land. A few nights later, one of the calves was found mutilated. The next night it was two calves, and he lost two more the next night.

"The poor man thought he had purchased a cursed home and asked your grandpa and me to bless the house for them.

"I wasn't there for thirty seconds, and I began to feel ill. Little did I know that the demon had no desire to stay with the Simmonses. Right from the start, it made me its mark and began to hitch a ride."

"Did Grandpa go to get Felicity when you got sick?"

"Lord, no. I wish we had. That demon was old and smart. Understand, your grandpa and I had successfully completed hundreds of exorcisms by this point. The old demon entered me quietly, and other than my stomach turning whenever I ate, I had no idea he was in me."

"When did you become aware that you had been possessed?"

"I think it was two weeks after being to the farmhouse. I knew something was wrong. It was partly that I could no longer stomach anything other than animal products in my diet. Plus, I had this constant urge to lash out whenever somebody aggravated me.

"I thought maybe I was sick, maybe I had caught a terminal illness, and it was how my body was dealing with it. But then, little by little, the demon began to suggest things in my mind. Not fully taking control—I think he knew I would've known that right away. Instead, he would take just a small portion of my mind, and in many ways, it felt like my consciousness debating itself in my head."

Granny pauses as she folds her hands in her lap. She takes a deep breath and continues. "That morning with the knife, Howard and Ralph were playing chase in the house. They were too old for that by then, and I remember thinking they would break something.

"As Ralph was chasing Howard through the house, Howard began to squeal whenever Ralph would get too close to him. That's when the demon took over just enough of my mind to make it seem like I was having a debate in my consciousness.

"Howard squealed again, and I heard a voice in my head say if he's going to squeal like a pig, you should carve him up like a piglet. I picked up the knife, I could see myself doing it, and I was horrified. But I could no longer stop myself."

"That had to be terrifying."

"It's definitely something I'll never forget." Granny locks

eyes with me. "That's the point, April. I never should have been playing around with exorcisms. I wasn't even close to having enough faith to control the situation. If Felicity Bell had not been around to rid me of the demon, I don't know what your grandpa and I would have done."

This seems like just another incredible skill with a dead end to it. It reminds me of when I learned that I had accidentally traveled in time. I was extremely excited to talk to Nana about it, and then she immediately forbade it. For good reasons, mainly being lost in the infinite. The proposition of being sentenced to floating in complete darkness with no sensory stimulation for eternity could give even the most reckless of girls pause.

On the excursions with our paranormal team, there have been opportunities where I could've helped the team, and specifically Liza if I had the skill of expulsion. But just like time travel, if I listen to people who know what they are talking about, I would only use it as a last resort.

"Now that just bites."

"Pardon me, honey?" Granny's white eyebrows draw together.

"Well, it's just why have the skills and abilities if it's too dangerous to use them?"

Granny chuckles. "Baby, expulsion is such a small part of the religious supernatural portfolio. There are other things, more important and beautiful things, the gift will bring you if you hone the skill."

"If you're talking about salvation, I need something a little more tangible for when I'm on an excursion with Dusty."

"Now you're just being rude." Granny favors me one of her rare "get your act together" looks. "What I'm referring to is the art of manifestation."

I wasn't sure if her pause was for dramatic effect or if she thought I didn't already know about her belief in manifestation.

"The ability to bring something into existence with your

mind."

"I'm familiar with it, Granny."

"You are?"

I give a nervous laugh. "I remember you mentioning it when I was younger. Back when we used to spend the summers with you."

"I see."

"Honestly, I don't find it to be very reliable."

"April, it's an extremely reliable art."

I'm not going to argue the point. I know my experience and my lack of "success." Any positive results I have had can be written off as a timely coincidence. I stand and gesture toward the door. "Do you want me to give you a ride over to the house?"

Granny doesn't stand. She crosses her arms, and her eyes form narrow slits. "You don't believe me."

"Not about the skill. Still, if you think it is reliable, I have to wonder if you have been drinking too many of those Long Island iced teas."

Granny rolls her eyes. I may have inherited the trait from her. "I've been doing manifestations long before I ever started drinking Long Island iced teas."

I pinch my index finger to my thumb and put it to my lip, pretending to take a long drag on a blunt. "You grew up in the 60s. Maybe you had a little too much of the wacky weed back then."

I earn a laugh from her as she stands. "I won't say we didn't partake. But I assure you my mental faculties are in full operational mode. It's your faith that is lacking."

"My faith?"

Granny slides by me and through the doorway, "Yes. I am absolutely amazed the little girl with the huge imagination and deep love for Bible stories has turned into a woman who can't grasp new ideas."

That's just so wrong. I don't have a hard time grasping new ideas. I'm the queen of grasping new ideas.

I follow Granny into the kitchen with my wounded pride.

I'm not particularly pleased with her at the moment. Especially considering she called me out here on false pretense to pick on me. Granted, she gave me a lead on the supernatural weapons project, but why not bring the book to dinner?

"What are you doing?" I ask.

"Getting my pies and casserole together, of course. It didn't sound like you were going to give me much time."

Now I feel six inches tall for making her think I was in a rush. "You're serious about this manifestation stuff? That it's reliable."

"Serious as a heart attack." She pulls a cardboard box onto the counter and sets the pies slowly in it.

"Then answer me this. Why do you bake? Why not just twinkle your nose and make a pecan pie?"

"That's ludicrous, April."

For someone like myself who doesn't know how to bake, it makes all the sense in the world. I would see endless possibilities for the skill if it were real. "Why?"

"We don't have to twinkle our nose." She covers her casserole. "How would that help your mental capacity anyway? If anything, I would find it distracting."

My entire family has this tendency to focus on the wrong parts of conversations when I am talking to them. Granny knows darn well there is nothing remarkable about someone twinkling their nose. The actual topic of the discussion is the magical production of food items that would win me praise at the next holiday dinner.

"Pies, why wouldn't you just manifest pies rather than bake them?"

Granny looks at me as if I have lost all good sense. "Because I *like* baking pies, and I'm good at it."

Well, there is that. "What do you use manifestation for, then?"

"Special stuff—the hard stuff—things that you can't do on your own. I like to use it only when I know that it is the only thing that can bring something to fruition."

"Like…" I still have this gut feeling that Granny is pulling my leg. It would be out of character for her. Still, this is too rich, and my results to date have been less than stellar.

"If a friend is sick or in need." She twitches her shoulder. "I might give them a little assistance."

I laugh in disbelief again. Something about this conversation makes me uncomfortable, nervous. "Granny, that's prayer. Besides, you have no way of knowing if it was your prayer or just coincidence."

"First off, I may call it prayer most of the time, but it is just marshaling the energies of the universe to create what I want. Second, I already told you I only like to use it for things that I know only the art of manifestation could have brought into existence."

I sigh. "Right. Now you sound like you think you have the same powers as God."

A smile forms on her lips. She studies me for the longest time. "Baby, if he made you with his energy, doesn't it stand to reason that there is just the smallest amount of that all-powerful energy within you? I'm not God, but I carry a tiny seed of his power that should allow me to tap into the universe's energy when I want to. It's my birthright."

I wait for her to burst into a laugh and holler, "I had you going," as she points her finger at me. Instead, all I get from her is that controlled, peaceful stare. I'm concerned for her. Is this a sign of early dementia? If so, I need to let Mama and Daddy know. They wouldn't want her to stay out on the farm by herself.

"Granny, you know that's not true. Right?"

"Of course, it's true." She shakes her head slowly, side to side. "Child, why has your faith died?"

"There's nothing wrong with my faith, Granny." There might be something wrong with you, but not my faith.

"I remember how excited you used to get in summer Bible school when you studied the fall of the walls of Jericho, Daniel in the lions' den." She points her finger. "And Shadrach, Meshach, and Abednego and the fiery furnace. You have to remember how you recounted those stories over and over to me."

"They're stories, Granny. Fairy tales."

"Excuse me?" Her stance shifts.

Whoops. Granny might be slipping in the mental capacity arena. However, she still has a keen grasp of what might be considered a blasphemous statement. I attempt to smooth over my careless words.

"They're fables, Granny. Parables." I correct myself. "They're meant to teach lessons through stories. It's easier for people to understand that way. It's just imaginary."

"No. They are accurate recordings of actual events."

I take in the wide stance of her five-foot-nothing frame and decide I have caused more than enough consternation today. I'll let Mama and Daddy handle it.

"Fine." I reach for the pie box. "You need a hand with this?"

The quick smack on my hand shocks me. Sure, it smarts, but more shocking is that it was the first time I can remember Granny ever striking me. "Ow!"

"Did that really hurt, or is it imaginary." She raises her eyebrows in a threatening manner when she asks.

"What?" She's lost her mind. I rub the back of my offended hand.

"I'm just trying to prove a point. If you write down that I struck your hand and it hurt, and then someone accuses you of making it up, does it make it less real? Did it not happen?"

Yep, she's certifiable. "Granny, I don't even know what you're talking about anymore. Do you want me to help you with the food or not?"

"What I want is for your faith to be as strong as it should."

I nod my head. "Strong faith. I got it. All good here, Granny. I'll work on it."

"I want you to visualize a feather. A unique feather. One that doesn't exist in the natural world."

That freezes me in my tracks. "You're serious."

"My granddaughter's faith hangs in the balance. Of course,

I'm serious."

"Yeah, I'm tired of this game, Granny." I reach for the box and hesitate as she raises her hand to strike my hand again.

"Feather, the more exotic, the better."

The funny thing is I've seen her like this before. Her face and eyes relax. On the surface she appears incredibly peaceful, but there's an energy, a growing power just below the surface. If she were a power line, I would swear I can hear the crackle of the electrical current crossing through her conductors. Just like a downed power line, I don't dare cross her path.

The feather. What the heck. As far as I know, pretty much all feathers look very similar, right? No, that's not the case. There are feathers from robins, cardinals, blue jays, and even chickens have different colors and sizes. But what would be a unique feather?

"Tell me a feather." She insists again.

"I'm trying!" Geez, it isn't like I'm picking from a catalog of feathers. "Okay, a hawk feather."

"Too common," she decrees.

I thought that was a pretty good selection myself. I consider about every kind of bird I can and believe I am out of choices until I remember... "A peacock. A male peacock tail feather."

"Almost as common as a hawk."

"No, it's not," I complain.

"Sure, it is. You see them in stores all the time. I said pick something unique. As in if I were to show it to you, it only could've happened through manifestation." Her eyes narrow. "What are you not understanding about this?"

I don't understand why I am still placating a crazy woman. Yet here I am, afraid to cross a five-foot-tall, ninety-pound septuagenarian for fear she might kick my butt. I don't care about any stupid feather. I just want to get Granny, her casserole, and the two pies loaded into the car so I can drive back home. "A one-and-a-half-inch long down goose feather, pink, with a purple spine." I feel the triumphant smile stretch across my face.

That's right. Press April too hard, and you're gonna regret it.

My smile is still stretching across my face when Granny raises her right hand and blows into it. My pink feather shoots out of her fist, floating toward me. I reach out, and it lands in the palm of my hand. I know, before I even look, the spine is purple.

"Wait. You did some sort of mind suggestion trick. You made me pick that feather, and you had it in your hand all along," I complain as I blow the feather back at her.

"That would be a powerful trick, too," Granny says with a smirk. "I don't have that ability, although I believe you might be capable of it."

I'm shocked by her statement. Oddly, it makes me grin. I'm not sure if because of the sheer preposterousness of her claim or because I'm thinking, "Oh, please let it be so."

I have always thought the power of mental persuasion would be one of the best skills in the universe. With a skill such as that, I might master the ability to get my dog to mind me, and he thinks it is his idea. That could be especially handy.

I'm not sure how Granny pulled off her trick, but I'm not ready to concede just yet. I make to lift the box again, then say, "Three-inch-long lime green feather."

Without a second's hesitation, Granny opens her left hand and blows a lime green feather in my direction."

"Two-inch, yellow with white polka dots," I call out.

The yellow feather floats lazily, side to side, down from the ceiling in front of my face. I won't say I'm a *believer*. Still, three well-timed coincidences in a row make for a strong case on circumstantial evidence. A case I can't argue against.

Looking up from the yellow and white polka-dotted feather descending to the floor, I'm surprised by the hazy glow surrounding Granny.

Chapter 30

"Do you need some more examples, April?" Granny laughs, the odd glow around her oscillating from a muted gold to a bright white.

"I'm thinking," I reply.

"I'll accept that apology anytime you're ready."

My face screws up. "Apology for what?"

"For doubting me. You should know your Granny would never lie to you."

That is a true statement on her part. Still, I just am not sure I'm prepared to buy into the possibility of creating something from a desire.

My reticence to accept what she tells me, especially after our feather magic routine, is illogical. How can I believe in ghosts, demons, time travel, spells, and potions, yet find it so difficult to think that I can bring something into the world by using only my mind?

I don't know. Perhaps because it sounds too good to be true?

Seriously, if someone can bring everything their heart desires into the world by using their mind coupled with extreme focus, why is there so much lack and want in the world? Or is it only a few people possess the ability?

Also, how could I ever value something I didn't have to work for? Is that important?

Bless it, my brain hurts. In so many ways, the idea of manifestation feels like Pandora's box. An addictive skill set is better left unused.

"Your turn. Why don't you give it a try?" Granny coaxes.

I huff as I realize we will not be leaving for the lake house until I appease her. "What sort of feather do you want?"

Granny wrinkles her nose. "Let's not do feathers. Why don't you think about something you've seen recently and pull it toward you?"

This is worse than the feather exercise. I'm at a total loss.

Pull something toward me? The only thing I want to pull toward me is my parents' house. I'm tired of this awkward demonstration and am ready to sit down to Thanksgiving dinner so I can eat until I am full as a tick and visit with folks I don't see every day.

"You're stalling," Granny says as she purses her lips.

That's Granny's disappointed face, and I can never weather it for long. It is the antithesis of "great job, April." I become anxious to perform her request.

Bring something to me.

Maleficent, the goat, comes to mind. I focus on her big, mischievous eyes and mentally ask for her to come to me.

"At least try, April."

"I am, Granny. I'm pulling Maleficent to me."

She nods her head. "That's a good one."

I close my eyes. Granny's face is distracting me.

My expectations are admittedly low. If they could be lower than zero, I'd be there.

How can I expect to draw a goat to me with my mind? Especially *that* goat. Maleficent has a mind of her own. This is the same goat no one can coerce to obey what you want when you offer her treats.

As I fall deeper into a state of concentration, I swear I can hear her nasally breathing and smell the scent of goat sweat in the room. I focus on Maleficent's eyes and visualize her staring at me. I complete the rest of her face and head, including her floppy ears. I feel the energy bubbling under my skin, causing me to become giddy with the prospects of the power.

I'm learning power is an intensely addictive drug. I first noticed it during my exercises. Nana had me practice them to master control of my budding abilities. Low-level telekinesis and the ability to ignite a fire plume. When I successfully complete an exercise, I'm never satisfied. I am left with a primal urge spiking the dopamine dump to my brain—a base desire pushing me to harness even more power.

Who wouldn't be excited about creating a spark out of thin air? That is so awfully cool. But the parlor trick in and of itself isn't the issue. Creating the flame is harmless. The pull of the power isn't necessarily without cause for concern.

Organizing the multitudes of charged electrons into my core and concentrating to critical mass feels like being pricked by a million straight pins all at once. The first few times the power came to me, it hurt and was scary. Now, what was once painful feels good as I know it signals the eminent pleasure of releasing the concentrated power.

There is no rush like a power rush exciting my body.

The connection with Maleficent is made. It's not as if I am her, still I can feel myself inside her thoughts coercing her, suggesting she come to me for a treat. It is more of an instinctual feeling rather than a language.

The excitement level I'm feeling peaks. This will work. I am going to be good at this.

I bear down with my focus holding the image of her walking toward me in my mind.

She is coming. I can feel it in my gut.

Who am I kidding? I can't even get that goat to stay inside the yard when I'm driving my car off the farm. I really believe I can get her to come to the front porch against her will?

In defeat, I open my eyes and slouch against the kitchen table. "I guess that proves I don't have that skill, Granny. I can't get that goat to come to me."

"Can't never could, April. You must have the correct attitude to manifest. To bring things into your life, you need to be positive."

"I'm positive I suck at this."

"April!" Granny crosses her arms. "Not in my home."

"Well, it's true." I shrug. "For one thing, I can't focus long enough to manifest anything."

"I don't know about that." Granny points between my feet. I step back as she pulls out the broom and dustpan.

I've seen what's on the floor at least a million times in my life. Still, I hold out hope it is not what I think it is. "What is that?"

Granny snorts a laugh. "Goat scat, I do believe."

"No!" I can't contain my horror.

Granny sweeps it neatly into the dustpan. "Yep. There's no mistaking it."

Great. I try to manifest a goat, and instead, I get a pile of neat little goat dung balls. That's worse than having a skill. I have a defective skill.

Granny opens the back door dumping the goat refuse off the side of the deck. "All gone."

"See. That's why I didn't believe you. I'm a failure at manifestation."

Granny chuckles. "Not the most stellar demonstration I've ever seen."

Still, the residual high from the release of the power remains. It pushes me forward, wheedling me to pull energy in and try again.

After all, manifestation could bring great good into the world. I should learn the skill so I can help other people with it.

The mental argument in my head is insincere. I know that, on the base level, still the desire is so great I buy into the falsehood.

"I need to try again," I say.

"I believe we should get over to the party. We don't want to be late," Granny says.

She's looking at me oddly. Does she know what I am wrestling with inside?

"No. Now that I know what I'm doing, I think I can make it happen."

"It takes a lot of energy, April. Maybe if you rest until this afternoon and try again at home, you can make it happen."

Granny moves toward the door, casserole in hand. I resign to lifting the pie box and following her to the front door.

With her free hand, Granny opens the front door. Maleficent lets out a cry. She looks me directly in the eye and cries again.

"It worked! Oh my gosh, it worked," I exclaim.

"Now it's my turn to be skeptical," Granny says. "I think she may be up here searching for scraps."

Granny can try to burst my bubble, but I know I brought that goat to the front door. I can't wait to manifest something that really counts.

Chapter 31

The Snow reunion is not for the weak of heart. Mama and Daddy have invited close to forty friends and relatives to this year's Thanksgiving festival. Some of the people we regularly see, such as the Neals and Rainses. Other guests, the only time we see them is on the holidays. Folks that fall into that classification would be cousin Lamont and Aunt Renée.

Daddy always drives down to pick them up for the holiday dinners as neither has a car. It's safer that they don't.

Cousin Lamont lives somewhere down in Jasper. He caught some disease from the oil fields burning in the first Gulf War and lives in a tent close to the rest area. Daddy has tried to help him get into the VA to improve his situation on numerous occasions. But as Daddy says, "It just wouldn't take with Lamont."

Aunt Renée is fruitier than a Fruit Loop in a box of Cornflakes. That's not to be mean, just to point out the obvious.

She has been diagnosed with bipolar, schizophrenia, manic depression, and several other psychological conditions I can't pronounce. She has been on disability for as long as I can remember.

Despite her doctors' many clinical analyses, Dusty's diagnosis of our aunt that he gave at the age of twelve still feels the most accurate. "She just ain't right."

These are my people.

Aunt Renée will tell you she has been married four times. In her head, that is the truth.

The rest of the family will tell you Parker Luis left her at the altar at the age of eighteen, four months pregnant with a baby. The child was stillborn three months later.

I'm not sure if her eggs were cracked before all that hardship took place. Either way, it is understandable that such a horrific year as a teenager could stunt someone's social growth for the rest of their life.

Granny has made herself scarce from me since we arrived at the lake house. I suppose she has convinced herself that I won't try to manifest anything without her assistance. That's funny. She should know that I've never had an issue learning on my own.

"Estoy cegado por tu belleza."

I have no idea what he said, but the voice is familiar, and I feel my skin tingle pleasantly. Luis's large, beautiful dark eyes and perfectly structured face greets me with a genuine smile as I turn to him. "You better not be talking dirty to me in Spanish, Luis."

He ducks his head in his usual shy deference, closing his eyes briefly and exposing the thickness of his eyelashes. "I respect you too much for that, my April."

My April, is it today? Somebody must be in a festive mood. "I'm glad you were able to make it today."

"I was thankful for the invite from Dusty and your mother. Holidays are difficult when your family is so far away."

"You know you're part of this family, too. As dysfunctional as it may be."

"And I am very, very thankful for that."

"Have you seen Liza since she's gotten back from the hospital? I'm afraid that I've been so covered up with work I haven't had the opportunity to check up on her."

Luis's brows twitch as if he is contemplating how best to word his question. "Have you been sleeping well?"

"Since we've been back?"

Luis nods his head. His eyes, usually full of humor, are serious, his expression expectant.

"Sure. I'm not getting enough of it, but I've been sleeping fine."

"Good. That's good."

I reach out and grab Luis by the arm. He is wearing a long-sleeved buttoned shirt, and I only receive some general energy impressions. He is concerned. *Extremely* concerned. "Is something wrong with Liza?"

Luis sighs. "You should probably ask her yourself."

"I'm asking you, Luis."

He hesitates before continuing. "She says she's having nightmares about the clown at the Baron home in Oaklawn."

She can try to do what I did. Block the oversized clown that set the attic on fire from her mind. I still get chills thinking about how close Liza and I came to becoming crispy critters. "A twelve-foot-tall clown with size twenty-four shoes has a tendency to wig out most people."

"It's not the ghost clown that she has nightmares about. It's the clown doll that was on top of the toy chest."

What? That's silly. We had two full-bodied hostile apparitions in the room. Why would Liza be focused on some old stuffed doll that went up in the fire? "You're right. I need to call her and talk to her."

Luis's face brightens. "She will appreciate that."

"Is she coming today to the party?"

"Oh, no. Every Thanksgiving, she goes into Gadsden and works the homeless shelter's Thanksgiving meal."

That is Liza. A real living, breathing dichotomy.

If you are meeting her for the first time, you would assume she is some sort of lousy attitude biker chick. To be fair, she might have a bit of that uncompromising attitude in her—but she also has a caring heart of twenty-four-karat gold.

"I'll check up on her tomorrow."

Luis squeezes my shoulder. The concern has faded from his face, replaced by hopefulness. "Thank you, I appreciate that. I know it will do her good."

I wander toward the kitchen in hopes of finding Granny. Instead, I find Mama and Daddy having a conversation with— Oh my gosh, it's him. Lee Darby.

He is more gorgeous than I remember. His six-foot-two frame has filled out nicely, and his boyish face has been replaced by a rugged manly profile complete with a cocky smile.

I watch as he relays a story to my parents. His facial features and hands are highly animated while he speaks. I am mesmerized by the energy he exudes.

He notices me in the doorway, his face relaxes, and a lopsided grin appears. "Hey there, stranger."

The timbre of his voice resonates with my soul. I'm positive I'm grinning like a loon. "Glad you could make it, Lee."

"What, no hug?" He extends his left arm away from his side.

Moth to the flame. Bee to the flower. Whatever you want to call it, I find myself walking over to him and giving him a hug as if I am magnetized to him.

I step back and notice both of my parents are looking at me with a most perplexed expression. I feel the need to explain. "I just remembered that Lee and I had homeroom together our junior year in high school."

"April used to help me with my first period Math during homeroom. There's no way I would've gotten through that class without her help," Lee adds.

Wow! He is smooth. That little white lie was so good I almost believed it myself. It did the trick. My parents are nodding their heads appreciatively.

"I was just telling Lee about two different interior designers I want him to meet with," Mama explains.

I'm not listening to her. I'm enjoying the electrical currents crackling deliciously across my body from the hug I gave Lee Darby. He has always been charismatic and good-looking. Now he gives off a sexual energy that is impossible to resist.

So, what the heck, why resist? Right?

"Vivian is determined to make sure the house she sold me is

not turned into a man cave. I suppose I can at least listen to the two interior designers. If I change my mind, Bobby Jo's Furniture Rental is just down the street, and I can turn it into a man cave in less than a weekend." He shoots Mama a playful sideways glance.

"Over my dead body," she says with a laugh.

She takes the bait.

"I can get me one of those singing basses to hang in the foyer. 'Take me to the river.'"

"I did not sell you a premier home for you to turn it into some sort of professional ballplayer party house. The fraternity house look is fine when you're in your late teens, but I'm sure there are people you want to impress now that you're older," Mama preaches.

Lee rubs the back of his neck. "I don't know. It's tough to beat a sofa on the front porch. Is that considered tacky?"

"No, absolutely not. You will not be denigrating that house by putting a sofa on the front porch," Mama continues.

"Viv." Daddy touches her hand. "He's just pulling your leg."

She glares at Daddy, then turns her stink eye on Lee.

Lee breaks into a full grin as he shrugs his shoulders.

"Oh, you are a wicked one." Her eyes narrow into slits in stark contradiction to her amused smile.

Tearing off a paper towel, she grabs a handful of chocolate chip cookies off one of the cooling racks and wraps them. "Take these and get out of my kitchen," she says as she shoves the cookies in Lee's direction with one hand while making a shooing motion with the other.

Lee accepts the cookies, makes eye contact with me, and gestures toward the glass door. I follow him out onto the porch without a word.

"You want one?" Lee asks as he slides the door shut.

"How does that even work? I would have to beg for a cookie. You jerk her chain, and she gives you enough for three people," I ask.

Lee leans against the railing, propping one foot against it. I watch as he unwraps the bundle, stacks the cookies, and lifts the top half, gesturing toward me. "Looks like your take is three."

He drops the cookies in my open palm. "You must have that woman in a trance. She doesn't normally reward bad behavior with cookies."

"People will surprise you."

Yeah, I'm feeling a little bit of that surprise right now. The Lee Darby I knew was good-looking, athletic, and occasionally clever. What he wasn't was intriguing or socially adept.

Something has changed in the last seven years. Something has made his personality fuller, more enticing to me. It is difficult to explain, but he draws me in effortlessly. It is as if I could stay entertained just watching and talking to him.

"Is that your new mantra?" I ask.

He nibbles a chocolate chip cookie as he studies me. "Just stating a fact. Do you see it differently?"

"I think most of us are predictable. People tend to be the same way. Over time, you can anticipate what their reaction will be to all manner of things."

Lee nods in agreement. "That's right. Until they don't do what you expect and surprise you."

There may be some truth to that. But Lee Darby was never the most profound thinker. Around me, in the past, most of his thinking was done below his belt. It is taking me a moment to catch up with the new Lee Darby. Maybe he's *surprising me*?

He gestures with his cookie toward me. "Take you, for example. The last person I expected to ever find in this town again—unless it was for Thanksgiving dinner—was April Snow. I thought you would be long gone to New York or LA or some other huge city by now."

It stings a little bit, but then I remember something about the Lee Darby who no longer exists. "And what happened to the Lee Darby who was never going to leave Guntersville? You may have a lake home here now, Mr. Darby, but I bet you have a bachelor pad in some big city and live out of a suitcase half the year. Tell me, what small town did you end up in?"

"Touché. I make my home when my home isn't a suitcase as you so aptly describe, in the cozy, quiet hamlet of Boston." He smiles, and my knees turn to jelly. "Still, you just made my point. We are both just full of surprises, aren't we, April?"

I quit staring into his gray eyes. I want to run my hands through his short-cropped golden hair and taste his lips. I lean toward him as close as I can without taking a step toward him.

"I'm sure in a small town like this, an educated, beautiful lady like yourself already has a fiancé."

I'm so deep into thoughts about gripping the hair on the back of his head that I have to shake the cobwebs from my mind. "No. I'm not seeing anyone right now."

Lee's eyebrows raise. "Seriously? I always knew the boys around here weren't particularly bright, but that's just plain stupid. You didn't like murder or castrate your last boyfriend, did you?"

I snort a laugh. I feel my face flush hot. "No. I might have thought about it once or twice, but now there's no police record on me."

Lee shakes his head slowly as he maintains eye contact. "Crazy. See, it surprises me that none of the boys in this town have the intestinal fortitude to ask you out." He shrugs his right shoulder nonchalantly. "Of course, you are intimidating."

"Intimidating? I'm not intimidating."

The good-humored grin disappears from Lee's face. "Oh yeah, you are. Educated, successful, from a good family, and then to top all that off with you being drop-dead gorgeous— yeah, you're intimidating, whether you want to admit it or not."

I halfway believe he is making fun of me. Still, my ego is eagerly lapping it up, so I decide to play along. "Tell me, are you intimidated by me too, Mr. Darby?"

"Nah. Just to be fair to all those other guys that are intimidated by you, I have an advantage."

"And what advantage would that be?"

"I've had the honor of making out with you. So, you see, you're already human to me. All the other boys still look at you as an unattainable goddess."

It's not just my face that flushes now; it's my entire body. I can't tell if it is anger, embarrassment, or pleasure as my mind goes back to our youth in the back of his father's car.

On the one hand, I feel I should be offended Lee would say something that hints at misogyny, but in the same sentence, he described me as a goddess. I'm thoroughly confused; I don't know what to say or how to react.

As he realizes he has befuddled me, his cocksure grin re-appears. "And I'm going to prove my point right now. April, I would love to take you out Saturday night if you would be inclined to join me."

Saturday. Something is going on Saturday. Lee's expectant look is not helping with my memory recall.

He sighs. "If I misread things, I apologize."

I reach out and grab his wrist.

Bad move. Oh my! I guess it's good to know that his level of attraction is equal to mine.

"No. You don't understand. I already have some sort of appointment Saturday night. I just can't—Oh, I'm working."

Lee's eyebrows draw together. "What sort of law practice works on Saturday night? Even night court isn't on Saturdays."

"No, I'm working with my brother Dusty. I help him do research for his books. We've had this date set up for Saturday for a while now. I really can't back out."

Lee gives an abbreviated laugh, the first hint of nervousness on his part during the entire conversation. "Okay, but before I make a fool out of myself again, it's a scheduling conflict and not a friend-classification issue. Right?"

"Absolutely!" Bless it—that sounds too eager.

"Okay, how about Sunday night?" He asks more tentatively this time.

"I'm looking forward to it."

"You didn't even hear what we're doing or what time I'm

picking you up," he says.

"You're picking me up at seven o'clock, and you just need to surprise me on what we're doing."

He wads up the paper towel in his fist as he eyes me. "I mean, what if I decide to take you miniature golfing."

"I'd say you better be a good sport about losing."

That coaxes a laugh from Lee, and I find it as intoxicating as his eyes. I'm glad we can't go out until Sunday. Hopefully, that will give me time to cool off. I'm not sure I would trust myself going out with him any time before Sunday.

The glass door slides open. Dusty pokes his head out. "Dinner is served."

"Dusty, what time are we meeting Saturday?" I ask.

"Sundown is about six thirty in the evening this time of year. We'll need to leave at five thirty to give us a chance to get all of our equipment in place before dark."

I turn to Lee placing my hands on my hip. "See. I was telling the truth."

"Geez, girl, I didn't say you weren't." Lee flashes me his lopsided grin.

It may only be pretending, but having a pseudo-boyfriend at my side for the dinner party sure does make being social easier. I even make nice with Jackie Rains for a few minutes without wanting to yank her baldheaded. What's up with that? I always want to do her bodily harm.

Lee stays by my side as I talk to each of our guests. He is polite with each of them when they ask about his sports career, even though he has to tell the same story at least twenty times.

Lee never puts his arm around me or holds my hand, but little tingles of electrical energy continue to jump from his skin to mine. I stay so worked up in his presence I don't even finish my dinner.

Dessert time worked inversely. I satiated my sexual urges with pieces of all three flavors of pies. They were tiny pieces. I wouldn't even consider them pieces—more like slivers.

"I know what we have to do if we ever go to the county fair,"

Lee says.

"What's that?"

"We need to enter you in the pie-eating contest."

Nothing makes me quite as self-conscious as a man I'm interested in pointing out that I love my sugars. Well, that and a man who opts for coffee when pie is offered.

"Do you not like pie?"

"I love pie. Just not that kind."

Another jolt lights up in my belly. I'm not sure if Lee really doesn't care for pecan, pumpkin, or key lime, or if it was double entendre, but my body is reacting to everything as the latter. Everything he says or does seems to carry some sort of sexual innuendo.

As I walk Lee out to his truck, he takes both my hands into his—his eyes hold me in place—and the visions coursing from him to me take my breath away.

"I feel like the luckiest guy in the world tonight," he says in a low voice laced with sexual promise.

I have sensory overload. The smell of oak and leather from Lee's aftershave, the sharp edges of his handsome face, the warmth of his hands, and the lustful visions flowing from his thoughts all work in tandem to lower my IQ precipitously.

"I had a swell time." Oh no. Please no. I want to take it back as soon as I say it.

Lee releases my hands as he chuckles. He dips his head as he runs his thumb across his lip. "Yeah. Okay." He gestures toward his truck. "I better get gone so you can help your folks clean up."

Swell. Who even says swell anymore? *Good grief, April.* I watch him open his truck door and pull himself up into the cab.

"Lee!"

He stops and peers over the top of the door. "Yeah?"

What? What, April? "I just want to say I'm thankful you came to dinner tonight."

He has a blank stare for a beat. He raises his chin as he

laughs. "Ah. I see what you did there. Cute. A little corny, but cute. Me too. I'm *thankful*, April. It was good to see you."

He flips a little wave of the hand as he shuts the truck door. I watch as he drives the big truck down my parents' drive, and I find myself staring at the end of the empty drive after he is gone.

Chapter 32

I cross my arms against the chill of the night. Something has gotten started tonight. What it is and where it is going—well, the last few months have taught me to get out of the predicting business. Still, at the minimum, it promises to be something I will remember. I'm willing to bet almost anything on that.

"He seems like a pretty good guy."

Daddy's voice pulls me out of my trance. He holds out a coffee mug toward me with one hand while holding a second mug closer to him.

I accept the pink princess mug. "Thanks."

Daddy blows on his coffee. "I think he likes you," he says, looking over the top of his mug.

"He asked me out."

"Hmm … How do you feel about that?"

How do I feel? Confused, worried… "I feel happy."

His eyebrows lift. "Happy is good." He returns his attention to his coffee.

We finish our coffee in quiet companionship while we enjoy staring at the bright winter stars. It's the way we did when I was much younger when I drank hot cocoa instead of coffee. Daddy is often a quiet man. Even when he is silent, he says a lot when we share moments like this.

I enjoyed seeing everyone and having the close company of

an attractive man. Still, I am relieved when the last guests have gone home and Daddy leaves to take cousin Lamont and Aunt Renée home.

My body had revved up to super-hot so many times over the last three hours that I'm exhausted. Good grief. I'm so out of practice, I wonder if the opportunity presented itself, if I could go without it being some embarrassing fiasco.

Stop it. It's just a date. Besides, I'll be lucky to get through the first date with my latest track record, much less have to worry about birth control.

I bring the last of the dessert plates into the kitchen. Mama is loading the dishwasher, and I rinse the dishes that won't fit in this cycle.

The silence feels awkward, so I ask, "Did everything go as you hoped?"

"I think it went well enough," Mama says. "How about you."

I look away to conceal a grin. My ears heat up. "Yeah. I thought it was a good time. The food was delicious."

"It was. The only thing missing was my daughter's dish."

I'm impervious to her ribbing tonight. "I think next year I'll take you up on the cooking lessons."

"Really?" She stops as stares at me.

"Sure. Why not? Maybe it's time I grow up and learn to cook," I say.

"We don't have to wait a year. Christmas dinner is coming up in a month, and I can work with you then."

"Uh—let's not get ahead of ourselves, Mama."

Chapter 33

On the way to my apartment, I notice the shadow at the end of the dock. I walk toward Puppy. As I near him, I hear his low growl. A bundle of fear rolls over in my gut. "Puppy?"

His eyes glint as he looks back toward me. He returns his attention to the water.

"Puppy. Let's go to bed. Leave Him alone."

Puppy offers the briefest of whines before walking away from the dock. He trots past me, pushing through his doggy door disappearing into my apartment.

As I slip into my pj's after brushing my teeth, my phone rings. It's Jacob, and I press to answer. "You missed out, buddy."

"Aww, Grandma Hurley had a pretty good spread put on, too," Jacob says.

"So you say. But there's no comparing home-cooked meals to Cheese Barrel."

"True. But at least I did get some turkey and stuffing."

"I guess it can't all be bad, then." After I say that, we fall into a long, silent pause.

"April, you know I've been trying to get you alone for a while to talk to you. But the more I think about it, I should just ask, even if it's just over the phone. I mean, life's too short not to get answers. I mean, for heaven's sake, it seems like just yesterday we were in grade school together. Time just flies by."

That reminds me. "Speaking of old schoolmates, do you remember Lee Darby?"

"Well, yeah. We played on the baseball team together."

"You're not gonna believe this. But he bought a house from Mama, and she invited him to dinner tonight."

"That's nice of your mama." Jacob's voice sounds funny to me. "Did he come?"

"Yes. He did. He looks way different. In a good way. Did you know that he was playing in the majors now?"

"I seem to remember hearing that from someone," Jacob says.

"It's all so crazy, you know. Like I hadn't thought about him in years, and then he just sort of pops up again. Guess what he did?"

"I don't know, April."

"Guess, Jacob."

"I don't want to, April. Just tell me."

"He asked me out! Can you believe it? Isn't that, like, the craziest thing?" Jacob is silent, so I add since it obviously hasn't registered with him, "The drought is finally over for your best friend."

The silence is deafening.

"Jacob, are you still there?"

He clears his throat. "Yeah. I'm still here, April. I'm always here."

That's an odd thing to say. I'm about to ask him what he means. He cuts in first.

"Listen, I'm happy for you if you are happy."

"Thanks." His voice still sounds off to me. "Is something the matter? You sound funny."

"No. I'm good."

I don't believe him. "You don't sound alright. You know you can tell me anything."

"I just said I was fine!"

My jaw falls open in shock, and I'm speechless. It is the first time I can remember Jacob being short with me.

"Aw heck, April. I'm sorry. I'm just exhausted and grouchy tonight. Just being around all that family wore me out, I suppose. I'm sorry I called in such a foul mood."

"It's okay." I offer to let him off the hook.

"No, it's not. Listen, I'm going to let you go. Goodnight."

He hangs up before I get a chance to say goodnight. Too weird. That is so un-Jacob.

Puppy works his way up to the top of the bed with his head on one of my pillows. I usually don't let him do that, but I don't feel like wrestling with him to get him back at the foot of the bed tonight. I fall asleep quickly despite his snoring.

Chapter 34

I set out early Friday morning to Sewanee University for my appointment with Dr. David Devereaux. Admittedly, for the two-hour drive to the campus, my mind is on anything except historical weapons that might be used during a paranormal excursion.

My mind is focused solely on Lee Darby. His beautiful gray eyes and cocky smile. I know, it's a lot of thinking about what should be a casual date of two people that have already attempted to date before. But either it feels like destiny, or the six months back home has built up a backlog of lust that I have no control over.

Regardless of which of the two reasons I'm driven to constant thoughts of Lee Darby. It bodes well that there may be some sort of physical activity between us soon. I know I'm certainly in favor of that.

The more complicated aspect of the whole deal is, what then? I'm not spending the whole drive worrying about what would happen if two adults had consensual sex. Instead, I'm trying to figure out how two disparate lives can mesh successfully. At times it feels like I'm taking out a pocket knife and whittling the edges off a square peg so it will fit in the round hole.

The only aspect that makes marginal sense is that Lee's team is based out of Boston. Boston is a big metropolitan city, which fits my life goal of working at a large firm. Nothing other than that really makes much sense, though.

I always had this vision of having two children in my mid-thirties. My husband, who would also have a high-level professional position, would co-parent them with me. Baseball players play over one-hundred and sixty games a year. Half of those are at home, and they expect their wives to attend the games. The other half of the games are away. For several months out of the year, I would have an absentee husband, and our kids would have an absentee father.

I kept rationalizing that it would be no big deal. Some professional players have successful families and marriages all the time, or at least that's my assumption. No matter how much I try to tell myself that it would work out, it continues to feel like I'm just glossing over the very inconvenient facts.

Sewanee's campus is beautiful. Set back on a heavily forested campus, most of the buildings are done in beautiful stone masonry that mimics some of the cathedrals you would encounter on a European tour.

I meet Dr. Devereaux in the lobby of the dean of natural science and history's office. He is a man of medium height, with a thick, muscular build, a large mustache dyed red—and a bald head.

He eagerly extends his hand. "April?"

"Dr. Devereaux?"

He shakes his head. "Dr. Devereaux is what they call my dad and granddaddy. Please, call me David."

"Okay ... David."

A devilish smile appears below his bushy mustache. I immediately can tell this man is a true character and was probably a complete rake when he was younger.

"How is Tutti?"

"Sir?"

He laughs. "Your Granny. Is she well?"

"Oh yes, sir." Hmm ... Maybe I was right about Granny's sudden flush of color when she mentioned David.

"I was delighted to get her call. I had not heard from her in years." He gestures over his shoulder. "How about we take a little walk down to my lab, and I can show you a few items that might be of interest to you."

If Dr. Devereaux, David, were not friends with Granny, I would have severe reservations following him to his office alone. But I fall in side by side as we walk out of the dean's office and up a flight of stairs.

"How exactly do you know my granny, David." I don't know why but it feels exceptionally awkward calling him David.

He shoots me a sideways glance. "Professionally. We met many years ago when we were both working on the same disturbance."

"Disturbance?"

"I believe the church might refer to it as an exorcism. I was only involved because it was a museum curator that I had been familiar with in the past. I suppose you could say he was a friend."

David stops in front of a door, unlocks it, and holds it open for me. "Welcome to my life's work," he announces.

I swoon as I enter his lab. There are so many varying and strong electrical impulses coming it is hard to keep focused.

David doesn't appear to notice as he walks over to a battery of large drawers built into the wall and begins to unlock one.

"As I was explaining to Tutti, I'm not sure just how much help I can be. You do realize that all of these weapons are designed for creatures that are only figments of scared people's imaginations."

"The weapons aren't real?"

His eyebrows raise in apparent amusement. "Oh, they're the real McCoy, alright. It's just what they were designed to defend against is not real. Vampires, werewolves, ghosts, and demons —they're strictly inventions of people's imaginations. But the weapons are very creative.

Thankfully, I can't speak to vampires and werewolves, but

David is sorely mistaken about ghosts and demons. I find it interesting that the man has been drawn to researching and collecting something that he must see as almost a joke. How obtuse do you have to be to have access to so much history and first-hand knowledge and still not be a believer?

"This one here is my favorite," David announces as he turns. He holds what I know to be a crossbow in his left hand and one of the bolts in his right hand. "Unger the mute, a lesser Bavarian king in the twelfth century, had this made specifically for his youngest daughter. It seems she was afflicted with nightmares about werewolves."

David holds the bolt tip out toward me. "You see that tip? Pure silver."

"How in the world is it in such pristine condition?"

David rolls his eyes as he returns the crossbow and bolt to their drawer. "That daughter later married an Austrian king. It was an arranged marriage for political gain, as most were during that time. Still, you will find it interesting that she came to be known as Agatha the slayer. Supposedly she slew a werewolf in her hamlet that had been devouring children that were searching for mushrooms in the woods."

"With the crossbow?"

"As the story goes. It seems the werewolf was one of her father's gardeners. If you're a cynic—" David raises his hand and twiddles his fingers. "You might think the princes accidentally shot one of the servants with her crossbow, and the whole story was cooked up to conceal the true manner of the gardener's death. In any event, the weapon was kept under glass in the local armory for centuries and later moved to the mayor's office. Sort of a part trophy and part 'in case of werewolf, break glass' artifact."

David amuses himself with his joke, but he fails to recognize the second possibility. That there are such things as werewolves, and the princess truly had saved the children in the hamlet.

It would be advantageous to have a weapon that was already

proven effective. Still, this isn't the manner of weapon I have in mind. Crossbows are inherently slow to load and extremely cumbersome. Besides, I have no prior knowledge of Dusty ever encountering a werewolf.

David retrieves something from one of the other drawers. "Now, this is one of my favorites." He holds out what appears to be a short, stabbing sword from the Bronze Age—of course, that couldn't be possible. By now, any blade from that period would have oxidized, pitted, and appeared like a piece of black Swiss cheese.

This blade is highly polished with a brass color and a prominent ridge running down the center of both sides of the blade. The edges are sharply honed, and the tip still suitable for piercing leather easily, two millennia after its production.

The blade gleams with energy. I can't decipher if it is some sort of blessing, curse, or residing entity generating the power. It does not surprise me it is one of David's favorites. Silly man, maybe he really can't identify the supernatural, but even laypeople are attracted to the power of magical items.

"This blade was rumored to be the blade Brutus, used when he betrayed Julius Caesar."

It isn't. I don't know how I know that, but I do. And I know David doesn't believe for a moment that it is Brutus's sword.

"Some of the citizens of Rome had come to believe that Julius Caesar might be the bastard of a Roman god. A half-breed, if you will. This blade is sufficient to kill any half-breed." David studies my face. I assume to ascertain if I understand the significance of what he just claimed.

Half-breed would include demons. He is telling me it is a demon sword.

He is correct.

Once he tells me that critical bit of information, the pieces fall into place, and I know exactly what is driving the high energy level of the sword.

Yes, we do run into demons from time to time. The idea of hunting them down and poking them with a sword doesn't exactly instill confidence in me. I'm looking for more of a quick fix to our issues.

"Dr. Devereaux, I mean David, do you have any weapons that are more, I don't know, twenty-first century?"

His brow furrows. "You mean like drones and missiles?"

"Uh, I was thinking of something more along the lines of a gun. Maybe a pistol or a riot gun?"

David pulls at his bushy mustache and the smile lines of his eyes crinkle. "I have something. It's a little hobby of mine, but of course, it's silly."

His personality has done a complete one-eighty. Moments ago, he was comfortable relaying solid facts, albeit with a somewhat condescending tone, of the original producers of the weapons he was showing me. Now there is a particular vulnerability and nervous energy about him.

"Mind you, it's just a theory. No, not even truly a theory because they don't really exist."

I watch as he bites his lower lip while squinting his eyes. He's fighting an internal battle. His excitement and pride want to show me something. His sensibilities and belief system tell him nothing goes bump in the night, so he doesn't want to say anything that will embarrass him.

Pride seems to win out. "With all the stories, there is one underlying factor that always baffles me. Each of these different"—he makes air quotes with his fingers—"monsters have a different method of being dispatched. Ghost dispersed with salt and iron, sometimes blessings, demons are darn near indestructible except with weapons blessed for that specific task, werewolves"—he shrugs—"silver bullets, silver in general, and then vampires, blessed items, crosses, garlic, silver, and a stake through the heart."

I wait patiently for his point.

He tosses his hands in the air. "What's a Van Helsing supposed to bring to the fight? Lord help you if you bring salt to combat a demon or a demon knife to fight a ghost. Do you see what I mean?"

I do. Rollo, the clown, was a perfect example where Liza's warding circle had no effect.

That is what makes the chore of selecting a suitable weapon system for the team so daunting. It is impossible to determine what sort of paranormal entity we will encounter once we arrive at our research destination.

How often have Liza and I discussed whether an entity will be affected by religious blessings or if Wiccan magic were in order? What would it be worth to us if we could do one chant or spell and cover both bases?

David holds out a small blue cartridge that resembles a miniature shotgun shell. It is similar in size to a .45 ACP. "Have you seen one of these before?" David asks of the blue round.

"I can't say I've seen that version."

"This is a forty-five caliber round. A standard round has a takedown capability second to none." He holds up the blue cartridge. "But when we load it with this bad boy, it becomes a second-to-none zombie killing machine. Plus, it can still be used for self-defense against the more common monsters. Men turned evil.

"Anyone who doesn't want to play by the rules, whether they are dead or alive, this weapon can handle them. The beauty of it is the shot load turns the gun into an all-around supernatural self-defense weapon."

"What's so special about it?" I ask. "Besides being blue and suspecting that it can still penetrate." I touch the plastic tip

David pulls the round back from me, takes a wrench, and pulls the thick plastic off the shot back. He dumps the contents in a metal tray.

Pointing with his pen, he says, "Here you have rock salt, iron ore birdshot, both for dispersing ghosts. These little beads here that look like silver, they are for your werewolves." He rolls six, small straw-sized cylinders away from the pellets. "These here are designed to break apart on contact. They are garlic infused with blessed holy oil."

"Get out of town."

"No, seriously," he says.

"I was with you until the garlic-infused holy water."

"It is. And I know what you're thinking—David, how can that all work together in a system? But it does. At least in theory. I've spent years developing these rounds, including thousands of slugs fired into ballistic gelatin to ensure that each part works correctly.

"That the round casing stays intact in the chamber holding the items together, penetrates a minimum of twelve inches, but then breaks apart, dispersing the shot load throughout the target.

"The most delicate aspect being the holy water. The outer shell dissolves seconds after being exposed to the atmosphere."

"Dissolves?"

David shrugs. "Yes."

I have serious doubts the shell works properly, but there is no denying the thought is super cool. "How accurate is it, David?"

"At fifty feet, it reacts similarly to standard ammo. Move out to a hundred feet, and there's no telling where it will end up."

Considering the vast majority of trouble we get into during our paranormal excursions is within twenty feet, I couldn't care less that the weapon is inaccurate at a hundred feet.

"This is much more along the lines of what I have in mind, David. Do you happen to sell the shells for different models of guns?"

David grins at me as if I am mentally challenged. "Like I said, it's just a prototype. I've been able to match up the shells for forty-fives, thirty-eights, and nine millimeters. I'm struggling with the smaller caliber guns. But I don't have any shells for sale. Understand, it's just a hobby of mine."

"Oh—I was hoping you might have a few boxes I could buy from you today. How long would it take for an order?"

"No. I can't." David frowns. "I would never risk someone else's safety with a novelty such as these. The packing of shells is not an exact science. One small mistake can manifest into a catastrophe.

"Maybe after I have a few more years of research on the reliability of the shells—I would never even consider making them available to the general public. I wouldn't want these fired with anybody else close to the general vicinity."

There is no guarantee the shells will actually work. There is a high probability the holy oil could rupture in the barrel and make a mess of the firearm. Still, after Rollo the clown, it is a risk I'm willing to take.

The opportunity is too good to pass up, but it is evident that David is so concerned about the safety of the rounds that I may never get my hands on any.

"That's cool," I say nonchalantly. "There's no way they'd actually fire anyway."

David laughs. "Yes, they fire."

I squinch my nose up in disbelief. "It's a cool concept, but the execution is lacking. There's no way a round filled with oil won't foul up a gun."

"No, it works. I tested it myself."

I nod my head. "Sure, you did in the lab. That doesn't mean it will hold up in field tests. Things work in the lab all the time only to fail in the field."

I gesture toward the original drawers he opened. "Do you have any other demon swords? Possibly ones that I can borrow or buy from you?"

David pulls aggressively at his mustache. "I thought you wanted a more modern weapon?"

"It would be preferred, but I would rather take an old-fashioned weapon like a stabbing sword over a weapon that doesn't work."

"I said it works!"

Chapter 35

"You'll tell Tutti hi for me, right?"

I set the small bundle consisting of two demon swords and thirty-six rounds of forty-five caliber paranormal pepper rounds gingerly in the trunk of my IROC. "Sure, but why don't you call her yourself? I'm sure she'd love to get together for a cup of coffee or something."

David's forehead furrows. "Do you think so?"

Does a cat have climbing gear? "Yes, I'm positive she would love to hear from you."

"I might just do that." His face turns serious as he points to the contents of my trunk. "Don't forget. You promised to wear protective eyewear to test those rounds."

"Sure thing." I slam the trunk shut. "I do appreciate you allowing us to demo them."

"It sounds like you and your brother know your way around a gun. That's the only reason why I'm letting you sample them."

That and your pride couldn't handle my questioning their serviceability. "I appreciate that. I'll also make sure to send you information on their performance."

"Thanks." He frowns. "I would like you to remember something."

"What's that?"

"Van Helsing, Dr. Frankenstein, hunter or creator, they all come to the same end. Hanging around monsters at the least will steal your sanity and at the worst gets you killed."

David shakes my hand and wishes me a safe trip back to Guntersville. As I drive out of the historic campus tucked away in the woods, I can't know for sure if my weapon search has been successful.

The knives and the gun shells seem like an adequate solution for our defensive needs, but until they are proven in battle —they are just hopes.

As I reach the gray asphalt of Highway 72, I have convinced myself I will ride over to check up on Lexi Bransford. Then I'll do a reconnaissance drive-by on J&B Body Shop even though the drive and morning conversation with David has left me exhausted.

Dropping by to check on Lexi was not on the agenda for today. But I began to have this niggling feeling a few hours ago. I know it will only worsen if I don't check on her.

If I learned one thing over the last year, I should always respect my gut feelings.

Besides, it is the polite thing to do, given she was not be allowed to see her kids on Thanksgiving. I can't imagine how difficult that must be for a mother. Checking up on her is both the right thing to do, as well as professional.

As I drive on autopilot toward town, I try to remember if any of our paranormal team members might have a forty-five. I know Luis and Miles are a hard no. The Early brothers and Chet most definitely have firearms, but what caliber, I'll have to ask.

I know Dusty would gladly purchase a couple for our protection. Still, we don't know if the rounds will be effective, and even if they are, it's the shotgun shells David promised to work on that I believe we should standardize on. Bullpup shotguns with David's paranormal load shells are what I have settled on as our dream weapon of choice. The forty-fives are only temporary to test the effectiveness of a paranormal round.

I have serious doubts that the weapon system will actually

perform as hoped. Still, it has to be worth a try regardless of how whacked it sounds. If effective, it can be a real game-changer for our team.

Besides, even if the shotgun idea doesn't work, firing an ineffective load at a poltergeist is still preferable to doing nothing except screaming as it kills me.

It occurs to me that if I ever tell Lee about my weekend side hustle, paranormal hunting with Dusty's team, he will either be a believer or a denier. If he is a paranormal believer, he might worry every time I leave the house. It sounds sweet for someone to fret over your safety—I have a belief, however, that it would get old quickly. On the other hand, he might be a denier, like my brother Chase, and think I'm a nut for spending my weekends chasing after myths.

I can't decide if it is better to have a boyfriend think you are in constant danger or just a nut. That probably plays into my indecisiveness about ever sharing my secret with Lee.

I reach Lexi's house and am relieved to see her van in the driveway. My luck is still holding out. I pull my IROC into her driveway and park behind her van.

I walk to her front door and ring the doorbell. No one answers.

I ring the doorbell again. Then I knock on the door as I pull my phone out to text Lexi.

Someone on the other side of the door makes a loud hissing "shhh" sound.

The curtains of the bay window to my left move. "Come on, Lexi. It's not like I'm blind. I see you there," I yell toward the window.

The silence seems to go on forever. I contemplate getting back in my car and driving off. So much for the *right* thing to do and professionalism.

Normally, Lexi's sketchiness would have angered me enough to find out why she won't answer the door. Presently I'm too tired to have that level of curiosity about anyone or anything.

The deadbolt on the front door rotates. The door inches open a few inches, Lexi's face appears in the crack. "What are you doing here?"

"I wanted to check in on you. I know it must be tough not to have been able to see your children yesterday."

Lexi's face tightens. I can't get an exact read as her anxious thoughts fill the air, except she has a profound fear of me finding out something.

I assume that *something* is why she hasn't invited me into her home.

"Did your mother-in-law soften up and bring them by for a visit?" I ask.

She shakes her head. "No. But I knew she wouldn't budge on that. She's too hardheaded for common sense."

Then again, she may think the kids' mother might be the worst influence for them. "I'm sorry."

She frowns. "I guess I'll survive."

I gesture toward the door. "Are you going to let me in or not?"

"Oh, yeah. I guess so." She steps back and opens the door a few inches more.

I squeeze through, and I'm immediately inundated with her emotions of fear, frustration, and confusion. I suppose those might be logical emotions for a woman who just lost her husband and the primary breadwinner. Still, there is a sharp edge to this fear.

It is laced with guilt. That makes no sense to me.

"Tell me you at least got a turkey dinner."

Lexi clasps then unclasps her hands in front of her. "I had some fried chicken. I guess that's sort of close enough for government work."

I laugh. That's one of Daddy's sayings. It's okay for him to say it. He's a government employee.

"Lexi, to be honest with you, I'm not stopping by just to check up on you. I'm hoping that you might have remembered something, anything, that might help us in identifying your husband's killer."

Her hands fidget with the knot of her robe's sash. She gestures over her shoulder. "Do you mind if I go put some sweatpants on?"

"Of course not. Go right ahead."

As she closes the door to her bedroom, I turn and scan the living room. It doesn't exactly take Sherlock Holmes to figure out what she is nervous about.

Two tumblers are sitting on the coffee table. Now, I've been bad off enough to think I wanted a drink in each hand—but I've never actually acted on it. I suppose there can be a first for everything.

All benefit of the doubt for Lexi leaves when I sit. There are intense sexual energies present on the sofa, new and so strong it is as if I can smell the hint of sex in the air.

I'm no expert on relationships and the dynamics of rebounds. Still, having a sexual encounter with someone only days after your husband is blown up in your driveway seems sort of callous, even messed up. At the very least, it seemed a little, I don't know—early?

So many unanswered questions rush through my mind I develop a subtle case of vertigo. Were these old energy imprints I'm reading? Doubtful. They feel recent, not even hours old.

The thing is, I don't know anything about the men in my client's life. I've never seen her husband … alive. I've also never met Tad Sapp.

I feel a portion of the imprint is Lexi; I know her energy, her feel. I have no idea about the rest of the vitality signature. It is male, but I have no way of identifying whom.

The voyeuristic nature of the energies I feel makes me stand. I pace back to the front door.

Lexi returns from her bedroom, and I must've cast a look of disgust back toward the sofa. Her eyes go from me to the sofa and back to me.

Her eyes widen slightly as her mouth opens, forming an "O." Her expression confirms the timeline for me. It was recent.

Following that thread, she probably changed into sweatpants to tell her lover, who is hiding in her bedroom now, who I am and how long it will be before she can convince me to leave.

She stands blocking her closed bedroom door, clasping her hands in front of her again.

"I meant to ask you, were you ever able to get in touch with Mr. Sapp?" I ask.

Her eyes widen further, and her voice strains. "No. It's been five days now since I've heard from him."

She keeps with the timeline of his disappearance, but the stress her body exhibits tells that she is lying. "Were you able to think of anything that maybe we didn't discuss earlier? Anyone else who might've had it out for Ben?"

She simply shakes her head.

"Nothing from the silent business partner? Maybe they have been coming around to figure out how to liquidate the business?"

She exhales loudly. "I don't know. I just don't know anything about the business. You could check in with Antonio at the shop. Ben sometimes had him run it when we were traveling. But I haven't heard anything."

Even if she has male company, there is so much strangeness in how she acts that I can't tell if she is truthful about the business anymore.

I have the feeling my client knows a lot more than what she is letting on about the business arrangements of her husband. But even with my "gifts," I have nothing I can prove.

"I'm sorry to hear your mother-in-law didn't change her mind. Is there anything I can do to help you with that? Maybe petition the judge for some visitation?"

Her face tightens ever so briefly. "No. I'm going to see this through first. Delilah won't change her mind until I'm found innocent and Ben's killer is behind bars."

Wrong answer. No mother would turn down help to gain the opportunity to see her children she hasn't seen in the last week. I don't have any idea what's up, but something is not right with Lexi Bransford. That much, I'm sure of.

I no longer have any doubts that my client is lying to me about *everything*. What I don't understand is why.

Her future hangs in the balance, and I'm the one person who can help her. The one person who cares. Why would she lie to me?

"Lexi, you need to make sure that if anything comes to you, anything that you think might be of help, no matter how trivial, that you tell me about it. In these cases, sometimes it's the smallest detail that turns it in your favor."

She can't focus for more than a second. She even makes one quick glance toward her bedroom door. "Okay," she says.

"All right then. I'll check in on you Monday," I say as I open the front door.

I receive another noncommittal "okay" from Lexi as I pull the door shut behind me. I suppose I shouldn't be surprised she doesn't walk me to my car.

Chapter 36

The drive to Boaz will take thirty minutes, so I decide to use the time to reach out to Liza. I want to ask her if she is going on this evening's excursion. I also want to get her opinion on the paranormal ammunition from Dr. Devereaux and my recent manifestation skill schooling at the hands of my granny.

I'm discouraged when my call rolls over to her voicemail. As I struggle to decide what I want to record, I see her calling in on the other line.

"Hey," I say.

"I prefer daisies," Liza says.

"And here I would've taken you for a belladonna girl."

"I believe Rollo ended any appreciation I have for that bloom."

"I heard that," I say.

"So, what? You leave me for dead last weekend in a Birmingham emergency room, and just now you're calling?"

"Liza—I didn't leave—you for dead," I stutter. "Dusty told me you were going to be okay."

"Oh, chill. I was just pulling your leg. But I am surprised I'm just now getting a call from you."

"I know. I'm a sucky friend."

"Yeah, I don't think you'll find anybody to argue about that with you." Liza punctuates it with a laugh, but she's salty.

"But you are okay?" I ask cautiously.

"Yeah. I have another doctor's appointment Monday morning. That's to make sure everything is clear with the concussion issue. My shoulder and ribs are still sore, but I can breathe without it feeling like someone is slipping a knife in between my ribs now."

"That's a positive. The breathing part. Are you cleared to drive? Do you need a ride to the doctor Monday?"

"I don't know—possibly. I really hadn't thought about it yet."

It is Liza, but without her usual hard-edged 'I planned for every contingency' attitude. This morning's version sounds fragile.

The night of the killer clown attack, everything moved so fast and was so fraught with mortal danger, I didn't realize then how hard Liza hit the wall when Rollo slapped her across the room. The memory comes back to me, and the visual is of a ragdoll being slammed so hard against the lath and plaster wall that it left an indent. In retrospect, it is a miracle she escaped with just the concussion and some bruises.

"You'll be glad to know that if anything Rollo comes at us again, I've got a little something special for him now."

"I've already seen your fireballs. If you don't mind, I'd rather you wait until I'm not in the room before you use those again," Liza grumbles.

That makes me laugh. She's right. The fireballs seemed like a good idea right up until the time the attic went up in flames. "No, I have secured something better."

"Ice shards, poisonous gas—again, whatever it is, just make sure I'm out of the room."

"No, silly. Not magic. I found, well Granny found, a professor who has developed a bullet that will disperse almost all the different entities we come across."

"Yeah, that won't work."

Her comment deflates my enthusiasm a little. "Well, it's worth a try. It can't turn out any worse than poorly aimed fireballs in an enclosed environment."

"You make a good point. I tell you what. If it works, bring a few rounds to my apartment." Liza's voice is uncharacteristically bitter.

I hesitate to ask, "Why? What's up."

"It's nothing."

"No, something is bothering you. Tell me what it is."

The crackle of static on the line increases dramatically. "You remember that stupid little clown that Moses had on his toy chest?"

My blood chills as a tingle runs up my spine. I find it difficult to hold my car straight on the highway. "Yes," I croak.

"He followed me home."

My mind's eye immediately fills with the vision of a porcelain-faced clown doll decked out in a medieval jester's outfit. The image comes complete with a semitransparent five-year-old boy dressed in powder-blue footies carrying the clown doll. I involuntary shake my shoulders.

"What do you mean he followed you home?" I whisper.

"I mean Tuesday when I got home, I went in to take a shower, and he was sitting in the bathtub. I nearly slipped and brained myself on the commode."

"Liza, that doesn't make any sense. We both saw the doll go up in flames with the attic in Birmingham."

"You would think. At least I know the attic burned up first, and we barely escaped. I never saw anybody carrying a doll past us, did you?"

"No." The only people that were there that evening were from our paranormal team. Even though we might occasionally like to goof around, we all take ghost hunting seriously. None of us would fake a spirit or needlessly scare one of our partners. "Where is he now?"

"Well—I just tossed him into the fire barrel the superintendent of my building likes to keep going for burning paper products."

Good. Liza might be partially concussed, but she still has enough wherewithal to properly dispose of a possessed item.

Getting rid of the spirit doll is much more important than figuring out how it got out of the house.

"For the second time," Liza adds.

My thought process freezes up again. "What do you mean 'the second time'?"

"I mean, it's the second time I've thrown him into the fire barrel. He didn't stay burned up the first time."

"Liza, maybe you should go somewhere. I don't like you being there by yourself." I become increasingly concerned for my friend. If the toy clown made it out of the attic fire, I must wonder what else might have made it out of the attic alive that we thought perished. Liza is in a weakened state, and I don't want her to have to face anything on her own.

"I'll be okay. It's not the first time something stray has followed me home."

I'm battling to decide between going and making sure Liza is okay and running by the body shop and doing surveillance. "I don't like you being there by yourself."

"It's no big deal. You and the boys are all just one phone call away if something starts to get out of control." The static on her line increases significantly again. "If the little sucker comes back, I might chain him to a concrete block and throw him in the river."

"Does that work?"

Liza laughs. "No, but fire doesn't seem to bother him. And you know what the definition of insanity is."

"Staying in your home alone with a haunted ghost doll?"

"That's hilarious. You missed your calling."

"I'm going to let you go, I'm running a little bit of surveillance on J&B's, and I'm pulling up in the lot now."

"That shady auto repair shop in downtown Boaz?"

The disdain in Liza's voice is strong. "Why do *you* say shady?"

"Everybody knows J&B's is just the shell for a drug distribution center."

"For real?"

"Yep. And you're calling me crazy for not letting a stupid stuffed doll run me off. You better watch yourself out there, April. People like that don't take kindly to nosy people."

I hadn't really considered J&B's to be a *real* place of danger for me. I won't be going back in like I did the first time. I just want to wait and get a feel for the place. I won't learn anything additional by sitting at home and reading regurgitated reports. Still, Liza's warning has placed the uncomfortable seed of danger in my mind.

"The workers have already seen me before. They don't have any issues with me." When I was posing as someone needing a car repaired, not a nosy lawyer.

"Hopefully, it'll stay that way," Liza says.

"Since you still have to be cleared by your doctor on Monday, I suppose you're not coming out Saturday night?"

"No. Too much at risk if I'm not well yet. The last thing I need is to be tossed up against another wall while my brain is still bruised. I barely have enough of it as it is."

"How does she do so much with so little?" I tease.

"I know, right? Hey, I'm serious. You be careful out there at J&B's, okay?"

"Will do. You go ahead and drown that little sucker if he dares to show up again with bells on his toes."

Liza laughs. "As long as I can catch him, I will."

I scold myself as soon as I disconnect the line. I forgot to mention what Granny demonstrated to me. Oh well, it will be a reason to check up on Liza soon. That's what a good friend would do, and I plan to improve in that department as soon as my schedule allows.

I angle my car into the vacant, used car lot across from J&B Body Shop. Pulling up close to the building, my car is partially obscured from anyone looking out from J&B's. I kill the engine, tilt my seat back, cross my arms, and settle in to watch the seemingly quiet business.

There is no real explanation for why I'm watching the body shop. Except for the fact that I become easily obsessed with the unexplained.

I have no real expectations of what I will discover. I have a gut feeling that I need to watch, and I will listen to my instincts now.

These are the times I really miss Michael VanDerveer. How I would love to simply call and ask him to do this research for me as I go about my business at the law office.

Vander has been gone two months now, and no one has heard from him. Howard had gotten word through one of his contacts that Vander had gone silent on purpose. None of his usual contacts know where he is or how to get in touch with him.

I've started the habit of saying a little prayer for him every night before I fall asleep. I don't pretend that it is actually working. I do it more for remembrance—respect if you will—also in hopes that I'll see him again.

I don't claim Vander and I are friends, but we are close business associates. I have a strong affinity for people I can count on. Vander is definitely one of those results-oriented people in the world whom I can count on.

It's not just his usefulness that has me fixate on Vander at times. There's a natural pull to him. Not like "attractive guy" interest, but more like a blood relationship. Which I know is a crazy thought considering I have such scant details on his life and I have only sat and spoken to him a handful of times.

Perhaps it's just the mystery that surrounds his existence. It might just be the attraction of one more riddle to solve that draws me to think of him.

A nondescript, brown American-made car drives onto the parking lot of J&B's. The driver unlocks the front office door and disappears inside.

I grin when the first overhead bay door rolls open. *Bingo*. The driver walks out of the repair bay, then pulls his brown car into the building.

It appears like Liza is right. The way the "customer" had a key to the front door is odd at best. The cautious manner in which the man scans the area, causing me to slouch down in my car seat before he pulls the door down, just screams sketchy.

Still, I realize there is a ginormous difference between sketchy and illegal. There is also a delineation between a criminal scheme and a crime cartel. The question is, what sort of an organization is J&B Body Shop.

More importantly—how will I find out?

Chapter 37

An hour later, I'm preparing to leave. Not because I'm bored; I have adrenaline strumming through my veins since I have convinced myself I'm surveilling a central distribution node of the cartel. However, the expiration date on my bladder has expired.

As I reach for my car keys, the first overhead door rolls open. Three men step out.

It's the driver of the brown car and two dudes who look like they take Anadrol six times a day. Seriously, guys. You can't even cross your arms.

Wait. The brown car is gone, or at least its outer skin. In its place is the aluminum frame and chassis of a small sedan.

The three men carry on a conversation at the front of the bay. The larger of the two men taking human growth hormones pulls an envelope from his back pocket, handing it to the driver. The driver tucks the envelope in his back pocket as they continue their conversation.

A red sports car pulls into J&B's parking lot, stopping in front of the three men. They continue their conversation undeterred by the new vehicle.

The driver's door to the sports car opens, and a lithe blonde woman steps out of the car and says something in the men's direction. The two bodybuilders laugh, and one of them slaps the driver on the shoulder.

The driver gets into the woman's car, and they pull off together. The two bodybuilders disappear into the garage and shut the first bay door.

This opens up a whole new angle on Lexi's case. If Ben was actively working as a distribution point for drug traffickers, one of his business partners would be a far more probable candidate for blowing him up. This bodes well for Lexi if I can figure out how to get some credible evidence for Judge Rossi to review.

I could call Agent Casey and ask him to have one of his agents investigate it. After Lexi's arraignment went so poorly, he might be willing to help clear her name. But if I am wrong, I will slide from a promising candidate to a conspiracy case loser in his eyes. For some reason, that is important to me.

The opening of the second bay door catches me by surprise. Moments later, two beautiful Harleys roll out of the repair bay. Each bike has one of the bodybuilders straddling the fat tail. They close the bay door behind them and drive off in the opposite direction of the red sports car.

My stomach rolls with excitement. I bet I can check out what is going on inside of the repair shop. Suppose I knew for sure that it was a drug distribution operation? In that case, I could ask Agent Casey for help with certainty that I wouldn't be embarrassed.

Those two had to be the only ones in the building. Right? There aren't any other vehicles in front of the building. Still, someone may have parked their rides inside the gravel lot. Nah. I'm overthinking this. They'll never be the wiser I'm in the office.

If I can just find something of prosecutorial value, I can confidently ask for Agent Casey's help. The last thing I need to do is be wrong about the connection to Ben's murder.

That's stupid, April. No, it's making sure I'm right before I go demanding the FBI take a closer look into the body shop. It's called professional preservation.

That's it. I'm going in.

Reaching for the handle of my door, as I pull the handle, I look up and scream. A man is glaring at me through the side window. Refilling my lungs, I begin to scream a second time, but my throat tightens, choking it off.

The man swings his fist against my car window. The window flexes inward—but that must be my imagination. Glass doesn't flex.

He swings his fist a second time, and again it bounces off the window. This time I notice the long knife in his hand, the hilt he is using in an attempt to shatter the glass. Chase has an emergency knife, and I know they are highly effective for breaking windows.

He will be in my car in seconds.

I must get away from this madman as quickly as possible. Turning the keys to my ignition, nothing happens. I try a second time, and bile rises in my mouth as I get the same result.

The man swings the blade again at my window, this time creating a rattle.

"Come on!" I yell at my car as I try the ignition again. Again nothing.

The window of my car explodes, sending shards of glass into my hair and filling my lap. The man reaches in with his free hand, gripping and tugging my shirt collar.

I slap at his hand as I attempt to dive into the passenger seat to escape his grasp. My seatbelt holds me in place.

"Stop it!" he yells at me.

By some miracle, my hand finds the button of my seatbelt and releases me from my binds. He yanks my collar again, and I crash my left forearm in an upward arc, breaking his grip, but earning myself a busted lip when his hand flies into my face.

I duck out of the retracting seatbelt, now tangled around his arm, and crab crawl over the center console onto the passenger seat, kicking at his hand as I go.

Oh Lord, this isn't going to work! Even if I get out the passenger door, he can run me down. I'm not safe in the car, and I'm not safe outside of the vehicle.

He leans in the broken car window, attempting to grab my leg. I kick out, this time connecting solidly with his fist. He draws back, curses, then dives forward, knife first.

I would do anything right now for a gun. I wish I had not put the ammo in the trunk, and I wish I had talked Dr. Devereaux into loaning me a pistol. A gun is the only thing that can save me from being knifed to death.

My attacker dives into the car again with his knife. I connect the sole of my tennis shoe with his knife hand again, making him recoil.

Angrier than ever, he yanks on the door. It's still locked, and he stumbles backward when his hand slips out from under the handle.

My glove compartment pops open. On top of all the maintenance records, there is the forty-five Chase insisted I take with me the other day. I grab the weapon, chamber a round, and point it at my attacker as I flip the safety off in one smooth motion.

The gun has a nice, balanced weight to it. It feels good in my hand; it feels like salvation.

The attacker doesn't notice the equation has changed as he reaches in to unlock the car door.

"You pull that lock up, and I pull the trigger!" I scream at him.

His tunnel vision shifts from the lock on the door to the gun in my hand. I swear I see his eyes stare down the barrel of the gun.

"Now back it up. You need to get lost before you get hurt!"

The attacker's face calms. "You won't pull it," he says. He yanks the lock upward.

I'm not sure that I mean to pull the trigger, but I do. The sound is deafening, leaving my ears ringing and a sulfur taste in my mouth. The air in the car is immediately acrid from the gunpowder.

My attacker stops. His eyes widen as his mouth opens. He

clutches at his right ear. Blood flows freely, painting his wrist bright red.

He briefly removes his hand, apparently still in shock, to examine if there is blood. I'm horrified to see he is now missing his right ear.

Despite the shock of having shot a man's ear off, I scream at him. "You better get out of here if you want to keep the other ear."

My attacker doesn't ignore the second warning. He runs across the lot, disappearing through an alley to the right.

What the heck! What was that all about?

The incident has left me shaken. I have enough awareness left to click the safety on the firearm.

I'm not about to put it back in the glove compartment until J&B's is well behind me in the rearview mirror. But I just shot a man's ear off unintentionally. I don't need to make the situation any worse by shooting one of my toes off, too.

I slide back over the console into the driver's seat, gingerly wiping the largest shards onto the floorboard.

I can feel the tiny pebbles of glass through my jeans, and a few more fall out of my hair. I want to clear the glass better, but I don't want to hang around and allow my attacker to regroup.

I try the ignition of the car. Again, not even a sound. I hang my head in defeat. The last thing I want to do is call one of my brothers to give me a ride home. It would be a non-stop scolding the entire drive home.

The correct thing to do is to call the police. I'm just the victim of an assault—or robbery—or I don't want to think about it. Still, I also just blew a man's ear off with a gun that isn't registered to me.

That's terrible optics.

I'm searching through the copious piles of legal training that resides in my head. None of it offers sound advice about what to do when you shoot a man's ear off.

I try to remember if this will be a felony. Also, if it is probable I'll be charged with reckless discharge of a firearm, and if I would be found guilty given the circumstances of the incident. Unfortunately, the lawyer part of my brain obviously went on vacation when the frantic girl took over and got trigger happy.

I open my eyes and exhale. What a pickle.

Looking down in defeat, I notice my gearshift looks odd. No wonder the car wouldn't start. I didn't put it in park when I pulled into the lot across from J&B's.

Rather than berate myself for doing something so mindless, I'm thankful it is something simple, and I can get home without causing a considerable stir. Putting my car in park is way easier than calling home and having to explain my situation.

As I pull onto the highway, I'm forced to drive way below the speed limit. Little chunks of glass vibrate off my dash, and more are flying free from my car door.

Suddenly, I begin to hiccup for breath. The waterworks are close behind, and I feel the warmth trickle down my freezing cheeks. I shake uncontrollably. It could be a reaction to the cool November air blowing through my now-missing window at thirty-five miles an hour.

I know it's not the temperature.

What the heck. Who was he? What did he want? I know he wanted something. That emotion rolled off of him like the stench of urine. His "want" emotions were even higher than his anger when he could not unlock the door.

But a want for what?

Chapter 38

I have almost gotten control of my emotions when I pull into my parents' driveway. When I see Chase sitting on the deck, I break into a fresh round of watery emotions. If he hadn't insisted and put that gun in my glove compartment, where would I be?

He looks up before I can park my car. His head tilts quizzically as I put the car in park and turn it off. Any hopes of slipping quietly into my apartment are gone as I see him walk toward me with that concerned big brother look that I both love and hate.

I'm sure to be the topic of discussion at dinner. "April got herself in trouble again. Good thing her big brothers look out for her."

I pull in a steadying breath as I pop open the car door and say the first thing that comes to mind. "One of those dumb dump trucks out on seventy-two kicked up a rock. Look at what it did to my window."

His eyebrows come together with a look of consternation. "But it's—"

I look back at my car and see what he is hesitating about. Stupid. "Yeah, isn't that the craziest? You wouldn't think a rock could've hit the side window. Do you think there's any way you can fix it for me?"

He scratches his head. "Yeah, but—"

"You're the best brother ever." I give him a quick peck on the cheek. "I have to get ready for work tonight with Dusty. Thank you."

"You're welcome?"

It is necessary to take a shower to get all the glass out of my hair. It is also essential to wash the fear off my skin. The longer I stand in the hot shower, the madder I become.

It serves that creep right. He's lucky I hadn't *meant* to pull the trigger because I wouldn't have missed if I had been aiming.

Two things come to me in a rush as the fear washes off. The attack might not have been random. It's possible the workers at J&B Body Shop had noticed my surveillance of the shop and decided to teach me a lesson. The more I think about it from that angle, the more it makes sense.

That isn't good. If that is the case, I wasn't just unsafe at J&B's, I could be unsafe anywhere. Criminal elements like those don't have a problem chasing down someone they view as a threat.

Case in point, Ben. Maybe he had crossed the wrong "partner." I would think criminal enterprises would consider assassinations as practical means of employee corrective action.

The second thought that comes to me is I may have just completed my first manifestation. How else do I explain the glove compartment suddenly opening? Didn't I *wish* for a gun? Didn't Granny say that the thought had to be accompanied by the strongest of emotions?

There could be no stronger emotion than what I felt as my attacker lunged at me repeatedly with his knife. My emotions were so strong that they shut out everything except the knife and my desire for a gun.

But I had no expectation a gun would appear.

Then it was there. How do I explain that away?

The revelation that I manifested the gun scares the bejeezus out of me. If I can wish something useful into my life that easily, couldn't I unintentionally wish bad things into my life by thinking about them?

Hmm … That would put a new urgent emphasis on the "not thinking negative thoughts" project.

This manifestation skill is undoubtedly a double-edged sword. But the other side of the equation, the good one, is making me grin as I rinse off. How cool is it that I can think into existence something I want?

So cool, you can't even begin to describe it.

Once more, this skill isn't just a theory anymore to me. I have actually done it. I know what is required to make it happen.

I can't wait to get back home from the Wagners' tonight and begin practicing my new skill. The only thing equal to it in animism that holds the same level of interest is the spontaneous creation of fire.

I'm not going to lie. If my inability to control spontaneous fire is any indication, I may want to take it slow with manifestation.

I hear a knock on my door. I hurry to wrap a towel around me. It is too early for Dusty to be ready to leave.

"Come in," I say.

Chase takes a look at me in my towel, frowns, and covers his eyes as he turns his head. "Come on, April. They make robes for a reason."

I pull my towel tighter around me, now made self-conscious. "Grow up, Chase. I have more covered than what a bathing suit would do."

Chase continues to look away. "Listen, we both know that a dump truck did not kick a rock up and cause that."

"What do you mean?" I only float the white lie because he is not looking at my face.

"Come on, April. Are you really going to stick with that, or are you going to tell me what happened?"

I consider his question. I'm going to stick with my original version. "Well, that's what happened."

Chase gets over my no-towel issue, turns, and fixes me with his "yeah right" look. "Okay. We'll play that game. Show me your hands."

I make a pointed look toward the towel I clutch closed around my chest. He picks up on the gesture.

"Then go put a robe on, but you're showing me your hands."

Being bossed around is one of my trigger points, and my guilty grin from telling a lie evaporates as my annoyance ticks up a notch. "What's your deal, anyway? If you don't want to fix the window, fine. I'll get someone else to do it."

"Like J&B Body Shop?"

It may just be a random guess, or coincidence on Chase's part, but it shakes me to my core. Both the silly lying grin and the put-out-little-sister glare evaporate. I'm in full-blown sulk mode.

"Fine." I rotate my hands, clutching my towel, and show Chase first my right hand, then my left.

"Good. Thank you. Now, would you like to explain why there is blood all over the door of your car?"

Big brother is landing heavy blows today. I feel all the air escape me in one quick exhale.

If I thought it was an option, I wouldn't answer him. I don't want to answer the question. But he is standing in front of me with his arms crossed, and I know he isn't moving out of my doorway until we finish this conversation.

Darn it. I can feel the tears coming down my cheeks again. I hate it when the boys see me cry.

"April."

"I'm gonna tell you!" I snap as I wipe away some of the tears. "I was out at J&B's running surveillance. While I was there, this guy started trying to break into my car. He broke the window out with the hilt of his knife. And then I shot his ear off with the gun you put in my glove compartment." It all comes out in a slurred rush.

Chase blinks several times in rapid-fire succession as he drops his arms to his side. He is quiet.

He appears to be having difficulty processing everything. Heck, *I'm* having trouble processing everything.

His eyes scan me from head to toe in a manner that brings my annoyance back. "Did he hurt you?"

I wrap my free arm over my shoulder. "No. Just scared me."

"And you shot his ear off?" Chase's eyes narrow.

"I think. It looked to be gone, but it was so bloody I can't be for sure."

Chase whistles as he shakes his head. "Sucks to be him. In addition to missing an ear, he's probably going to feel like somebody cracked his head with a baseball bat for the next couple of months."

"He deserved it," I reply.

"Heck yeah. Hopefully, he'll learn from it." He crosses his arms again. "Why didn't you tell me in the first place? Why the lying?"

"I don't really like the word 'lying.' I think it was more along the lines of not wanting to tell the story yet."

"Uh-huh. I think that would've been 'I'll tell you later, Chase. I'm too shook up to talk about it at the moment.' Not what just went on."

There really is no arguing with his point. "Okay," I croak.

"And second," he begins.

No, not a second. I can't deal with a full-blown sermon right now.

"You got no business running surveillance on any place. You're not a cop or a detective, or a private investigator. You're a lawyer. If you want to do surveillance, get you some training and some real self-defense courses. Going out there on your own and not knowing what you're doing is just a recipe for disaster."

Well, big brother, that pretty much sums up my life to this point. It seems like all I've been doing lately is running into things unprepared and then finding out that there's a lot more to the world than what I know.

"Do you hear me?"

"Yes, I hear you." I look up from the floor, and we stare at each other. I know Chase. Unless you make eye contact, he won't believe you have heard him.

"Good. I'm happy you're okay, and the entire time I'm fixing your window, I'm going to be grateful for that."

Chase's words bring fresh tears to my eyes, and I will myself not to let them fall. He moves toward me as if he will hug me, pauses, separates his arms, and waves them in and out. It's sort of a bear hug-air hug.

He points at my towel. "I'll rain check on the hug." He winks at me then leaves.

As I stare at the door, all I can think is, I could have really used that hug right now.

Chapter 39

I'm more than ready to leave my apartment by the time Dusty texts me. I've managed to shake off most of the emotions from being attacked earlier in the day, and I believe the distraction of a ghost hunt will do me some good.

Besides, it is at the Wagners' home, and Dusty had only asked Luis, Miles, and me to accompany him. It couldn't be too big of a deal if we are heading out with just a skeleton crew. Right?

Luis is leaning against our paranormal hunting van when I come out of my apartment. He is watching something on his phone and laughing.

"What are you watching, Luis?" I crane my neck to see his screen.

He laughs out his answer as he turns the screen toward me. "Kids."

I'm expecting to see a version of *America's Funniest Video* complete with little kids running around at a birthday party when he turns the screen to me. Instead, the type of "kids" Luis is referring to are baby goats.

"They are so cute and so beautiful. The way they are so full of joy, they make me laugh and smile," Luis says.

I'm not buying it. I don't see why he's so amused. I am about to ask where Dusty is when one of the kids jumps up on the back of one of the adult goats.

Darn it if I don't start chortling along with Luis.

Spending summers on Grandpa and Granny's farm, I have had plenty of experiences with goats. Somewhere along the line, I had forgotten how cute the kids can be when they are playing.

It is like a drug. My happy pill. I lean against the van next to Luis as we watch two more kid videos in a row.

"Load up," Dusty hollers coming out of the sliding glass door with Miles in tow, seemingly in high spirits. My brother is carrying a cooler, and Miles has grocery sacks in both hands.

"I got shotgun," Miles announces.

Shotgun. Shells. Ammo. I forgot the special ammo from Dr. Devereaux. "Hold on a minute."

Dr. Devereaux had only today promised he would work on shotgun shells for me, the ammo for the ultimate paranormal weapon my mind is keyed on now. I pull the forty-five-caliber ammo from my trunk.

I close the trunk and pause. The plan was to load the forty-five Chase had given me with the ammo and give the rest to Dusty.

That is a solid plan. Except touching the gun is going to immediately bring back the bad memories of this afternoon's attack when I just cleared them from my mind.

I clutch the handle on the passenger door while taking long, deep breaths as I set the ammo on the roof of my car. *You've got this. You've got this, April.*

"Hurry up. The sun will be going down soon," Miles says to me.

"Just a minute!" *Do it. Do it.* I yank open the door, slap open the glove compartment, and retrieve the gun.

I don't know what I was expecting, the gun to feel oily and evil, or possibly to be like a firebrand to the touch, but it is none of those things.

Instead, it feels like a well-balanced firearm in my hand. Cool.

All the weirdo clowns in the world better watch out. I'm armed and dangerous.

"What was that all about?" Miles does his best ticked-off schoolmarm scowl.

I show him the ammo box as I step up into the van through the side door. "Paranormal ammo."

"Is that a real thing?" Luis asks.

I eject the clip from my pistol and open the box of ammo. "I don't know. I guess we're gonna find out. Dusty, do you have your forty-five?"

Dusty doesn't say anything as he pulls out of our driveway. He presses the console next to his right knee, and a four-inch by four-inch square slides open twelve inches deep. I can see the Colt holstered neatly in the spring-loaded, pop-out box.

Wow! My big brother is like 007. He extracts his pistol, checks the safety, and hands it to me.

"You need to be careful with those. I don't want us to go on into someplace and shoot it up," Miles frets.

"Miles, chill." It is more of a suggestion the way Dusty says it.

Miles shrugs and looks out the window. "All right. But I'm just saying."

"I'm sure Dusty and April have had lots of training on the safe operation of firearms," Luis adds hopefully.

I finish loading Dusty's gun and hand it back to him. He holsters it and closes the compartment. "Maybe we'll get an opportunity to see if they work tonight."

I hope not. The last thing I want to do is fire that gun a second time today.

Chapter 40

As we pull into the Wagners' driveway, they are waiting for us on their porch. That strikes me as odd. The weather is pleasant for sitting outside with a fire pit—but still a bit chilly to be on the porch.

As I watch Vance and Leslie stand from their rocking chairs and walk toward us, I smile. I remember how foreign they were to me when I was assigned Vance's case a few months back.

Vance and Leslie can be most easily described as hard-working, country, and tough. They're also extremely high on the survivor scale and a touch more than crazy, which generally keeps you a little uncomfortable when you're talking to them.

The other thing about Vance and Leslie you need to know is they would die for each other. I know people say that all the time. But I have proof.

Leslie endured a brutal beating by two thugs to protect Vance and his company, and Vance chased down the same armed men and killed them in action-hero fashion. No, they *truly* would die for one another.

I believe I could do with a little less than the full-blown, die-for-me thing. Still, it would make my heart sing to have a man look at me the way Vance looks at Leslie. They have nothing but complete adoration expressed when they lock eyes and often grin as if sharing a secret.

"Ms. April," Vance begins with a broad grin, "it sure is good to see you again."

Leslie grabs my hand. "It is. How have you been? Did you have a good Thanksgiving?"

My face is stretching into the same crazy grin they have. It must be contagious. "I did. How about you?"

"It was beautiful. I even talked my daddy into coming and having dinner with us this year." Leslie gestures over her shoulder. "I mean with the new house and all."

"Y'all have done really well for yourselves," I say.

Vance's face turns serious, and I almost lean back with apprehension. "It's because of you, Ms. April. Without your help, they would have thrown me under the jail just for defending my family."

"I don't know what I would have done if they had done Vance wrong like that."

At that moment, it comes to me who Vance and Leslie remind me of—Bonnie and Clyde. It is as if I teleported back in time, and I'm hanging out with the best-known criminal couple of all time. I did the world a favor by getting Vance off. Otherwise, Leslie might have busted him out of the county pen and gone on a crime spree across North Alabama.

Stranger things have happened.

"What are you doing out on the porch. Isn't it too chilly for that tonight?"

Leslie purses her lips. "It started up again?" she says, more as a question than a statement.

"We thought we would just wait out on the porch until the experts arrived," Vance adds.

"It?" Dusty asks.

Leslie wags her finger in the air. "That stupid ghost. It started making a big old ruckus again about half an hour ago. I think it's about wore us smooth."

Vance shrugged. "So, we came out here to wait."

Makes sense to me. I'd be more than happy to wait out on the porch with the Wagners, but I doubt Dusty will pay me if I do.

"That's good," Dusty says. "If it's active tonight, maybe we'll be able to identify the source and help you get rid of it."

"I was sort of hoping that by you showing up, it would just decide it was time to move along," Vance grouses.

"A spirit will rarely move on without some sort of interaction," Luis adds.

Vance and Leslie stare at Luis as if he has two heads. "Typically, we have to make contact between the living and the dead to affect change," I explain to them.

They both nod in agreement.

"If you'll give us a tour of the home and let us know where the most energy is coming from, we'll go ahead and pull out our gear and get set up for the night," Dusty says.

Vance jams his hands in his back pocket. "I guess we better get this over with."

I follow Vance into their home. Luis, Dusty, then Miles follow us. Leslie decides she would rather stay on the porch by herself.

The first thing I notice is that the home was probably built in the late 1800s. The second thing I notice is either the prior owner completed a tremendous amount of remodeling to maximize their profit or Vance has been hard at work. There are new baseboard and crown molding that shines brightly from heavy coats of high-gloss paint and no scuff marks or dents.

"Vance, was the house redone on the interior when you bought it?" I ask him.

He opens the door to the basement and flips the switch. "Nah, it was all that old plasterwork. It even had the old-timey crawlspace behind it. Once I furred it out, and drywalled the walls and the ceiling, it actually gave us an extra foot in either direction."

I'm tired just listening to him describe how much work he has already poured into the home. Then again, that doesn't surprise me with Vance. He's always been a hard worker.

I'm thinking about the remodeling he has done at the house

as I take the last step into the basement. Immediately I feel a low hum through me. It is feeble, and I can't get a good read, but it feels neutral.

"Occasionally, when I'm down here doing the laundry"— Vance points at the fluorescent light above the washer and dryer unit—"those lights go to flickering something fierce. That's about it. But it is worrisome.

The energy source is so low I am forced to drop my mental barriers altogether. It is weak, as if it is one of the spirits close to letting go of this side of the veil. All in all, I don't really believe the spirit would be anything to worry about. Maybe an aggravating occasional flickering light, but it really isn't long for this side.

"Miles, do you mind setting up a couple cameras down here and monitoring them?" Dusty asks.

"Whatever you want, chief," Miles says.

Vance starts back up the stairs, and I follow him. We walk to the kitchen, the dining room, and the family room. The only room on the main floor with any energy imprints is Vance and Leslie's master bedroom. But they are the source of those.

Vance gestures for me to follow him up the stairs. Luis and Dusty fall in behind me.

"Wow, this house is huge, Vance," I comment.

"Leslie says she wants six kids. I figure you might as well do it right the first time. I don't care to have to do all this remodeling a second time."

Smart guy. "Well, it looks fantastic."

"Thank you." He looks genuinely pleased with my compliment.

When I step on the top floor, I feel emotion floating in the air. It is sadness or possibly loneliness. It is again so faint it is hard to determine which.

"Ms. Green, the elderly lady who lived here, had used two of the rooms up here for storage and closed off the other. There is some roof damage, and I had some water damage I had to deal with in the rooms after I threw out the junk she had left."

"She just left her stuff?" I ask.

Vance makes a sideways grin. "Now, Ms. April. They always say you can't take it with you."

I tilt my chin up as I understand what he is alluding to. "She died."

"Yes, ma'am. Downstairs is the master bedroom. Could you feel her?" He suddenly looks embarrassed. "That's what Leslie told me. That you feel things. Ghosts."

I shrug. "Something like that. Some of the times."

He eyes me suspiciously. "Did you feel one in the master bedroom? Leslie says there is one in there, too."

I feel my ears heat up. "No. I didn't feel anything in the master bedroom."

He appears pleased as he opens a bedroom door. "Good. I think it might be hard to sleep if I knew a dead person was eyeing me. You know what I mean?"

"I believe I do."

I follow Vance into the freshly painted room. It is bright pink and yellow.

"This would be a great little girl's room," Luis comments.

"That's the idea," Vance says as he leads us back out into the hallway.

We step into a huge Jack and Jill bathroom. I don't feel anything in the first section or in the tub section. When we walk through to the adjoining vanity, I get a slight flutter. I turn to see if Dusty felt it, too, and catch a small white face in the bottom right-hand corner of the mirror. By the time I turn my eyes back to that location in the mirror, the face is gone.

"Hey, hold on a minute, Dusty."

I know I'm not seeing things. I saw a little old lady as pasty white as if she had never been out in the sun. But now she is gone.

"What is it?"

"I thought I saw something. But I must've been mistaken."

We catch back up with Vance as he is opening the second bedroom. I now sense a slightly higher energy level than in the bathroom. Scanning the room, I see nothing out of place other than a couple of unused towels on the king-size bed. This room is painted a bright violet color.

"This would work well for girls, too," Luis critiques the room color again.

Vance exits the room, and I begin to follow him, then stop. A foot down from the ceiling in the far-left corner, a slight variation catches my eye. It is a cross between a very faint smoke cloud and a mirage.

It is a tear in the veil.

I would investigate the third room, but I believe I have found ground zero for the disturbances. A tear in the veil is no minor occurrence, and it nearly guarantees the presence of a spirit.

I study Dusty's and Luis's faces. They do not appear to notice the portal to the dead that I see. It is best to keep it to myself for now. If they don't see it, I can wait and investigate it on my own.

"This concludes the Wagners' tour. I hope everybody enjoyed the ride," Vance jokes.

"The disturbances that you've been experiencing," Luis begins, "other than the basement, where else have you experienced them?"

Vance doesn't move from the third bedroom doorway. He points toward the bathroom and second room. "Between those two rooms. You can hear it off and on during the night. It sounds like somebody getting up to go to the restroom."

If I didn't have my "gifts" and hadn't just seen the troubling tear in the veil, I might try to convince Vance he simply heard the expansion and contractions of the home framing.

"Is it just the sounds you hear?" Dusty's pointed question seems to concern Vance. He takes his time weighing the positives and negatives of telling Dusty the truth before he is candid.

"Sometimes I see shadows. Most of the time shadows. But every once in a while, I see a little old lady holding dolls."

Luis steps closer to Vance. "Mr. Wagner, do you have a picture of Ms. Green, the woman who passed?"

"No. I'm sorry I don't."

I know where Luis is going with his line of questioning, but it is a dead end. If Vance had a picture of Ms. Green, he would've easily identified her ghost.

I point toward the second bedroom. "If you don't mind, I think I want to set up in here. You two can set up in the other bedrooms."

Dusty and Luis exchange a brief look before they shrug in tandem.

Within the hour, I'm set up in the violet-colored upstairs room. I have placed my lawn chair in the opposite corner of the tear in the veil. It has been a long time since I have seen a stable tear, and this one is nearly thirty inches in diameter. I don't want to get too close and accidentally slide through unexpectedly.

"Are you sure you'll be okay in here?" Dusty says as he gives the room another scan.

His eyes do not even hesitate on the pulsating smoke on the ceiling across from us. If his motion had paused even momentarily on the veil, I would've thought that maybe he felt or saw something out of place. Instead, he is simply going on his gut that if I selected an area, it is for a reason.

"Sure. I just thought this room was peaceful."

Dusty tilts his head slightly and grins. "Yeah, right." But thankfully, he doesn't press me any further. "I'll be in the pink room, and Luis is next door. Just make sure to holler if you need us."

"I will." I'm hoping he will move along so I can get a few minutes to examine what I'm seeing.

Dusty finally tires of crowding me, like only an older brother can, and leaves for his room of the investigation. I give it a few minutes to ensure he is gone and shuffle slowly toward the tear.

Despite it being a more significant tear than usual, it is without a definite split. The undulating mass contains a line down the center that appears to be more concentrated than the rest of the veil. Almost as if the opening had closed over with thick scar tissue, leaving the tear sealed for all eternity. This is the first time I have ever seen this and never have heard anyone else speak of it before.

With no active tear available to investigate, the only option left to me is to sit and observe.

I adjust my weight in the lawn chair, trying to get more comfortable. Something doesn't add up with the sealed opening.

Pulling my forty-five from my belt, I eject and check the odd, blue rounds in the clip, reset the clip, and check the safety. I have no expectations of another awkwardly tall clown appearing. Still, I won't be caught unprepared if lightning strikes twice.

My phone rings, and if I hadn't set the safety on my gun, I would've shot a hole in Vance's excellent violet paint job. Looking down at the ID, I smile when I see Lee's name displayed. I shove the gun back in my belt and answer my phone.

"Hey. How are you?"

"I'm doing great. I'm looking forward to seeing you tomorrow night. I just want to double-check and make sure we are still good," Lee says.

"We sure are."

"Good. I was afraid you might've backed out."

"Why would you have thought that?" I ask.

"I don't know. Maybe it just seems too good to be true. To be getting a second chance with you."

I nearly melt into a little puddle in my lawn chair. In my dealings with ultra-confident alpha males, this is the sweetest thing I have ever heard. "Then I guess you better make the best of your second chance."

Lee laughs, a slow, low rumbling timbre that connects directly to my sexy meter.

"I definitely intend to take full advantage of my second opportunity."

I hear the bathroom door open. I begin to get up to peek out the bedroom doorway to see who is going into the bathroom. "You are, are you? How do you intend to do that?"

"I'm not gonna tell you," Lee teases.

I peer down the hallway and see Dusty flipping pages on a notepad. Looking in the other direction, Luis is typing on his laptop. Neither is looking in my direction. More importantly, both are seated and appear to have been settled in for some time.

"Okay. Lucky for you, I like surprises." I'm not really paying attention to the phone conversation anymore. I can feel my anxiety level tweaking upward as I search for an explanation of why the bathroom door has seemingly closed on its own.

The sound of water comes from the bathroom, and I feel the fear creep across my skin. When the commode flushes, I fall violently ill. "Lee, can I call you back?"

The sudden change in my tone alarms him. "Are you okay? Is everything all right?"

"Yes. Everything's fine," I lie. "I just need to take care of something really quick. I'll call you later."

"Okay."

I hit the disconnect button and pull out my forty-five. I hold my gun in my right hand and my phone in my left like some gunslinger from the old Westerns waiting for whoever or whatever is behind the bathroom door to make the first move.

I know it isn't Leslie or Vance. They left to spend the night at the Better Western hotel in Guntersville when we started to unpack the van. The only other person in the house is Miles. He would have passed by two other bathrooms on the way to the upstairs one, and it makes no sense for him to be in the Jack and Jill bathroom.

Visions of the killer twelve-foot clown pop into my mind's eye, and I shrink back into the violet room in terror. It is him. He has followed me from Birmingham, and he is about to flop one of his size twenty-four shoes outside the bathroom door.

I can't handle it. I would just die. As it is, fear has gripped my heart and lungs and is squeezing them so tight they are beginning to fail.

I cower in the far corner of the violet room next to the twin-sized bed. The veil pulsates above my head, my eyes are fixed on the open bedroom door.

There is a tiny squeak that echoes down the hall as the bathroom door opens to the hallway. I watch the doorknob, just outside the open doorway to the violet room, turn. I wait for the large, preposterous shoe to flop into the hallway as it appeared from the closet in the Birmingham attic, and my breath seizes up.

All oxygen to my brain has now ceased. My lungs burn from the lack of oxygen.

It's at moments like this when I question my sanity. What the heck am I doing here? Why am I risking my life like this? It sure isn't for the money. Well, money does play a small part in it.

But for heaven's sake, I'm a highly educated professional. I don't have to put myself in harm's way to make a good living. Didn't the frickin' FBI all but offer me a job this week.

Sure, it might not be my dream job. Still, the experience would be world-class. It would be a great stepping stone toward that coveted partnership at a law firm in the large metro area that is my goal.

Someone is having a coughing fit. Maybe the killer clown has caught emphysema from inhaling too much smoke during the fire in Birmingham?

There is no way to hold my breath any longer, and I gasp in a fresh breath of air. I curl myself into an even tighter ball in the corner. I sit still in front of the foot of the bed in hopes of concealing myself.

Every muscle in my body tenses when I catch movement from the bathroom to the doorway of the room I occupy.

I'm confused as I stare at the diminutive figure staring at me, her eyes in a squint.

She is barely three feet tall and thin, very thin. The cotton gown she wears hangs loosely from her shoulders. There is nary a wisp of hair on her head. Her eyes are sunken, with shades of dark encircling them. Her body appears to be broken down by illness and stress, giving her the appearance of a miniature old woman. She holds a ratty doll with a chipped porcelain face in the crook of her left arm. The apparition is nearly sixty percent solid and absolutely pathetic looking.

"Who are you? Why are you here?" she asks with a suspicious tone.

Briefly, I consider acting like I don't know she is talking to me. That I'm like every other human and can't see her. But she is staring at me dead in the eyes, and I know it won't work. She knows I can see her.

I move from my curled position into a squat where we are now at eye level across the room from one another. "The nice new people who bought this house are concerned that someone is up here and needs their help. Do you need help?"

The little girl wraps her right arm around the doll, pulling it closer to her chest. "I can't find my mommy."

There is a tug at my heart from the desperate inflection in her voice. I fight back the emotion to work the job at hand. "You're separated from your mommy?"

The little girl nods her head mutely.

"Do you want me to help you find her?"

The little girl steps closer. "Yes. But I've already looked everywhere."

There is an odd strobe of light off the bedroom wall. I look up at the veil above my head and can see electrical impulses rotating below its surface. "Do you know your name? My name is April Snow."

"My name is Amelia Green."

"Amelia is a beautiful name."

"My mommy said when she was a little girl, she always wanted a baby sister, and she wanted to name her Amelia."

"I see. When was the last time you saw your mommy?"

The little girl pulls the doll even closer to her. "I don't know. It's been a long time."

A long time means decades if my thoughts are correct. I had not bothered to ask how old Ms. Green was when she passed. Still, suppose she made it to her seventies, just accounting for average childbearing age. In that case, Amelia has been walking the upstairs hallways for three to four decades. Given that she is still at sixty percent materialization, I know she has a strong desire to remain.

"Amelia, if you don't mind, can you tell me what's wrong with you?"

Her thin lips nearly disappear at the question that obviously annoys her. "I just have this tummy ache. Mommy says that the doctors will fix it, and it's all going to be okay. Once I'm all better, she's going to take me on the roller coaster." She lowers her chin and knots her eyebrows. "Mommy promised."

"Does your tummy hurt?"

She nods her head.

"Now?" I ask.

"Always. It always hurts, and I'm always cold." Her shoulders give a minute shiver that ripples the gown hanging loosely from her narrow shoulders.

My heartbreak for the little girl. I'm not going to cry. This has been like a record crying week, and I'm not going to allow myself that again. I draw a long, deep breath and will back the tears as my nose tickles and stops working for me.

I'm can't decide how to move Amelia forward with the least amount of hurt and confusion. How do you tell a little girl who wants to be alive that she and her mommy are dead? But that is precisely the task that has fallen to me.

"April?"

I jerk my head in the direction of the male voice. Dusty and Luis are standing in the doorway. Both have concerned, questioning looks on their face. Why shouldn't they? Neither can see Amelia, which means I am in a squatting position in a room talking to myself.

Amelia looks over her shoulder at the two men and dismisses them, turning back to me. She understands they can't see her.

I hold up my finger toward Dusty to signal for them to give me a minute. "Amelia, I have something very important to tell you."

She moves forward a few more steps and releases her clutch on the baby doll. "Is it about my mommy? Do you know where she is?"

"Yes, honey, I do. I need to ask you a favor. Can you do me a favor?"

Her facial expression tightens momentarily, still she nods her agreement.

"Thank you. What I need to ask is that you be very strong and brave. Even stronger and braver than you normally are. Can you do that for me?"

There is no hesitation from her as she bobs her head in agreement this time. That brings a smile to my face. It's an incredible thing to see such a small and sick soul be so brave.

"Amelia, your mommy is in heaven. And she's waiting there for you. Do you want to go to her?"

My foolish expectation is that Amelia will immediately say yes. Instead, she bows up, and her lower lip begins to tremble in a fit of rage.

"No. We're going to go ride the rollercoaster. Mommy promised. She told me I would get all better, and we would ride the rollercoaster together." Her features are set with new determination. "*You* don't know what you're talking about."

My knees begin to ache. I stand. "I'm sorry, Amelia. I know it's disappointing and hard to understand. Your mommy wanted you to get better. I'm sure she hoped and prayed you would. But you were too sick. Sometimes parents are wrong."

Her face squints tightly, and she clenches her tiny gray teeth. "No. You're just wrong."

"I wish I were. And I know your mommy wishes she were right, that you would get better, and that she was alive to take you to a rollercoaster, but things don't always happen the way we hope they will."

"It's not nice to tell lies," Amelia snarls. "Bad lady."

If the home belonged to anyone besides Leslie and Vance, I believe I would leave now. In a rush, I have an epiphany that I just do not have the energy to fight any more this week.

I'm tired, a borderline emotional wreck, and what do I care if a little girl ghost wants to live in her own reality a little longer. Who am I to break her heart?

We stand in silence, staring at one another.

Her snarl dissipates, and her lower lip begins to quiver again. I know she remembers the crossing.

"Do you remember now, Amelia?" I whisper.

She favors me with a brief nod of her head, and the tears stream down her cheeks.

"I'm so sorry, honey. So, so sorry."

Hugging the doll now close to her cheek, she convulses in tiny sobs. "She promised," she protests with a hollow, haunting voice.

"I know. I'm sure it broke her heart to not be able to keep her promise. I know she wants to take her special little girl to the fair. You know you're special, don't you, Amelia? So brave and patient."

She gives the slightest of shrugs, still unable to stop her intermittent sobbing.

I feel absolutely horrible now, and Amelia's tears must be catching because I feel them flowing freely down my cheeks, too.

"Amelia, don't you want to go see your mommy? I know she is missing you terribly."

She gives another quick nod of her head, and I cry even harder. "But I don't know where she is," she cries.

"I think you do." I point toward the oscillating cloud in the corner. "She's just on the other side of the veil."

Amelia wipes her nose on her arm. "But I can't get to the other side. And I'm scared."

"Would it be easier if I hold your hand? Hold your hand so you can peek on the other side? To see if she is there, Amelia?"

If you'd asked me earlier in the day if that is even possible, I would've said no. But now I'm filled with the certainty that if I want Amelia to be able to, if I want it bad enough for her and concentrate long enough, I can hold Amelia's hand. I can hold her hand, so she doesn't have to be alone on such a scary mission for such a little girl.

"Could you?" Her eyebrows lift in a hopeful manner.

"I think I might if you can help me. And either way, I think we should try. Do you want to try?"

She tucks her doll a little tighter in one hand as she lifts her other hand toward me. Her face is set with grim determination as she approaches me, closing the gap between us. Closing the gap between her and the tear in the veil.

I extend my hand, giving thanks for the ability to hold her hand all the while. When her cold, delicate fingers touch the palm of my hand, I am not surprised. I close my hand gently over hers.

"You're such a brave girl, Amelia."

She appears to gain strength from our touch. She stands a little taller and straightens her neck. "Mommy says I'm a warrior princess."

"Your mommy is a smart lady, Amelia. Yes, you are such a brave warrior princess. Are you ready to go see her?"

Amelia looks over her shoulder. I feel her doubt washing away her newfound bravery.

It's difficult to leave the familiar behind.

"I know it's scary to change, but I also know your mommy would love to see you."

Her eyes come back to me, and she squares her emaciated shoulders. "I'm ready."

"Okay." I have no clue what I am doing. At this point, I'm going strictly on instinct as I lead her to the corner just under the veil. I drop to my knees. "We need to think really hard on opening this shiny door again. I know your mommy is on the other side of this door, but only you and I can open it for her. Do you understand, Amelia?"

Amelia drops to her knees next to me as if she must mimic me. "I understand. I'll help."

Her thoughts are loud. I can hear her wishing to see her mommy again, as if the thoughts are my own. I focus on the scar tissue of the veil splitting open so she can journey to the other side.

A sensation tingles on my back and shoulders. I open my eyes, staring at the scarred seam of the veil as the ugly mound running through the center begins to dissipate. The bits of flawed energy that once held the tear closed rain down on the two of us like electrically charged confetti.

As the seam opens, I feel the energy against my skin, like the sun warming me on a hot summer day.

"Are you ready, Amelia?"

I can feel her fear, yet she nods her chin with fierce determination. She is a warrior princess, indeed.

"I'll hold your hand the whole time." I point to the opening in the veil. "That's the doorway for you. You can look in first. If you get scared or don't want to go, I'll be here for you. I'll be here for you if you change your mind. If you see your mommy, you can just let go of my hand."

"And you promise *you* won't let go?"

"I won't let go, Amelia. *You* will have to let go. And only if you see your mommy."

We stare at each other in silence. Her tiny hand in mine. She looks back to the swarming tear. As she does, her body levitates off the floor, and I move with her closer to the veil.

As she approaches the veil, the spider-like webbing across the tear flickers and lights in quick succession as if it is becoming excited, preparing to accept her.

Amelia first reaches out the hand clutching her doll into the veil's split. The veil illuminates so brightly I am forced to squint my eyes.

She pushes her face through the seam while I hold her hand tightly. I will not fail to keep my promise.

The excitement and expectations she feels flow freely

through my hand. She tugs her hand in mine as the immense joy lights us both up from the inside out. I fight the urge to hold on even tighter to her hand. I don't want to let her go.

Then, I release her hand. She disappears into the seam of the veil.

The lights of the veil slow their oscillation and finally stop altogether. All is silent.

Amelia is gone.

Chapter 41

It's irrational. I feel a sudden sense of loss.

I hope the joy I felt coursing through her tiny hand is that she saw her mother. Unfortunately, until I cross the veil, that will be a mystery to me.

"April."

My eyes focus on Dusty and Luis in the doorway. I had forgotten they were there. "There was a little girl ghost, Dusty. She was the daughter of the last owner."

Dusty points to where I'm standing. "Just now? Where you are?"

"A minute ago. She's gone through the veil now."

Dusty turns to Luis. Luis shakes his head. "I didn't see anything, either."

"Go get your laptop. Let's see if we captured anything," Dusty says to Luis.

As Luis leaves to get his laptop, Dusty returns his attention to me. "Is that it? You think that is everything?"

It is tough to say, but yes, it feels like everything has been resolved now. "I think so."

Dusty takes a look at his phone. "Wow, it's not even ten o'clock yet. I wonder if the Wagners would rather come back tonight?"

Given the opportunity to sleep in my own bed rather than at the Better Western, I know I would rather be at home. "We need to call them anyway to give them the good news."

"True." Dusty walks away as he dials their number.

When he is out of sight, I lean my back against the wall and slide down it until my butt lands on the floor. I pull my knees in toward me and wrap my arms around my legs.

I feel a migraine coming on.

I also feel like I am made of glass, just shattered into a thousand pieces.

Logically I should be happy. I have successfully helped a troubled spirit traverse into a more restful state. That's a good thing.

But I also have to face the fact that life is so brief and fragile. Something I'd rather not acknowledge.

"Go figure, they're coming back home." Dusty's jaw drops as he starts towards me. "Are you okay? What's the matter?"

I raise a hand toward him. "I'm fine. I'm just drained. It's been a rough couple of days."

"I understand. Can you wait for the Wagners? Leslie said she wants to talk to you."

I rub my temples. "We all came in the same van, Dusty. I can't leave until you do."

"Oh, yeah."

Sometimes it still amazes me how smart he is and yet how stupid he can be. But that is probably just the shooting pain in my head making me think those mean thoughts.

"Dusty, look at these electrical signals we got."

I watch as Miles shoves a laptop to Dusty. As he examines what Miles is showing him, Luis looks over Dusty's shoulder.

"Good gosh. Look at the density of that electrical field." Dusty's excitement is palatable. "Hey, April, did you feel anything? It looks like the ghost was touching you."

I debate whether or not to tell Dusty the truth. It is odd enough that I can sense and see ghosts. If I can touch and hold her hands, too, that makes me an ultra-freak. Something to examine even closer.

Not today. "I think I felt something cold a couple of times, but nothing more than that."

I can tell by Dusty's look that he isn't buying it. I'm too tired and in too much pain to care what his impression is at the moment. I can share the complete version later, once I don't feel as if I may vomit.

Chapter 42

The boys spend the next fifteen minutes arguing about the best way to flesh out the electrical surges they have captured with their equipment. I have lost all interest by this point and am just trying to recoup enough energy to walk to the van and let them drive me home.

When Leslie and Vance arrive home, I struggle to my feet. I make it downstairs, and Leslie immediately crushes me with a hug.

"Thank you, thank you, thank you. I just don't know what I would do without you, April Snow. This is the second time you have fixed something in my life, and we're complete strangers. Nobody has ever done something like this for me."

Vance extends his hand to me as well, and I shake it. "We just can't thank you enough, April. We are truly blessed to have you as a friend."

I wasn't expecting the "friend" word. I didn't know we were there yet.

But then, why not? You can't have enough friends. And besides, if I ever were to get into a fight, Leslie and Vance are two people I would love to have on my side.

The boys take a few minutes to show the Wagners the information they captured. Then there is the signing of release papers before we leave, so Dusty can use the material in his books.

We pile into the van, and my relief is immeasurable. I lean the side of my face against the cold window and enjoy the sensation.

After the boys' initial excitement and discussion on how to best animate the electrical pulses into a believable ghost, they have all but fallen quiet. I think I ruined their fun.

They agree to get together tomorrow and work through the night if necessary to complete the documentation. That will mean more questions tomorrow. Which is good. I'll feel better tomorrow, and I can fill Dusty in completely on Amelia's story.

Just not tonight. Tonight, the emotions are still too raw, and I don't feel physically well.

The trip, by paranormal standards, is an indisputable success. In less than four hours, we expelled a ghost, had functional electronic imaging, and a complete historical record of the spirit. A case like the Wagners' used to take at least a weekend, if not several, and a slew of manpower hours expended.

Good haunting stories don't come cheap.

When we pull into our parents' driveway, Dusty parks the van and swivels in his seat. "I thought I would drop you off before I take the boys home. I think you need some rest."

I bark a short laugh. "That's an understatement."

"Are you okay, April?"

I pull open the van door. "It's all relative with me, isn't it?"

Dusty smiles. "Don't do that. You have a beautiful skill. I thank you for your work tonight, and I know the Wagners are especially thankful that you were with us tonight."

I favor my big, lovable brother with a quick smile that I'm not feeling and press the button for the side door to close. As I fumble with my keys to my apartment, my only hope is that Puppy is inside. I could use a hug and a shower.

Puppy doesn't disappoint me. He is waiting on me when I come in. It is like he knew I needed him.

After a doggie hug and rough petting session—Puppy likes it rough—I step into the shower and brace against the tile as I let the warm water wash the scent of stress from my skin.

I towel dry and put my pj's on as I consider calling Lee. I'm sure ten minutes before midnight isn't late for a professional ballplayer, but I'm way too tired to try and sound sexy. I don't want to fall asleep and let him hear me snore.

Pushing Puppy out of the center of the bed, I stretch my legs as I turn out my nightstand light.

"'Night, Puppy."

Chapter 43

Through the darkness, I become aware something isn't quite right. I can hear traffic, the occasional stray voice, and a few doors opening and closing. Those are things you shouldn't hear when you live out in the country, on a lake, on top of a boathouse. An occasional outboard motor, maybe. Cars and especially stray voices, not so much.

I sit up, realizing I'm not in my room.

When the hand touches my thigh, every muscle in my body contracts, and I gasp. I roll to my right off the bed and stick the landing.

I was in Liza's bed. She is facing me. It is dark, but I can see her face from the dim light reflecting through her curtains.

She holds a finger up to her lips, then points over my shoulder. "Do you see him?" she whispers.

What the devil?

Him who? I don't know who she is talking about or how I'm here.

Stepping forward, I sit down on the edge of her bed as I struggle to figure out just what in tarnation is going on.

I am disconcerted in every way possible, and the idea of my best friend being afraid of whoever *he* is, isn't making it any better.

I crane my neck to scan the room. Nothing. Or at least nothing that would be referred to as "him."

A kitchenette is to the left of the sofa and a loveseat is eight feet in front of me. The apartment door is in between them. To the right are bookshelves and a small TV. And crucifixes, lots of crucifixes, all over the walls.

I bend over, closer to her face. "I don't see anything. What am I supposed to be seeing?"

"Over by the kitchen island. Wait, he'll show himself again."

"Who will?"

"The stuffed doll clown."

Weird just got scary. The last thing I want to see now in my compromised mental capacity is the clown doll Liza claims she has already burned up twice.

I've never heard of a spirit surviving a burning. I'm not sure what it means, but it seems to allude to a certain amount of indestructibility on the part of the spirit.

This doesn't make me happy. Not happy at all.

I'm in bed enjoying a well-deserved sleep with my puppy mattress warmer. Then I end up in Liza's bed, searching her dimly lit apartment for a possessed clown doll. I must've been a mass murderer in my previous life. I can't explain why all these bad things seem to happen to me.

My breathing is shallow as I look around the room again. When my eyes are in the direction of the bookshelves, I catch quick movement in my peripheral vision and swing my head back toward the kitchen area.

What was that? And what moves that fast?

"Did you see it?" Liza asks as she presses her hand against my knee.

"I don't know. Maybe?"

Liza is handling me appearing in her bed unannounced a lot better than I am. She is acting as if it is no big deal that I suddenly dropped in, and she even seems to appreciate the support.

I wish I could be that cool about it. I suppose it's a good thing the freaky clown is keeping my attention, so I can't fixate on how the fudge I got here to begin with.

Something leaps onto the counter, and I watch two long utility knives pull out from the sharpening block.

I'm concentrating on the shadow on top of the kitchen island when its head rotates a hundred and eighty degrees, and I see its red eyes light up across the room.

I know I'm awake. This is too real to be a dream.

"How long has this been going on?" I whisper to Liza.

"The moving around where I can see him moving just started tonight. The rest of the time, he's never exposed his ability to move."

"Why now?"

"I suppose he's getting tired of me throwing him into the fire bucket. I burned him a fourth time tonight."

I can understand that. It's reasonable to believe that if someone threw me in a fire bucket, I'd probably want to cut them, too.

"Shouldn't the fire have ended him?"

"Yep. We are definitely in uncharted territory now," Liza confirms my worst fear.

As I am getting my bearings and am about to recommend we gather the rest of the team for assistance, the evil little clown does a flip off the island countertop and runs toward us. I move to jump off the bed, but he is way too fast for me. As I put a foot down, he slides by me on his back, making an incision on my calf before disappearing under Liza's bed.

Holy cow, that hurts! And that little sucker is way too fast. He's like a little blue blur. If it wasn't for the bells on the tips of his slippers, I'm not sure I could keep track of him.

"Did he just cut you?" Liza asks incredulously.

I grasp my calf muscle as I quickly pull my legs back up on the bed. My blood is warm and sticky under my grip. "Bless it. That really smarts."

There is pressure under the mattress and a tearing sound. Liza and I separate to opposite sides of the bed as the tearing sound continues.

"He's cutting through the mattress."

"There's no way he can get through the box spring *and* the mattress," Liza says.

I see the first chunk of mattress foam flip out from under the bed, and I know Liza is wrong. It might be a lot to cut through, but with determination and a sharp knife, it will just be a matter of time.

"We're going to have to make a break for it," I insist.

"What? What do you mean?"

"I mean that if you don't want to get poked by a blade, we've got to get a better position." I search the room. Our options are limited. "We need to take a break for the kitchen island."

Liza's voice cracks as she says, "But he just hopped up there."

"Yeah, but he can't cut through the bottom. Besides, if he wants to hop up on the bed, it would've been easier than the counter, and we will be able to see him coming."

I can see Liza shaking her head in the dark. "No. There's no way you can convince me to run to the island."

The tearing sound picks up its pace, as does the foam coming out from under the bed. "We don't have a choice. We've got to move."

"I said no."

A nine-inch blade comes up through the middle of the mattress. I draw back in horror, and Liza makes a break for the kitchen island.

She dives on top of the island as I jump off the bed. I run and jump.

I think I have gone high enough to clear the counter, and my thighs slap the edge as I flip awkwardly onto the countertop.

Pain tears through me. I don't think it could hurt any worse if someone had just swung a baseball bat at my legs. Despite the pain, I stand and arm myself with a twelve-inch cast-iron skillet from Liza's stovetop.

"Hey, I was going to use that," she complains.

I'm not about to give up the skillet. "You snooze, you lose." I gesture toward the knife block. There is still a wicked-looking stainless steel cleaver on the side of the block.

Liza picks it up, seems to consider it, and grins. "Yeah, this should be the ticket."

Sharpy, the clown, has gone quiet under the bed. I think I like the sawing sound better.

"What are we up against?" I ask Liza.

"Honestly, I'm not sure. All I know is whatever was going on in that house in Birmingham is way wrong."

We both gasp as we see the blue blur run out from under the bed and roll twice, blades clacking on the floor like a special ops soldier until he disappears behind the loveseat.

"What is he doing?" Liza asks.

"I'd say trying to flank us. Step closer to my side. We have to make sure that we're both facing him if he comes at us."

"He's so fast. I'm not sure I can hit him with the blade."

I have doubts of my own. Even if I see him coming, I'm not sure I can swing a cast-iron skillet quickly enough to make contact with him. He's freakishly fast.

Why couldn't I have appeared at Liza's house fully armed? Would it be too much to ask that I had some of the unique shells that Dr. Devereaux was making for us?

"Yeah, I'm not sure I can hit him with the skillet either," I whisper. "But I'm going to act like I can."

"Why don't you call your brother. He'll know what to do, and he can bring the rest of the team."

"Well, I'd love to. Except, in my haste to come over, I seem to have left my phone on your bed."

"Oh yeah." Liza moves toward the edge of the counter. "I can make a run for mine."

I grab ahold of her shirttail. "Absolutely not. That's the last thing we need to do. We can handle this."

"How?"

As if to mock me, the clown does two more somersaults as he moves from the back of the loveseat to the back of the sofa. He is fewer than eight feet away from us.

How is an excellent question. After the results from Birmingham, I really do not want to try fire again. Burning someone out of their apartment, I believe, could ruin a good friendship.

I keep coming back to the gun. I just wish somehow I'd had the pistol on me.

The doll rolls out from behind the loveseat and taps the tip of the blades to the floor. He marches toward us, scraping the edges on the tile as he moves closer.

I just know before I reached my hand behind me. There is a sudden extra weight tugging at the back of my pj's.

Sharpy pulls his lips back, exposing long, viper-like teeth crowded all along his jawline. His eyes glow red, and his overall disposition is insatiable bloodlust.

As I watch him approach, dragging the blades, I slip my right hand behind my back and grasp the handle of the familiar forty-five caliber. I must be ready. I'm a good shot, but hitting a moving target is one thing, and a moving target as fast as Sharpy will not require just excellent skill, but a lot of luck.

"It's time to pay the bill. For being such a peel," Sharpy chimes as his porcelain lips move freely. Major wig out.

I didn't know the clown could talk. His scratchy, high-pitched voice sends ice down my spine. I'm not sure I can even fire my weapon.

Still, I ease my left hand behind me and chamber a round in the weapon while I hold it in my right. I thumb the safety off.

As the safety rotates to the off position, Sharpy makes his move. He does a somersault, landing hard on his feet before he pushes off, coming directly for me.

My right hand comes forward on instinct, and I fire a round into the chest of the doll, which explodes into sparkling sand, showering down on Liza and me.

"What the heck was that?" Liza asks excitedly.

I'm laughing hysterically. "The new protection system I'm working on."

"I'd say it works," Liza says. "Do I get one, too?"

I shake the sand out of my hair. "Yeah. We're going to be

doing shotguns once they have them ready."

Liza slides off the countertop. "Sweet."

My legs are hurting even worse now that the adrenaline pipeline has been closed. "I hope you have some ibuprofen. I'm going to need a handful."

"For the cut?"

I had forgotten about the cut on my calf. The welts on my thighs must be even worse than I thought. Still, on the positive side, shorts season is over. Nobody will see.

"Do you think he's gone for good this time?" Liza asks as she rummages through her cupboard.

I touch my thighs gingerly and wince. "I sure hope so. I don't think you can swing into the local surplus military store and buy nuclear weapons."

"Sure would've been nice to have that gun in Birmingham when *too tall and too weird* was after us."

I collapse onto one of her kitchen chairs. My legs really hurt. And I am still disoriented about having woken up in the wrong bed and with a possessed doll attacking me.

Liza sets a bottle of vodka in the center of the table with one hand while setting two glass tumblers and a bottle of ibuprofen in front of me. "So, what gives?"

If ever there was an open-ended question. I rub one hand roughly over my face while I grab for the ibuprofen. The container sounds like a baby's rattle due to the sudden tremors I have in my hands. I set the bottle down and hold it to the table while I open the top. "Darned if I know."

Liza makes a clicking noise with her tongue. "Please. Who do you think you're talking to?"

I empty a handful of ibuprofen into my left hand and reach for the bottle with my other. Liza snags it before I can grab it.

She unscrews the top and pours half a tumbler for each of us, and slides one to me. "Don't think for a minute that I believe you don't have a theory."

I toss the pills into my mouth and take a swallow of vodka. Oh man, that's rough.

"Yeah, I have a theory. My life sucks. That's my theory."

When I look up, I'm surprised to see Liza frowning at me. Her lips narrow as she shakes her head. "You just don't get it." She takes a sip of her vodka and stares at me over the rim.

"Oh, please. Please spare me the speech about how lucky I am to have all these weird talents. Or having all this family that's always in my business."

"No." Liza's shoulders convulse, and I see tears welling in her eyes. "What I was gonna say is how lucky I am that I have a friend who cares so much she appeared out of thin air to save me."

I take another long draw of the vodka. It is easier this time. "I think you're exaggerating."

She laughs, and a single tear runs down her right cheek. "No. I had tried everything to get rid of him. If you hadn't shown up, he would've killed me tonight."

I hadn't realized how serious and scared she was, but the facts line up for me. If it had not been for the pistol manifesting in my hand, I'm not sure we would have been able to defeat Sharpy, even as a team. I can't imagine having to do battle with that ultra-fast little creep on my own.

"It kills me how you go through life making these huge waves that affect people, and you don't even notice it, April May."

"You're crazy. I'm the girl who can't even get a job in her own profession. I definitely don't have any influence in other people's lives."

Liza reaches out and grabs my hand. "Listen to me. You know I'm not the biggest people person in the world. The first time I met you, I took you to be some spoiled rotten princess who wouldn't be able to carry her weight. Pretty much a waste of good air."

I knew she hadn't taken right to me, but that surprises me. "Hey."

She raises her eyebrows. "It's true. It's also true I was wrong. I am very thankful that I met you."

A little awkward, but really sweet. "Me too," I whisper.

She exhales then purses her lips. "Okay, since I have you here. How did it go last night?"

Liza and I sit and talk and drink until the sun comes up. Besides, I knew my legs hurt too bad to attempt to drive home. Plus, I didn't have a car.

I call Daddy for a ride, but he is already at church with Mama. Dusty isn't answering his phone, which meant he is probably sound asleep.

That leaves Chase.

Chapter 44

Chase peppers me with questions the whole drive home. *When did you leave to go to Liza's? I didn't see you leave. Did she pick you up, or did somebody else? It's awfully early to be drinking. Don't you have a date tonight?*

Chase should've been a cop. He'd be great during interrogation. I assure you anybody spending a few hours with Chase would become so confused about what they said, he would be able to claim they changed their story twenty-five times. As it is, I'm thrilled to make my escape when we pull onto our parents' driveway.

"Thank you for the ride." I shut the car door and walk to my apartment. The way I figure it, I can still get a five-hour nap before Lee shows up, and I need sleep desperately.

Puppy is nowhere to be found. Of course not. He's probably waiting in the kitchen for Chase to cook him breakfast.

The thought of scrambled eggs and bacon makes my stomach rumble. But as hungry as I am, I know I need to sleep more.

I'm just getting comfortable in bed, and someone knocks on my door. Really? "Who is it?" I yell.

"Chase."

Now what? "It's unlocked," I holler at the door before rolling back toward the wall.

The door opens, and I hear Chase's boots striding toward me

and a familiar tap-tap of Puppy's paws on the hardwood.

"Your buddy wants to take a nap with you, and I brought you some breakfast."

My brother is a saint. I greedily accept the plate with two eggs, a grilled cheese, and bacon.

"I can't eat all this."

Chase shrugs as he walks to the door. "If you don't, I'm sure Fang will finish it off for you."

I'm so thankful for the ride and breakfast I don't even argue about my dog's name. "Thank you."

"You're welcome."

Breakfast cost me thirty minutes of my planned five-hour nap. I'm surprised that I eat everything on my plate. Feeling warm and satiated, I curl up with Puppy for my nap.

Chapter 45

I pull off my second ruined blouse because I broke out in a nervous sweat while putting on my makeup. I put a T-shirt on. The plan is to change into my third blouse at the last minute. I don't believe that will stop me from breaking into a spontaneous sweat once I'm on the date with Lee. Still, it is the best I can do.

It aggravates me that my body sometimes reacts to guys like I'm a middle-school virgin. My hope is that when I settle down one of these days with my man, my body will normalize. But until then, weirdness it is.

It makes no logical sense that I would be the least bit nervous about a date with Lee. I mean, we have been out a lot before. There is no *news* there.

Yeah, I keep telling myself that, but my body isn't buying it.

The boy I went out with during high school no longer exists. This is a kinder, worldlier, and hotter version of Lee, and I'm extremely into this version of Lee.

I suppose, deep down, I'm nervous about what he thinks about me. *If* he thinks about me.

Our relationship had been more than a quick fling. If it had not been for my driving ambition, I probably would have been thrilled to settle down with Lee and have children not long after we graduated high school.

So, I suppose in a roundabout way, my ambition had driven his dream, too. If I had not been so driven, his dream would never have had the time and space to grow into a professional ballplayer career.

But his dream came true, and mine didn't. For some reason that is significant to me.

I'm ready twenty minutes early, which is highly unusual. I decide to step outside into the cool November air just in case my body tries to break out into the nervous sweats again.

Puppy brushes past my leg and breaks out into a chubby boy run. No wonder. Dusty and Chase are sitting next to the grill drinking beer. I consider going back into my apartment, but Dusty spots me before I can turn around.

"Hey there, sis," Dusty says in his casual manner that doesn't match his stare. "Come and talk to me for a minute."

"Lee is supposed to be here in a minute to pick me up."

Dusty pulls another wrought-iron chair over to where he and Chase are sitting. "Just until your boyfriend gets here."

"He's not my boyfriend," I grumble as I shuffle to the porch.

Dusty hands me a beer as I sit down. "Rough night?"

"You should know. I was with you," I say before taking a sip of my beer.

"That's funny because Chase told me he had to give you a ride home from Liza's."

I shoot a burning glare at Chase. He looks away. "So, it is a crime to visit a friend now?"

Dusty chuckles. "Nope. I'm sure she enjoyed the company. I'm just trying to figure out how you got over there."

I take another sip of beer and ignore him as I rub Puppy between the ears.

"Liza's not supposed to be driving because of her concussion." He pauses as if waiting for me to say something. When I don't, he continues, "Unlike some people, she usually follows directions, and I know it was too far for you to walk, so I'm trying to figure out how you got over there."

That is so interesting because I was trying to figure out why it is any of his business. I take another sip of beer and rub Puppy's fur harder.

"So, what, you just won't answer me?"

Even if I wanted to answer Dusty, which I don't, I wouldn't know what to tell him. As it is, I have a lot of questions for Nana when Thursday rolls around.

"Well?" Dusty asks again.

"I didn't want to tell you, but Nana showed me how to use a flying broom. I didn't want to tell you because I know you get upset if anybody is on a bicycle without a helmet." I pat the side of my hair. "I'm not going to put a bike helmet on this regardless of what you think."

"You expect me to believe that?" Dusty says.

"Hello?" Lee walks around the side of the house.

"Right on time." Chase whispers.

I stand and hand Dusty my half-empty beer, "Thanks for the beer, Dusty."

"That's it?" he complains.

"Wow, look at you," Lee comments.

I take his hand to pull him away from the porch before my brothers can get started. "Come on."

"Hey, you kids be good," Chase hollers at our backs.

"I'd forgotten how beautiful you are," Lee comments as we approach his truck.

For real? I cut my eyes to Lee. Either he is being genuine, or he is taking lying to a whole new level of skill. "Thanks."

He opens the door for me. "I have to admit to you, I've been sort of nervous all day about the date." He makes the declaration with a disarming goofy smile on his face.

"Really? You shouldn't be. We've been out a lot before." Thank the Lord I'm not the only one nervous. I try to steel my nerves as I watch him cross in front of the truck and open the driver's door.

"I suppose. But people change, and I just hope that we're enough of who we were that you'll still connect with me."

Chapter 46

Neither of us should've been nervous in the least. We spent the next six hours together picking up like we had never quit dating.

Lee took me bowling and then to dinner at the Catfish Palace. After dinner, we buy a bottle of wine, park his truck next to the river, and sit on his tailgate while we talk some more and drink the wine.

He asks if I want to go back to his place. I want to, but I feel it is too soon, and he agrees without any complaint.

As we pull up to my parents' home, I am glad to see that nobody is on the back porch.

"Can I walk you to the door?" Lee asks.

Am I ready for a kiss? Yes. I'm definitely ready for a kiss. "I'd be disappointed if you didn't."

I wait and let him come around to open my door because I want him to. When I step down, he slides his hand into mine.

"I had a great time tonight."

"You say that to all the girls," I tease.

"No. I mostly don't talk to other girls."

I lean up against the door to my apartment. "Why is that?"

He wrinkles his nose as he shakes his head. "I don't know. They all seem like they have some agenda or life plan that they're working on. It's like they're not real people, more like robots." He levels his eyes to me. "You're not like that. You're real."

"Am I now?"

He leans in and braces his arm against the door. "Yeah. And you're really pretty."

The way he says it tickles me, and I giggle. Then I clutch his collar pulling him closer to me. "Shut your mouth."

He edges closer until I can feel his breath on my lips. "I'm going to kiss you silly," he says.

"I'll be the judge of that," I purr as my eyes shut.

Electrical sparks fry my brain as our lips meet. Raw waves of passion wash all coherent thoughts I had out to the sea of love.

He angles his head as the tip of his tongue traces lightly across my lips. Leaning into him, I enjoy the flashes of heat that fill me. Sensations that leave me breathless, disoriented, and dizzy.

Lee pulls back as I'm losing all self-control.

A small whimper escapes me. It should embarrass me, but I'm beyond caring.

The laugh he conceals forces his chest to bounce. "You're cute."

I'm something else, too, right now. Cute doesn't begin to describe how I'm feeling.

He pulls further away from me, and I must fight the urge to whimper again. I recall that my body always did respond to him. Still, it had been more of a physical attraction and curiosity. Curiosity had been replaced by hunger and urgency.

"I want to see you again," Lee says.

I nod mutely. At this point, I'm afraid if I say anything, it will be "come on in." My apartment. I meant my apartment. Or at least to start with.

He gestures over his shoulder. "I better be going. I know tomorrow's a workday for you."

Again, the mute nod from me.

"I'll call you tomorrow. Maybe if your workday's not too bad, we can hang out tomorrow night." He drops his hands from my waist and walks back to his truck. As he gets in, he stops and waves.

I return the wave.

It's a darn good thing he left, I think as I watch his truck pull down the driveway. I'm thankful one of us has some common sense, because every ounce of caution I ever had disintegrated under his kiss.

I'm not exactly sure how I feel about a man having that sort of effect on me.

Not surprisingly, I have dreams about Lee all night. They are good, hot, and steamy dreams. Although none of them satiated me like I would have been if I had invited Lee into my apartment last night.

I must admit that a part of me is extremely disappointed that I didn't just appear suddenly naked in Lee's bed. That would have been awesome, but no, I only appear in my girlfriend's bed, and when she is under attack from a crazed, possessed clown doll.

What good is a weird skill like spontaneous transference if it isn't occasionally a bonus play for me? Is it too much to ask that just once one of these "gifts" I have will do something that benefits me?

Chapter 47

It is only 3:00 AM, and I can't sleep. The main reason, of course, is Lee.

The other reason is Lexi. Something is going on at J&B Body Shop. I don't know what, but it plays into Ben's murder, and I know it is the key to getting Lexi off.

I kick back the covers and pad barefooted to the bathroom for a quick shower.

Drying off, I pull on yoga pants and an extra-long sweatshirt before heading out.

I'm only a few minutes down the road when I realize the error of my ways. I should've grabbed a coffee on the way out.

When I make it into Boaz, I pass by J&B's. I want to see if there are any familiar cars. There aren't. At least if there are, they are inside the building.

I pull around the city square and, this time, park an entire block down from J&B's. It will be more challenging to see what is going on from here. Still, hopefully, I will not attract the attention of another homeless man.

The longer I sit in the dark, the more foolish I feel. I'm not sure what my expectations were, but I feel slightly crazy—obsessed about this storefront.

I should've called Agent Casey and discussed what I saw the week before at J&B's and let his men do their job. I guess a part of me is still cynical that the prosecution will only reveal items that strengthen their case, regardless of what the law says about discovery.

At 5:30 AM, I'm finally sleepy again. At this point, I'm wishing I was back home in my bed.

I could drive into Guntersville and take a nap at the office.

A white minivan pulls up, followed by a black Escalade. Interesting.

I know that minivan. Sure, there's a lot of white minivans on the road, but only so many of them have the monogram CSB on the back window in cursive and a stick family of a dad, mom, and three kids. Lexi steps out of the van, and when she does, a man exits the driver's side of the Escalade. He moves toward her, and they have a lengthy discussion.

What in the world could she be discussing with this man? Who is he? Was he her husband's silent partner? Why did I park so blasted far away?

The door behind the driver's seat of the Escalade opens, and a second man exits. My breath catches, and my eyes bug out when I see the colossal gauze patch on the side of the man's head. It is the homeless man whose ear I shot off yesterday.

I now have even more questions flood my mind. But the only question that really counts to me now is how quickly can I get away from J&B's and can I do it without being noticed.

I go to turn the ignition key of my IROC in hopes of making my getaway when a sharp knock on the driver's side glass makes me flinch hard to the right. I think I might have peed myself.

It takes a second for me to place the familiar face. He makes a gesture for me to roll down my window.

I balance the terror of seeing my attacker from yesterday against my trust in the man from the FBI.

Reluctantly, I roll my window down. Only because I trust Agent Casey for some reason, and I want some answers.

"You can't be here, Counselor Snow." King's facial expression is stern. He is noticeably upset but doing an outstanding job of keeping it harnessed.

"It's a public road," I reply without thought.

He doesn't appear to find that amusing. "You're getting involved in things you can't understand."

"Try me. I'm not nearly as dumb as I look."

King blows out an aggravated breath. "Listen, you don't have to worry about Lexi or her kids anymore."

"Why's that?"

"Because I'm telling you that. She's no longer your client."

It probably isn't smart to aggravate tall, dark, and dangerous, but he isn't exactly alleviating my curiosity, either. "You're going to have to give me a better explanation than that."

"You're just going to put Lexi and yourself in danger."

"Now you're threatening me?"

King grasps the window with his hand. "No, I'm telling you the facts, and you need to trust me."

"Trust you? I don't even know you."

We stare at each other for a full minute. He appears to be considering something. He frowns and then pulls a pad from his pocket and scribbles something on it. "He warned me you wouldn't listen." He grumbles before he tears a sheet of paper from the notebook and shoves it through the window at me.

"What's this?" I ask.

"Just dial the number, please."

I guess because he said please, I could consider it. I stare at the ten-digit number on the piece of paper. It doesn't look familiar.

"You say you want answers. Then just call it. Get your answers," King urges.

King's request seems simple enough. Getting answers to all my questions sounds like a good thing. Still, my hands are frozen in front of me as I continue to stare at the number.

There is something significant here. Something I can't put my fingers on. An immense amount of energy is on the scrap of paper I hold in front of me.

Is it King's energy? If so, why?

I notice the one-eared homeless man, now dressed sharply in a black suit, take notice of my vehicle and begin to cross the road. I am not sure why I hesitated to make the phone call, but my time consideration is drawing to a close. I either make the phone call Agent Casey requests now or attempt to run from the FBI.

Running from the FBI seems to have little to no up-side. I type the phone number into my phone, and to my surprise, King steps back from the driver's door and motions for the one-eared man to stop where he is and not come closer.

The call is answered after the first ring. "Snow, don't you have something better to do than shoot off the ears of unsuspecting FBI agents?"

The voice is familiar. It is like a voice from the dead causing a rush of confusion, relief, and excitement through my body. "Vander? Is that you?"

It sounds like my friend who has been missing for the past few months. Whenever I think about him, the friend, I feel sick to my stomach that he is probably lost to the world. It almost seems too good to hear his voice and know he is alive.

"It's me."

"Where are you?" I ask. "I've been asking Howard for information, and nobody can tell me anything."

"I'm sorry, April. But I can't tell you. Believe me when I say the less you know, the safer it is for you."

"Why? What are you doing?"

"It's not important. Listen to me, please. I know you're just doing your job. I warned them not to let you be pulled into this. I told them there's no way that you wouldn't stay after this until you figured out what the truth was, and they didn't listen to me. But I need you to listen to me now. You must stand down. You have to turn around and act like nothing has happened."

Stand down? How am I supposed to do that when I saw that there is obviously some sort of collusion going on between the FBI and Lexi. What did that mean to the murder of Ben? Was

Lexi innocent, or has she copped a deal to help the Feds in return for her freedom?

"What's going on, Vander?"

"It's not nearly as important as you probably think it is, April. It's just business as usual."

"No. No, it's not. This is not business as usual. You need to tell me what's going on."

My demand hangs in the air for several seconds before he answers. "You do not understand me. You have accidentally stumbled into something that you cannot even fathom the size of. I am asking, no, begging you, walk away. Forget any of this has happened."

I know he is sincere. The level of emotion his voice has is unusually high for Vander. He is stressed, and he urgently wants me to obey his request.

"I'm an agent of the court, Vander. It's my responsibility to make sure the laws of the land are followed."

"Does that include you going to prison for twenty years for attempted murder?"

His question is so absurd. I haven't done anything but my job. You don't go to prison for defending your clients. "What are you talking about?"

"The agent whose ear you blew off. Most jurors don't take kindly to people who shoot our law enforcement agents."

"That's not what happened. Besides, I didn't shoot to kill. I didn't even pull the trigger."

"Yeah, why don't you listen to yourself. If you are a juror, would you buy that? Especially after I show you pictures of our agent's bloodied hole in the side of his skull where his ear should be."

"I didn't mean to shoot his ear off," I grumble.

"And I'm sure you didn't mean to land in the middle of several years' worth of FBI preparation, either. All the same for your safety and career longevity, I'm asking you, as a friend, please stand down. That's all I need. The rest of it, my team will handle. But you've got to help me."

I'm torn. What Vander is telling me, even though it isn't all the information I want, makes sense. Plus, it is Vander, so I want to believe it. Still, it isn't right if they killed Ben to get to Lexi.

"I'm sorry, Vander, I really am. But an innocent man has been killed. I can't just turn my back on that."

He makes an abbreviated laugh. "Ben Bransford is not an innocent man. He's also not a dead man. He's worth way too much to my investigation for him to be dead."

Vander's statement rocks me to my core. Ben is alive? "But there was a body in the car."

"Darn it, April. This isn't twenty-one questions. There are bodies everywhere. Just because you saw a burned-up body in Bransford's driveway doesn't mean it was Ben."

If I were talking to anyone other than Vander, I would think they were lying. But to date, Vander has never led me astray. "And Lexi?"

"She didn't know anything until this morning. She and her children will be gone this morning, the same morning that the last person in Guntersville will see Tad Sapp.

It's a small town. People will talk and draw their own conclusions. It isn't exactly a secret that the two of them were having a fling on the side. Ben had civilly requested that he does not have to deal with Lexi any more or his kids, but that they are taken care of."

"What a shmuck," I growl. "Somebody should've blown him up in his driveway."

Vander laughs. "True that. It's definitely a nest of losers."

"I hate it for the kids."

"It's not optimal," Vander says, "but it's probably not gonna be a bad thing to get them out of the dysfunctional family, either. Who knows, maybe Lexi can turn over a new leaf without Ben and become a better mom for her kids. From what I've seen, I think she loves them."

I know from my experience with Lexi that Vander is right. But I'm not ready to cut her any slack just yet.

"I need to know that I can count on you to walk away from this and not mention anything to anyone, April."

"If I don't agree?"

"It's out of my hands. I can tell you the agent you shot yesterday believes in an ear for an ear."

At first, I believe Vander might be joking. But the lengthy silence confirms that I really have no choice left in the matter. I need to do as Vander requests and walk away.

"So, you're working for the FBI?"

"Not exactly. Do I have your word? I need to hear you say it."

"Oh, you knew you were going to get me to agree when you first answered the phone."

"I don't hold foolish expectations, April. Even smart and reasonable people like yourself occasionally make decisions that don't benefit them."

I can walk away from the case. If for no other reason than I can't imagine anyone more capable than Vander.

But now, a new riddle afflicts my curiosity, and I have a burning desire to get to the truth. "Where are you, Vander?"

"Not where you are. That's all I can tell you."

"Are you being safe?"

I hear another short laugh. "Come on, April. You know that's not my style."

"Are you coming home soon?" I ask.

"Honestly, I have no clue at this point. But I promise you that if I do make it home, I'll buy you as many margaritas as you want and I'll fill you in on all the details that aren't classified."

The "if" part of his statement does not elude me. It twists like a knife in my heart, bringing forward a tiny bit of anger and resentment. What is he doing that is so important he can't tell me? Why does he have to put his life on the line?

More importantly, why do I even care?

"Lee Darby is back in town. We went out last night. We had a really good time together." I don't know why I tell Vander that. Still, it seems important.

"Yeah, I heard about that. I know you can and do whatever

makes you happy, but I know Lee really well. As a friend, I would recommend you be careful. He has a long track record of breaking people's hearts."

"Well, he's here in town, and he's interested in me. And I'm interested in him. We're going to hang out again tonight."

During the long silence that ensues, I feel dirty and petty about what I said. But it is true. Who is Vander to throw shade on Lee, when at least I know what Lee does for a living, and he is around so I can talk to him?

"If it makes you happy, I'm happy. Thank you for giving your word on standing down. I know it is tough."

His voice has shifted into the cold, impersonal professional tone, and it makes me sad. "Sure."

"I'll see you when I see you," he says with no emotion.

"Goodbye, Vander."

I disconnect the line and take a deep breath. It means nothing to me. Vander is just a passing acquaintance in my life. A boy, now man, I once knew. Nothing more and nothing less.

I notice Agent Casey gesturing to my left. When I turn my head to him, he arches his eyebrows.

In response, I give a bow of my head and start my IROC. Agent Casey backs away from my car, and I pull down the street.

As I drive back into Guntersville, I hit Lee's number.

His voice is thick with sleep. "Hey, beautiful, I'm glad you called."

I smile as I ask. "How about pizza and a show tonight? My treat."

The End

Never miss an April May Snow release.
Join the reader's club!
www.mscottswanson.com

Coming December 24th, 2021
Foolish Fantasies
Click to pre-order

Have you read the prequels? *The Gifts Awaken* stories are the prequel series to the *Foolish* novel series of April May Snow.

Click to get your copies today!

The Gifts Awaken Prequel Series

Throw the Bouquet

Throw the Cap

Throw the Dice

Throw the Elbow

Throw the Fastball

Throw the Gauntlet

Throw the Hissy

M. Scott lives outside of Nashville, TN, with his wife and two guard chihuahuas. When he's not writing, he's cooking, or taking long walks to smooth out plot lines for the next April May Snow adventure.

Dear Favorite Reader,

Thank you for reading April's story. You make her adventures possible. Without you, there would be no point in creating her story.

I'd like to encourage you to post a review on Amazon. A review from you is a powerful way to support authors you enjoy. It allows our books to be found by additional readers, and frankly, motivates us to continue to produce books. This is especially true for your independents.

Once again, thank you for the support. You are the magic that breathes life into these characters.

M. Scott Swanson

The best way to stay in touch is to join the reader's club!

www.mscottswanson.com

Other ways to stay in touch are:

Like on Amazon

Like on Facebook

Like on Goodreads

You can also reach me at mscottswanson@gmail.com.

I hope your life is filled with

magic and LOVE!

Made in United States
North Haven, CT
07 September 2022

23799535R00176